The Dead Chase
The Twelfth in the Murray of Letho Series

Lexie Conyngham

First published in 2021 by The Kellas Cat Press, Aberdeen.

ISBN: 978-1-910926-64-2

Cover illustration by Helen Braid at www.ellieillustrates.co.uk

ACKNOWLEDGMENTS

As always thank you to Jill, Nanisa, Bryony and Kath, valiant beta readers, and to the Facebook UK Crime Book Club, rather a good way to get through lockdown.

Dramatis Personae

Sir Joshua Akehurst, self-made man and signals enthusiast
Lady Akehurst, his wife, a lady who makes her presence felt
Amanda Akehurst, his grand-daughter, heiress to his fortune and therefore a desirable bride
Paul Paulison, his devoted secretary
Alester Blair, with his daughter Isobel, guests of Sir Joshua, and Blair's man Smith
Adolphus Payne, known to his friends as Fussy, great-nephew of Sir Joshua
Mr Lawrence, Fussy's godfather
Harry Holden, Lady Akehurst's great-nephew and far from ornamental to the household
Barnabas Ketchell, another fashionable young(ish) man, facilitator to Mr. Holden's nocturnal entertainments
Trent, Sir Joshua's butler
Jackie and Rosie, junior servants unexpectedly raised to temporary responsibility

Charles Murray of Letho
Henry Robbins, his manservant
Old Donald McKenzie, his coachman
Young Donald, his groom, nephew to Old Donald

Additionally:
Beatrix Pirrie, a woman with a past (some of which she shares with Murray)
Miss Crockett, anxious about Frenchmen with knives
Lt. Harold Munnings, R.N. (retd.), keeper of the semaphore tower at Newhaven
Nathan Worthing, blessed with two opposing guardians

Chapter One

'It's not as if,' said Murray to his neighbour, 'it's been a very good year.'

His neighbour, Miss Fairbairn, a young lady of some intelligence, had been placed there by her mother the hostess, in order to snare a rich, handsome and still relatively young widower – Murray. Murray and the girl were comfortable in each other's company chiefly because they both knew very well that her affections were engaged elsewhere. Murray found her a good dinner companion, but not quite good enough: he had been scarred by marriage once, and had no idea of entering into it again without great care.

The young lady gave a laugh that contained all the irony he might have expected.

'No, not at all. The King is dead, long live the – oh, heavens, the Prince Regent! Freezing cold winter. Soaking wet summer. Uprisings in the west. Plots to kill the Cabinet. Caroline of Brunswick back in the country and the King trying to orchestrate a divorce – a divorced King! The next thing we know is that France will invade just out of pity for us, and that will be that.'

It was Murray's turn to laugh.

'I suspect that borders on seditious talk, Miss Fairbairn – take care!'

'Ah, well, perhaps indeed we should turn the conversation, before it causes general dyspepsia. Let me see, what might a conventional question be? Are you in Edinburgh for the season, Mr. Murray?'

'I believe so, for most of it, anyway. I'll go to the country for

Hogmanay, for my daughter is staying with her cousins in Fife.'

'Oh? She must be growing fast! What age is she now?'

'She is four,' said Murray proudly, but managed not to list her current accomplishments. Fortunately Miss Fairbairn nodded and went on.

'And your friend Mr. Blair? I don't believe I have seen him this whole year!'

'We were in the north country together in December, but he and his daughter are a good deal in Sussex these days, with his late wife's family.'

'I have never been, but I hear it is a fair county.'

'Yes, indeed.' Chalk hills and sunshine, flint walls and fat cattle. Though from all Murray had heard his friend Blair say, the old man would rather be at home here in Edinburgh. Murray was not sure what took him so often and for so long down to the south coast. Whatever it was, Murray regretted it: it looked as if he would go through another Edinburgh season without Blair's eccentric but entertaining company.

Alester Blair was not, however, in Sussex. He was in London, though his mind was set, even more firmly than usual, on Edinburgh. And, as it happened, on Murray himself.

'My dear Charles,' he wrote, his pen lashing the paper with great black loops and whorls. 'I trust you are well, and Augusta too, and your whole household, and particularly Mr. and Mrs. Robbins, of course, and my man Smith also joins with me in wishing them well, though of course he would not be so impertinent even after so many years of service as to request me to begin my letter with his salutations. I write to ask you a tremendous favour –' he paused, drove a line through 'tremendous', and then, after more consideration, he extended the line to take out the whole sentence. 'There is something' – 'something' went the same way as 'tremendous' – 'a matter'. No. A circumstance, on which I should like your advice.' 'Benefit from your advice' – 'be most grateful for your advice'.

'Oh!' He slapped his pen on to the table, oblivious to the little squirt of ink that flew from the nib. 'If I cannot write the preliminaries, how am I ever to explain the matter itself?'

Isobel raised her head from her sketchbook. Curled into the

windowseat she could observe a cast of characters on the street below that had come to populate this particular book over the last weeks, the only benefit, as far as she could see, from staying in London. Street traders, cab drivers – and their horses – Waterloo veterans with half a leg, carriages collecting or depositing those of a higher status, glimpsed as bonnets or feathers or the tail of a cloak as they hurried from vehicle to doorway or back, puffed-up pinks in the highest fashion squinting in the unaccustomed bright air of an autumn afternoon, they all appeared in sharp little lines on Isobel's pages.

'He would come if you asked him, Father. Then you could explain in person.'

Blair sighed.

'He would come if I asked him, yes. I think so.' He eyed his daughter blearily. 'But have I the right to ask him? All this could simply be my fancy. I could be imagining it all.'

Isobel closed and set aside her sketchbook, and rose.

'I don't think it is all your fancy, Father. From what you've told me, anyway, there seems to be something odd going on. Of course, it may be harmless –'

'But if it proved not to be …'

'Exactly.'

Blair eyed her upwards and sideways, like a man trying to peer at the sun.

'Are you offended, then, that I want Charles' opinion, when I have yours so readily to hand?'

'Well, obviously mine should be good enough for you,' said Isobel, making a mock hurt face to tease him. 'But I know how you and Charles rely on each other. And as I say, he would come here if you asked him.'

'I wish we could just go there, instead.'

'Yes,' said Isobel, rather more solemnly this time. 'Yes, that would be – a relief.'

Blair reached out a hand, and she took it.

'I'm sorry, my dear,' he said wearily. 'I should never have accepted this invitation. Or I should never have brought you with me.'

She came closer, leaning down to rub his shoulders fondly.

'No matter, Father. We were on our way to Sussex anyway.

And what has to be done, has to be done.'

'That, at least, is true! And clear, and unambiguous. But what has to be done?'

'Ah,' said Isobel. 'Yes, there's a question. But I think the first part of the answer must be that you write and ask Charles to come to London.'

With Isobel's input, some kind of coherent letter was finally drafted and Smith, the manservant, was summoned to take it to the mail, bypassing the household's own mailbag. Blair watched Smith go with a sigh, but Isobel gave her father a swift, one-armed hug.

'He'll come,' she said, 'and then if nothing else you'll feel better for having his company.'

A smile meandered over Blair's face.

'His father was an awkward man to have as a friend,' he said, 'very, um, determined, and his sense of humour was sometimes difficult to discover. But I confess I value young Charles' friendship more than I can say. He takes after his mother, and she was a delightful lady.'

'Time to dress for dinner, Father,' said Isobel, who had heard these reminiscences more than once recently. 'And then, who knows what may happen?'

Isobel Blair, who had in her life received two proposals of marriage and accepted one, was nevertheless still single at the age of twenty-something – not precisely an unclaimed treasure, not yet, but perhaps teetering perilously towards the edge of that unflattering description. Though she was aware that this state of affairs distressed her father, who would have been greatly relieved to see her happily established (and 'happily' was the key word here) in her own household, she was not in any hurry to change her situation. Whether this made the experience of staying for a few weeks at the heart of London society any more or less enjoyable was a matter of some debate in her head. There had already been too many nights when she retired to bed late and weary and befuddled by lights and music and dancing and far, far too many people doing far, far too many strange things in their senseless pursuit of novelty. To have felt herself obliged to seek a husband in all this madness might have given her some focus, but the task seemed hopeless, for she had barely met a man she could tolerate for longer than an evening.

Yet she knew she was lucky, for the household in which they were staying was not entirely made up of that kind of person: there were one or two at the dinner table who regarded this as closer to breakfast, and merely the preliminary to the drink and debauchery of the night before they staggered back to rattle through the building at dawn, and finally fall asleep. Next to her, for example, was young Harry Holden, barely awake, making a monumental task of transferring his soup in a shaking spoon to his loose mouth. His face was mostly teeth and nose, and remarkably little chin, with a tuft of assertive hair making up for the doubtful wrinkling of his long forehead. Directly across the table, as if they could only sustain themselves by a clear view of each other, was his friend Barnabas Ketchell, allegedly aged five and thirty, but doing a passable impression of a man in his sixties, impeccably turned out as to his clothing but with skin the colour of dust and an interesting yellow tint to his eyes. But they were secondary members of the party.

'Miss Blair!' Her hostess' voice, the sharpness of a damp finger down a window elevated to the volume to be heard across vast drawing rooms, scoured down the table towards her. They were only ten at dinner and the table was not a long one. Several of the guests winced. Behind Isobel, she heard the butler clatter dishes together. 'How did you enjoy Somerset House?'

'Very much, thank you, ma'am,' said Isobel at once.

'You'll confess that there is no place equal for a display of fine art either in London or anywhere else.' Lady Akehurst settled her breadth back in her chair, satisfied that Isobel would agree. There was such a weight of her, Isobel thought, that it must have been some strain to keep herself upright all the time.

'Certainly I have never seen its equal,' Isobel conceded obediently. And the gallery's contents had indeed been very fine. 'I only wish it had been a little less crowded, for it was hard to pause in the crowds and absorb the details of any one painting, which I should have been delighted to do.'

Her father, seated on Lady Akehurst's left, gave a little whistle of agitation, and she could hear his feet tapping the polished floor. The man opposite him, Mr. Lawrence, long acquainted with the Blairs, surveyed her father with distaste. The butler leaned past Mr. Lawrence with the burgundy, and several drops scattered like blood over the white cloth.

'The crowds demonstrate its popularity amongst those with the taste to appreciate the art,' said Lady Akehurst, nodding. Her head seemed to bounce on the cushion of her chins, then settle. 'One knows the spectacle is worth it when there are plenty there to admire it.'

'Quite,' said Isobel, not in the least agreeing. Plenty of the ladies and gentlemen in Somerset House had been paying more attention to their own appearance than to the merit of the paintings. 'Yet is difficult to admire anything from behind someone's well-tailored shoulder or expansive bonnet.'

She glanced up and caught the eye of the girl opposite her. Amanda Akehurst's lips had parted in dismay at Isobel's words: she was far too unimaginative a young lady to disagree with her grandmother like that. Lady Akehurst enjoyed her own opinions, and did not see why anyone else should not take the same pleasure in them. Isobel winked. Amanda's face flushed in irritation.

'We had a charming turn in the park this afternoon.' A more agreeable member of their party broke into the conversation as though he had just remembered how to speak. Adolphus Payne, Fussy to his friends, sat up and surveyed the company with a friendly grin. 'There was a hint of autumn in the air, the lightest chill, but the sun shone. My very favourite kind of weather! Do you agree, Miss Blair, or do you like it warmer?'

'A bright, chill day is delightful, Mr. Payne, I quite agree!' She quite liked Fussy: at least he spent more than half his time sober, unlike Harry Holden and Barnabas Ketchell.

Amanda Akehurst shuddered.

'Oh, no, Miss Blair! Surely you cannot! I must have the sun warm so I can sit in the shade and still abandon my shawl!' Amanda gave her shoulders a little wriggle, drawing attention to their plump rosiness. Isobel half-expected her to rattle. As so often, Lady Akehurst had adorned her grand-daughter with some of the family jewels. They were very fine, but, in Isobel's opinion, far too heavy for a young thing like Amanda, like a carthorse harness on a child's pony.

'Well, in our changeable country perhaps it is as well that different people like different things,' said Fussy Payne peaceably. 'Then at least some of us are happy at any moment.'

Isobel smiled at him, admiring his efforts. She had paused with a piece of gravy-rich pastry balanced on her fork: the butler bumped her shoulder from behind, and the pastry flew, a newly freed bird, and landed with a faint plop in the gravy boat. Sir Joshua Akehurst beside her paused in conversation with his secretary and raised his eyebrows, but nobody looked at the butler.

Isobel struggled to remember his name. She was the kind of person who tended to pay attention to other people's servants – nosy, perhaps, was the word for it – who spoke to them, and listened to them, and knew a bit about them. But in this household she was not even sure that she had heard anyone speak to the butler, let alone any lower rank of maid or manservant. She resented any idea that this might be the proper way to behave. She had always taken a keen interest in her father's servants, and thought that households worked better that way. Why on earth would they not?

Lady Akehurst cleared her throat.

'And what are your plans for this evening, dear Harry?'

Harry Holden, toying with a fragment of pastry, abandoned it to rub his eyes.

'Thought we might take a look at the Italian Opera,' he said. 'Didn't we, Barnie?'

Barnabas Ketchell roused himself just a little.

'Oh, yes!'

'Are you an admirer of Italian opera, then, Mr. Ketchell?' Lady Akehurst's voice had an edge to it. Isobel was reminded of her Latin lessons: Lady Akehurst was not expecting the answer 'yes'.

'An admirer of opera? What on earth does that have to do with it?' Mr. Ketchell demanded, then seemed to recollect himself. 'The music is very splendid, of course: some of the performers have quite exquisite voices. But as to my being an admirer, Lady Akehurst,' he said, warming up to behave as a good guest should, 'I fear I cannot aspire to those levels of expertise. I can only say that the performances I have heard have been very fine.' He was almost upright in his seat now, arranging the front of his coat more neatly, sliding careful fingers through his thin hair to settle it. 'And the ones I have seen,' he added, half to Harry Holden. Harry chortled.

'Oh, yes, we've seen some fine performances there,' he agreed. 'Very, um, accomplished.'

It was obvious there was something to which they were

referring that was not opera. Isobel assumed either drink or women, neither of which, of course, it would be seemly for her to mention. Not that she had any wish to encourage their conversation, but she was a little surprised that Lady Akehurst still looked so benevolently upon her nephew Harry for bringing the subject, however allusively, to her dinner table. Harry seemed to be a favourite.

'But dear Harry, you could come with us if you wished to Lady Fanshawe's ball. The whole household was included in the invitation – even you, Mr. Ketchell,' she added, through tight lips, then brightened as she returned her gaze to her nephew. 'We shall all be there!'

'I shall not,' said Sir Joshua suddenly. The butler dropped three knives with a clatter on to the broad sideboard. 'I am going to the House.'

'Oh, my dear, must you?' Lady Akehurst's chins wobbled with disappointment. 'You know we must make a fine appearance. For Amanda's sake.'

For a moment, both Sir Joshua and Lady Akehurst shone looks of gleaming devotion on their grand-daughter. Amanda seemed oblivious.

'I shall be honoured to escort you, my lady,' said Blair. 'If it would be helpful.'

'I, too,' said Mr. Lawrence at once, eyeing Blair with disapproval. 'I am sure we can be no substitute for Sir Joshua, but we shall have some splendour, my lady.'

'Indeed two escorts might look a little over-splendid,' Blair muttered.

'What was that, Mr. Blair?' Lady Akehurst asked with a puzzled smile.

'It will indeed be splendid,' he enunciated more clearly. Isobel could not quite see his face but she could imagine her father's look of open innocence.

'I so look forward to a ball!' said Amanda, angling her little head in a manner Isobel felt sure she thought alluring. She had seen it several times directed at eligible young men. 'They are delicious occasions! Such finery, such refreshment, such dancing! I swear I had three offers for every dance at the last ball! And such delightful company!'

Such standing about, thought Isobel, such over-crowding,

such heat and sweat, clogged powder and damp hair and stale perfume. She would rather stay at home and read a book – or if she had to attend, she would prefer to find a quiet spot on a balcony and fill her sketchbook. But the husband hunt was still a novelty for Amanda. No doubt it would not be a long one: Amanda was, well, not conventionally pretty, and so far Isobel had seen little evidence of intelligence, but she was Sir Joshua Akehurst's grand-daughter and sole heir. That would be quite sufficient to find her a train of suitors, no doubt.

'But, Sir Joshua, the meeting about the signals!' Sir Joshua's secretary was young and almost universally monochrome. His hair had turned early and it seemed that he dressed in mourning for it. Even his voice was colourless, and Isobel had never heard him speak above a whisper. He was rarely far from Sir Joshua's elbow. Just now he shuffled the papers beside his plate and chose one to wave gently. 'You made an especial point of making sure all the right people would be gathered for it.'

'Yes, Paulinson, thank you. Mr. Paulinson has gone to a great deal of trouble over it my dear. I cannot possibly abandon it now.'

'But my dear!' squawked Lady Akehurst.

Blair tapped his nutmeg grater on the edge of the table, then jumped to see that everyone was looking at him.

'I beg your pardon!' he said at once, wide-eyed. 'What kind of signals, Sir Joshua? It's a fascinating subject.'

'It certainly is,' said Sir Joshua at once. Isobel saw Harry Holden close his eyes hard – not so fascinating, it appeared, to him. 'We are rebuilding the semaphore towers we used in the Wars – there was a line from the Admiralty to Portsmouth. The speed at which messages could be sent was astonishing! But the new towers will be even better. Brick built, with internal controls so that you can set up each letter at prodigious speed. I must show you some of the sketches – Paulinson, do you have the folder there?'

'I beg you, my dear, not at the table,' said Lady Akehurst quickly, with a glance at Harry. 'You don't want them to be spoiled. And we have not settled about Lady Fanshawe's ball!'

Isobel would go where she was taken, with little choice in the matter. She let the conversation sweep over her, and considered their host. Sir Joshua Akehurst, elevated to a knighthood only very recently for services to the financial wellbeing of the Prince Regent, had more money than he knew what to do with. In fact, his principal pleasure in it seemed to be its accumulation ('not always,' Fussy had told her, 'entirely honourably, for there have been stories of men ruined and children and wives abandoned to the poorhouse while Sir Joshua has reaped the profits. Rumours of desolation and self-killing, if you can believe it!'). And with his only son dead, the wealth, such of it as had not already been spent on trying to find her a husband a social step up from the knightage, was destined for Amanda. In the meantime, though, others could try to seize a share, in one form or another. Harry Holden and Mr. Ketchell, valiant Corinthians, had emptied their wine glasses again and Ketchell was eyeing the butler, hoping for a refill.

'Anyway,' said Lady Akehurst at last, after glaring at Ketchell, 'we need to make the most of our time in London. Take any advantages we are able to.'

Ketchell snorted, grinning. Lady Akehurst waved the butler over to her and drew him down to listen to some whispered instruction. The butler, bending low to hear her, lost his balance and had to catch the edge of the table with one hand, tugging the cloth a little. Mr. Lawrence steadied his own glass, which was still full.

'How long do you plan to stay in London, Lady Akehurst?' he asked. The butler stepped back from the table, and pointedly looked away from Ketchell, who was now holding up his empty glass towards the butler.

'Oh, not perhaps much longer,' said Lady Akehurst, ignoring the pantomime. Her speculative gaze fell on Amanda. No doubt she was trying to calculate how much longer they would have to wait for a proposal.

'And then you plan to go to Leamington Spa?' Mr. Lawrence pursued. 'You will not wish to take your whole household with you, guests and all!' He tweaked his mouth briefly into a dry smile, trying to make it look like a jest, but his eyes were on Blair.

'But I have no intention of going to Leamington now, Mr. Lawrence! I have heard that the water there is not at all good for our purposes, and the society quite limited this season. No, we shall go into Sussex as usual, and relish all that our new home county has to offer.'

Oh heavens, thought Isobel, she means Brighton. Surely they

would not have to go with her? But Mr. Lawrence looked almost as dismayed as she felt.

'Sussex?' he repeated. 'But that is where I myself intended to go. You know that my home is in Lewes.'

'Of course, Mr. Lawrence. I believe you did mention it. I found it a little surprising that you so extolled the merits of Leamington when you have Brighton on your doorstep!' She leaned towards him, teasing. Isobel hoped she would not topple from her chair, or they would never lift her off the floor. 'You are a little disloyal to your county, are you not? Dear me, Mr. Lawrence!'

The stiff smile reappeared stoically on Mr. Lawrence's grey face.

'As I said, I had heard very good things of Leamington. Lady Akehurst, you would not have me recommend somewhere to you out of loyalty only, would you? When I believed that a different place might prove beneficial?'

Goodness, thought Isobel, his flirtation might have been made out of starched linen, stiff with disuse. It was painful to watch. And what, now, was Mr. Lawrence up to?

Of those around the table, it was only Mr. Lawrence and Fussy Payne that she had met before this visit. Fussy Payne was amiable and kindly, if a little vague, and always easy company. Mr. Lawrence was his godfather, and neither amiable nor kindly nor indeed vague. Mr. Lawrence had married, many years ago, a lady named Jane Olliver. Jane Olliver had had a sister – both ladies were now dead – who had, even more years ago, married Alester Blair. Mr. Lawrence was, then, Isobel's uncle. And he and Alester Blair had detested each other for ever.

Chapter Two

'We're away to London?'

'Aye, lad: there's a thing.'

Murray's coachman, Donald McKenzie, had been to London before and was unimpressed. His nephew, however, Young Donald, a man approaching twenty, had seen less of the world.

'To London?' It was less a reiteration of the question, and more an awed echo. 'My … My pals in Glasgow will never believe it!'

'If you don't get that harness smartened up we'll no be going any road,' Donald's uncle pointed out. 'And make sure your livery's clean and your boots polished. I'll no have you letting me down, never mind Mr. Murray.'

'Aye, Uncle, I'll make you proud of me!' A minute or two of enthusiastic polishing later, and another thought had struck him. 'Do you think I would have time to get a letter off to my mother? Just to let her know where I'm off to? She'd be that proud!'

'Aye, of course, lad,' said his uncle. 'Nettie'll want to know all your news. Away and do that now while the light's good, and tuck it in the bag for the carrier, and then you can settle down to your polishing.'

'Thanks, Uncle!' cried Young Donald, and was up and out before the harness he had been holding hit the bench.

'Aye,' said the coachman to himself, addressing a particularly stiff new bit of leather with his cloth and brushes, 'the lad's got energy, right enough.' He sighed, then smiled to himself. Young Donald had brought a bit of a sparkle into life in the mews, there was no doubt about it.

'Are you sure, Robbins?' Murray asked for what he thought

was probably the fifth or sixth time. 'You're happy to come to London?'

'Aye, sir.' Robbins, who had been Murray's manservant ever since Murray's father's death, nodded his pale head. 'Who else would go?'

'Well …' It was true that Murray had had a succession of dubious and dim lads over the last year in an attempt to train them up to replace Walter. Walter had not been a brilliant manservant, but he was now making good progress at the University of St. Andrews, a much better place for him. Murray had shaved himself more often than he had let any of the lads shave him, and had grown used to baths of various temperatures, clothes inadequately brushed, bedsheets unwarmed and either being left to sleep late in the mornings or being brutally awoken by the clattering of fire irons and the like.

'And you'd not want to take William or Daniel.'

'No …' William and Daniel, no longer lads, had their own faults, and their own families, too. But then Robbins had a wife, and two children.

'Are you sure Mary – Mrs. Robbins – would not mind?'

'She let me come to Edinburgh, sir,' said Robbins, the least smile in his pale eyes.

'Ah, yes, but London!'

'It's Mr. Blair, sir. And Smith, too.'

Of course. Robbins would consider loyalty to be owed not only to his master, but also to Mr. Blair. And Smith, Blair's man, was an old friend, too. Murray reminded himself that it was not only his own obligations he should think of here.

'Well, there's no doubt I'd be glad to have you. Is Old Donald happy? Are the horses fit, or would he rather, do you think, that we took the mail?'

'He tells me everything is fine, sir. We'll be ready to leave tomorrow, if you are.'

He continued silently rubbing glasses – Murray had discovered him in his pantry – while Murray glanced down again at Blair's letter.

'"A matter of some concern,' he read aloud, 'and though I have no <u>reason</u> to think it urgent, my <u>heart</u> tells me that it may be so, and that the lady is already in danger." The underlinings are quite firm. I think he is really worried.'

'He would not summon you like that, sir, if he were not.'

'No.'

'He does not name the lady?'

'He would be too discreet to do so in a letter. Or Isobel would remind him, anyway, for I'm sure she had a hand in this one.'

'Miss Blair is there, too?'

'Yes, she is. So whatever the problem is, it is something that he does not feel that he, and Smith, and Isobel, are capable of handling together.'

Robbins' eyes widened just a little.

'That could be interesting, sir.' He set the glass down on the bench. 'I think if I put it to Mary, she would make sure I went with you.'

'If only to hear the story later,' Murray agreed. Robbins nodded.

'Mary likes a good story, sir.'

The carrier brought his bag early the following morning, just in time for Murray to receive his letters before his departure. There were a couple for Robbins, too, from Letho, and one for the groom, Young Donald. Donald blushed as he took it and, at a curious look from his uncle, tucked it into the front of his livery coat. He did indeed look smart.

'My mother's reply,' Murray heard him breathe to the coachman before he stooped to arrange the steps at the carriage door. Murray put off climbing them as long as he could: the carriage was generously built, but anyone with his long legs would never be perfectly comfortable in it. He watched Robbins ensuring that every box he had packed was in fact on the carriage and not abandoned in the hallway, watched the coachman checking over the harness and the horses' hooves, watched the horses anticipating hard work and variety, watched the curious gazes of a couple of maids, peeping from the window while pretending to dust. But at last it was time to fold himself into the dark box and allow Robbins to climb in after him – as a senior servant he was permitted, but as a travelling companion, particularly as Murray could not easily read in a carriage, he was invaluable.

There was a nip in the autumn air and they arranged blankets over their laps, already appreciating the hot bricks wrapped amongst them. Murray would leave the windows open as long as he could. Young Donald flipped up the steps, closed the door, checked the leather handle and disappeared. They could hear him clambering up to his perch. A couple of words exchanged with his uncle, a firm 'Go on!' to the horses, a lurch as the wheels found their way over the cobbles, and they were off.

At the hour at which the carriage was setting off from its mews in Edinburgh's New Town, no one was remotely awake in the tall white house in Fitzroy Square. No one, that is, except Alester Blair.

His room was at the front of the building but he had already padded silently through some other parts of the house to obtain a view to the rear, to the yard and stables. He had observed a man whipping a horse he had no right to whip. He had seen a woman begging for food at the back gate, being turned away by one servant, then after a moment being pursued by another servant who swiftly passed her half a loaf and an apple. He had watched the stable cat, as interested in the scenes of life as he was himself, perching on a low roof to wash in peace after finishing off some morsel she had brought with her. Like the cat, Blair was not looking for anything in particular: he wanted to take in the day, and see what was going on in the world.

It felt intrusive to be about before the family appeared: he was in the world of the servants, sneaking from room to room making sure he was not disturbing any of them at their work. But like the family, the servants here tended to sleep late – how could they not, when the family had them waiting up to receive them at all hours of the morning? – and Blair slipped alone through grey shuttered rooms, weaving about the shadows of furniture, blinking into dark corners and tiptoeing up and down stairs. For a moment he hesitated in the passage where Miss Akehurst had her bedchamber, but he saw nothing out of the ordinary, and slid away again.

He returned to his own room and perched for a while on the windowseat where Isobel had sat to draw the other day. Why was she not married? he asked himself, his eyes following a street sweeper as the lad worked his way along the railings opposite. She was a bonny girl – woman, now – with a good fortune to come to her, and more than her fair share of wit. It was a familiar question and he had no good answer, so he let his mind meander on. Miss Akehurst would not wait so long before marrying, he was sure, though even her late mother must have admitted that her principal attraction was the inheritance due to her from her grandfather Sir Joshua Akehurst.

Blair tended to be charitable when it came to the charms of young females, but even he found it difficult to say anything positive about Miss Akehurst. While other well-rounded young ladies looked blooming and bright, she looked like undercooked dough. Her skin had a dusty look. It was unfortunate, but if she had been a different person it would have mattered less. Miss Akehurst did not try to be pleasant company, though. Her smiles were insincere, her conversation focussed chiefly on herself and on the young gentlemen she had met or hoped to meet. If she were well-informed, she hid it extremely well. Her drawing and singing were of little merit, her playing worse. And her eyes, so often the saving grace of anyone for whom he struggled for a compliment, were of a perfectly ordinary blue and rather too small, her lashes pale and her eyelids puffy.

But her fortune … that was her charm, and also, quite possibly, her downfall. For Blair was convinced that Miss Akehurst was in danger.

He had come upon her in the drawing room early one morning – well, not so early for him, but early for the household. She had been reading a note, and though she crumpled it quickly when she heard him enter the room, once she saw it was only old Mr. Blair she began to straighten it out again, smoothing each crease gently.

'Oh, I am sorry to have interrupted you!' said Blair at once.

'Not at all, Mr. Blair,' said Amanda with a sigh.

'For I am all too aware that elegant young ladies, on receipt of a love letter, prefer to be alone,' he went on.

'A love letter! But how did you – I mean, I don't suppose Miss Blair ever …' Confused, she subsided a little, allowing Blair a moment to restrain any resentment he might have felt on his daughter's behalf. Certainly Isobel had received love letters, but he chose not to comment, merely waiting. Inevitably, Amanda Akehurst could not resist an explanation.

'I believe it is a love letter, indeed, Mr. Blair,' she allowed, turning an unflattering shade of old rose. 'Though – well, it is a bit of a mystery! Clearly my admirer is shy!'

She gave the note a final pressing, and handed it to Blair. He puffed and squinted, and with her permission carried it over to the window for clearer light.

'Sweet angel,' it began, rather to his surprise. 'My every thought is of you. You shall belong to none but me. I cannot wait until you are entirely mine. I cannot rest. You will come to me when the time is right. Your devoted admirer.'

'Gracious,' he remarked.

'Of course one receives these things,' said Amanda with a small, irritating toss of her head, and another blush that made her out to be an exaggerator, at least. 'Yet there is a sincerity to this one, I confess, that intrigues me.'

'An intensity, yes,' said Blair thoughtfully.

'What was that?'

'It strikes me that this young man would not make, um, a comfortable admirer.'

'Comfortable? No!' she said, misunderstanding him. 'As he declares, it seems he will never be comfortable until or unless I choose to make him happy! Poor fellow,' she added, with a simper. 'I wonder who it could be? Lord Kemleigh's son, perhaps? He asked me to dance four times at Lady Chambers' ball, you know!'

'I do know,' said Blair sadly. She had announced the fact at every meal since the event, besides that he had been present at the ball himself. Lord Kemleigh's son had struck him as a young man with an eye to the best benefit for himself, but then so had several who had attended Miss Akehurst with interest. It did not mark him out as someone who would go to the trouble of writing mysterious billets doux.

'Or Mr. Horston-Privett?' Amanda pondered. 'He too danced with me several times, and would have filled my card if I had let him!' It rather proved his point. There was nothing much to choose between her apparent admirers. Yet the writer of this note demonstrated something like possessiveness. He shivered, then reprimanded himself. It was only the one note, after all. The man who wrote it might well be young and inexperienced in such things, and had happened to hit on the wrong tone.

'What does your grandmother say about it?' he asked. 'She is best placed to give you good advice.'

'Oh, no! Grandmamma must not know!' Amanda was breathless with alarm. 'No, he said so in his very first note!'

'You mean there have been more?'

'Of course! Look.' She drew three more pieces of paper, all small, from the depths of her cleavage. They were all very warm, and a little damp. Blair fingered them with caution.

'This must be our secret,' the first one ended. 'Tell no one,' said the second. 'I speak no word of my devotion to any but you, and you must do the same,' the third began, and all added sentiments similar to those in the note he had seen first.

'Have these been arriving for some time, then?'

'Oh, only a few days. One a day,' she said. 'He is certainly determined!'

'And you have no idea who it might be, beyond guesses? No one has made it clear to you in person, and there have been no details that might help you identify him?'

'Details?' she asked vaguely. 'Like what?'

'Like … well, "The pink dress you wore last night at the ball was particularly charming".'

'I don't often wear pink,' she said, frowning. Blair blew out a sigh through loose lips.

'Or "Did you enjoy the recital as much as I did?" That kind of thing. Something that might tell you where he had been, where you might have seen him.'

'Oh! No, nothing about recitals. Or gowns, or anything like that.'

'Hm,' said Blair. The notes could have been written at any time, to anyone. None of them contained her name. 'How do you receive them?'

'Oh, with the greatest of pleasure!'

He rubbed his forehead vigorously.

'No, Miss Akehurst,' he said, 'I mean how do they arrive?'

'Oh! Under my door, early in the morning. This one,' the one she had first shown him, 'came just now.'

Blair blinked.

'Then someone in the household is involved.'

'Oh, don't be ridiculous, Mr. Blair! Who in this household

might possibly be sending such things?'

'Well, either that or someone is capable of sneaking in and out again, four times, without anyone seeing him. Or he has bribed a servant.'

The possibilities seemed to baffle her, and a little smile bloomed on her face.

'He is really most devoted, is he not?' she sighed.

He shook his head and excused himself, and went back to his room to ponder the matter.

And he had pondered it since, while making it part of his daily routine to see if he could spot anyone where they had no reason to be around the house, early in the morning. He had debated the matter with Isobel several times.

'Harry Holden,' she suggested each time, committing little sketches of each man to her book. 'Or Barnabas Ketchell. Or Fussy Payne.'

'I can't see any of them doing it. It's not Mr. Payne's style at all. Barnabas …'

'Isn't ever sober for long enough,' Isobel would remind him. 'Nor, really, is Harry Holden. But you're right: Fussy is far too nice.'

'One of the servants, rising above his station?' he had suggested more than once.

'It's possible – though you say it was an elegant hand. It's less likely. The only servant who seems to be of that level is poor Mr. Trent.' She had gone and found out the butler's name, though not, as yet, why he was so nervous.

'Never steady enough to write a whole note.' Blair nodded agreement. 'Could that be the reason for his nerves? Is he the one bribed to slip the notes under Miss Akehurst's door?'

'Surely he would not take that risk. He would lose his place at once. Yet,' she went on, 'there is certainly something affecting his nerves. He might not be able to keep his place much longer as it is.' That was the evening that Trent had dropped a gobbet of hot potato from a pie down the back of Isobel's gown. She still had a scar inside her lip where she had bitten it.

Blair sighed, remembering all these conversations. There was so little to go on, so little even to mention to Lady Akehurst. And when did he ever get a chance to talk to Lady Akehurst anyway? She, and her summons, were the reason he was here in this awkward household, but though he and Isobel had borne with the whole place for over a week, suffering the glares of Mr. Lawrence and the irritations of Harry Holden and Amanda Akehurst, and the self-important if fascinating lectures of Sir Joshua, Lady Akehurst had not once been available for private conversation nor shown any inclination to tell Blair why she had wanted him in the party.

The glares of Mr. Lawrence … An educated, intelligent man, with an elegant hand. A man he detested, with a loathing that he could not remember ever feeling for anyone else in his whole long life. Instinct told him that Mr. Lawrence was the man in the house most capable of sending unpleasant, ambiguous little notes to a young lady. But in the case of Mr. Lawrence, Blair knew that he was more than likely to be biased. That was why he needed Charles Murray.

Charles Murray himself was making uncertain progress down the country, in weather most generously described as autumnal. The new groom, Donald, seemed to spend more of his time on the ground than actually on the carriage, wading through mud and hauling the horses out of potholes. Murray was annoying himself, never mind Robbins, by opening the window for fresh air and slamming it closed again in the face of driving rain, then opening it again to gasp at the narrow aperture. On a few occasions the pair of them also dismounted and walked, slithering through soaked grass, to help Donald loosen a wheel or add their strength to a party of locals trying to shove a cart out of the ditch, or into the ditch – it was not always easy to distinguish.

'Young Donald's shaping up well,' Murray remarked to Robbins as they ate their supper in a foggy inn parlour that night, steam oozing from every inch of them. 'His uncle must be pleased with him.'

'Aye, it would seem so,' Robbins agreed. 'He has a gift with horses.'

'Did he work with them in Renfrew?'

'I don't believe so. But he was glad enough to get the post with us.'

'Why the move?' Murray would usually have known the background of all his servants, but he had been away for some time recently: he needed to catch up.

'That bit of trouble in the west, sir,' said Robbins, precisely removing the last of the meat from his lamb chop.

'He was involved in that?'

'Not directly, sir. As I understand it, he came to Edinburgh to escape the business. You know what it's like with young men in a group: when one or two get themselves into bother, the others are quickly drawn in. He left before it could happen to him.'

'Good lad,' said Murray. 'I hope he finds the position to his liking.'

'Old Donald takes good care of him, anyway,' said Robbins, 'and he keeps contact with his family. That was a letter from his mother, apparently, he received just as we were leaving.'

'A good sign,' Murray agreed. 'Now, if we could only find a housekeeper as easily ...'

The talk turned to staffing problems, and their energies to praying for better weather to come.

'A letter from Charles?' Isobel queried.

'He's on his way,' said Blair.

'I knew he would come if you asked him.'

'I wish he could be here sooner.'

'Has she had more notes?'

'A few, yes. Almost every day.'

'And you've still seen nothing in the mornings?' She sketched a shadowy figure in a corridor, hovering beside a door with a paper in its hand. Looking at it she shuddered, and tweaked it to make a smiling face in the shadow, but it was still somehow unpleasant. She scored a line through it.

'Not a thing.' Her father sighed heavily, jiggling his knees. 'I've tried all kinds of times, but short of making up my bed in the passage outside her room I can think of no way to be certain of either seeing him or stopping him.'

'And if she found you there she would take you for another admirer, no doubt,' said Isobel with a grin.

'I had wished,' said Blair, 'that Lady Akehurst would tell me why she had asked me to be one of this party, and let me oblige her or not as was fitting, and let us go, but now I do not want to leave until I think Miss Akehurst is safe. Which is just as well, as Lady Akehurst still has not made her intentions known. Sometimes,' he added, looking like a child promised a toy which was being kept out of reach, 'she gives me a significant look, as if to say that after dinner she will tell me everything. And the rest of the time she looks through me, as if she has no idea why we should be in her house at all.'

'Perhaps she is mad,' said Isobel. 'Perhaps we all are, or we would not be here.'

Chapter Three

'Good day to you, cousin!'

Isobel looked about her, over the back of the sopha, and saw Fussy Payne's amiable face in the doorway.

'I don't think that's an entirely accurate salutation,' said Isobel, waving him into the parlour. 'Mr. Lawrence is your godfather, not your actual father.'

Fussy shrugged.

'Mr. Lawrence is kinder to me than my real father was, and besides, at least Mr. Lawrence is alive.'

'It is an advantage, certainly.' Isobel grinned. 'Well, then, honorary cousin by the rite of baptism, what are you up to this morning? I hope you know that no fashionable person rises this early.'

'Your father has been up for hours.'

'Proving my point,' said Isobel.

'And you yourself seem up and alert.'

'Again, this supports my argument, not yours. There is nothing fashionable in our family.'

'Then I am honoured to be an honorary member of it,' said Fussy with a bow. 'Anyway, I wondered, seeing you were up and no one else is and it's a fine morning and no one much will be about taking up space, if you cared to go for a promenade?'

'What, in the park?'

'Just across the road, yes. I had no intention of troubling either a coachman or my boots – they are new, and nip most terribly.' He surveyed his well-polished feet with a glum expression. 'A breath of air is all I seek, and if it is available then a little gentle conversation.'

Isobel was not at all averse to the idea.

'I shall fetch my bonnet,' she said.

Furnished with bonnet, as well as spencer, gloves and umbrella, Isobel ventured forth on Adolphus Payne's arm a few moments later. Despite his enthusiasm for the outing, he winced as the low autumn sunlight glanced across his eyes.

'Not just the boots that are nipping, then,' Isobel observed. 'You were out with Harry Holden and Mr. Ketchell last night, weren't you?'

'Mmm,' said Fussy, shielding his eyes with his free hand.

'Sampling, perhaps … what did they call it? Blue Ruin?'

'That's one name for it,' Fussy agreed.

'Is gin blue?' Isobel asked, with an artist's curiosity.

'There's a blueishness to it, I suppose,' said Fussy. 'Sort of like the blue in lead. It might even be lead. In the kind of place we were drinking, I wouldn't trust them to serve a glass of pure anything if they could eke it out with something cheaper and nastier.'

Isobel chuckled. What Fussy did was up to him, but he was usually more sensible than to venture into the London night with a couple of dissolute would-be Corinthians like Harry and Mr. Ketchell. They reached the iron gates of the park belonging to the houses in the square: private and well-kept, it made for pleasanter exercise than strolling in the sight of the most analytical members of society in Hyde Park.

It had not yet rained this morning – the sunshine trickled through the trees to continue its torment of Fussy's poor head – but the laurels' leathery leaves were lined with diamond droplets, eager to spoil a silk gown. Fortunately for Isobel she rarely bothered with silk during the day, and the wool of her spencer protected her from the infiltration of any cold water. Fussy did his best to hold back branches with his cane, but he was not adept. The most he achieved was a shower of drops down his own sleeve, causing him to exclaim in disgust.

'So where did you find yourself last night?' Isobel asked once they were on a wider path.

'All Max,' said Fussy.

'Almack's? I didn't know you had a ticket.'

'No, All Max,' Fussy repeated, spelling it. 'It's a pun, don't you see?'

'Ho, ho.'

Fussy grinned apologetically.

'It's near the Tower of London. Max is another word for gin, too. No ticket required. And to be accurate, I didn't so much find myself there as lose myself. Maybe we went on somewhere else later, but if we did I have extraordinarily little recollection of it.'

'You're lucky you came home at all.'

Fussy grunted agreement.

'I don't think Ketchell did. Harry and I saw each other back.'

'And where did Mr. Ketchell end up?'

He slid her a sideways look of warning and alarm.

'Better not to ask!'

'Oh,' said Isobel, imagining five different things at once, all of them dreadful. She thought Mr. Ketchell capable of any of them.

'Why is Mr. Ketchell staying with the Akehursts?' she asked suddenly. It was a question that had been bothering her. Fussy blinked.

'Oh! Well, he's a chum of Harry's, you know.'

'Heaven protect me from chums such as those,' Isobel murmured. 'But why, then, is Harry staying with the Akehursts? Is he a relation?'

'Of Lady Akehurst's, yes. Some kind of nephew or cousin or some such.'

'Another of your cousins,' Isobel teased. 'He seems to be a favourite of hers.'

'Yes, that's right, though I can't imagine why. Favourite enough to make her tolerant of Ketchell's being there, too.'

'Extraordinary,' said Isobel. She would not have tolerated Mr. Ketchell in her house for as long as it would take for him to drink a bottle of Blue Ruin. 'Even more extraordinary that you should have decided to go out with them,' she added. 'It's not like you at all, is it?'

'Ah, well, they were very persuasive,' said Fussy.

'I'm still surprised.'

'Ah, well,' Fussy repeated, defensively. 'I'm a bit surprised myself. Still, when you're in London you have to see London, don't you?' He sighed, trying to ease his shoulders back in his tight coat. Isobel had noted that men's coats were becoming rather broader in the shoulder: Fussy was a step behind fashion, but then he was not a great one for the town.

'I don't feel any need to see London,' Isobel said. 'Nor indeed to be here.'

'Oh? Then why are you here?'

'Because …' Isobel hesitated, but she trusted Fussy: she had known him for years. 'Because Lady Akehurst wants my father's advice, or help, or something, but she has not yet told him why.'

'Ah,' said Fussy, 'that may be my fault.'

'Your fault?'

'She said she had a problem and wanted help. I knew Mr. Blair was good at that kind of thing – hasn't he been involved in murders and things, in North Britain? I mean, in finding out who did them, of course, not in committing them. Hasn't he?'

Fussy's wide-eyed anxiety over getting things right was touching.

'Yes, yes he has,' Isobel reassured him. 'But surely there is no murder at issue here?'

'Oh,' said Fussy, flicking his cane over some dreary autumn shrubs, 'I have no idea what it is. But she seemed pleased to be told someone could help, and asked me at once for Mr. Blair's directions. And, well, I like to keep in with Lady Akehurst. And Sir Joshua, of course.'

Isobel waited, not quite sure why she did but hoping that if she said nothing an explanation would follow. The park was quiet except for a croaking of rooks in the bare trees. For a few paces, they continued in silence along the sandy path, footsteps dulled. After a moment, Fussy fulfilled her expectations.

'Oh, it's rotten being poor when you're wanted to put up a respectable appearance! And, well, I suppose I have no real hopes of the Akehursts – Amanda is Sir Joshua's heir and that is that, but I'm the next in line – Sir Joshua was my father's uncle – and I did wonder if he might leave a little to me and still give Amanda enough to see her well settled. There is a great deal to go around – if only he would let it go a little further around.' He heaved a weary sigh. This was clearly a long term concern.

'You could always marry her,' said Isobel, a little mischievously. But Fussy had already contemplated that.

'I could, if she'd have me,' he said. 'Though I don't like the idea of marrying only for money. One should have some feeling for the lady, surely?' He looked thoughtful, and then seemed to realise what he had said: he glanced at Isobel apologetically. 'But as I say, she would never consider me. Amanda has her eyes on a title, at the very least, and if possible a match of fortunes. No hope for me at all!'

'Poor Fussy!' said Isobel. 'You'll just have to turn to crime, and become a highwayman!'

He laughed, and nodded.

'That's the perfect solution. I can ride passably well, and let off random shots as inaccurately as anybody. Of course I should have to borrow the horse and probably pay for its keep, and then balls and powder have to be paid for, too … I shall have to go into the whole thing, and see if it could be made profitable.'

'I shall stitch you a mask,' said Isobel generously, 'for if anyone were to recognise you, they would be so shocked they would probably faint, and might do themselves an injury in falling.'

'Oh, quite right! I thank you for the thought. I have no wish that anyone should suffer injury. Or alarm. Or loss of any kind … which makes it unlikely that I should be much of a success.'

'Then I don't know what is to be done with you. You will just have to make out an advertisement for a wealthy young lady who will be amenable to your charms and whom you will find completely captivating. Make them apply in writing, first: you can tell a great deal from a good letter,' she added, then thought of Amanda's love letters. 'You don't know, do you, Fussy, of anyone who might be paying court to Amanda? A secret admirer, perhaps?'

Fussy considered.

'No, I don't think so. Of course, if they were successfully secret, I should know nothing about it anyway. I'm not very good at spotting clever things like that.'

'She hasn't mentioned anything to you? You haven't seen anyone perhaps watching her at a ball or at the theatre, without her being aware?'

He laughed.

'At any one time Amanda has a mark on every young man in the vicinity, whether or not they are paying her any attention. I doubt that anyone could watch her without her being aware.'

Any young man, thought Isobel to herself. Any young man,

yes, but what if the man were older? Something about those letters, as her father had described them to her, spoke of an older man – an experienced, watchful, controlling man. She shivered.

'Are you cold?' asked Fussy at once – he was always attentive to his companions. 'Would you like to go back?'

'No, no,' said Isobel, 'let us complete our circuit. You are almost a natural colour again, and I shall not see you go back to the house without being fully recovered.'

Fussy was much better on their return, and in that he was considerably ahead of Harry Holden, whom they found slouched over a tray of tea in the parlour. Their hostess Lady Akehurst was with him.

'Poor Harry is most unwell this morning!' she exclaimed when she saw them. Her voice bounced off each crystal of the chandelier in turn, and Harry's cup clattered on its saucer. His face was an interesting yellowish-grey colour, and his eyes were puffy.

'I'm very sorry to hear that,' said Fussy, and Isobel thought he looked genuinely concerned. Fussy was a very nice man.

'An oyster, at Vauxhall, I think,' said Harry indistinctly.

'Have some more tea, Harry – it is sure to wash things out!' Lady Akehurst refilled his cup and Harry looked as if something were going to wash out forthwith.

Isobel felt herself braced to step back sharply.

'Perhaps you should try a little fresh air. It has brightened Mr. Payne up tremendously,' she said, very slightly louder than was necessary. She had established her opinion of Harry in the few days they had been in the house, and thought he was a fool. An easily-led fool, too – and where was Mr. Ketchell today? She hoped that wherever he might have laid his head last night, it had been spinning when he lifted it this morning. She had no doubt he was a bad influence on both Harry and Fussy.

'And plenty of milk with your tea,' Lady Akehurst added. For a moment Isobel wondered if she were actually trying to cause Harry more pain under the guise of tenderness, but it seemed Lady Akehurst really thought milky tea would help. Harry leapt up and ran from the room, dropping and treading on his saucer in his haste. Even the nasty crack it gave did not make him pause.

'Oh!' said Isobel, stooping to pick up the two pieces of

china. 'That's unfortunate.'

'Poor dear Harry,' said Lady Akehurst, oblivious to the saucer. 'I wonder if I should summon my physician?'

'I think a little rest will help him, and later some fresh air, as Miss Blair suggested,' said Fussy. 'I'll keep an eye on him, and make sure he grows no worse, anyway.'

'That is very good of you, Adolphus,' said Lady Akehurst, though she still stared at the door as though willing Harry to return. 'Oh, will you take some tea, Miss Blair? Adolphus?'

She rang for replenishments.

'I hope Miss Akehurst is well this morning,' said Isobel. 'It was a late night last night.'

'She is not up yet, though she is awake and quite well, thank you,' said Lady Akehurst. 'It was a very successful evening. So many offers of dances! She is quite doted on by the young gentlemen in our circles.'

'Of course she is,' said Isobel as warmly as she could manage. 'Why would she not be?'

'Well, indeed! And some of them scions of the finest families in the town! It is such a shame the same good fortune did not come to you, Miss Blair!'

Out of the corner of her eye, Isobel saw Fussy flinch as if Lady Akehurst had struck out physically, but Isobel decided to ignore the remark.

'No doubt a suitable match will be found for Miss Akehurst very soon!' she said. 'Will we be delighted by an announcement before the end of the season, do you think?'

Lady Akehurst flushed a little, a pleased expression settling on her face.

'I should be very surprised if there was not something, Miss Blair. Very surprised indeed. There are three, or I may perhaps say four, very promising candidates who are all prodigiously interested in Amanda and are showing her the very greatest attention. Any one of them would be a – well,' she leaned forward towards Isobel as if Fussy would not then be able to hear her bellow. 'A triumph, you know?'

Isobel nodded approval, trying to look impressed. A triumph for what? For Lady Akehurst's matchmaking skills, or Sir Joshua Akehurst's fortune? It seemed very unlikely to be Amanda's charms, but there: Amanda was to be married before the season was out, while she, unclaimed treasure as she was, perched on her shelf to observe the way the world worked. She made a quiet wager with herself that this time next year, all other things being equal, she was likely to be happier than Amanda.

'Is there a ball this evening?' she asked, politely enthusiastic.

'Ah, alas, no,' said Lady Akehurst. 'There will be the theatre, though, and then I thought perhaps a turn in Vauxhall before supper at the Littleboroughs. There will be several of Amanda's friends in each place, I am sure. But I had thought that this afternoon you might care to accompany us in the carriage around the Park? A little fresh air, as you so rightly advised, brightens the complexion very favourably and will ensure that Amanda is quite fresh before the evening begins.'

'I should be very happy to make one of the party,' said Isobel, for each time she had gone to Hyde Park she had found more grotesques for her sketchbook, even if she had to commit them to memory and draw them later. Gentlemen and ladies squashed and spread into the most fashionable shapes, whatever nature might originally have intended – old fools drooling over young flirts – the society leader turning her back on some hapless individual and cutting him out of the rest of society for who knew what faux pas – the band of young pinks strutting about trying to catch everyone's eye … it was a treasure trove.

'I wonder would you be good enough to include me, too?'

They all jumped as Alester Blair stood suddenly from where he had been unnoticed in a high-backed chair by the window. He bowed humbly to Lady Akehurst.

'I should be very grateful if I might make one in the carriage. I'm afraid I am no horseman.'

Isobel smiled to see her father. He was extraordinarily good at not being noticed when he wished it. And she would be very glad of his company this afternoon – some of the conversation might be intelligent, and at least they could talk it over afterwards in private. Along with telling him all Fussy Payne had said, too.

There was perhaps a minor mystery to it, though, which Isobel was keen to solve.

'I thought you hated riding in the Park, Father,' she

murmured to him as they waited in the parlour for the others to be ready. It seemed to be taking an interminable time. The parlour was still as over-heated as it had been earlier and Isobel would have much preferred to have waited in the hall, but it was narrow and awkward.

'I don't like it very much,' Blair admitted. 'Or at least, I should far rather walk than sit in a carriage where you can only talk with people who happen to be about when it stops, or who trot alongside you. And in an open carriage I feel as if I have been laid out like a joint on a dish, ready for inspection.'

'Then why did you ask to go?'

'I found this this morning.' He rummaged in his massive pockets and, for a wonder, quickly produced a piece of paper. It was relatively fresh-looking, though he had to detach several threads and a piece of wax before handing it over to Isobel.

'Soon, my love, my enchantress, I shall come for you,' it read. 'Do not resist: I cannot live without you. I cannot say but that I might cause harm to others in my determination if you delay me.'

She handed it back to Blair.

'Has Amanda seen it? I take it this was for her.'

'He had not quite pushed it far enough under her door. I cannot decide whether I should give it to her or not. But in any case, I thought it wise to be near her when she goes out.' He scowled. 'I do not like the tone of these notes. Yet all Miss Akehurst sees in them is admiration and adoration.'

'Rather than threat and possessiveness,' said Isobel, nodding. 'It's a shame none of the young men is coming. Though I cannot think that Harry Holden or Mr. Ketchell would be much use in an emergency. Fussy doesn't have a horse, of course.'

'It may be enough that we are keeping alert: whoever he is, he might not strike if he sees that people are watching.'

'He must be a bold fellow, though, if you think he will strike in the middle of the promenade in Hyde Park. Unless, of course, he tries it on the way to or from the Park.'

'It could be anywhere,' said Blair, puffing out sadly through loose lips. 'He could follow her tonight, or he could be hauling her out through her bedroom window even as we speak.'

'We'd hear the screams, I'm quite sure,' said Isobel, not quite reassuringly.

The parlour door squeaked behind them – they had left it open so that they could see the rest of the party assemble. But in the doorway was Barnabas Ketchell. He gave Isobel a smile, the kind of smile that made her want to hide in the depths of a heavy and concealing cloak.

'Good day, Miss Blair, Mr. Blair. Are you off somewhere entertaining?'

'Only Hyde Park,' said Blair innocently.

Mr. Ketchell emitted a spurt of laughter.

'Only Hyde Park! I had not thought either of you so unimpressed by our London sights! What takes you there today?'

'Lady Akehurst's invitation,' said Isobel briskly. 'I think I hear her now.'

'Then I wish you well. Perhaps, Miss Blair, I shall have the good fortune to see you there later?'

'Perhaps,' she replied, taken aback at his manner. Fortunately at that moment Amanda Akehurst appeared behind him.

'Aren't we going?' she demanded, and the party gathered themselves instantly around her and Lady Akehurst, and made their way out to the carriage. Isobel, glancing back despite herself, saw Mr. Ketchell on the doorstep, bowing elaborately. The sardonic smile had not left his face once.

The Park was busy, as it always was on a Sunday. The coachman paused for a moment before urging the horses on to force a gap in the slow promenade, and Amanda primped the flowers on her bonnet, eyes already surveying the crowds for promising young men. Lady Akehurst divided her time between a similar scan and checking to see that Amanda was as perfectly presented as possible, parasol angled ungratefully against the gentle autumn sunlight.

The general division was ladies in carriages and gentlemen on horseback, though a few carriages included escorts like Blair, and in one or two cases a group of young pinks had a carriage to themselves and steered it close to promising young females. Bejewelled dowagers summoned elegant Corinthians to their sides with a flick of their gloved hands, demanding attention for their wards. A few horsemen tried their paces a little over to one side, showing off their skills, though most were content to impress with high fashion, glowing boot leather, and a fine seat. At some points the promenade was barely more than one carriage wide, while at others, where perhaps a particularly popular person had slowed, several carriages were bound to stop and horsemen milled about them. As the Akehurst carriage drew to a halt, Isobel, seated facing backwards beside her father, could feel his agitation: he glanced all about him, quicker at scanning the crowd even than Amanda herself. Isobel watched her: she was poised in what she seemed to think was a relaxed position, head a little on one side, more of the overdone Akehurst jewels weighing down her puffy bosom. Then she became aware of a little stirring in the crowd around them.

'Oh, look, Grandmamma – who on earth is that?' Amanda pointed with her parasol handle. One of the points struck Lady Akehurst's bonnet sharply.

'Amanda, be careful!'

'Miss Akehurst!'

For somehow, suddenly, there was a hand around Amanda's waist, and she was being hauled clear of the carriage into the arms of a masked horseman.

Chapter Four

'Mr. Blair! Good gracious!' cried Lady Akehurst, still trying to straighten her bonnet. 'What are you doing!'

But Blair was incapable of speech: he had lunged across the carriage and grasped Amanda hard around her knees. Isobel, armed with her furled parasol, struck the horseman hard across the arm, then decided poking him with the point would be more effective.

'Help!' she cried. 'Kidnap! Assault! Help!'

And to her astonishment, the horseman abruptly let go, spun his horse very neatly, and managed somehow to dart off through the crowd. The whole thing had lasted around ten seconds: the people around them had barely had the chance to take it in, and though a number of quizzing-glasses were raised in their direction, no one had the wit to pursue the attacker.

Blair sagged to the floor of the carriage. Amanda, far from the primped and polished young lady she had been a few moments ago, struggled back into the carriage from her perilous position flung over its side. Isobel helped her to straighten her fichu and bonnet, decency more important for the moment than shock or question. Her skirts were irredeemably crushed, and her face was a bright and unbecoming scarlet.

'What is happening?' Lady Akehurst had not yet caught up with events. 'What on earth were you doing, Mr. Blair? What is going on? Edwards, draw off to the side, man, at once! I shall not tolerate such behaviour! What were you doing to my grand-daughter?'

The coachman, who knew no more than anyone else of what had occurred, wisely ignored Lady Akehurst's confused gabble, and took the horses calmly off to the side of the path, but the little party was followed, irresistibly, by the rest of the ton, always desperate for novelty. Carriages and horsemen clustered around them, like hens around a handful of grain.

'He came for me!' Amanda gasped. It was not wholly clear whether she was excited or alarmed, though Isobel guessed from the way she was holding herself that the episode had not been without injury. Her ribs at least must be bruised. The horseman had dropped her like a stale piecrust. Isobel abandoned her parasol for the moment, and leaned over to help her father back into his seat. He was red and breathless, eyes wide. She helped him settle, then, glancing at Lady Akehurst she realised that their hostess had really seen very little of the incident, what with her bonnet being pulled over her eyes and her distraction with Blair's lunging forward so suddenly.

'A masked horseman,' said Isobel. Lady Akehurst very reasonably looked baffled. Isobel expanded, speaking more clearly. 'A masked horseman was trying to abduct Miss Akehurst.'

'A masked horseman!' someone next to her picked up the words, and she heard them rustling through the crowd, leaves blown by a gust of wind. 'Abducting Miss Akehurst!'

Lady Akehurst, still not quite sure what had really happened, was less than impressed. She began to scowl at the crowd, then remembered that they were better placated, and tried a light laugh. It did not become her.

'What? You are making a joke! It is all a joke,' she repeated, a little more loudly. 'Don't be ridiculous, Miss Blair! What a strange sense of humour you have! What would a masked horseman be doing in Hyde Park? In broad daylight?'

'Trying to abduct your grand-daughter,' Isobel replied, with what she thought was monumental patience. 'He rode a dark bay or black horse, wore an unexceptional green coat and hat, and had a black silk scarf tied about his face. I'm not sure I could reliably say more about him. Could you, Miss Akehurst?' she asked pointedly. Now was the moment for Amanda to tell her grandmother all about the disturbing notes.

'I could see nothing,' said Amanda, without looking at any of them. Indeed, she seemed to be scanning the crowds for the masked horseman. Isobel had no doubt he had whipped off his scarf and merged into the general population, possibly still in the park itself. If anything specific had marked his presence, it was confidence. Still, she could not resist her own survey of the crowd, recovering her parasol and holding it like a sword, trying to pinpoint any coats in that particular shade of green. But everyone milled about, as if deliberately trying to obscure the villain, while continued repetitions of 'A masked horseman!' sussurated back and forth. Then a figure came much closer than the rest of the crowd and Isobel jumped, her hands tightening on her parasol.

'Lady Akehurst,' said a familiar voice. 'Miss Akehurst. Is something amiss?'

Even if she had not recognised Mr. Lawrence's voice, the unhappy grunt from her father would have told her who it was. Blair had hunched over as if punched in the stomach. Mr. Lawrence had somehow guided his horse through their audience, and arrived at the side of the carriage, blocking as much of the view as he could contrive to give them some privacy. Unable to see their entertainment, the mob of decorative society principals began to move off, as no doubt Mr. Lawrence had intended. He was not one for public display. Just out of interest, Isobel noted that his coat was a dull grey. He seemed an unlikely kidnapper.

'Mr. Lawrence! We are just about to go home. I cannot have Amanda seen in such a state, not in the Park.' The facts of the case seemed to be sinking in: Lady Akehurst was breathless, a hand pressed to her bosom. 'What kind of place is this becoming?'

'Of course. Allow me to help clear your way.' Mr. Lawrence turned, and began to urge those nearest to move back. Gradually he made room for Edwards to manoeuvre the carriage, closely escorted by him, towards the gate of the park and out once more into the relative anonymity of the public street. Maintaining his distance, he rode beside the carriage, grim-faced and silent, all the way back to the house.

At the door, Lady Akehurst tugged Amanda rapidly out of her seat and up the steps, leaving the Blairs and Mr. Lawrence to follow at their own speed. Blair, who had slid out of the carriage first in order to hand Lady Akehurst down, was almost knocked over by Lady Akehurst's passing. Isobel and he steadied each other, making faces, then hurried into the house in frank curiosity, to see what might happen next.

Lady Akehurst and her grand-daughter had vanished into the parlour, and as the door had been left open the Blairs followed. Mr.

Lawrence must have abandoned his horse to a groom for Isobel felt at once the tension that always rose when he and her father were in the same place. Blair shambled off to the chair he had occupied earlier, huddling himself into its ungenerous upholstery. A rustle of pages told Isobel that he was hiding behind the latest edition of Ackermann's Repository. The Akehursts did not appear to notice him.

'Now, Amanda, I want you to tell me what just happened. I have never known such a thing before! And for it to happen to us! In the Park, in front of everyone!'

'A masked horseman seized me about the waist,' said Amanda, managing to convey a kind of sulky triumph. Only the most successful society ladies, she implied, could attract that kind of response – praise, rather than censure, was due.

'But how ridiculous! I said before that it was ridiculous, a joke. How could there have been a masked horseman in the Park? Who would wear a mask, when the whole purpose of being there is to be seen? And why would he choose to seize you, Amanda? Did you know of the fellow? For I cannot imagine it was anyone of our acquaintance.'

Amanda blushed.

'I don't really know who it was. I couldn't really see him.'

'It's true, Lady Akehurst,' Isobel agreed. 'He seized her rather clumsily, and her face was crushed into his coat.' He hadn't anticipated just how much she weighed, Isobel suspected. Had he really seen her before? If not, how had he known who to attack? Or had it been a chance encounter? But with the foregoing notes under Amanda's door, the coincidence would have been too great.

'Your face was crushed into his coat?' Lady Akehurst was still struggling with the details, as if a reputation could be ruined on such a small thing. Well, of course, it could, but by comparison with being snatched up by a masked horseman in the middle of Hyde Park, and having an elderly gentleman do his best to drag you back down again, it seemed a trivial point.

'Did he smell of anything?' Isobel asked suddenly. Both Akehursts turned and gaped at her. Mr. Lawrence let out a sharp, disgusted sigh, but a faint shaking of the pages of Ackermann's told her her father was listening. Good heavens, it was exactly the kind of question he would ask – which explained Mr. Lawrence's disgust.

'I mean, perhaps it would help to identify him if there were any kind of aroma about him. A strong smell of the stables, perhaps. Or of spirits – perhaps he was drunk?' She was sure he had not been: his movements, barring the struggle to lift Amanda, had been very precise.

'Goodness,' said Lady Akehurst, giving Isobel a hard stare. Then she turned to Amanda. 'Well? Did he seem drunk? It might at least explain such extraordinary behaviour.'

'I don't think so,' said Amanda, but Isobel thought that was not quite the whole answer. She might have the chance to ask Amanda again later.

'And then he let you go? Just like that?' Lady Akehurst preferred to pursue the more definite evidence.

'Well, Mr. Blair grabbed my legs and pulled me back away from the man,' said Amanda. 'It was most uncomfortable.'

'Did he?' asked Lady Akehurst. Isobel received another stare. 'So that is what he was doing on the floor of the carriage?'

'Yes, my lady,' said Isobel. 'I believe he simply acted as swiftly as he could to help Miss Akehurst and save her from the attacker.'

'I see,' said Lady Akehurst, looking more favourably at Isobel. 'And did I observe some work with a parasol?'

'I did my best, my lady,' Isobel admitted.

'Then we owe a debt to the Blair family,' said Lady Akehurst, much more kindly. Mr. Lawrence snorted in disdain, but the pages of Ackermann's were silent. 'Have you any impression of who the man might have been, Miss Blair? It seems to me you had the best view of the event. Had you seen the man – perhaps in the street, taking an interest in us?'

'No, I had not, my lady, to my knowledge, but there was nothing so extraordinary about his appearance aside from the mask. I don't believe I should have noticed him particularly without it.'

'But did you not think he was a handsome man?' Amanda exclaimed. 'A good seat, and fine eyes?'

'I beg your pardon, Amanda!' Lady Akehurst, who had been standing splendidly before the hearth to hold her enquiry, sat dramatically in an upright chair.

'I mean … from what I could see, Grandmamma.'

'But you said you could see nothing!' This time Lady

Akehurst's glare was for her grand-daughter. 'Amanda, tell me the truth: are you in some way acquainted with this man?'

'How could I possibly tell, Grandmamma?' Amanda asked, struggling with an air of concerned innocence. 'I could barely see him. I was simply imagining … I mean, I was wondering … And anyway, how could I have become acquainted with someone like that?'

'I should say he was a gentleman, or the better type of merchant,' said Isobel. 'I mean, you might have met him somewhere. I think he was the quality of person you – we – might have met.' The Akehurst ladies were watching her again, as if they thought she might produce a snake from her muff, or a puff of smoke from her ears. 'It was a very fine horse, and though the man's coat was unremarkable it was exactly the right kind of unremarkable – beautifully cut, from good cloth. And the mask was silk. There was money there, and taste, I should say, if nothing else.'

Amanda Akehurst's smug look had returned.

'There!' she said.

'Whatever his background,' said Lady Akehurst obstinately, 'attempting to abduct a young lady from her carriage – in the middle of Hyde Park,' she added, as though that somehow exacerbated an abduction rather than making it all the more challenging, 'is hardly the way to go about a respectable courtship. If he is one of your suitors, I shall be asking him some very serious questions as to his intentions. And if your grandfather were to hear of this –'

'To hear of what?'

'My dear!' Lady Akehurst started as the parlour door swung wholly open to reveal her husband framed like one of Raeburn's slightly sterner portraits – a minister, perhaps, with aspirations to be Moderator. 'My dear, had I but known you were at home …'

'I was working in my library,' said Sir Joshua, sourly, 'when I heard what appeared to be a legion of the Roman Army marching up the steps and into the house. I trust we have not been invaded, and that all it was was your return from the Park?' Paul Paulinson, his secretary, hovered behind him, ready to repel boarders, presumably.

'Well, yes, you see – well, Amanda felt a little faint – a slight headache, that is all – and dear Mr. Lawrence helped us to turn the carriage, and we returned early.'

No one in the parlour met anyone else's eye during this interesting speech.

'A headache?' Sir Joshua broke the little silence that followed it. He peered at his grand-daughter anxiously. 'You look flushed, it is true.'

Amanda dropped him a quick curtsey, rather than trusting herself to words.

'Always so very crowded and busy,' Lady Akehurst added. 'You know. And noisy, very noisy. I felt quite headachy myself.'

'I don't know why you bother going,' said Sir Joshua. He considered Amanda for another moment. 'You should go and lie down with the shutters to, my dear. Nothing else for it.'

'A glass of wine, perhaps,' suggested Lady Akehurst.

'Not at all,' said her husband. 'Do more harm than good. You're overtired, Amanda, dear.' He raised an eyebrow at Lady Akehurst as though challenging her to defy him, then turned on his heel and left the parlour. Paulinson hesitated for a moment, as if Sir Joshua had carelessly left his shadow behind.

'Is everyone really all right?' he asked in his papery voice. 'Sir Joshua will worry, you know.'

'We are all quite well, thank you, Mr. Paulinson,' said Lady Akehurst after a pause. 'Go along. Sir Joshua will need you.'

'My lady,' said Paulinson, brightening slightly at the thought of being needed. He padded quickly away. After a few seconds, they heard the library door shut firmly against the world. Isobel breathed again.

'There will be no more said of this for now,' Lady Akehurst decreed. 'Nothing at all. Miss Blair, you seem as I say to have seen this – this person most clearly. Should you be able to identify him again you will inform me at once.'

'My lady,' said Isobel, not entirely committing herself one way or the other.

'Amanda, you will indeed go and lie down in your bedchamber. I shall write to Mrs. Pyecroft and give our apologies for this evening – I shall say you are unwell.'

'Oh, but Grandmamma!' cried Amanda. 'There will be several gentlemen there who have expressly –'

'I shall be watching your suitors a good deal more closely after this,' Lady Akehurst swept on. 'There will be weeding, my girl

– a great deal of weeding. Your grandfather will not have an unsuitable match made.'

But in the end, of course, Lady Akehurst could not resist indulging her grand-daughter and displaying her at yet another social occasion, and the Blairs found themselves once again guarding their little corner of a crowded drawing room, watching as Amanda flirted ferociously with every handsome young man who presented himself, and Lady Akehurst gossiped and grinned and signally failed to weed anything at all. The young men were virtually all individuals Isobel would not have trusted to the end of the road: she could almost see them counting over Amanda's prospective fortune as they fawned over her plump hands and failed quite to meet her little eyes. But she could not see in any of them enough initiative to tie on a mask and attempt a very public abduction. In fact, she thought, watching them closely, none of them seemed capable of an original thought.

'It's so very warm in here,' murmured one young man, and indeed he did appear to be sweating prodigiously. 'I am sure you would benefit from a little fresh air. Allow me to escort you out on to the terrace: it is a clear night, and we can see the stars!'

Isobel seriously doubted it, in the flood of lights glaring from Mrs. Pyecroft's generous windows. But Amanda seemed charmed.

'The stars? Really?'

'Though,' said the young man, and this time Isobel had to strain to hear him, 'they are as nothing beside the stars in your eyes.'

'Goodness,' said Isobel abruptly, trying very hard not to laugh, 'isn't that Miss Pyecroft calling you over, Miss Akehurst? I believe she wishes to show you something.'

She was about to march Amanda smartly off to meet their hostess' daughter, but the unpromising young man divined her intentions almost at once, and, bowing low to Amanda, abandoned them.

'Dear Miss Akehurst,' said Isobel swiftly before the next fortune-hunter could make his approach, 'you must take care not to allow yourself to be compromised. A worthy suitor would not attempt to trick you into an awkward situation – or a lonely terrace.'

'He was only seeking my company, Miss Blair,' said Amanda dismissively. 'If you had as many admirers as I have, you would know that they struggle to spend a little time with me.'

Isobel swallowed a retort. Amanda's eyes were still scanning the crowd.

'I don't believe he is here,' said Isobel, perhaps a little less kindly than she might have a few minutes before. 'Your attempted abductor.'

Amanda sighed.

'Yet you said you thought he was a gentleman.'

'Or similar. That does not mean he has to attend every assembly in the town. He may be wary of being seen in your company so soon after this morning, in case people work out who he is.' She spoke absently, and regretted it: Amanda's eyes lit up at the thought of her abductor's clever strategies.

'Of course! He will come for me in some other way!'

'Miss Akehurst,' Isobel lowered her voice, 'do you really want to be abducted? Is that really – does that really seem like a good idea to you?'

'If he loves me so much that he would do that for me ...'

'If he loved you so much he would brave your grandparents, instead of sneaking about in a mask,' Isobel pointed out. Amanda waved a plump hand.

'There is no thrill in braving grandparents.'

No thrill, Isobel thought, but any suitor would find Sir Joshua quite intimidating.

'And what if Sir Joshua should punish his actions by changing his will? Making someone else his heir?'

'Grandpappa would do no such thing,' said Amanda, without even a hint of discomposure. It was probably true. The more likely action of a man prominent in society would be to pay off the gallant if impatient suitor, and make sure a quiet marriage ceremony occurred as soon as possible.

However, Isobel had not taken into consideration the possibility of a pre-emptive strike.

They returned to the house a little after midnight, no later than usual, and were surprised to find Sir Joshua pacing the narrow hallway, still dressed as he would be for the House. When they appeared in the doorway he stopped, and adopted a look of thunder. Isobel suspected he had had it prepared for several hours.

'What's this I hear about an incident in the Park?' he

demanded.

Lady Akehurst, who had had a little too much punch, quivered before him.

'An – an incident, sir?'

'You know what I mean. The whole House is talking of it. Some fool of a man in a mask attacked the carriage!'

'Well …'

'I have heard the whole story,' said Sir Joshua, dismissing them all with a brusque gesture. 'Can you imagine how embarrassing it was for me to find it out from the general gossip?' He turned on his heel, slowly, making sure each of them, the Blairs as well as his own family, felt the import of his words. 'We shall discuss the implications in the morning. And there will be implications. No one will be permitted to endanger my grand-daughter.'

It seemed only reasonable to agree: even Isobel, who was quite tired of Amanda, had no particular wish to endanger her. Only Blair looked anxious, and Isobel was sure he was thinking of those love letters, with their hints at force and control. But Sir Joshua, having given his warning of morning judgements, had moved on.

'Now, has anyone seen Paulinson? Was he with you this evening?'

'Mr. Paulinson?' Amanda almost giggled. 'At a party? I don't think so!'

'Then where the devil is the man?' Sir Joshua. 'I haven't seen him since dinner!'

'Not at all?' asked Blair. 'Had you sent him on some errand?'

'He said he wanted to fetch something from his room. I went into my study to gather my thoughts for the House. I expected him to join me, but when he did not I carried on alone.'

Blair cleared his throat politely.

'Did you think to send someone up to look for him, sir?'

Mr. Lawrence narrowed his eyes at Blair, his mouth disapproving.

'Of course I did, Mr. Blair,' said Sir Joshua. 'Apparently he was not in fact in his room. I concluded that he had misunderstood me and perhaps gone ahead to the House, thinking he was to catch me up there. It is rare for Paulinson to misunderstand,' he added, with a tremor in his voice. 'I confess I was puzzled, as well as concerned. As I still am.'

'It is unusual,' said Lady Akehurst, which Isobel thought was an understatement. Paulinson was so close to Sir Joshua in his work that she had occasionally thought she had spotted a collar and lead. 'Perhaps you missed him on the way: perhaps he arrived at the House, could not find you and came back, then finding you had already gone he went back to the House. Do you think, my dear?'

Sir Joshua looked at her as if he could not quite remember where he had found her. He was not a good colour.

'Do you think I spend my evenings in ridiculous dances like that?' he demanded. 'Back and forth and back and forth – I might as well go to one of your dreadful balls. I'm going to bed,' he added suddenly. 'In the morning, I shall deal with these things.'

But the morning was not at all what Sir Joshua had expected.

Chapter Five

It was the butler, Trent, who first opened the front door in the morning, just before dawn. It was part of his usual routine, unlocking what was only locked at night time, ensuring that the door's white paintwork was clean, that the step did not need sweeping, that no tramp or drunkard had found it a pleasant place to spend the night. He was the first, therefore, to find the man sprawled across the step, but when he went to poke the fellow with his toe and suggest he find other accommodation, the man did not react. Then the butler saw the blood. He screamed.

When Blair came down to the entrance hall a moment later, the butler was clutching the railings and shaking so violently he could barely stand. Blair patted him solemnly on the arm, then went sideways, heart trembling, to peer at the man flung on the step. There was no doubt the fellow was dead, but it was no tramp. Horrified, Blair realised that it was Paulinson.

'You'll have to go and tell Sir Joshua,' said Blair, pulling himself together enough to speak kindly. It would be warmer inside, and having a purpose might help the man to control his shivers. He nodded his head in the direction of the body, causing his hastily-assumed wig to lurch. 'I'll stay here with him.'

The butler pulled himself towards the front door, and vanished inside. Blair could hear his toes scuttling over the tiled floor, as if the murderer might be following him. He waited half a moment, then ducked down to look more closely at Paulinson's body.

He was lying with his feet on the street and his head towards the front door, on his stomach, his face turned to one side and one arm out as if he had been reaching for the door. It was hard to shake the impression that he had been pursued and had almost made it home. But where had he been? A hat could have been lost in the chase, if there had been a chase, but he was wearing no gloves, or overcoat, or cloak. Blair touched him gently on the neck. He was cold, and the blood had darkened to a sticky pool on the step. On a night like last night, he had probably been there for a few hours. Had he cried out, but they had all been asleep? Or had someone from the house pushed him outside, stabbed him and left him, locking the front door against him? Blair looked at Paulinson's shoes – shoes, not boots, but not slippers either. They looked fairly clean, but then the day had not been wet. They were inconclusive, he decided, nodding solemnly to himself. He stopped when he realised that a few people were beginning to gather across the street, wondering at the figures on the step.

While Paulinson's left hand was stretched towards the door, the right was almost hidden beneath him, down near his waist. Blair tipped the body very gently and with some difficulty, for it had stiffened. But there was his right hand, ungloved too, pale and smooth as always – and with something in it. A crumpled handkerchief? A piece of paper? He leaned over and delicately plucked it from Paulinson's fingers. Paper, with writing on it.

'What's this? Has that fool of a butler made some kind of mistake?'

It was Sir Joshua, of course. Blair straightened and turned, and moved aside so that Sir Joshua could see clearly. He clutched at the door post.

'Paulinson? Is he – is he dead?'

There were a few gasps from the little crowd, delighted to have a name and a circumstance. The word 'Paulinson' echoed along with 'Dead', and finished with one raised 'I told you so!' which was immediately shushed.

'I'm afraid so, sir,' said Blair. 'And has been for some hours.'

'But – what happened?'

'There's a good deal of blood,' said Blair. Behind Sir Joshua he could see Lady Akehurst now, and Fussy and Mr. Lawrence. Oh, dear: Mr. Lawrence would not like this. 'But I'm not sure yet where it came from. There are no marks on his back, that I can see, and I have not yet turned him over. He's stiff.'

'I'll help, if I can,' said Fussy, coming forward. Blair noted that he was dressed: the rest were in night clothes still. He looked back at Paulinson more closely. The body was dressed for dinner, not for the morning.

Between them, Blair and Fussy turned Paulinson over on the step, so that now his left hand was palm upwards, pleading. The look of shock on Paulinson's face was very horrible to see, almost worse than the black gash across his throat.

'He knew it was coming,' Sir Joshua murmured. Fussy swallowed hard, then stepped into the street and was sick in the gutter. Sir Joshua covered his own mouth with a long hand. 'Poor Paulinson. Poor, poor fellow.'

He detached himself from the doorpost, and stooped to close Paulinson's eyes, then straightened and surveyed the dead face sorrowfully. There was a little sigh from the crowd. Blair made a decision.

'Sir, I found this in his hand,' he said, handing over the piece of paper. Sir Joshua looked startled, then reached out for the paper as if he were not quite sure what to do with it. After a moment he straightened it and tilted it towards the light from the doorway.

'Good Lord,' he murmured.

'What does it say, sir?' asked Blair, reckoning that Sir Joshua was most likely to tell him when he was still shocked.

'It says, "Never think you can escape the Cato Street heroes. Let this be a sign unto you." I – is it my fault he's dead? Oh, Paulinson! Was I supposed to die here instead?' Sir Joshua's face trembled with uncertainty. Then he rammed the paper into his hand and squashed it. 'He must be taken indoors. He cannot be left out here as a public spectacle. Fetch a board, carry him to his room. He must be treated with all dignity.'

'Have you a police office nearby, sir?'

'A police office? I shall report this directly to the magistrate.' Sir Joshua summoned a couple of the footmen with a look. 'You, clear these people away. You, fetch something to lay over Mr. Paulinson's body. Hurry up with that board. Paulinson! Oh,' he stopped, shocked. 'I thought to call him to help. What am I to do without him?'

'He did seem very dependent on Mr. Paulinson,' Isobel agreed when Blair had the chance to give her a full account after breakfast. 'But I am surprised to hear that he admitted it. Goodness, poor Mr. Paulinson!'

'I wish I could work out what had happened,' said Blair sadly. 'If he was dressed in indoor clothes, what happened to him after dinner? Where did he go, and why did he not take a pair of gloves, at the very least? Where was he in between going up to his room for something and being killed on the doorstep?'

'And has this anything to do with what happened to Amanda?' Isobel added suddenly.

Blair pursed his lips alarmingly.

'Could it? I don't know. I thought that might just be for the money, you know? But money cannot have anything to do with Paulinson's death, or not Sir Joshua's money, anyway. Can it?'

'I don't see how it could,' Isobel agreed slowly. 'Nor how the Cato Street conspiracy could have anything to do with a masked man trying to abduct Amanda. But it's all very odd, isn't it?'

'What I'd like to know,' said Blair, 'is whether or not any of the rest of the Cabinet is similarly targeted.'

'Maybe the magistrate will be able to tell us that.'

The magistrate, no doubt very happy to do the bidding of a Cabinet Minister, turned up sharply and asked, with a blend of authority and respect, if he could see the gentlemen of the household in the drawing room at their earliest convenience. Isobel, irritable at being excluded, took her sketchbook and went to find Amanda.

'It's awful about poor Mr. Paulinson, isn't it?' she began. Amanda would sit and talk as long as Isobel was drawing her.

'Awful. I shan't be able to look at the front doorstep!'

'What will the neighbours think?' added Lady Akehurst. 'I hope there is not much talk!' But it was clear her thoughts were concentrated on the drawing room: she was restless, setting down her needlework and taking it up again.

'I think the last time I saw him was when we went into the drawing room after dinner,' said Isobel. 'He was still in the dining room then, wasn't he?'

'Of course: he would not have left early,' said Lady Akehurst firmly.

'But he never came into the drawing room, did he?'

The Akehurst ladies frowned in unison, then shook their

heads.

'I hadn't noticed,' said Amanda.

'Sir Joshua says he went upstairs to fetch something,' said Isobel. 'I wonder if anyone saw him after that?'

But her innocent pressing brought no response. Neither of the ladies claimed to have seen Mr. Paulinson from dinner until this morning – and Amanda had not even seen him then.

In the drawing room, Blair thought the magistrate was clever, but not quite as clever as he thought he was. At least he asked a few reasonable questions: he noted down exactly where each of them had seen Paul Paulinson last. For almost all of them that had been in the dining room, when Sir Joshua had mentioned his imminent departure for the House. Paulinson, knowing he would be expected to attend his master, had asked if he might be excused to fetch something from his room, and Sir Joshua had nodded.

The gentlemen had not lingered long in the dining room, and though Sir Joshua had led the way to the drawing room it had only been Fussy who had glanced up the stairs and seen Paulinson's legs disappearing upwards.

'Are you quite sure that they were Mr. Paulinson's legs, sir?'

Fussy blinked, a little pink.

'It had not occurred to me that they could be anyone else's, but as I immediately followed Sir Joshua into the drawing room I had no chance to make sure, anyway.'

The magistrate nodded.

'Who else would it have been?' Sir Joshua demanded. 'The servants would not be on those stairs, and the rest of us were together.'

'Did anyone else see or hear Mr. Paulinson after that point?' the magistrate persisted. He scanned the room. Mr. Lawrence and Sir Joshua sat in upright chairs, both very proper. Fussy shared a sofa with Harry Holden, who was draped over one of its arms like a hungover rug. Blair was sure the magistrate had recognised Holden: no doubt the young man had come up before him more than once on some night time jollity. Barnabas Ketchell, perhaps for similar reasons, had managed to keep himself in the shadows, slightly out of the magistrate's line of sight. Blair himself was perched on a stool where he could see as many of the room's occupants as possible. Like Sir Joshua, he found himself occasionally surprised that Paul Paulinson was not there, in attendance, his master's constant shadow.

'The servants might have,' Mr. Lawrence pointed out tightly, as if he had been waiting for the magistrate to realise that, and had given up on him.

'I shall be questioning them, of course,' said the magistrate with a stern look at Mr. Lawrence that Blair liked very much. 'With your permission, of course,' he added hurriedly. Sir Joshua waved a hand to grant it.

'What were Mr. Paulinson's connexions?' asked the magistrate, more confident.

'His connexions? He was my secretary.'

'Of course, sir, but had he friends? Enemies? Family here or elsewhere?'

'He was my secretary. He had no need of friends, and no time for enemies. As to family, I believe he had parents in … was it Norfolk? Suffolk? But his life was here.'

'Did he go out much?' asked the magistrate, slightly more cautiously.

'He went out when I told him to,' said Sir Joshua. 'Look, sir, I have shown you the piece of paper that was discovered in his hand. It is obvious that he was killed as a warning to me. His acquaintance, limited as it was, has nothing to do with this.'

The magistrate gave up.

'May I question the servants now, sir?'

'That would be for the best,' said Sir Joshua, and rose to leave the room, forcing everyone else to stand, too. The magistrate left in his wake.

'Do you think that's true?' asked Blair generally. 'Do we all think that Mr. Paulinson was killed as a warning to Sir Joshua?'

'Sir Joshua thinks it's all about him,' muttered Harry Holden. 'He always does. I suppose it might be,' he added, subsiding.

'He is a very important man,' said Fussy. 'You know, government and the Admiralty and everything. And everything is still so unsettled, even now they've hanged all the Cato Street fellows. Maybe he's right.'

'Why him, specifically?' asked Blair. 'That magistrate said

he didn't know of any other threats to other cabinet ministers.'

'One has to start somewhere,' said Ketchell suddenly, making them all jump. He made it sound unpleasant, though it was a fair point. He smiled, seeing the effect he had had.

'I don't suppose Paulinson went out with you two last night, then?' said Mr. Lawrence acidly.

'Paulie? Of course not! He wouldn't be seen dead with us!' said Harry with a laugh, then looked sick.

'No, he wasn't keen on our company,' Ketchell confirmed. 'A bit too rich for him.'

'But he must have gone somewhere,' said Blair. 'He was outside, and no one could find him in the house.'

'I don't imagine anyone looked too hard,' said Ketchell. 'One of the servants knocked on his door, maybe looked in his room. But no one knows if he was in another room. We were all downstairs.'

Blair nodded. Ketchell was not stupid: it was useful to remember that. But why on earth would Paulinson have gone to another room? Could he have been deliberately hiding, or doing something covert? Both seemed unlikely. But then again, if he had not been in the house – and at some stage he left the house, obviously – why would he have gone outside without any gloves, hat or overcoat?

'I hope,' said Mr. Lawrence, 'that you will not feel obliged to meddle in this, Mr. Blair.'

'Me?' said Blair sweetly. 'I never meddle in anything. Nothing at all.'

But he was quite keen to hear what Smith would have to say about the magistrate questioning the servants. That would be interesting.

'Well, it's interesting in a way, sir,' Smith said, once again bringing order to Blair's particular brand of chaos. 'No one saw him at all.'

'Do you believe them?'

'Most of 'em, sir, yes: I don't think they care enough about the household to be bothered lying. That butler, though, Trent. I still don't know what to make of him.'

'Does he drink?' asked Blair. The man certainly shook far

too much.

'Don't they all, sir? Barring Mr. Robbins, of course. But there's something more than that wrong with Trent. The least little thing and he jumps fit to knock himself out on the ceiling.'

'Nerves gone,' said Blair, sympathetically.

'Yes, sir – but how? He wasn't a soldier, as far as I can gather, or in any kind of dangerous situation.'

'Do you think he's that kind of nervous man who might be dangerous?'

Smith shrugged.

'I'd be surprised, sir. But he's not all there, that's for sure.'

Blair sighed, and poked at some gloves Smith had just paired up and smoothed. One halfway down the stack caught his interest, and he pulled it out, fiddling with the fingers.

'Mr. Lawrence tells me I'm not to meddle.'

'Does he, sir?'

'I'm not altogether sure I can help it.' He heaved another bottomless sigh. 'I wish Charles were here, though. He's good at meddling.'

But there was to be very little chance for meddling, at least at the scene of the crime. It was only mid-morning when Sir Joshua marched into the parlour and addressed his wife and grand-daughter.

'Prepare to leave town. Our departure will take place as soon as possible.'

'Leave town, my dear?' Lady Akehurst dropped her embroidery into her lap and stared at him.

'As I said.'

'But what about poor Mr. Paulinson's funeral? How is that to be managed?'

'I shall make arrangements,' said her husband firmly.

'But where are we to go? You cannot expect us to abandon all our social engagements!'

'There will be no further objections. There will be no more riding in the Park, either. You are off to Brighton tomorrow. You may begin to pack.'

'To Brighton!' cried Lady Akehurst in dismay.

'There should have been much greater care taken,' Sir Joshua paid no attention to her. Isobel thought he looked frightened, though he tried to appear in control. 'Much greater thought given to our security. When those traitors attempted to destroy the whole Cabinet only months ago – and now our work is so much more crucial – there are threats everywhere, even in London.'

'But Brighton!' Lady Akehurst was not interested in crucial work or national threats. 'Husband, I have several suitable young gentlemen who are very interested in Amanda – nothing has been said yet, of course, but only a few more weeks – days, perhaps, and I am convinced at least one of them will make an offer for her!'

'I daresay there are young gentlemen in Brighton, too,' snapped Sir Joshua, 'and perhaps less worldly ones. Assassinating my secretary on my very doorstep! Abducting my grand-daughter in broad daylight! And not a word from any of you about that – from my own family, keeping me in the dark! No, the house will be cleared tomorrow. The carriage will depart at nine.'

It was clear that the Blairs were included in this exile, but Isobel had assumed that, despite the apparent threat to his safety, Sir Joshua was not coming. Surely he would not miss Mr. Paulinson's funeral, even if it would not take place from Fitzroy Square. Surely he could not be spared from his crucial work at this time – and she had rather relished the thought of leaving him behind with his endless talks of semaphore over the dinner table. But no: at a quarter to nine the next morning, he was ready in the hall and marking the time with his large pocket watch. Isobel was very glad that she and the manservant Smith had hurried her father into readiness in good time. Mr. Lawrence was also prompt, with his godson Fussy: they had their own carriage, as had the Blairs. Lady Akehurst was flustered, running about and fetching last minute scarves and reticules, changing her mind over which muff she wanted on the journey, over which bonnet Amanda would wear in the carriage. The servants quaked at her booming voice. Isobel saw the butler was to come with them: his hands, in their woolly travel gloves, were shaking. Amanda threw a fit over having to walk past the stain of Paulinson's blood on the step, there despite the best efforts of the maids, but on the other hand Amanda could not be expected to leave by the servants' entrance and, when a cloth had been thrown over the stain she managed to struggle past it, hand pressed to her lips. Gradually the carriages were filled, the luggage arranged, and Sir

Joshua climbed in at last beside his wife and grand-daughter with a final grim survey of the little convoy. The footman raised the steps and closed the door, and they were off.

'Did you leave a letter for Charles, Father?' Isobel asked suddenly.

'Yes, yes,' said Blair, making a horrible face. 'I have left it, for I have no idea where he might be. The last I heard he was stuck in a flood in some little village in Yorkshire. I hope he might not be long in following.'

'At least the house will not be empty when he arrives,' said Isobel.

'No … though I daresay Mr. Ketchell and Mr. Holden will not be quite what he expects to find on his arrival.'

Perhaps not, thought Isobel. Barnabas Ketchell and Harry Holden, both impressively still drunk, had staggered in as their party left the house, and waved in bewilderment at their departure. Or Harry did: Mr. Ketchell's expression was much more thoughtful.

Chapter Six

'I wonder,' said Murray thoughtfully, 'when we'll start to see someone rounding up animals two by two?'

Robbins nodded. The rain seemed unceasing, but at last they had managed to negotiate the bridge across a swollen river that had been holding them back for a few damp days. Their stay in the low-lying Yorkshire village had been interesting, but they had no regrets about leaving it.

'Maybe we should have gone by sea, sir.'

It was not a joke: there were some very comfortable coastal services from Leith to London. But though Murray's stomach had survived some expeditions outside Aberdeen harbour last winter, it was not a mode of transport to which he naturally inclined, and besides, it was comfortable to have one's own carriage.

'It couldn't have been much wetter,' Murray acknowledged. His face was misted with spray as he gazed out of the carriage window. Robbins was too polite to huddle deeper into his blankets.

'At least it allowed Mr. Blair's second letter to catch up with us,' he offered.

'Given the eccentricities of that village's carrier's office, that in itself is a minor miracle,' Murray agreed. 'Yes: it was good to be reassured that nothing disastrous had happened yet, though he's clearly still worried.' He closed his eyes, recalling a few of Blair's words. He spoke them aloud. '"She thinks it's love. I'm convinced it is danger. And I think I know who threatens her."'

'An unhappy love affair?' Robbins suggested. Murray frowned.

'But if that were all it was, then why would he say he thinks he knows who threatens her? Do you see – if it were a matter of an unsuitable suitor, it would be obvious who it was.'

'I suppose so, sir. Unless Mr. Blair suspects that there is something more beside the young man's suit. Someone directing the matter?'

'That would certainly be strange,' Murray said. 'But given what little we know, it's hard to do anything but speculate. And he makes mention of danger in both letters. I think we do right to go as swiftly as we can.'

'What strikes me as curious, sir,' said Robbins, 'is that Mr. Blair thinks he knows who is behind it, but that he is waiting for you, even though the young lady may be in danger.'

'That had occurred to me, too. What does he need me for?'

'Two heads are better than one,' said Robbins.

'But he has Isobel. And if it's force he needs on his side, he has Smith.'

'Smith is not a young man,' said Robbins, with a touch of sorrow. 'Nevertheless, sir, if it were only strength he needed, he should surely be able to hire someone to help. No,' he went on, 'there is a puzzle, I believe, sir, that he and Miss Blair cannot work out without you.'

'Very flattering,' said Murray gloomily. 'Anyway, there is one good thing. I'm sure Miss Blair helped him to word at least his first letter, and I'm sure if the problem directly concerned her he would have said so, even if he had been discreet enough not to name her in a letter that might go astray. Whether Isobel can help him or not with this problem, at least it seems that she is not the young lady in danger. That is some comfort.'

The journey passed in a dismal series of inns and muddy roads and people hunched miserable under shawls and broad hats, and only the buildings they passed seemed to show much variation to mark their progress down the country. Stone changed colour and then turned to brick, roofs rose and fell, windows widened and narrowed – the fields were empty of crops and told them little except how the soil went from red clay to dark peat to yellow sand. The cattle were universally damp.

Murray and Robbins, as well as the coachman, had all visited London before, but even in the few years since his last arrival there Murray thought the streets had extended further north and the crowds had crept with them. Now they were so close to their destination he grew impatient with their speed, just as Donald the coachman had to slow for carts and carriages and everything in between. What had, on his last visit, been villages, now submitted to the irresistible wave of London flowing along their high streets and among their cottages and churches, the land between them and the capital now almost London, too.

They made their last stop at an inn on Hampstead Hill. Their night's accommodation was expensive – Murray was not surprised – but it gave him and the servants a chance to straighten themselves before they arrived at the house where Blair and Isobel were staying. He went to look for his coachman in the coachyard the following morning, and spotted Young Donald at the gate of the inn, staring down the hill.

'Earth hath not anything to show so fair, apparently,' said Murray lightly. Young Donald jumped.

'Is that it, sir? Is that London?'

'I'm afraid so, yes.'

'All of it?'

'Yes, one way and another.'

Young Donald surveyed it again, hardly breathing. Murray looked too. From here you could nearly capture Wordsworth's awe: the autumnal mists mingling with the smoke of thousands of morning cooking fires gave his towers and domes, theatres and temples, the look of some mystical Eastern kingdom, a golden cloud palace half a world wide. Of course from here you could neither hear the clamour nor inhale the aroma of so many people and animals living and dying in close proximity.

'You canna see either side of it hardly,' said Young Donald at last.

'Well, on this occasion we'll not be going round it. We're heading almost straight down there – well, round to the left a bit first, I think, for comfort.'

'Right into the midst of it, sir,' Young Donald sighed. 'Will we ever find our way out again?'

'Your uncle is a good driver, and knows the town,' said Murray comfortably. 'Don't go wandering off, now, when we reach the house. There are hazards in London even Renfrew has never thought of.'

'Exciting, eh, sir?' Young Donald turned to look at him at last. His eyes were shining worryingly. Murray smiled and turned away.

'We'll be down there soon enough, Donald,' he said. 'No need to rush into it.'

In the coachyard, Old Donald had finally appeared with some harness he had been polishing: he and it smelled sharp and clean. Murray waited until he had set the gear down by the carriage.

'This is the address, Donald: I think you should have no trouble finding it.'

'Aye, sir,' agreed the coachman, squinting down at the piece of paper. 'I ken Fitzroy Square – that'd be the one with only the twa legs to it.'

'So I believe,' Murray agreed. Used to the endless construction of Edinburgh's New Town, he found no peculiarities in the idea of a square with only two sides. 'I'm not sure to what extent we are expected at the house: it might be best if you and Young Donald made sure you had a good breakfast here after you've cleaned the worst of the mud off the carriage.'

Old Donald surveyed the state of the carriage with a sour mouth, but Young Donald was already with them and on his toes.

'Shall I fetch a bucket, Uncle?' he said. 'And maybe twa three clouts?'

Privately Murray wondered if the two or three cloths would be enough, but at least it was a start. Young Donald was full of enthusiasm: no doubt the carriage would be spotless in no time. No doubt he wanted to make a good impression on London, ignorant of the fact that London would be almost entirely oblivious to yet another party of newcomers cluttering up its busy streets.

Back inside the inn, Murray found Robbins ordering a substantial breakfast to be brought to a private parlour – a little peace after the endless rattle of the wheels on the road would be very welcome. Then they would tidy themselves up and make themselves fit to be presented to an unknown hostess who might, if they were lucky, find them space to stay. Otherwise they would be off to another inn.

Fitzroy Square … Murray had read of it, for the Scottish Adam brothers had had a hand in some of its design. Blair could find himself – and make himself at home – in any company but this sounded like a household of some status in society. There would be room and food for their arrival, but perhaps no welcome. With Blair, anything was possible.

And of course, Isobel would be there – sensible, clever Isobel, with her witty drawings and her ability to manage her father's most outlandish eccentricities. It would be good to see Isobel again: he had not seen her in far too long.

While they waited for their food, he stared through the window at the bustling Hampstead street outside, half-repulsed, half-excited by this foreshadowing of the city to come. He found little delight in the busyness of London, in its grubby streets and poverty and the contrasting arrogance of the fashionable elite, so bored with their rich lives. Yet there was no doubt that there was a charm to the chance of seeing some of the sights, and even some of the people, one read about as far away as Scotland. He wondered if he might hear some good new music, too, or have the chance to view one of the art collections. And anyway, he was here to help Alester Blair, his oldest friend, and in order to help a friend one should be prepared to go and stay wherever one was required to. He grinned at his own severity, and turned away from the window to make the most of his expensive breakfast.

Had a crow been passing, and elected, for a purpose of which only crows could be aware, to fly straight from Hampstead Hill to Fitzroy Square, he would have found that the distance amounted in human terms to about four miles. For a carriage and four, the matter was less straightforward.

There was no direct road between the two places, and even to take a slight detour would mean using streets not suitable for their equipage. Instead Old Donald directed the carriage to the fields of Islington, lush even at this time of year with the preparations for fattening cattle for Smithfield Market. Here the road was fine and broad, but the closer they came to Smithfield the more the carriageway was littered with the detritus of St. Bartholomew's Fair, a wild occasion by all accounts. Crowds still lingered, some of them simply too drunk still to move anywhere else. Animals, vegetables, and substances it was better not to investigate too closely obstructed the way, and the traffic into London was dense. Old Donald was not the kind of coachman who rose up and swore on his master's behalf, whip cracking about the other road users – nor would Murray have wished him to be. It would likely have done no good, anyway, and though he had grown impatient, so near to their destination, Murray sat and waited. Four miles took rather more than four hours: it would have been quicker to walk.

Fitzroy Square was, indeed, still lacking a couple of the terraces it would take to make it satisfy the definition of 'square' for any geometrist, but what it had was very fine. The south and east sides were grand, white-faced edifices, with first floor wrought-iron balconies and neo-Classical windows designed to cause any inhabitant of Edinburgh's New Town to feel instantly at home. Only shallow steps and a stone bridge spanning the basement area divided each house from the street, and Robbins, with a nod to Old Donald, crossed the short space to ring the doorbell on Murray's behalf. After some time Murray realised Robbins was still standing waiting. He was about to call Robbins back to confer, when the door was opened by a diminutive and not very lively looking lad of about ten, his over-sized livery coat evidently borrowed from a larger servant who had not explained to the lad the function of buttons.

Some conversation passed. Robbins was not a physically demonstrative man, and he had his back to Murray, so it was not easy to tell his reactions to the boy's helpless gestures. At last, after what seemed to be a lengthy lecture from Robbins at which the boy had looked more and more alarmed, the lad opened the front door wide and stood by it, as straight as the heavy coat would allow. Robbins slipped back to the carriage, and gestured to Young Donald.

'There appears to be some confusion,' said Robbins, as Young Donald adjusted the carriage steps for Murray. 'This is undoubtedly the house where Mr. Blair and Miss Blair have been staying, but he seems unable to tell me where they are or when they might be back. The house, though, belongs to a Sir Joshua Akehurst.'

'The Cabinet member?' Murray knew the name, but not much more about the man. He had appeared in newspaper accounts of those who had escaped death in the Cato Street affair.

'There may be two,' admitted Robbins, diffidently.

'Blair has never mentioned him as an acquaintance, but if Blair listed all his acquaintances ...'

'Quite so, sir,' Robbins agreed. 'I asked if any of the family was at home, but that seemed to be a question for the university professors. After some discussion on appropriate behaviour for a young person required to attend the door of a knight's household, the person has agreed that you might wait in the parlour. I thought you might like a change from the carriage, sir.'

'I gather you're not impressed?'

Robbins made no reply except for a brief widening of his odd, luminous eyes, and escorted his master to the door where the young person waited obediently. Murray nodded at him, leaving it to Robbins to communicate more fully. The lad skipped to slam the front door, then scuttled ahead of Murray to open the door to a parlour, cold and with the curtains still drawn, to the left of the hall. The furnishings were fine, but would have benefitted from a little dusting. Murray seated himself by the fireplace, more in hope than in expectation, but the boy, with a bow, shot off into the inner workings of the house.

Robbins, who would never have permitted such behaviour from a servant in the New Town of Edinburgh, stood with his hands behind his back and presented a calm appearance to the world, though Murray was sure he was frustrated inside. They waited, listening to the silence of the house. Not even a clock ticked. Outside, Old Donald had evidently decided that their welcome was not assured enough for him to take the carriage off just yet: there was no sound, through the thick curtains, of the horses moving. The rain pattered on the windows. Something distant rustled in the chimney. There was so little evidence of human existence that for a moment Murray was visited by an uncomfortable phantasy that Blair and Isobel were lying upstairs in some equally desolate room, murdered and abandoned.

It was fortunately interrupted by footsteps in the hallway. There was whispering: the door opened abruptly and the lad shot into the room as if he had been pushed.

'Rosie –' he began, but broke off at the sound of a sharp cough from the hallway. His eyes swivelled back and forth, then he darted back into the hall. More whispers.

'Excuse me,' he said, reappearing. He crossed the room, and began to tug on the curtains to try to open them. After a moment, Robbins took pity on him, and went to help. Wet autumnal light dribbled into the room, barely improving matters. The boy returned to the doorway, handy for any necessary escape route. 'I'm to say,' he began again, 'that the family are from home and that Mr. Blair and Miss Blair have gone too.'

'The family is that of Sir Joshua Akehurst?' Murray wanted confirmation, for want of anything better.

'Yes, sir.'

'Where did they go?'

'Mr. Trent didn't say, sir.'

'Mr. Trent is apparently the butler, sir,' Robbins put in, from information previously extracted.

'Odd,' said Murray. 'And have you been left in charge?'

'Oh, no, sir!' This caused the lad to hiccough in panic, and for a moment he was rendered completely useless. Robbins patted his back. 'No, sir, not me. Rosie's in charge, sir.'

'And who is Rosie?'

'She's … she's Rosie, sir.' There was another cough from the hallway. The boy stuck his head back round the doorpost, and in a moment returned. 'She's the kitchenmaid, sir. She's not supposed to be above stairs.'

'I see,' said Murray, who sort of did. Rosie was presumably directing operations from the hallway. 'Well, then, did Mr. Blair –'

But at that point there was a noise on the stairs – a scratching, rattling, thumping noise, that caused the lad to jump a foot in the air and then run towards it. By the sound of scurrying footsteps, Rosie, by contrast, had run away. In a moment the boy reappeared with a feeble gesture, and a young gentleman entered the room.

'How di do?' he enquired politely, swaying a little.

'Good day to you,' said Murray, with a bow. The man was about five and twenty, he thought, though by his complexion he might have been fifty. When he smiled, it was to display several square yards of teeth. Murray noted that under his silk banyan, which trailed behind him, his waistcoat was done up wrongly. 'My name is Charles Murray of Letho, and I am sorry to disturb you. I had hoped to find my friend Alester Blair here.'

'Of Letho?' the man queried, as if it had been the only bit of the speech he had caught. Then he pulled himself together. 'I must apologise, sir: you have caught me – at a bit of a disadvantage. Last night went on a bit late, or a bit early, if you see what I mean.' He rubbed briefly at his towering forehead, then made an effort to smile. It was not entirely unsuccessful. 'Ah, Mr. Blair was here, you know. And Miss Blair. Were you looking for Miss Blair, too?'

'The Blairs are family friends,' Murray explained. 'I understand that they and the family have moved on somewhere. Can you tell me where, please?'

'Oh, I beg your pardon!' the young man exclaimed. 'I should have introduced myself. I am Harry Holden, Lady Akehurst's nephew. Yes, I'm afraid the Akehursts have gone on. She asked me to go too, of course, but I was having far too much fun in London! And she does like me to be enjoying myself.'

'Excellent,' said Murray, now suspecting he was dealing with someone whose mind was not as quick as it might be. 'And when they went on, where did they go?'

'Oh … south, somewhere,' said Holden, with a wave of his hand that turned into a quick snatch at the back of a chair. 'Forgive me, I fear I do need a bite to eat. You'll join me? Settle the stomach, you know? I find, after a night on Blue Ruin, the world seems a little hazy until I have filled my belly. Not that I can't take it, you know? Straight as a soldier till – till whatever time I came in this morning.'

'Perhaps we should return later,' suggested Murray, 'for I'm afraid it is extremely important that I find out where the Blairs have gone. Did they leave with the Akehursts?'

'They did, they did. Here, come and sit down with me and we'll get some food sent in. Here, you, um, Jackie!'

The boy in the livery ran over at once.

'Yes, sir?'

'Fetch in – what'll you have, Letho? A couple of hens, to start. A pie or two. I fancy veal, I think. Let's be going on with that. Did you hear that, Jackie? And something for yourself and Rosie, of course.'

'Yes, sir!'

Jackie darted off, but at the parlour door collided with another diminutive figure – presumably Rosie the kitchenmaid. There was a short spell of muttering, and the boy turned back.

'Sir,' he addressed himself to Robbins. 'Please will you come to the kitchen door, sir? Rosie – your coachman wants a word.'

Robbins bowed to the gentlemen, and went. Murray, resigned to having to deal with Mr. Holden for a little longer – and not disinclined to eat, certainly, after four hours stuck in the carriage – sat at the parlour table by the window, opposite his apparent host. Harry Holden, the after-effects of the night before now obvious in the aroma of spirits about him and his reddened eyes, made Murray feel terribly old. Holden had propped one elbow on the table to shield his face from the daylight, dull as it was.

'Don't know if I like it better or not when my Aunt Akehurst is away,' he confided. 'I can do what I like, but she takes all the good servants with her, and I'm left with just the children. Have to shave myself, brush out my own clothes, everything. What's the good in that? And I know she'd have left me one of the decent ones if she could have, that's the annoying thing, only Uncle Akehurst wouldn't let her. Ridiculous.' But Murray thought his petulance was forced, as if real resentment might take up too much energy.

'Did the Blairs leave with the Akehursts?' Murray asked.

'Oh, yes, the whole shower, off they went! Only Barnie and me left – and the serving brats. Not that they're bad brats, but they just don't have a notion what to do.'

'And they went somewhere south?'

Holden waited while Jackie returned with some ill-assorted cutlery.

'The things are coming, sir,' he told Holden, who nodded, and scuffed the lad's hair with a trace of affection.

'Good boy,' he said, dismissing him. 'South – yes. Sussex. I think Aunt Akehurst said they were off to Brighton. It was all very sudden – something to do with Amanda, I think.'

'Amanda?'

'My cousin. Sort of. Well, yes. Aunt Akehurst is my great aunt, you see, and Amanda is her grand-daughter. Sir Joshua Akehurst's heir.'

'*I think I know who threatens her*,' Blair had written. Could this be the girl he had meant?

'Had she been taken ill, that they wanted to remove her to Brighton?'

'Ill? Amanda? I doubt it! No … well, I don't know,' he said, then leaned forward conspiratorially. His breath was terrible. 'I heard that there'd been an incident in the Park. It was all the talk of the ton, you know! And Aunt Akehurst wouldn't like that, not at all.'

'An incident?'

Holden straightened, nodding with great solemnity. 'That's what I heard,' he said, as if it said everything. 'An *incident*.'

Chapter Seven

Before Murray could ask more, Robbins appeared in the doorway, followed by the lad, both of them carrying covered dishes. Robbins straightened the cutlery, produced napkins, and swiftly effected some kind of order to the meal, whatever it might have been – a very late breakfast for Mr. Holden, anyway. Murray knew Robbins well enough to note the stiff angle of his shoulders and the tightness about his pale eyes: Robbins was quite clearly appalled at the standard of service in the household, even given that the owners were away. When both gentlemen had been served, he cleared his throat politely.

'Sir, the coachman informs me that one of the horses is lame, and will need a night's rest, which he hopes will not inconvenience your plans.'

'Oh!' Murray's first thought was to wonder which horse, and how distressed it might be, but that was not conversation for now. If he had been ready to depart straightaway, it would have been frustrating, but another horse could perhaps have been hired – but as it was, their long delays through Islington and Smithfield meant that it was already a late hour for setting out for the south. 'Mr. Holden, will your servants be able to direct my coachman to a good stable for the night? One that can take a carriage and four horses? And we will need a convenient inn, too, for it seems we will not be able to carry on to Sussex until tomorrow at least.'

'Oh, stay here!' said Holden with an eager wave of his hand, as though he thought Murray might have forgotten he was there.

'I couldn't possibly impose –'

'No, really! Barnie and I are rattling about in here and it

would be good to have a new face to look at! And there's plenty of room in the stables now Uncle Akehurst's carriage is away, I'm sure – I don't believe I've ever been in them but they're round the back somewhere. Stay as long as you like! Do you know London at all?' The idea seemed to have roused him a little from his dulled state.

'I've visited on several occasions, though I would not say I know it well.'

'Then come out with us this evening!' Holden was quite excited now. 'See some of the sights! There's nothing like a night in London to let you see mankind at its best and worst, and all things in between. And there's no one like Barnie to show us around: he really seems to know everyone and everything and all that is happening.'

A night out in London – that could be entertaining. Looking at Holden, Murray reckoned there would be likely to be drink involved, but perhaps also there might be the theatre, or music, or, if he were lucky, a bit of dancing. He liked dancing.

'Thank you,' he said, 'I believe I should enjoy that.'

'Then eat up – we can send out for more at any time – and line your stomach! And the lad will show your man to your room.'

By the time they had finished eating – Holden had taken a fancy to send Jackie out again for turtle soup, and then again for an apple pie – Robbins had managed to find the wherewithal to light a fire in the room to which he had been shown, and had begun to unpack a few pieces of clothing and accoutrements. When Murray appeared in the doorway, tentatively, wondering at first if he had the right room, Robbins rose and bowed.

'Have you anywhere decent to sleep, yourself, Robbins?' Murray asked. 'Will the Donalds be settled well?'

'I believe so, sir,' said Robbins. 'The stables are well-appointed, and there are several horses there at present with a very respectable man from Essex looking after them. He was very happy to accommodate the Donalds. I have secured a room in the attic for myself.'

'Warm, I hope?'

'It will be, sir.'

Murray smiled.

'A strange set-up, don't you think? I have yet to meet this

Barnie gentleman. No doubt his stomach will remain unlined.'

'Do you wish me to attend you this evening when you go out, sir?'

'I don't think so, thank you. But I'll do my best to keep a clear head – I suspect that Mr. Holden is in the habit of overindulging, and who knows where we might end up? I'd like to return with my pockets secure, at least.'

'That's what I mean, sir. If I were to attend you there would be less chance of mishap.'

'I know, Robbins, but I think I'll be all right. I'd be happier if you were here, preferably getting a good night's sleep, but in any case making sure all is safe here.'

'Well,' said Robbins, 'I shall lay out your second best coat and waistcoat, sir.'

Murray contained a grin at Robbins' cautious disapproval.

'Quite right – better keep the good stuff for Brighton. I gather society is quite grand down there.'

'Do we know how to find the Blairs, sir?'

'I think that will be straightforward. It is not a very extensive place, I believe. There cannot be too many Sir Joshua Akehursts in the town. I just hope we can make a start in that direction tomorrow. I think it is around fifty miles away, so that will be another couple of days, if the horses stay well.'

'If you don't need me this evening,' said Robbins, 'I shall write to Mary and let her know where we are going.'

'A good idea. Right, is there any chance of hot water in this place?'

Harry Holden was waiting for Murray in the parlour a few hours later, wearing much the same as he had been earlier except that the silk banyan had been replaced by a black coat of dubious cleanliness – to judge by some of the smeared marks Holden had had a go at removing some of them himself, then given up. His trousers were so tight they barely clung to the fashionable side of decency. His cloak, gloves and hat lay over the back of an armchair.

'Excellent!' he said. 'Now we just need Barnie. I'm sure he'll not be long …' He broke off at the sound of footsteps on the stairs. 'Here we are! Barnie, here is Mr. Letho. Mr. Letho, may I present Barnabas Ketchell.'

The figure in the doorway bowed, one hand on the door jamb for support. Already Murray, not bothered about correcting his name in this company, could see that he was scrawny, but when the man straightened he revealed an unhealthy pot of a belly, and a grey, grainy pallor in the sagging jowls of his face and throat. Only his nose was a splendid crimson. His neckcloth was yellowish, his hands, already sliding into worn leather gloves, claw-like. His expression, if anything definite could be said about it, was wary.

'Good evening, Mr. Letho. You'll be a friend of Sir Joshua Akehurst, I take it?'

His voice had been cultivated – Murray had the impression it had been left to run to ruin, overgrown with brambles and nettles. It was rough.

'Ah, no: I came here to find my friend Alester Blair, but I hear he has left before me. I have not the good fortune to be acquainted with Sir Joshua.'

Ketchell nodded.

'Are you to accompany us this evening?'

'I believe so, Mr. Ketchell, if it will not inconvenience your plans.'

'Not at all,' said Ketchell, with a rueful grin. 'It's not as if we had tickets for Almack's, after all. Fresh from the country, eh?'

'Not particularly,' Murray said cheerfully. Certainly he was no longer a young innocent, and something told him that Ketchell enjoyed taking young innocents – probably well furnished with their father's money – about the town. Ketchell was the kind of man that made one check one's pockets. He nodded at Murray, ambiguously, and looked him up and down out of the corner of his eye.

'Oh, yes: well, no doubt all three of us are all the go, on the town.' He sighed. 'Are you ready, then, Harry? Shall we sport a toe?'

'I'm always ready, Barnie – I'm on the fret!'

'Then shall we go?'

As it turned out, even gentlemen on the fret, eager to be off, were slow to start. Ketchell and Holden led the way out into the street, then the fresh air seemed to hit them and they both paused, clutching the railings and surveying the scene with care. Murray looked about him, too, at nothing in particular, then noticed a dark stain on the broad flag of the doorstep. In a moment Ketchell saw him looking at it.

'Oh, yes, poor Paulie,' he remarked, casually.

'Who's Paulie?' Murray asked.

'Oh, that was terrible!' said Harry Holden, turning a little green. 'Sir Joshua's secretary, dead on the doorstep!'

'Dead?' A chill finger crept up Murray's spine, but the two young men seemed comparatively untroubled.

'That's right, with his throat cut!' said Ketchell, lugubriously leaning towards Murray. His breath was unpleasant.

'But who did it?' asked Murray. Ketchell shrugged.

'Street thieves? They'd have been better to wait: if he'd had his way he'd have inveigled his way into some of Sir Joshua's money, and been much more worth the effort.' He shrugged. Harry, clinging to the railings, gave the darkened bloodstain a long stare, but Ketchell distracted him.

'Where's the best dancing this evening, then, Harry?' Ketchell asked. This started a lengthy debate as Ketchell drew them slowly away from the doorstep. Much of their chatter was in St. Giles Greek – the local slang employed by pinks and Corinthians – and Murray suspected that Holden at least did it less from nature and more to show off his local knowledge. The fact that Murray understood most of it was something he chose not to bother sharing, for now.

'There's dancing at the Cranbourne,' Ketchell was saying, 'if we had the rhino.' He cast a speculative glance back at Murray who was a few paces behind. The bloody doorstep was not going to leave his inner eye for a while. Was it something connected to Blair's worries?

'I've got enough to see us in and furnished, Barnie,' said Harry. 'Aunt Akehurst gave me a bit before she left.'

'Did she now?' said Barnie, grinning. 'Then the Cranbourne it is. And do you like the Opera, Mr. Letho?'

'I'm sure I should find a visit very interesting, Mr. Ketchell,' Murray acknowledged. He had to put the thoughts aside for the moment. A dance and the Opera – the evening was boding well. He just hoped that whatever crowd attended the Opera this evening was there for the music, and not just to be seen.

Yet even then, with the decision made, it took an

ité

unconscionable time for the three of them to go anywhere. Harry Holden wanted to stop and see if anyone of interest was in Ben Medley's parlour: the old pugilist had a reputation for attracting the best conversations to his couches. But Medley, his face battered from old fights like a field after the pigs had been in, said he had a rheum and they would be better not to catch it: his parlour was empty, and though he gave them a glass of hock each and let them warm themselves by his fire, it was clear their host was in no humour to cope with guests. A violent bout of sneezing prevented him even wishing them a proper good night.

'I have never seen him so low!' Harry Holden was half-apologetic, half-disappointed for himself. 'I tell you, seeing him in his misery has made me miserable myself. The thought of dancing at this moment is as unwelcome as being taken up by the traps.'

'The police won't want you this early in the evening,' said Barnabas Ketchell quickly, with a glance at Murray. 'You're barely bosky and you've fought no one, nor broken anything. You would be a dull enough man to arrest. Look, there's a sluicery I know between here and the Cranbourne: let's drop in for a jug. Only to watch out for the buzmen, Mr. Letho – guard your pockets well!'

The sluicery was in a clean enough street and, of its kind, not completely foul. A girl with a pretty face, as yet unraddled by the gin they were serving and no doubt her other sources of income, sang an old song in a sweet, if faint, voice, and the drinkers were impressed enough to make an effort to listen. The gin did not appear to have too much in the way of foreign bodies in it. Murray contrived only to sip his. No doubt someone would finish off his cup after he left.

Holden and Ketchell emptied the jug between them, and stood firmly enough, not even wilting when the fresh air hit them outside in the street. The street was briefly flooded with ladies and gentlemen in masks, laughing and joking: one was dressed as a Harlequin, one as a farmer with leather gaiters, one as a Bishop – though it appeared to be a lady.

'A masquerade at the Watlington house tonight, it seems,' said Ketchell.

'A shame we had no invitation. I like a masquerade,' said Harry Holden, pausing to cast a longing glance back at the masqueraders. 'I do a very good Frenchman, Mr. Letho – often my friends don't even recognise me! Je suis Array Oldang,' he announced, twirling the sidelocks of his hair into what presumably he believed to be a French style and adopting a murderous accent. 'Je swee charmong ah roncontree voo.'

'Very convincing, even without the mask,' Murray agreed with a smile. It was hard to know how sincere Harry was, but he seemed genuine.

'Barnie taught me the lingo. I never remembered any of it at school.'

'Well, it's always useful, even if you don't go to masquerades.' Barnie had drifted on ahead a little, or Murray might have asked him where he had learned his French. Murray liked languages. But Barnie Ketchell turned to see what was keeping them and waved them on.

'Nearly there!' he said. In the lamplight at the Cranbourne's doorway, Murray could see that Ketchell's cheeks were already flushed – though it might have been the cold air.

The Cranbourne was a disappointment. The place had the air of events drawing to a close: the band looked tired and the dancers were sweaty and bedraggled. Supper was just being served but the food was as jaded as the people: Holden and Ketchell nevertheless seemed determined to make the most of their ticket money, and Harry ate a plateful of curiously drab morsels while Ketchell found the punch and secured rather more than his share. Murray looked about for any young ladies – or he would have happily danced with older ones – who seemed nimble on their feet, and managed to secure the first two dances after supper with a girl whose chaperone was prepared to take him, his card and his reputation at his word. But the band was even more sleepy after their break – 'off to meet with the Dustman', Harry Holden remarked sympathetically as the horn player broke off to yawn excessively, and the young lady, though pleasant and keen, seemed just as drowsy and kept apologising for making mistakes. In the end Murray was happy enough for their party to move on, and they left the Cranbourne quietly, careful not to disturb the doziness of those remaining.

'The Opera, then?' asked Harry, only a little put off his evening's fun.

'The Opera,' Barnie Ketchell agreed.

It seemed quickest to walk, though Harry expressed some interest in chairs: for all that he was the youngest of the three of them, his constitution did not seem strong. Barnie Ketchell, on the other hand, though he looked near death's door in the wrong light, possessed a determination to see all there was to see and to show it to Murray. He gave him some history of the Italian Opera as they went along, even though Murray already knew much of it.

'And now Taylor runs the proceedings more from the debtors' prison than elsewhere,' Ketchell summed up with satisfaction, 'and barely a farthing of your ticket money will go anywhere near a singer, or a player. And going by the past no doubt the place will burn down again in a year or so, the management will change again, and who knows what will become of it then?'

'They're building another theatre in the Haymarket anyway,' said Harry from a few paces behind them, dragging his feet. 'That will ruin the Opera entirely.'

Ketchell turned to let his friend catch up, a knowing smile on his face.

'And where will all the pretty birds go then?'

'Barnie,' Harry groaned, 'I need some daffy before I face them this evening. Let us stop and find a jug.'

'Aye, a grand idea,' Barnie conceded.

Another delay, another gin-cellar. This time the gin was downright nasty: Murray could bring himself to do no more than sniff it, even though he had paid for it. He set it down carefully, convinced that if he splashed it on his coat it would eat right through to the bone. Barnie knocked his back as though it were mother's milk to him. Harry drank with focussed dejection, and when he had emptied his cup he knocked it hard on the counter.

'Right,' he said, 'I can face it now.'

Despite the lateness of the hour Pall Mall and the Haymarket were still dotted with street sellers. Murray was amused that he would have been able to buy a knife and some sealing wax, had he felt a need for them. Harry and Barnie paid them no attention, but drove forward as if the Opera had been the end goal of a lifelong pilgrimage, arriving triumphant at the door and blinking in the hard yellow light that flooded the pavement.

'Here we are!'

Murray's heart lifted as he heard, distantly, the strains of a

Rossini opera, performed surprisingly well if Barnie were right and the singers were hardly being paid. He paused, then realised that Barnie and Harry were not heading towards the auditorium at all, but off to the side somewhere. In the hope that they were going to secure a box, he followed.

The room they entered was not upstairs, but down, a staircase leading into a room crowded mostly, he thought, with women. And it was only a moment before he realised what kind of women these were.

To be fair they were not what Barnie would probably have called flash mollishers, low, cheap prostitutes. These were well turned out, fashionably dressed, and in some cases alarmingly young and fresh looking. Each group surrounded a mother hen, an older woman nicely bejewelled, keeping an eye on her income more sharply than any society chaperone. One, even now, was watching Harry Holden with wary concern, as he sidled up to a charming young lady with bright blue eyes and a winningly modest expression. Clearly Harry and she had met before, and just as clearly the young lady's guardian had done some investigation into Harry's financial potential, and found him wanting. Harry looked wretched.

Barnie was touring the room, examining the stock, you would say, if he had been at a country fair. Murray could not quite bring himself to regard the women in the same way. Certainly the prospect before him was very pleasing, but that was only until you began to think of what lay behind it. He was trying to think of an excuse to leave – preferably to go and listen to the opera – when one party of ladies gathered themselves together to depart, and brushed past him on their way to the stairs. The closest woman bumped against his elbow, stepped backwards with an apology, then looked up into his eyes with a start.

'Charles!'

'Beatrix?'

'Come along, Beatrix, we're going,' said the mother hen, and the party surged up the staircase to the exit. But Murray stared after them, as Beatrix, head down, hurried along with her companions, leaving him astonished.

Beatrix Pirrie … how many years had it been?

He found himself a table and sat, while a waiter placed wine before him. Something about his expression must have made the women leave him undisturbed for now. Beatrix Pirrie.

Long ago, when he had just left university, he had worked as a kind of secretary for an unusual man by the name of Lord Scoggie. Beatrix, a poor relation, had lived in Scoggie Castle as companion to Lord Scoggie's capable daughter. And then she had left, in the company of a man whose reputation was as tarnished as his peculiar charms were powerful. Murray had tried to warn her, to explain how she herself would suffer in the eyes of society, but he had been young like Beatrix and consequently unconvincing. She had gone, and he had missed her, and from that day to this he had barely heard her name spoken. But here she was, primped and powdered and in the worst of society. Part of him longed to say 'I told you so' – and part of him wanted to weep that he had been right.

'Mr. Letho?'

It was Barnie, an unappealing grin on his face.

'Ah, yes – some wine?' Murray offered.

'Alas! Unless you have found a young lady to appeal to you, Harry asks that we should move on. His lady-love has once more spurned him, and he wishes to retreat to the arms of his beloved daffy. I think we should find some scran first, or he will be helpless by midnight.'

The rest of the night was a blur, even though Murray avoided most of the spirits offered him. The food was not bad, and the effort of keeping Harry just on the near side of lusky, as Barnie described it, kept Murray's mind mostly away from memories of Beatrix. But once they had lurched into the house in Fitzroy Square and bundled Harry into his bed, Murray retreated to his own room in a daze of recollection and speculation. Robbins was waiting for him – well, had fallen asleep in a chair, as was only sensible – but Murray had no words to explain yet how he felt. When Robbins had gone off to his own room, Murray sat in his nightshirt on the edge of the bed, staring into the candle flame on his night table, and thinking of the past, of Lord Scoggie, now dead, of his sons, Murray's erstwhile pupils, of cold and dank Scoggie Castle and all that had happened there, good and bad. He had learned a great deal at Scoggie Castle, and he still, sometimes, saw young Lord Scoggie and his brother Robert. And their sister Deborah, who had made a good match and now ran her own household with happy competence. But Beatrix

Pirrie, abandoning society with her seducer, had vanished. And now what kind of life was she living? She had looked, he thought, running over and over their brief encounter, healthy and well, at least, smartly dressed and adorned, looked after. But to be amongst that crowd in the Italian Opera, looking for custom …

Eventually he sank into uneasy sleep, tormented by dreams of the past and the possible present. Light was already edging around the shutters when he heard Robbins bringing in hot water and stooping to light the fire.

'What time is it?' he asked, not relying on his cloudy eyes to peer at his watch just yet.

'It's nine, sir, and I regret to say there is a problem.'

Murray sat up wearily. He hoped it was a simple one.

'The horse?' he asked.

'The horse, sir?'

'The one that was lame.'

'Ah, no, sir, though I believe Old Donald feels a longer rest would be appropriate. No, but the problem is related to that.'

Murray rubbed at his face and ran fingers through his dark hair, trying to revive himself.

'Go on, then – what?'

'It's Young Donald, sir. He's disappeared.'

Chapter Eight

Groomed and dressed and still not entirely conscious, Murray went to the stables, which were, indeed, somewhere round the back. Old Donald, the lick of his hair pushed back wildly over the top of his head, was brushing one of the horses with steady sweeps, murmuring to the animal in a voice that was incomprehensible but soothing. As soon as he stepped away to bow to Murray, a look of deep anxiety returned to his face.

'Sir, I am so sorry that Donald has done this! And you good enough to take him into your stables!'

'Let's not mind that now, Donald: let us try to work out what has happened. You're content that he left of his own free will?'

Donald's agitated expression gave way to a look of bafflement.

'Whysoever would he not? I'm sorry, sir, I mean I cannot understand why he would have left of his own free will, but how could he not have? Who would have taken him?'

'Fair enough. Now, did he tell you that he was going? Or did he leave a note of any kind?'

'A note? A note? No: and I should write to my sister, his mother. She must be told what he has done.'

'Then we don't know if he intends to stay away. It could be that he went out, for whatever reason – to see the sights of London, perhaps – and has become lost. He may have every intention of returning, but as yet has not found his way.'

'If I find he's under a hedge drunk, sir, I'll skelp him myself!' exclaimed Donald, again jumping off into unmentioned byways. The horse next to him twitched, and Donald put out a hand automatically to calm him, though he looked as if he could have done with calming himself.

'Let's find him first. Now, have you any idea where he might have gone? Did he mention anything that was of particular interest to him? Some grand sight, perhaps, he wanted to see?'

But already Donald was shaking his head.

'He said nothing, sir. He was excited to be in London, right enough, but what with the horse going lame – poor Midnight, here,' he put in, stroking the shoulder of the horse he had just been grooming.

'Oh, it's Midnight!' Murray had wondered which horse. For a moment there was intense discussion about the heat in the fetlock, the benefits of poulticing, the cleaning out of hooves and the nasty things one found on the roads around Smithfield Market. Midnight enjoyed some attention, and then of course the other horses had to be spoken to as well, to make things fair.

'So you see, sir, another day's rest would do poor old Midnight no harm at all.'

'And we could make use of the time in seeing if Young Donald comes back, could we not? Give him a chance to find his way home.'

'But you needed to get on to Brighton, sir.' Old Donald's voice wavered, caught between responsibility to his master, care of his horse, and duty to his family members.

'If Midnight is still not right tomorrow morning, Mr. Robbins and I will continue to Brighton by some other means, and you can follow on when that leg is better and Young Donald is safely returned.'

Robbins had been to fetch breakfast of a kind from some neighbouring establishments, and served it to Murray at the table in his chamber.

'But what if he did not intend to return, sir?' Robbins asked. 'He's a young man: he may think he has a better chance here in the city.'

'Yes, it's possible,' said Murray, 'though I should have thought he might have mentioned that to his uncle, or at least left him a note. They can both read and write.'

'Old Donald is a loyal man, sir: I'm sure if Young Donald told him to his face that he intended to leave, he would have tried to stop him. I daresay Young Donald would have wished to avoid that.'

'You seem determined that Young Donald is gone with no thought of returning, Robbins: have you any reason to think that way?'

Robbins sighed.

'No reason, sir, none at all. Just – what Mary might call a feeling, sir.'

'I see. Hm.' Murray waited while Robbins poured him another cup of coffee. 'Well, we are here for the day and another night, assuming that Mr. Holden does not decide that we have outstayed our welcome. Any sign of him yet?'

'None,' said Robbins, tight-lipped, 'nor of Mr. Ketchell, either.'

'Then the question is, if we have another twenty-four hours in London, how to make best use of it? We could try to look for Young Donald, but where on earth would we start? Particularly as we don't know whether or not he actually wants to be found. We can't help Mr. Blair, as we don't know what his problem is, specifically – what is it, Robbins?'

'Well, sir, we might have something by way of a trail.'

'How's that?'

Robbins produced a paper from within his waistcoat pocket, and unfolded it, handing it to Murray.

'The children below stairs, Jackie and Rosie, they eventually remembered that this had been left for me.'

Murray glanced at the back of the paper. It was addressed to Henry Robbins, and from the signature he realised that it had been left by Blair's man Smith, a man of some experience and resource.

'Dear Mr. Robbins,' it read, 'I have some small hope that this might find you here with Mr. Murray – and if instead he has brought another man I trust he has chosen a wise one. We have been urged on to Brighton, and I believe a house has been taken by Sir Joshua Akehurst somewhere near the London road. We leave in the morning. In case Mr. Blair's missives go astray I'll tell you that his concerns centre on Miss Akehurst who has been receiving love letters which my master considers threatening, and today there was an attempt to abduct her in Hyde Park by, if it can be believed, a masked stranger on horseback. Miss Blair saw him more clearly than anyone but she has had no time to make a drawing of him to leave for you. And if that were not enough, Sir Joshua's secretary then was found dead on the front doorstep with his throat cut. A magistrate was called and has spoken to all, but there is no solution to the mystery, though we are to leave anyway.

'I can at least say that both Mr. Blair and Miss Blair were quite well when they left town. We are to take Mr. Blair's carriage, so at least we are to some extent independent. And of course my master is very familiar with the county of Sussex. I am heartily pleased to be leaving London, but I shall be happier still to part company with the Akehursts and their household. There is a butler here I would not employ if he were the last man at the agency: yet everyone seems conspiring to pretend that there is nothing in the least wrong with him. At the same time I think my master would rather be out of it as well, for he is not sure why he is here at all. I wish I had better or at least clearer news to leave you. All this uncertainty pleases me not.

'I pray you will be able to follow at good speed to Brighton and I wish you a swift and safe journey.

'Your humble servant,

'A. Smith.'

'I wondered if it were possible, sir, that Mr. Blair might have left something similar for you but that it had not come to light yet.'

'Or perhaps between them they thought the servants' hall more reliable than Mr. Holden or Mr. Ketchell,' Murray suggested. 'Though this butler does not sound a very dependable person. I wonder what Smith finds objectionable about him, and why no one else seems to agree?'

'No doubt he has gone down to Brighton anyway, sir,' said Robbins. 'But as we have a day here, should we perhaps see if there is anything else we can discover about this murder? Though if it is in the hands of the magistrates, should we perhaps instead look at the abduction? Or attempted abduction?'

'That's a very good idea, Robbins. It was Miss Akehurst's safety that concerned Blair, and I cannot see what the death of a secretary in the street might have to do with it – or not enough to do anything about it, anyway. I believe the ton go to the Park regularly for their Grand Strut: it's more than likely that anyone there today would also have been there when it happened. Doesn't Smith say it happened the day he wrote the letter?'

'Yes, sir – on Sunday, apparently. They'll have left town on Monday morning.'

'Hm, yes – and it's Thursday today. They'll have reached Brighton yesterday or they'll be there today, if their journey has been without incident. Thursday in the Park … not as busy as on a Sunday, but no doubt there'll be some gossip. Not yet, though: the beaux-ideals won't be out of their beds yet, nor their ladies, either. We'll take a turn about the adjacent streets, and see if we can find Young Donald in a gutter somewhere.' It was his turn to sigh. 'A daft needle in a not very comfortable haystack, I think.'

Beginning with the fenced garden opposite, Murray and Robbins covered the whole of Fitzroy Square including the rough land set aside for the other two arms, poking their sticks into bushes, checking hollows, and even peering up into trees that seemed sturdy enough to form an appealing refuge for a man not quite able to make it home. They had no luck, and ventured further abroad, trying an eastwardly direction in case it had been the draw of fashionable places that had taken Young Donald out. Murray found himself in streets he had seen last night after dark, even more crowded now with street sellers and beggars, carriages and chairs. Buildings that had had a certain charm lit by many little lamps were now dull and unappealing. The damp autumnal air here was thick with the smoke of coal fires and in some streets it was hard to see clearly to the end of them. The bitter aroma no doubt added to the universal coughing and sniffling around them. Sweet chestnuts, roasting over a griddle at the corner of two streets, could barely be detected six feet away, and Murray felt sorry for the stout woman selling them. He bought two pokes with a screw of salt, and handed one to Robbins.

'It's impossible to know where he might have gone,' he said, jiggling the bag in his gloved hands. He would have to pull a glove off to peel the chestnuts, even if it meant burning his fingers. 'Do we even know if he had any acquaintances in London?'

'None that his uncle knew of, sir.'

'Would he have gone to look for a servants' agency? If he planned a change of employer?'

'He'd be a fool,' Robbins commented, then straightened his shoulders. 'Aye, I can see a young lad like that might think he had a better chance of advancement here than at Letho, if that's the kind of advancement he was interested in.' It was clear from Robbins' tone that it was not a kind of advancement of which he himself approved. 'But even if he did, and if he thought he would do it without telling his uncle – and I can see why that might be the case – why would he do it late at night? There isn't a respectable agency would be open. Even supposing there is such a thing as a respectable agency.' Robbins' lips thinned. Servants' agencies were the last resort for both staff and employers – it was much better to rely on word of mouth and personal recommendation. But in London, perhaps, it was the only possible way for a newcomer to find a place.

'So let's think: he went out to see the sights and lost himself, and has yet to find his way back to Fitzroy Square. He went out and found a gin sluicery, drank himself into oblivion and spent the night in a gutter – and has yet to find his way back to Fitzroy Square. He deliberately left to find a newer, brighter life in London, but left no note. He deliberately left to fulfil some arrangement of which we know nothing. Or he was taken against his will and – and, well, who knows what?'

'I don't fancy either of the last two, sir,' said Robbins. 'We don't know that he knows anyone or anything enough here to have an arrangement. And who would want to kidnap him?'

Murray pondered, dipping the creamy flesh of a chestnut into the salt and munching.

'I suppose I added the kidnapping possibility just for completeness, but then, apparently Miss Akehurst was almost kidnapped only a few days ago.'

'Aye, sir, but that's different, isn't it?'

'Is it? We don't know much about her, except that she is Sir Joshua Akehurst's grand-daughter. And she is presumably young, and unmarried, and the recipient of peculiar love letters.'

'And a masked stranger tried to abduct her, sir.'

'A masked stranger, yes. Like a highwayman from some broadsheet ballad. In Hyde Park, in broad daylight. You'd hardly believe it except that Smith says that Miss Blair saw him clearly. Hm, yes, Robbins – when you put it like that it almost seems possible that someone might have come back and taken Young Donald, too.'

Abandoning their fruitless search around midday, Murray and Robbins returned to Fitzroy Square to find that Harry Holden and Ketchell had not yet appeared. Unfortunately, when they went to the stables they found that the same was true of Young Donald.

'What if he hasn't come back by tomorrow morning, sir?' Old Donald asked anxiously.

'We'll leave a message with Jackie and Rosie,' said Murray, 'telling him to stay here till we return. We'll make sure to come back through London and see if he has contacted them.'

'Thank you, sir. That's more than good of you, sir.'

'Not at all, Donald. We can't leave him abandoned in London if he's just lost and trying to find his way here. He'll be safe enough until we return. Now, do you think we could take one of the horses to the Park? Or two – Robbins?'

'Ah, no, sir. I'll stay on my own two feet.'

The only animal Robbins felt safe riding was an elephant, and unless they took a long diversion to the animal collection at the Tower of London his opportunities were limited.

'No doubt you'll be able to find people to ask on foot,' Murray agreed. 'Would any of the horses be available, Donald?'

'Aye, sir, you could take Coalman: he takes well to the saddle. If we can find a saddle, of course, sir …' He glanced around the stables dubiously, though they seemed very well appointed.

'I'll go and change,' said Murray, allowing him time to negotiate with Sir Joshua's stableman. 'I'll be back in about half an hour. Robbins?'

'Aye, sir, your clothes are out. I'll fetch some hot water, if I can.'

Robbins surveyed the scene in mild disgust.

'It's like Cupar on market day,' he observed.

'You're not far off there,' Murray agreed, from his seat of vantage on Coalman.

The promenade moved slowly before them, carriages, horses, and the occasional pedestrian, and behind them and around them surged the steady flow of others to join it. Every person was dressed in the highest of fashion, arranged to very best advantage. It was not actually raining, and ladies dared open carriages, though they were well wrapped in furs and velvets. Jewels glinted dull in the misty air. A few flash young men galloped past, showing off their horses' paces, and a high gig spun by at a similarly reckless speed, one wheel off the ground altogether on a corner. There was the sound of high-pitched laughter, verging on hysteria, as it vanished amongst the trees.

'Where do we start?' asked Robbins.

'Good question. What about those young bloods over there? They look bored enough to be interested in a distraction of any kind.'

'Aye, sir, and I'll try the fellows over there watching – I think they're waiting for their masters.'

'I'll see you back here in an hour, if you find other likely people.'

'Sir.'

Murray pressed Coalman into a gentle trot, not to look too eager, and approached the group of three men constrained into the tightest of breeches and the smartest of coats, hats jauntily arranged on knowing haircuts. In a moment they had realised he was heading their way, and regarded him with some interest. Murray reckoned he was being assessed more sharply than by any protective dowager with a daughter to marry off.

'Good day to you!' he said from a suitable distance. 'My name is Murray, and I'm trying to find people who were here last Sunday – people with an observant turn, preferably.' He smiled, hoping for co-operation.

'I'm observant,' said one, almost still a boy now that Murray could see him more clearly. 'I'm damned observant. Fellows are always telling me so.'

'You!' One of the others cackled, almost as young and possessed of extraordinary pale blue gloves that showed every turn of his knuckles. They had probably cost around as much as Murray's horse. 'You barely recognise your own servant when he brings you a message! I'm much more observant than you! I'll wager you I've noticed more than you have even this morning.'

'It's me you need to talk to, sir,' said the third, solemn-faced but with a fan dangling from one wrist, studded with something that looked like emeralds. 'These two are too busy with their own affairs to notice anything. And I was here last Sunday.'

'So was I!' cried the second man again.

'I was, too, of course,' said the young lad. 'Someone needs to keep an eye on these two, or they would be in trouble in eight different ways before dawn every night.'

Murray could believe it.

'Of course, you needed to be in the right part of the park, too, I daresay,' he went on. 'I gather there was an incident involving, if it is to be believed, a man in a mask.'

'Oh! Goodness, yes, what an excitement!' cried the man with the gloves. 'I heard he tried to seize a young lady!'

'Miss Akehurst, that's what I heard,' said the youngest. 'Sir Joshua Akehurst's grand-daughter.'

'What did he want to snatch her for?' asked the second.

'I heard he couldn't lift her and had to ride off without her,' said the man with the fan. 'No doubt he had thoughts of a ransom. There's a good deal of rhino in that household.'

'Safer than marriage, then,' said the young man judiciously. 'Get the money, return the girl, move on to the next one.' He caught Murray's eye and had the grace to look a little ashamed of himself.

'So rumour is rife,' Murray remarked. 'Does rumour have any theories as to who the man was?'

The three young men looked at each other, puzzled.

'Who he was? But wasn't he wearing a mask?' asked the young one.

'Or was that a rumour, too?' asked the one with the gloves.

'You can recognise people even when they are wearing masks,' said the one with the fan, impatiently. 'But I don't know that anyone did. No one is admitting to it, anyway.' He flapped the fan out, opened it, and fanned his face irritably. From the way the other two smothered their grins, it seemed this was a recent affectation. 'He can't have been one of the ton.'

'I think,' said the young one after a moment, 'that I might actually have seen him.'

'You?' said Blue-Gloves. 'How would you have seen him?'

The young one frowned, applying himself to concentrating. Murray suspected he did not try it too often.

'Well, you know nearly everyone just goes round and round.' He gestured to the circling masses in their carriages and on horseback. 'Round and round,' he repeated, waving his hand appropriately, just in case they might have misunderstood. 'There was one fellow who wasn't going round and round. He was just heading straight over there, and from what people have said, I think it was round about the right time.'

'What did he look like?' Murray asked after waiting for the young fellow to go on.

'He had a damned good seat on his horse,' said the boy. 'But his clothes were a bit unexciting. You couldn't say he was a dashing fellow, at all.'

'Anything else about him?'

'A green coat,' said the boy, closing his eyes tight as if he could squeeze the information out of his brain like that. 'And the horse was dark, a dark bay, I'm almost sure. I can see a black tail …' He allowed his eyes to open slowly, and shrugged. 'But the fellow had his back to me, so I can't even say for sure if he had a mask.'

'Nevertheless, it might be useful,' Murray conceded. 'You don't remember if you saw anyone pursuing him? Meeting him? Calling out to him?'

But the boy was shaking his head already.

'I just have the memory of that figure heading off across the park, that's all. There's nothing else in my head.'

Murray was prepared to believe that, at least.

'Well, thank you for your help, and your time. It's a start!'

Maybe Robbins would have found out something more.

But they questioned and queried, prodded and cajoled, and by dusk, when the very last of the groups of weary socialisers had at last agreed that they would return home and change and meet again at the next fashionable venue, Murray and Robbins had virtually no information to share beyond what they had already discovered. Robbins' boots and Coalman's hooves were thick with mud and grit, and all of them were hungry and fed up.

'Let's take a short cut,' said Murray, sliding down from Coalman's high back to join Robbins at ground level. 'I've seen more than enough of this promenade for one day. Through those trees over there – I think that will take us directly to the gate we want.'

A discussion on food followed as they plodded wearily across the grass and into the trees. There was a good deal of undergrowth they had not noticed from a distance, and in the failing light the shadows under the branches were much darker than they had seemed at first. Nevertheless they were two grown men and fairly capable of protecting themselves, so they ploughed on.

A muffled scream brought Murray to his senses. Before they could sort out its direction, they heard running footsteps, heavy and determined.

'Who's there?' Murray shouted sternly, hoping to put off an attacker.

No reply. Light, quick breathing not far away, then the patter of lighter steps. A pause. Then a figure clad in white burst from the trees, stumbled, and fell into Murray's arms.

It was Beatrix Pirrie.

Chapter Nine

'Charles!'

'What's the matter, Beatrix? Is someone chasing you?' The heavy footsteps had ceased, but there was tension in the air.

'Yes, oh, yes. Help me, please!'

'Stay with us. Robbins?'

Robbins' blank white face loomed in the dusk.

'Sir.'

'If you will keep to Miss Pirrie's side, and a little behind. Beatrix, take the horse's reins and I can wield my cane. Now, we were making for the gate over there – will that do?'

'Gate? Oh, yes, yes. Anywhere away from this park, please, Charles.'

'Then let us make some speed.'

He tried to measure his long stride so as not to hurry Beatrix and Robbins too much, but they made good time across the rest of the park, better than they would have done before in their fatigue. He noted as they walked that Beatrix had no coat nor cloak, that her bonnet strings were undone, that one of her gloves was missing, and her gown was muddy to the knees. What conclusions should he draw? He refrained for the moment. At the gate, they paused.

'Where can we take you, Beatrix?'

'Take me?'

'Where do you live? Are there friends to whom we can take you, where you will be safe?'

'Friends!' Her laugh was breathless, ironic. 'I think I have no friends. The man –' she glanced at Robbins, but he was looking politely the other way – behind them, in fact, in case of pursuit. 'The man who has befriended me in recent years … he wants to kill me.'

'To kill you!' It seemed extreme, but looking at Beatrix again, her grubby gown and her dishevelled appearance, he was ready to believe it, at least for now. 'Is that what you were running from?'

'Oh, yes,' said Beatrix, looking back over her shoulder at the wood. 'That is exactly what I was running from. And I don't imagine he is going to give up.'

'Then let us move again.' Murray guided her between them towards Fitzroy Square. It was perhaps not the best solution, but it would do until at least they had some food and heard Beatrix's story.

The evening streets were beginning their transformation from the daytime town to the night-time one, lamps being lit, the gentry hurrying home to change, the streetsellers thinning, the beggars rising to go and spend the day's earnings, stretching stiffened limbs. Robbins tipped the last crossing sweeper before the entrance to the square, but kept watching about them. Murray knew he would not relax until they were safely in the house, and possibly not even then. He would be wondering what on earth was going on, and who this woman was who addressed Murray by his Christian name so readily.

It was quicker to go round with Robbins and the horse to the stables than to wait on the front doorstep for the lad Jackie to summon up the courage to open the door.

'Any word from Young Donald?' Murray asked as they handed Coalman over for his rub-down and supper. Old Donald shook his head.

'Not a sign,' he said sorrowfully. 'I doubt the lad is lost altogether.'

'We kept an eye open for him all day, but saw nothing,' said Murray, 'though we were only around the Park. He might still appear.'

'I think we'll be off to Brighton without him,' said Old Donald. 'I've written to his mother.'

'And I'll leave instructions here for him, as I said.' He patted Coalman's neck, and then led the way into the house, sending Robbins with orders to the kitchens. What they would be able to do in a household with no hostess and barely a host Murray was not sure, but a hot bath and a brushing down of muddy skirts would be a start. He led Beatrix into the parlour, and sat her down by the cold fireplace. There was no sign of Harry or Mr. Ketchell, for which he was duly grateful.

'When Robbins comes back I'll send him out for food. I apologise for the accommodation.'

'Is this your house, Charles?' Beatrix looked about her, quick and observant. 'Rented, perhaps?'

'No, it is more complicated than that. The house belongs to Sir Joshua Akehurst, the Cabinet minister, but we are not acquainted: I came here to meet a friend of mine but the family and their guests had had to move down to Brighton. We are to follow them tomorrow.'

'So none of the family is at home?'

Murray had the impression she was talking in order to stop her teeth from chattering. In a moment, though, Jackie appeared in the doorway with a warm shawl, and hurried forward to light the fire. Robbins followed him: you could tell that Jackie was well aware of Robbins' presence as he swept and worked at the hearth.

'Sir, there will be hot water in an hour, apparently. Would you like to eat before or after? I gather that Mr. Ketchell and Mr. Holden have already gone out for the evening.'

'Oh, good,' said Murray. 'Beatrix, would you prefer to eat first?'

'You'll be hungry,' she said at once, no doubt remembering him as a young man. 'Please, do not hold back on my account.'

'Very well, then, since the water will be so long. Whatever food you can find that is edible, Robbins, please.'

Robbins nodded, and summoned Jackie with a twitch of his chin. They left.

'You aren't still with my uncle Scoggie, then?' asked Beatrix with a smile. In the parlour candlelight it was harder to ignore the powder on her face and her reddened lips. He was struggling to fit this Beatrix together with his memory of her.

'My lord Scoggie is dead, I'm afraid. Henry is Lord Scoggie now, and doing very well. Robert is in the army. Deborah is married and settled.' He cleared his throat. 'And you? Are you – is it still – is that man still your companion?'

Another of Beatrix's breathless laughs, entirely devoid of humour.

'Oh, no: no, he is long gone. But I suppose I should be

grateful to him: at least he saw to it that after his departure I had another friend to protect me. Lord Scoggie dead, eh? That is sad, though he was a strange enough gentleman.'

'He was very kind to me,' said Murray, 'and remained so after I inherited my father's estate.'

A smile curled the painted lips for a moment.

'You were always fair,' she said. 'And wise, for your age. Have you married? Have you family?'

'I have a daughter,' said Murray, though for once he felt disinclined to discuss her with this stranger. 'My wife is dead.'

'Not much regret there?' A different kind of smile this time, one he did not quite like – one he could not fit at all with his memories of Beatrix, as if she had bought it somewhere and fastened it on.

'It was a little while ago.' He waved a hand slightly, moving the subject away. 'But what about you? This friend with whom he left you – is this the man you say wants to kill you?'

At this, she leaned forward suddenly, her head in her hands.

'I am sorry,' he heard her say through her fingers. 'One grows so used to – to conversation … But no, no, this is not that man. That was … three men ago, I believe. All gentlemen, you know. All of good station.' She sat back again, her expression mocking. 'I am accommodated well, dressed finely and in the best of fashion, fed and entertained … there are worse lives, I believe.'

To begin with, Murray thought, but did not say. Beatrix was still quite young, after all, and under the powder she was still – not beautiful, no, she had never been that. But somehow healthy looking, attractive enough, and no doubt attentive to the needs of her gentlemen friends. She had always been kind. Perhaps that was what they paid her for. He stopped there, not wanting to allow his imagination to wander further.

And again she was skirting about the events of this evening.

'So, it's your current friend who wants to kill you?' he pressed.

'That's right.' She grew solemn again. 'He's quite an important person, and sometimes – sometimes he arranges meetings in my little apartments, you know, private meetings, when men have important business to discuss. I arrange everything, act as hostess, and then of course I leave them to their brandy and their business and I know no more about it. But last night – well, of course it was an accident –'

'You overheard something?' he prompted.

'I maybe did,' she agreed. 'Something secret. Something dangerous. And now – well, I'm disposable.'

'So why wait for today?' asked Murray after a pause. 'Why not kill you last night?'

She looked at him in surprise.

'That's a very – a very practical question to ask!' she cried.

'Forgive me,' he said, 'I've known a few murderers over the years. Perhaps this is more familiar ground to me than you might think. But if someone is trying to keep a secret and finds that there is a danger of it being let out, he is not going to wait until the following evening to do something about it if the person who has found it is free to go about and talk to whomsoever she wishes in the course of the day.'

Beatrix blinked.

'I – I had not thought of that,' she said. 'Well, by the time the others left last night he was lusky. They drank me dry, between them. He nearly fell down the stairs. It was as much as I could do to help him into a chair and send him home to his wife, so I don't suppose he had realised till this morning what had happened, if his head let him. And then, well, I don't know what else might have delayed him. We didn't have much conversation in the Park. He sent me a note asking to meet me at the tail end of the Grand Promenade, and I did and he led me to that woodland, and the next thing I knew he was telling me I had heard too much and must be got rid of.'

'And how was he going to do that?' Murray asked, earning himself another shocked look. 'Had he a knife? Was it to be throttling?' He was a little surprised at himself: he was not sure that he would have spoken this way to a lady, or even some innocent servant girl, but this was Beatrix, who had turned her back on respectability. But that should not mean that she was any less sensitive when it came to violence, particularly violence against her. He told himself to be more gentle.

Beatrix's shoulders had hunched in, and he regretted his hard words even more.

'How did you escape?' he asked kindly.

'It was a knife,' she said, twisting her hands in her lap. 'He had pulled off my cloak, and I think he thought it would give him a better, well, target, but it made him clumsy. He should just have dropped it. But he fumbled with the cloak and the knife, and I ran.'

'Good for you!'

He made himself smile encouragingly. Beatrix had always been practical, as well as kind. Maybe that was why he felt he could talk to her without being over-delicate. She and her cousin Deborah had worked hard to make Scoggie Castle, with its draughts and its eccentric owner, as warm and welcoming as possible. He had always liked them both very much.

He realised the smile had lingered on his lips, and that Beatrix was smiling back, that new-bought, unfamiliar smile. He straightened.

'But the thing is, what do you want to do now? Would you talk to the Bow Street Runners, or a parish constable? If they have them here.' He was not sure of the police structures in London, but Beatrix was already shaking her head.

'Do you really think that they would believe me against him? I told you he is an important man, a gentleman, of some standing. And what am I?'

Murray did not answer that.

'Is there somewhere you could go to be safe? To friends, perhaps?' Though her 'friends' were what had caused the problem in the first place.

'I have no friends in town where he would not find me – and I would not bring danger to any of them,' she added, with a little lift of her head.

'And elsewhere? You had no family apart from the Scoggies, as I remember.'

'No,' she said, 'none. And I don't believe I could go back to them, now. Not after everything.'

'I'm sure Deborah still misses you,' he said. But Beatrix shrugged.

'No, that boat is burned. It is one thing to miss a former companion, but to accept her back in different circumstances, when there is a husband and a family to take into consideration – that is quite another thing.'

She was probably right. Murray sighed.

'But – wait, Charles, tell me I'm right. Did you say you were to set out for Brighton tomorrow?'

'Yes,' he said slowly, 'yes, I did.'

'Then – oh, if you could do me that favour! I have friends in Sussex, not far from Brighton. If you were to set me down, even outside the town so that no one would see me, see you with me, then it would do you the least harm and me the greatest service! Would you? Could you? It might be the saving of my life!'

'Yes,' said Murray, 'of course I could, if you truly think you would be safe there. Your friend – your gentleman friend – he doesn't know about these other friends?'

'I don't believe I have ever mentioned them to him, no. I knew them and they left for Sussex before he would ever have noticed me, I'm sure, and there is no reason why I should have told him about them. Oh, Charles, if only you could!'

'Then consider it done,' he said, 'but we leave early tomorrow morning, if the horses are fit.'

'I shall be ready – oh, if I could find a cloak, and brush my gown!'

'There's nothing else you need?'

'There are all kinds of things,' she said with a grin, 'but I shan't embarrass you by listing them. I don't think I should be safe to return to my apartment, do you?'

'Not at all, if he is really set on killing you.'

'Then I shall just have to manage,' she said. 'I have my reticule with some money. I wonder – would there be anyone here who could lend me a cloak?'

'I'll find out, or Robbins will,' said Murray. 'And I believe that is him returning now with the food.'

Thank goodness, he added to himself: dealing with killers, in his worryingly broad experience, was not best done on an empty stomach.

As it turned out, Beatrix was not afflicted by a poor appetite, either. They were halfway through demolishing rather a good meal when there was a clatter in the hallway, and in a moment the parlour door opened.

'You still here, Letho?' said Harry Holden, not unfriendly – as he might have every right to be. 'If we'd known we'd have waited for you – but you could come out with us now if you fancy it.'

'My,' said Ketchell, coming into the room behind him, 'what have we here?'

Murray was on his feet.

'Mr. Ketchell, Mr. Holden, this is Miss P – Paterson,' he said. He hesitated over her name, wary that somehow she might be linked with her past. Beatrix curtseyed as modestly as if she had never left Scoggie Castle. 'Forgive me, Miss Paterson is an old acquaintance and suffered a robbery in the street just as we met. I hope it will not be too much of an inconvenience to find her a room here for the night before I escort her back to her family in Sussex tomorrow, Mr. Holden.'

'Oh, of course! I mean of course not!' said Harry, blushing at the proximity of a female. 'There's plenty of room!'

'Thank you, Mr. Holden,' said Beatrix quietly. 'As Mr. Murray says, we shall be away in the morning, I trust.'

'We're just back to fetch some other gloves,' said Ketchell. 'His are covered in – well, something sticky.'

Harry Holden made a disgusted face.

'Best not to know what!' he said, 'but they are fit for nothing but the midden!'

The two men left noisily. Murray wondered how drunk they were, and how much they had taken in. Beatrix's powder and paint? His own change of name? Not that it mattered – and they would be gone tomorrow.

He waved Beatrix back to her chair, and sat down opposite again.

'Mr. Holden is related to our host's wife,' he explained briefly, 'and Mr. Ketchell is his friend.'

'They are generous with their accommodation,' said Beatrix.

'They are. One of my horses injured its fetlock, and we have been staying here overnight.'

'Oh! They are the two gentlemen you must have been with at the Italian Opera last night! I saw them, but I had no idea they were with you.'

'Ah, yes. They very kindly invited me to join them.'

Beatrix laughed a little.

'I suspect you would rather have been listening to the music than visiting that room downstairs.'

Murray nodded.

'I did hope to hear a little of the performance, yes.'

'You always were musical, I remember.'

Murray felt uncomfortable remembering the days at Scoggie Castle, before Beatrix's departure – the change that had come over her. He cleared his throat and set down his cutlery.

'So,' he began, 'do you think it might help if you told me what it was that you are not supposed to know? The secret you accidentally discovered? If both of us know it then it might be harder for him to kill you.'

Beatrix looked at him, then down at her plate for a long moment. He had already given up hope when she shook her head.

'My protector – ha! A protector who threatened to kill me! – he is an important man, as I say. He's powerful, in government circles, you understand.' Her face was solemn. 'This secret – it's a government secret. I do not believe on my honour that I could tell anyone, or not yet, anyway. No doubt one day it will all be revealed.'

'I see. Very well.' Murray had had experience of government secrets before, and on the whole preferred an honest corpse. 'Now, you say you don't want to go and fetch anything, but don't you have a maid?'

'I do, of course,' said Beatrix with a shrug, 'but I don't trust her. She was employed by him – that's where her loyalties lie. Oh, this is dreadful! This time yesterday none of this had happened – everything was just as it usually is!'

Murray was still trying to arrange the practicalities.

'Should we find an agency and employ someone?'

'It's only for a couple of days,' said Beatrix. 'I can manage. In the light of everything else, not having a maid is a small matter.'

'You can, I'm sure,' Murray agreed, 'but think how it will look. I'll ask Robbins to find someone this evening. I'm sure he'll think of something.'

'Poor man, he's already running round sorting out dinner and hot water!'

'He likes to make sure everything is organised. It's almost time for your hot water to be ready, but I have no idea what room has been found for you. He'll be here shortly.'

There was a pause, as if they expected Robbins to appear in the doorway.

'On the way to Sussex,' said Beatrix, struck by a sudden

idea, 'will we be going through Kingston at all?'

'I daresay we could. Why?'

'There's a place there called Coombe Warren. I wondered if – if we could stop and see it?'

'Why?' asked Murray again, trying not to sound ungracious. Once they were off he would be eager to get to Brighton and find Blair. He had been delayed too long already.

'There's something on the hill I – I need to see,' she said, frowning. Murray was also visited by a thought.

'Is this something to do with what you're not supposed to know?'

'Um,' said Beatrix, 'you're too quick off the mark, you know?'

'Then Coombe Warren it is,' Murray agreed, without smiling. And then Robbins was at the door.

'Your chamber has been prepared, madam,' he announced. 'Rosie will show you the way.'

'Thank you for dinner, Charles,' said Beatrix as they rose from the table. 'And thank you – for agreeing.' With a smile at Robbins, she left the room.

'Rosie?' Murray queried.

'It was the best I could do, sir,' said Robbins. 'She has her wits about her, but that's about all that could be said for her as a lady's maid.'

'Right, Robbins, I owe you an explanation. Here's what's happening.' He explained quickly how he knew Beatrix, what her condition was now, and what they were to do the following day. Robbins remained silent throughout, until Murray stopped and raised a hand to invite Robbins' contribution.

'A government secret, sir? That does not sound like something to involve oneself in.'

'I agree, Robbins, but I could hardly toss her back to be killed, could I?'

Robbins shook his head abruptly.

'Of course not, sir. Not once you'd helped. I'm just not sure where it might end.'

'Well, we'll be out of town tomorrow: that at least is a start, and we can deliver her to her friends and that will be the end of our responsibility. My responsibility, I should say.'

'Well, sir –'

The parlour door opened once again, and Murray turned expecting to see that Beatrix had forgotten something. But instead it was Mr. Ketchell, his paunch pressing out his waistcoat buttons, a thoughtful look on his face.

'Brighton, didn't you say, in the morning? Where Sir Joshua and Lady Akehurst have gone?'

'That's right. My friend is staying with them, and we hope to find him there.'

'See, Harry and I have a fancy to go down to the coast, and to catch up with his dear auntie. We take up prodigiously little space, and I understand you have rather an out-and-outer of a carriage – how would it be if you gave us a ride?'

Chapter Ten

Isobel raised a hand to shelter her eyes. The sun was shining, a harsh, cold sun, and the wind was flicking grit from the pebbly beach up and into her face. Still, it was a pleasure to be outside in the fresh air and, to all intents and purposes, on her own and away from the Akehursts.

Not that the Akehursts were dissatisfied with Brighton, not at all. Well, at least Lady Akehurst and Amanda were in their element. Brighton society was well-furnished with eligible young men on the lookout for a marriageable young lady, and Amanda considered herself the toast of society. Dressmakers and milliners had already been kept busy, glovers and shoemakers found themselves comfortably rewarded, and Amanda appeared in a new gown almost every minute, dazzling with the Akehurst jewels and flirting with every young man who took an interest in her – or her fortune. Isobel, watching more warily than Lady Akehurst, wondered what Amanda would be like when she eventually found herself a husband. If she had been one of the suitors, Isobel thought, she might not have liked all that flirtation with quite such an assortment of men.

Yet one thing seemed to have been achieved for the peace of mind of all here by the sea: as far as Alester Blair knew, no further dubious love letters had been received. And there had been no second attempt at abduction. Isobel was still convinced that the man in the mask had to allow his back to recover before he tried again, and was probably trying to work out the safest way to haul Amanda out of her carriage – or to think of some other method altogether.

'How do you like Brighton, Smith?' she asked the manservant as she turned from viewing the sea.

'Not greatly, miss,' Smith said. 'It seems to me like a fishing village with ornamentation.'

Isobel smiled. It was rare for Smith to find anywhere particularly charming. But at least the smell of fresh fish made for a pleasant change from London and its heavy, sooty air. She could see why the Prince Regent – no, the King, he was now – might come here simply to feel a bit cleaner.

When she returned to the house the Akehursts had rented, Isobel found her father pacing the parlour, a look of regret on his mobile features.

'Have I summoned Charles for no good reason?' he asked her at once, without bothering with a greeting. 'Here we are with nothing to show him.'

'I'm sure Charles will forgive you,' said Isobel, pulling off her gloves. Her face tingled with the warmth indoors after the wind outside. 'Is it not better that Amanda should be safe?'

'Of course it is, of course.' Blair tutted away to himself, still bumbling about between the chairs and sophas. 'It is much the better that she should be safe. But is she? Is she really, or are we just waiting for him to catch up?'

'You think he will follow us here from London? Why should he take that risk?'

'He has already taken at least one risk, trying to snatch her in the middle of the Grand Promenade,' said Blair, stopping to wave a finger at his daughter. 'And I still do not know how he managed to convey the letters to her, to her very bedchamber. What risk did he take to do that? At the very least, he bribed a servant, and who knows but that the servant would take the bribe and tell his master anyway? And then where would he be?' His mouth slapped shut, eyes wide, emphasising his point.

'And are you sure she has received no more since we arrived here? I think she would tell you before she would tell me,' Isobel admitted. Amanda seemed to see Isobel as a strict older sister, determined to stop her fun.

'I asked her,' Blair said, 'and when she said she had not she could not seem to help looking upset – and rather cross – that her suitor, as she thinks of him, has abandoned her. I do not think she was pretending.'

'It certainly seems a subtle pretence for someone like Amanda,' Isobel agreed. 'So where is he? When will he appear? Does he have commitments in London that prevented him from following at once? Or has it taken him some time to find out where we have gone?'

'That should be easy enough,' said Blair. 'He would only have to ask the servants. And I am sure Sir Joshua would have left word where he had gone, and could be contacted.'

'But he might not want to be seen to be asking,' said Isobel. 'For that would be another risk. But if he does appear, Charles cannot be far behind, surely: and then you will not have asked him in vain, and you and he can consult all you want to over this.'

Blair went and laid a hand on his daughter's shoulder.

'Your ideas and information are invaluable, too,' he said, 'you know they are. I should like all three of us to consider this matter. And who knows, perhaps at last Lady Akehurst will tell me what she wanted me in her house for, for in the last few days she has done nothing but arrange Miss Akehurst for the next party, and avoids me entirely.'

'Do you think Mr. Lawrence might know?' Isobel asked.

'If he did, of course he would not tell me. Unless he thought it would be of some inconvenience for me to know.'

'Well, Fussy has no idea, anyway. Though as I said, it was his idea to ask you to help.'

'I wish he had not,' said Blair miserably. 'He is a good young man, but I wish he had never mentioned my name. Or that he would prompt Lady Akehurst to be more forthcoming about her problems.'

'Perhaps what concerned her was in London,' Isobel suggested. 'She has left it behind and forgotten all about it.'

'Perhaps so,' said Blair. 'But if she does not tell me soon – and if we believe that Miss Akehurst is safe – I should like to leave this household and be on my way to somewhere I feel more at home. Somewhere with books, and warm colours, and a fire blazing.'

'Now, with that I can happily agree,' said Isobel, and gave

her father a hug.

They were, Murray thought, an odd assortment leaving Fitzroy Square the next morning.

Despite his best efforts, the coachman, Old Donald, could not conceal the fact that he was in tears, convinced he would never see his nephew again and overwhelmed by the thought of the effect this would have on his sister, Donald's mother. The horses, by contrast, were keen to be going, after a couple of days stuck in unfamiliar stables. Harry Holden and Barnabas Ketchell, not much more than tiddly – a relief to Murray who had expected them both to turn up drunk – lounged inside the carriage, facing Murray and Beatrix – Beatrix was enveloped in a cloak borrowed, perforce without her permission, from presumably Miss Akehurst. It would have gone twice round Beatrix. Also borrowed from the Akehurst household was young Rosie, the kitchenmaid, who was sitting on the outside back seat with Robbins to see that she behaved herself. Rosie, however, had never left London in her short life and was so desperately excited to be going to see the sea that there was nothing she would do to risk being sent back now.

A dismal-looking Jackie waved them off from the front door, now left completely in charge of the Fitzroy Square house. Murray hoped he would not be faced with anything complicated until they could at least return Rosie to him. Servants had deserted under less difficult conditions.

Old Donald managed his distress well enough to take them out of the town as quickly as he could, forsaking better roads for quieter ones: he was a country driver when he could be. They crossed the Thames by the new bridge at Vauxhall then made good progress through the market gardens of Battersea, the river still often visible on their right as they headed west. It was hilly country, with frequent and well-kept villages and some rather grand manor houses, conveniently sited close, but not too close, to London's commercial and administrative lures. Putney and Wimbledon passed by, and then, before they had even reached the town of Kingston down on the next swinging loop of the Thames, Beatrix leaned forward to point through the carriage window.

'I believe that might be Coombe Warren there, do you think?'

Harry leaned forward to see – Ketchell was much more relaxed – while Murray knocked on the roof and called to Old Donald to make enquiries. There was a deal of shouting – Old Donald had evidently asked someone with hearing difficulties – then a slow, straining start as the horses drew the carriage uphill.

'Wait!' Murray called, and they stopped again. 'I think we can walk – Miss, er, Paterson, would you be happy to walk?'

'We could do with stretching our legs, couldn't we, Harry?' Ketchell's elbow struck Harry in the ribs, and woke him from his staring. Robbins opened the carriage door, doing his best to replace Young Donald – goodness, thought Murray, it was hard to keep track of who was doing what at present, with kitchenmaids attending ladies and butlers seeing to steps.

'Up yonder, sir,' Old Donald called down. 'If it's the hill itself you want. But it's all hilly around here.'

'What's that up on the hill?' Beatrix asked, peering upwards. 'It looks like some kind of – I don't know, a windmill?'

'That would not be unusual around here, I believe,' said Murray. 'We've seen a few along the way. It's hard to tell through the trees, though.'

'Shall we walk up and see?' Beatrix asked. Murray did not question. Whatever it was she sought, he was sure he would find out more simply by following along, and not by asking her to elaborate. They set off steadily, and to his surprise Harry Holden and Mr. Ketchell began to trail along behind them.

'Breath of fresh air,' said Ketchell, grinning. 'Harry's not used to it, you know, Mr. – Letho.'

'My name is Murray, by the way, Mr. Ketchell,' Murray corrected him at last. 'I believe Mr. Holden picked it up wrongly, and I did not correct him.'

'Ah!' Ketchell's grin widened. 'I did wonder. Murray, eh?' He dropped behind a pace or two to walk with Harry Holden, and Murray could not hear what they might or might not be saying.

If the tower at the top of the hill was a windmill, it was certainly an odd one, and not yet completed. A red brick construction rose to a height of around a storey and a half, including a basement, for the area of perhaps a generous cottage, as yet unroofed, but complete with chimney and spaces for well-sized windows. In the centre, however, the building continued to rise, and was already twice the height of the wider construction. A solitary bricklayer perched at the top of a long, sagging ladder, demonstrating that they were not finished yet. It was hard to say what it might be intended to be: the window apertures continued up the central tower, in a way that did not look quite typical of a windmill. The fine brickwork was too grand, and the whole thing rather too tall.

After a moment's puzzled survey, they noticed a wooden hut beyond the new building, and wandered over. This, too, was tall, but weathered and a little neglected, with a kind of lean-to appendage at one end. From the doorway, there was a fine view over Kingston and the Thames, and points both north-east and south. On the top of the wooden hut was a tall metal spike, red in colour. Light began to dawn.

'It's a semaphore tower!' Murray said at last. 'From the war – but they seem to be building a new one!'

'Oh, of course!' said Harry Holden, trying to control his panting as he caught up with everyone else. 'That's what it is. To send signals to the coast, wasn't it?'

'And back,' said Murray. 'All the way between London and Portsmouth. In minutes, I think.'

'The Popham system. Replacing the Murray system,' said Ketchell, staring up at the red spike with a little smile on his face. 'Lord George Murray, you know, and his semaphore discs.' He looked pointedly at Murray, but Murray was more interested in what Beatrix was doing. She seemed to be looking about her closer to ground level.

'Is there anyone about who could tell us more?' she asked. 'This is very impressive! Minutes, did you say? Really? All that way?'

'This is only an old station,' Ketchell murmured. 'Aren't they building new ones, or something?'

But as if he had heard Beatrix's words, a man appeared from the central doorway of the wooden hut. He was smartly dressed for the situation, in clothes with a naval look to them.

'Good day to you!' he called, 'Sirs, madam. Have you come to see the contraption?'

'We're allowed to see inside?' Beatrix stepped forward eagerly. 'Can you show us how it works?'

'Step this way, madam. I'd be happy to show you.'

For all his apparent lack of interest, Ketchell was right behind her as they approached the hut. Harry was more intent on recovering from his unaccustomed exercise, but Murray hurried into the hut after Ketchell and Beatrix: he was not at all sure that Ketchell was entirely focussed on learning more about a signalling system. He seemed very interested in Beatrix.

'These levers hoist arms up and down on the mast you saw on the roof,' the man was already explaining by the time Murray had reached the doorway. The interior of the hut was much smarter than the outside, with every piece of metal shining and every surface free of dust. Two small boys with telescopes kept watch at windows pointing in almost opposite directions, elbows resting steadily on the sills while their feet shifted from side to side to keep the blood flowing.

'My sons,' the naval man explained with pride, gesturing to the wriggling rear views of the boys. 'Even in peace time there are plenty of messages going back and forth – so I can't move the levers for you, madam, or who knows what message the Admiralty might think I was sending! My word, what a disaster that would be!' He laughed.

'And what is the new building across the way?' Murray asked. Beatrix was fingering the polished levers, her gloved hands sliding on the clean wood, as if admiring the work of the tower-keeper's housemaid. Ketchell seemed to be standing far too close to her. Murray was not sure how he could discreetly manoeuvre himself between them.

'That's our new signal station,' said the man proudly. 'Much taller – you can easily see the next stations on the line from the top of that already, and it's not even finished yet. Coopers Hill down that way, and on the line back to London it's Putney Heath to the north-east. Each of my lads is watching one of them, so that if they should signal we'll see it at once. Half a minute each letter and the signal's off to the next station. It's a wonder, and with the new station it'll be a marvel!'

A government building, Murray thought, absently watching as the man explained the purpose of the signals to an eager Beatrix. Ketchell was still far too near, one arm hovering as if it might well settle about her waist. A government building, and Beatrix's protector, for want of a better word, was, as she had said, a man powerful in government circles. Someone at the Admiralty, perhaps? But the new line of signal towers was hardly a secret, was it? Could it be, when this pleasant naval gentleman was so happy to explain it all to a party of complete strangers? But there must be some connexion, or why would Beatrix, running to Brighton to find safety, have asked particularly to come this way and to stop to see the tower?

'Aye, we used to use discs,' the man was telling them, apparently in response to some question of Ketchell's. 'Six discs in a mighty big frame, twenty feet tall it was. But this is quicker and neater. And in the new tower we'll have wheels to raise the arms, instead of these levers, and then who knows how fast we can go? It's the nearest thing there is to standing and telling a man yourself what he needs to know: I don't think you could go any faster over the distance.'

There were times, for the rest of that day, that Murray wished he could go a good deal faster over the distance between London and Brighton.

Autumnal views of Surrey villages and open downland did not make up for the tedium of sharing a carriage with Harry Holden and Barnabas Ketchell, who had no conversation other than their flash talk of the quality of gin at this sluicery, or the nature of the entertainment at that cockpit. Even when they occasionally strayed into sport they managed to make it all about the gambling surrounding the event, and not the standard of the pugilists or the horses. Most of their conversation was directed at each other, though Murray had the impression they also aimed, or at least Ketchell aimed, to intrigue Miss Paterson, as they knew her. Ketchell seemed fascinated by her. Did he know her from somewhere? Murray hoped not: the fewer people who were aware of where Beatrix had taken refuge, the safer she would be.

And he himself could not converse much with Beatrix without giving her away, whether they discussed their present lives or their past shared acquaintance. He tried mentioning a few books he thought she might have read, but it seemed she had less opportunity to read than she had done in the past, and had barely heard of them. She had never been particularly musical, and the exhibitions of art she had seen in London were not ones that he had had the chance to visit yet, though for a few miles it was pleasant to hear her describe some of the paintings and statuary in Carlton House. Murray amused himself for a little while trying to imagine what kind of conversation Robbins might be having on the back seat with Rosie, but when he decided that it was probably much better than his own in the privileged interior, he grew mildly resentful, and tried to think of something else.

They made good time in the fine weather, with the roads dry and clear, and reached Crawley, a market town on the edge of the High Weald, in time for dinner. There, there was a choice of coaching inns: being on the route from London to the Prince Regent's – the King's, now – favourite recreational town of Brighton was no doubt very good for business. The George, the oldest and best known amongst travellers, was full, but Murray knew of a decent little place a little further out, the Hand in Hand, where the beds were clean, the food unusually fine, and the prices a touch lower than the better placed inns.

He had half-hoped that a day's travel would lessen the enthusiasm of Harry and Ketchell for an excursion, and that they might change their minds and head back to London, but they seemed intent on staying. Ketchell even urged Harry to leave the wine alone at a reasonably early hour and hurried him off to his bed. Beatrix, too, tired from all her excitement, headed to her room accompanied by little Rosie, and at last Robbins and Murray had the chance of a walk around the neighbourhood and a talk about the day.

'Rosie's bright, sir: I'm not sure she'd have the delicacy for a lady's maid, but she'll do the job while she's needed. Though if she spends tomorrow asking as many questions as she did today, I think I might walk, sir.'

'I can imagine. She was beside herself this morning.'

Robbins discreetly stretched his shoulders, easing out his back. Murray could sympathise, having spent the day trying not to tangle his long legs with Ketchell's.

'Coombe Warren was interesting,' he told Robbins, 'but I'm not sure yet why we had to go there. A semaphore tower – you've heard of them?'

'Oh, aye, sir, for signals down to the coast. I'm sure it was indeed interesting.'

'Ketchell seems to find Miss Beatrix equally fascinating, I'm afraid.' He sighed. 'I'm not sure he's the kind of protector she might be looking for – if she is considering continuing in her present line of business – but I worry that he has worked out what she is, or has seen her before somewhere. After all, she was at the Italian Opera, and he clearly frequents it, to ogle the women there. And if he knows what she is, he may consider that she is fair game.'

'He does not strike me as a pleasant man, sir.'

'No, nor me. Yet I know nothing particularly wrong of him except for his ogling women and drinking too much daffy. Gin.'

'Aye, sir. And perhaps, if I may say so, encouraging Mr. Holden to do the same.'

'Indeed: true enough. And that is not a good thing. I wonder what Lady Akehurst's opinion of him is? After all, if Mr. Holden is her nephew she might have a say in his friendships and behaviour.'

'I wonder what Lady Akehurst will say generally, sir – when we arrive unexpectedly, with her nephew, his friend, and her kitchenmaid purloined for other duties.'

'And no groom. You did a good job today, Robbins.'

'Thank you, sir.' The ghost of a smile misted Robbins' face for an instant. 'I hope Young Donald returns safely soon, though.'

'From wherever he might be … I wonder what our welcome in Brighton will be like? And how Blair and Isobel are? And if the young lady is recovered from her abduction?'

'Not long now, sir, and we'll know.'

'Yes – I only hope we shall not be too late.'

Chapter Eleven

'Another new gown?' Isobel asked, trying to sound intrigued rather than appalled. Amanda spun to show off the tailed skirt, almost flattening her dressmaker.

'I simply must,' she said firmly. 'There is to be a reception at the Royal Pavilion this evening, and we are invited! Imagine!'

'The Pavilion? I thought that was still more or less a building site,' said Isobel, then added quickly, 'But I'm sure it will be very grand. Are we all to go? Or is it you and Sir Joshua and Lady Akehurst?' Though she was curious to see inside the extravagance that was the Pavilion, she had no particular wish to go to a reception. Lots of standing about, not enough to drink in the way of fruit juices, far too hot and crowded and a long queue for carriages afterwards.

'Yes, yes, you and Mr. Blair and Mr. Lawrence and Fussy are all to come, too,' said Amanda impatiently. 'Though I daresay that is all because you are staying with us.' She glared down at the dressmaker, still on her knees with a cushion full of pins on her wrist. Unfortunately glares did not seem to make the woman work any faster. 'Miss Blair,' said Amanda, as if she had contained the question long enough, 'why are you staying with us? Fussy is of course family, and by extension so is Mr. Lawrence, I suppose, but it is a very long extension indeed to include the two of you.' She favoured Isobel with a look which she might well have learned from her grandmother. Isobel attempted to remain patient.

'We're here at Lady Akehurst's invitation,' she said, and just managed to sound casual. After all, she had no idea whether or not Lady Akehurst had taken her grand-daughter into her confidence on the matter, and Isobel was not going to be the one to question Amanda as to Lady Akehurst's motives. Talking to Fussy had been a different matter. But she could not resist adding, 'I was not aware that we had to be related to be her guests.' She tempered it with a smile.

'No,' said Amanda, reluctantly, 'I suppose not.'

The dressmaker finished pinning, and with the help of Amanda's maid lifted the dress up and over Amanda's poised head. She watched it as the dressmaker carefully arranged it over a chair to be stitched.

'Is it not the most beautiful cloth? You're an artist of sorts, Miss Blair – don't you find it exquisite?'

Isobel found the vivid apple green with its embroidered hem fussy and a little too brash, but that was not the way to please Miss Akehurst.

'I think it will look lovely on you – it is just your colour,' she said, mentally crossing her fingers. It would make Amanda look bilious. Amanda smiled.

'I should think my suitors will admire it greatly. Did you know I have just as many admirers here as I had in London? And I had thought it might be dull here!'

Just as many admirers – or rather just as many young men who could sniff out a fortune. It was a wonder offers had not been made already, when Lady Akehurst was making it so obvious that the merchandise was available for purchase. Or was Amanda herself the problem? Isobel was sure that, even if she had been a very impoverished young gentleman, she might well have thought twice before offering for Amanda.

'Well, society moves here much as it moves in London, I think,' said Isobel. 'I am glad you find it favourable. I wonder if any of your London beaux have followed you here?' It was a chance thought, but the memory of those love letters and the man in the green coat lingered.

'No ...' said Amanda, after a moment's thought, 'no, I believe they are an entirely new set. But of just the same quality,' she added hastily. She looked at Isobel from the corner of her eye, and Isobel suddenly saw in her a moment of self-knowledge. She knew what her attractions really were – her grandfather's money – and had no idea how to do anything to enhance them other than to buy more new gowns. It seemed unlikely that Lady Akehurst was much able to help her. Poor Amanda.

'Of course,' said Isobel. 'I should not have expected anything else. And I daresay an array of them will attend this reception, too.'

'An array of beaux …' Amanda, her moment of doubt slipping away, gave herself up to a happy sigh.

'Will the King be there?'

'Oh, the thought that he could be my beau! Of course it is possible!' Isobel was sure that the thought had already crossed Amanda's mind, but she was clearly delighted to imagine that Isobel had suggested it, too. And after all, the King always needed money. But Amanda assumed a very proper expression. 'Though he is, of course, a married man.'

'Of course.' It had never stopped him before, but Isobel doubted that even Lady Akehurst would approve. 'It would not really be ideal. Perhaps limit yourself to dukes?'

She meant it as a joke, but Amanda took it as a serious suggestion.

'Well, there are one or two sons of dukes who have assured me of their admiration …'

'As long as they are unmarried, they sound much better than the King!'

Amanda, once more clad in a day dress, sat carefully on the sopha beside Isobel.

'You are from Scotland? From North Britain?'

'That's right, yes.'

'How did my grandmother even know of your existence?'

Isobel smiled. Clearly Edinburgh was beyond civilisation.

'My late mother was from Sussex.'

'From Brighton?' Amanda regarded her dubiously, wondering if Isobel and her father should be allowed to be a degree better than they had seemed previously.

'From Lewes.'

'Was she Mr. Lawrence's sister?'

'Not exactly, no. Mr. Lawrence married my mother's sister.'

Amanda had not asked these questions weeks ago when they had arrived at Fitzroy Square. Isobel wondered what had stimulated them now. There was a pause, though, perhaps while Amanda considered her next enquiry.

'You say my grandmother invited you to stay, you and your

father. Was there a reason?'

'I'm not sure,' Isobel fudged. 'Why do you ask? Is Lady Akehurst in the habit of requiring reasons for inviting her guests?'

Amanda sat back, thinking. It was not something Isobel had noticed her do much, and for a moment she studied Amanda's face, itching to draw that unaccustomed frown of concentration. Then Amanda met her eye and Isobel looked away.

'Mr. Blair is quite odd, that is all,' she said. 'He is not at all like my grandparents' other guests. I can see why she might have invited you, for you can accompany me to balls and so on and it would be all quite proper and no suitor is going to be distracted by you, but Mr. Blair is ...' She struggled to explain, while Isobel grinned inwardly at the insult. 'He is a very easy person to confide in, isn't he?'

'People have always found him so, yes,' said Isobel. 'He is an intelligent man, but very kind.'

'That's what I thought,' said Amanda. 'Very kind. As for intelligent, well, who knows? But kind, yes, and I suppose sensible?'

'Yes, indeed,' Isobel agreed.

'I see ... That's what I thought,' she repeated. 'And discreet, that too?'

'That, too.'

Amanda sighed.

'Yes ... discreet. I must talk with him again.'

'If you are anxious about anything, he is certainly a good person to talk with,' Isobel assured her. She glanced over at the maid and the dressmaker, busy about the new gown. Now was not the time to invite a confidence herself, and she knew her father would do it better. 'I believe he is out at the moment, but he should be back soon, no doubt. Shall I mention to him that you would like a word?'

Amanda considered, staring at the gown absently.

'No,' she said in the end, 'no, I shall catch him at an opportune moment. When I'm ready. Soon.'

'Then if you will excuse me,' said Isobel, 'I had better make sure I have something suitable myself for this evening. I know that I shall look like nothing in particular beside you, Miss Akehurst, but at the same time I have no wish to let you down.'

'No, not at all,' Amanda agreed distantly, and waved Isobel away. Really, thought Isobel as she made her way to her own chamber, one had to laugh or one would simply have to slap her.

There was a reasonable coaching inn at Clayton, a place to rest before the straight Roman road rose again over the South Downs. Old Donald's efficient driving had almost brought them there when there was a cry of deep annoyance from up ahead, and the carriage drew to a halt. Murray, almost as hungry as Harry Holden was regularly professing to be, opened the carriage door and leaned out to see what the matter was.

'A broken cart, sir,' Old Donald called down, as lugubrious as if he had foretold the whole disaster. 'The wheel's off and it looks as if she was carrying timber, for it's all over the road.'

'Is the driver on his own?'

'Ah, wait, now, sir …' Old Donald must have stood in his seat to see better. 'Aye, I think he might be, sir.'

Murray glanced down the road behind them. There was no sign of any traffic following them.

'I suppose we'd better give him a hand, then.' He jumped down, not bothering to wait for Robbins to pull down the steps. Beatrix looked out after him.

'You'll not be much use,' he told her with a grin. 'Let Mr. Holden and Mr. Ketchell past.'

'What?' Harry objected. 'You want us to move some kind of wood around the road? Do you know how expensive these gloves were?'

'Take them off, then,' said Murray. 'If we don't give the man a hand, it will be a long time before you see your dinner.'

Harry Holden groaned, and perched in the doorway while Robbins folded the steps down. Ketchell followed, not quite so reluctant but seeming to find some distant humour in the whole prospect.

'What about your driver?' asked Harry, 'and your rainbow?'

Murray did not think of Robbins as some anonymous liveried servant, and waved Harry along towards the broken cart.

'My driver is too elderly, and besides, someone has to make sure the horses are not disturbed. And as you see, Robbins is already going to help. Come along: it will help you to work up an appetite.'

'But I already have an appetite!' Harry complained, though despite himself he pottered along the road after Murray and

Robbins. Ketchell, looking about him as if marking where they might be, followed at a short distance. Glancing back, Murray saw that Beatrix and little Rosie were watching with interest.

Murray and Robbins and the carter, whose choice of language was very educational, did the bulk of the work, lifting rough timbers clear of the flat bed of the cart and laying them against the high hedge to await collection.

'The axle has gone,' the carter explained, though he added several expressive adjectives. It was the first time for a while that Murray had heard that deep Sussex accent, and he took a few minutes to attune his ear. 'I sent for the wheelwright, but he's gone off the other way and won't be back maybe hours yet, or days, or who can tell round here?'

Given the load of timber, Murray was not the least surprised that the axle had gone. The driver must have been trying to save time or money by overloading the cart. The pair of oxen which had been drawing it seemed entirely unconcerned by the event, as well they might, and a small boy was overseeing their ponderous pillaging of the field on the other side of the hedge. The timber seemed never-ending, even when Harry and Ketchell pitched in properly – though neither of them had much strength to offer, and could only really pick off the lighter pieces. It was dusk before they finally cleared enough of the road for Donald to steer the carriage past: there was still no sign of the wheelwright, who may indeed have been acquainted with his potential customer, and Murray and his party had to leave the carter and his boy by the side of the road. Beatrix and Rosie were chilled while the men were sweating freely with their exertions, and despite their delay Murray decided that if there was room they would spend the night at the inn at Clayton, instead of just stopping for a meal. This, not surprisingly, met with general approval, although Murray noted a discreet conversation between Ketchell and Harry and a quick counting of money from Harry's pockets. Murray did not offer to pay. Ketchell and Harry had wished themselves on him in any case, and he had a suspicion that they thought he might be generous.

'Ten miles or so to go,' Murray remarked to Robbins when they reached the inn. 'Surely we'll find the Blairs tomorrow.'

'I'm sure we will, sir.'

'Mr. Murray.' Murray glanced round in surprise: it was

Ketchell. 'May I have a word?'

Here comes the request for money, no doubt, Murray thought as he turned to listen. But Ketchell had other matters on his mind, and a more serious expression than usual on his drawn face.

'Of course, Mr. Ketchell: what is it?'

'This may seem an odd question, Mr. Murray, but is there any reason why someone would be following us?'

'Following us?' Murray could not resist a quick look up and down the road outside the inn.

'I've only seen him distantly, but I'm sure I have seen him several times since we left Fitzroy Square,' said Ketchell. 'And when we stopped to help the carter, I'm convinced I saw him leave the road some way behind us, and presumably take to the fields.'

'A man alone?' asked Murray. Who could it be? Young Donald, trying to catch up? Or much worse, Beatrix's attacker?

'A man alone, yes,' said Ketchell, nodding in emphasis. 'A man in a green coat, and riding a fine black horse.'

But almost more remarkable than this information was the look in Ketchell's eyes. He seemed, if Murray was any judge, to be throwing down a challenge.

For a building site, the Royal Pavilion was dazzling.

At first sight, Isobel put that down to the sheer quantity of candles in the chandeliers. Then as her eyes grew used to the glare, she saw that the light was reflected back by so much gold leaf, so many rich details on the walls, on the pillars, in the sweeps of luscious fabric, and then of course by the clothing and jewels of the guests attending the reception, that even a few candles would glow like the heart of a bonfire. How, she wondered, would anyone portray this on paper, or canvas?

'What do you think, Father?' she asked. Blair was still blinking at the spectacle.

'Extraordinary,' was Blair's response. 'Extraordinary.'

'I wonder what Charles would think of it? Is it really like something you would find in India? He would know.'

Blair brightened at the mention of Murray.

'When he arrives we could perhaps bring him here, if part of it is open to visitors. I should be interested to hear his opinion.'

The splendour knocked the breath from Miss Amanda

Akehurst only for a minute or two, unfortunately. A footman dressed as an Indian king announced them at the door, and another ushered them forward into the huge room. If the King were there, it was hard to tell – and Isobel had heard that he was not a man easily missed even in a crowd.

Sir Joshua, unexpectedly accompanying them this evening, was not doing so with good grace. He followed them in, muttering to himself, examining the décor with distaste.

'What's wrong with plain walls?' he demanded in a low voice. 'Who needs all this nonsense? That's what I detest about Brighton,' he carried on, regardless of audience. 'All money and no sense. All entertainment and no useful business. Not that I can do anything without Mr. Paulinson,' he finished sadly.

'I wonder, Sir Joshua, that you did not simply stay in London?' said Blair. Only someone with his innocent expression could have interrupted Sir Joshua's grumpy soliloquy without suffering for it: Sir Joshua glared, but responded calmly enough.

'But my grand-daughter was in danger in London. That is why I came. My wife, sensible enough woman, but she will not be satisfied until Amanda is married off, and she's convinced it has to be done this year. I'd rather she stayed alive, and not abducted.' He was growing more intense. 'There you have it, Mr. Blair: if Amanda must be paraded in front of as many useless wastrels as will take an interest in her or in her interest in my fortune, then I shall be here to see that she is safe.' He stopped, a little breathless, his face pink.

'In your position I should do exactly the same,' said Blair humbly. 'Yet is there any idea that what threat there was has followed her from town?'

Sir Joshua snorted. His colour was still high, and Isobel felt suddenly concerned for his own wellbeing.

'There is no notion at all that she might be in danger here. But someone tried to abduct my dear grand-daughter in the middle of Hyde Park – it should not be beyond their cunning to follow her to Brighton and find her again. Don't you think?' he asked, suddenly less sure of himself.

'I think it is a possibility we should not ignore,' Blair agreed. Sir Joshua laid a hand heavily on Blair's shoulder, and Blair looked up at him, wide-eyed, looking for a moment like a faithful serving lad receiving his master's praise. Isobel wanted to laugh, but at the same time there was an anxiety in Sir Joshua's face that was deep and real – and still that high colour that worried her. 'Come, Sir Joshua,' said Blair, turning and beginning to shamble through the crowd, 'I believe some punch would do you the world of good.'

There was indeed some very fine punch, Isobel discovered when she followed them. There was apple juice, too, and all kinds of refreshment. Perhaps it was worth braving a royal reception. She paused with her glass to her lips, and looked about, trying to find Amanda and Lady Akehurst. A ladder, she thought, would be helpful. Or someone tall, like Charles.

In a moment, though, she spotted Fussy and Mr. Lawrence, who had chosen to walk to the event and had arrived separately. Fussy raised his glass to her, and hurried over.

'I'm glad to see you've arrived safely, and found the refreshments!'

'Is the King here?'

'Not that I know of, or not yet. I believe everyone else must be, though. Lord, what a crush!'

'Have you seen Lady Akehurst and Amanda?'

'Um,' said Fussy uncertainly, scanning the crowds around them. 'It's hard to say, isn't it? I have seen Amanda since we arrived – wearing a kind of spring green, isn't she?'

'A kind of, yes,' was as much of an opinion as Isobel would allow herself. Exactly as she had expected, the gown on Amanda made one think at once of a choppy sea after a rich meal.

'She looked prodigiously happy,' Fussy remarked. 'But she was on the arm of a young man she seemed to know.'

'Was she, indeed? I wonder who that could have been. She has very few acquaintances in Brighton, as far as I am aware.'

'Dark-haired fellow? Only caught a glimpse but I thought he looked familiar – I'm sure I've seen him before. Amanda looked very happy. No doubt Lady Akehurst oversaw it, anyway,' said Fussy comfortably. Isobel wished she could be so sure. She had little faith in Lady Akehurst's chaperoning skills.

'Miss Blair.'

'Good evening, Mr. Lawrence.' She curtseyed: there was no diminution of formality even if he had married her aunt.

'Is Mr. Blair here?'

'Of course, sir. I believe he is talking with Sir Joshua.'

'I hope he will not behave – peculiarly – this evening. There is a chance that the King himself will be here.'

Isobel smiled politely.

'That would be very exciting, I'm sure. I have never seen him, have you?'

Mr. Lawrence paused, perhaps unwilling to leave the subject of Blair's behaviour.

'I have seen him, once or twice. When he was the Prince Regent, you know. In Lewes, and elsewhere.'

'I did hear,' said Isobel carefully, 'that the Prince Regent's behaviour, in Lewes at least, was, on occasion, peculiar. The incident with the coach and four on Keere Street, wasn't it?'

Mr. Lawrence stiffened, if such a thing were possible, even more than usual.

'Any young gentleman will have moments of high spirits and, if relieved of responsibilities, even of some recklessness. I am sure our King never strayed from the outer limits of propriety on any occasion. Whereas your father ...'

'Oh! Excuse me, Mr. Lawrence, but I see Lady Akehurst and I have something most particular to tell her. Forgive me, Fussy!'

Isobel curtseyed and fled. It was true she had at last spotted Lady Akehurst gossiping with some cronies across the room, but it certainly made for a good excuse to abandon an unpleasant conversation.

'Lady Akehurst,' she managed to inveigle her way into the conversation after a few moments.

'Miss Blair!' Lady Akehurst smiled happily. 'Is this not a delightful evening? I so love to see all the colours again – I pray there will be no more cause for court mourning for many a long year.'

'Indeed – my lady, have you seen Miss Akehurst? I gather she was arm in arm with a young gentleman.'

'Was she, indeed?' Lady Akehurst looked more pleased than concerned. She straightened to look about the crowd. 'I'm afraid I've rather lost track ...'

'Your grand-daughter?' one of the ladies with her asked, a glint in her eye. 'I'm sure I saw her go through that doorway, not ten minutes since.'

'That doorway? But where does that go?' Isobel asked,

alarmed. The lady shrugged.

'I imagine there are powder rooms through that way – you know,' she leaned closer to Lady Akehurst, 'the plumbing in this pavilion is quite extraordinary!'

'Where is Amanda?' came Sir Joshua's voice over Isobel's shoulder.

'She's gone – out for a moment,' said Lady Akehurst quickly.

'For ten minutes,' added Isobel. Her father was with Sir Joshua still.

'Alone?' he asked, catching her eye.

'I'm not sure,' she said, 'but I've a feeling we should go and look. Now.'

They pushed through the crowd to the corner of the room, where a footman stood by a discreet door. He did not seem disposed to stop them, looking past them as if they did not exist. Blair was right behind Isobel, and Lady Akehurst, now catching some sense of panic from the others, almost shoved them through the doorway.

The passage beyond was empty of people, lined with prints in gilt frames on crimson walls. A movement caught Isobel's eye. Ahead, the passage turned a corner, and something beyond had tickled the reflection in the glass of a print. There was a heavy thump, and a kind of breathy cry.

She hurried forward, the others following, pressing her hands into her skirts to quiet them. She turned the corner.

Amanda lay sprawled amidst her sickly apple green skirts, clashing terribly with the scarlet carpet – and with the blood that flowed about her ashen face.

Isobel swooped forward, aware of a figure disappearing down the passage – surely that was not a green coat? She was on her knees beside Amanda, searching for a pulse in her throat, pushing back her gloves to find it more easily. One wound at least was there, close to her elaborate necklace. Was that a flutter of her lashes?

'I think she's alive. We need help,' she snapped, looking up at the others.

Sir Joshua's eyes shot upwards in his head. He clutched his chest, and fell solidly to the floor.

Chapter Twelve

At the inn next morning, Murray was in no mood to tolerate further delays. Unfortunately, nothing was going quite according to plan.

The inn at Clayton had changed hands since his last stay, and it was clear that though the prices had gone up, the money was not being spent on the food. A greasy, half-chilled plate of chops was sent back to the cook, only to be replaced by an equally noxious pie contained in pastry that would have been better used as a building material. It could well have been applied to the stables, for they were in a bad state. Heading for an early bed, still hungry, Murray found that his room had a lingering odour of someone else's sweating feet, and that he was sharing the room with not only Robbins but also Harry and Ketchell, while Beatrix and Rosie were consigned to an attic with a back stair that Murray was not at all happy about.

Perhaps Harry and Ketchell were equally dismayed at the thought of sharing with Murray, for they did not retire to bed until past three in the morning, and were not delicate in their movements then. Murray was already awake, partly worried about Beatrix and partly convinced, having woken from a disturbing dream, that Blair and his party were now in greater danger than ever.

When he finally managed some sleep he was wakened by the village church bells reminding him that it was Sunday, but after a tussle with his conscience he thought it would be better to push on to Brighton and make sure that Blair was all right. Breakfast was tolerable, if one avoided the stringy meat available and stuck with bread and coffee, but even after he had finished it and visited the stables and assured himself of everyone's safety, and observed Ketchell touring the village with his nose in the air, Harry had not yet made an appearance. His patience very near its end, Murray took Robbins and went upstairs once more to roll Harry off his lumpy mattress and dip his head in a basin of water that had, at some point, been hot for washing, but was now stone cold. Harry was contrite, and in less than an hour was grey-faced in the carriage, not moving any more than he had to and clutching his mouth every time they went over a bump. Ketchell grinned, but he and Beatrix remained silent. Murray was unsympathetic.

The last few miles to Brighton were accomplished slowly, the traffic increased even on a Sunday and dense around village churches, where Donald brought the horses to a respectful walking pace. Murray attempted to restore his own equilibrium by silently reciting a few psalms to himself. It sort of worked.

As the carriage descended slowly into the town, they all watched the buildings along the street, few of them more than twenty years old, by Murray's reckoning. Brighton must have changed radically in the last seventy years: a fishing village, a spa town and now a royal playground. Murray imagined that some of the older locals they passed still had a shocked look about them, wondering what had happened to their home, but in truth he saw fashionably dressed promenaders, heading home from church or taking the fresh sea air, without a trace of the fisherman about them. To remind the passerby of the health benefits of a stay here, there were as many wheeled chairs and frail, elderly carriage passengers as one would see in Bath or Harrogate, as many delicate young ladies hanging on their companion's arm. As they progressed on a slow straight line down towards the sea, there were also well-wrapped people marching ahead of them, no doubt for their morning's sea bathe. Murray hoped they had a warm fire to return to afterwards: the weather was definitely autumnal.

'The house they take is just off the Steine,' said Harry unexpectedly. 'I've been here before. Keep going a bit further … There! That street there.'

Murray called directions to Donald, who neatly turned the horses and slowed even further while Harry tried to remember precisely which of the narrow, stuccoed houses was his aunt's.

'It's rented, you know,' he explained. 'They left town so suddenly they were lucky it was vacant for them. There – that one, the one with the blue door.'

Donald pulled up in the narrow street, and Murray heard Robbins hop down from the back seat.

'The blue door, Robbins,' he directed, and watched as Robbins rang the doorbell. A certain sense of déjà vu came over him, as Robbins waited politely on the doorstep. But here there would be no pathetically liveried Jackie to be pushed to the door by Rosie. Here, no doubt would be the more senior staff, properly attired and well-trained and organised. Here, they would not be kept in the street for twenty minutes …

Robbins looked back at the carriage, caught Murray's eye, and gave the least shrug.

'What's wrong?' asked Harry, squirming round to look through the carriage window.

'No answer,' said Murray. 'Are you sure it's the right house?'

On the doorstep, Robbins stepped back to survey the height of the house. Murray could see nothing moving inside, no lamps or candles lit. The shutters were open, though: the house did not look completely abandoned.

Robbins returned to the carriage.

'I'll see if I can find the kitchen door, sir,' he said.

'Very good.'

Robbins wandered a little further along the road, and found some kind of lane that would allow him access to the back of the terrace. He vanished. Murray shivered. This was not good. There was something silently ominous about that blank-windowed house. Was Blair inside? Was he injured? Incapable? Was he alive?

Robbins seemed to be away for hours. Donald climbed down to soothe the horses, edging the carriage closer to the side of the road so as not to block traffic. Beatrix, who had fallen asleep an hour or so before, stirred and woke.

'Where are we? Are we stuck again?'

'We're apparently outside the right house,' said Murray, 'but it seems to be empty.' Where did Beatrix want to go? He did not want to ask her in front of Harry and Ketchell, but she had said it was somewhere outside Brighton. He might have to ask Donald to drive her back up the road a bit. Well, once they knew what they were doing and where they might be going.

At last, Robbins appeared at the corner of the access lane,

face expressionless. He returned to the carriage and came to the door.

'It is the right house, sir,' he said at once, 'but they've gone. They left this morning.'

'The Akehursts?'

'It seems so, sir.'

'And their guests?'

'For all anyone in there could tell me, yes, sir. The staff inside are the employees of the owner, come to clean the building before it is rented again. They only knew the name of the tenant, nothing of the number of people or their condition. Except, I suppose, that they knew how many beds had been slept in.'

'And nothing of the family is left inside?'

'Nothing, sir.'

'My aunt has moved on?' Harry was catching up. 'But when did they go?'

'Early this morning, sir,' said Robbins. 'Unexpectedly, I gather.'

There was something in his face: Murray knew there was more to say. He pushed the carriage door open and Robbins stooped quickly to unfold the step for him. Murray guided his manservant a little way along the street.

'What is it, Robbins? I have a bad enough feeling about all this.'

'The cleaners told me there is nothing inside belonging to the Akehursts. But they were upset about one thing, sir. In one of the bed chambers, they found a deal of blood.'

'Blood?' Murray's heart thumped.

'On a pillow, and down the bed curtain. As if, they said, someone had been injured about the head somehow. The woman who found it was not at all happy about it.'

'No, indeed.' He tapped his foot on the pavement, trying to sort it out in his head.

'I went to take a look, sir, but they had already stripped the bed and burned the worst of the cloth.'

'Blood on the bed. Everyone leaves unexpectedly, early in the morning. What on earth is going on here?' He frowned hard, as if it would aid concentration. 'I think, Robbins, we're going to have to take rooms somewhere nearby, get Donald and the horses settled

– perhaps see Miss Beatrix on her way and maybe, too, let Mr. Holden and Mr. Ketchell make their own way somewhere, and we'll come back here and see if there's anything we can find out. Perhaps the neighbours saw something. Perhaps the cleaners can tell us who the owner is, and the owner may know something.'

'Aye, sir. Do you know of an inn nearby?'

'After last night I'm hesitant to recommend anywhere. I'll see what there is. Donald may know of a good place.'

But it was more difficult to shake off their passengers than Murray had expected. Beatrix claimed to be exhausted after their journey – and after the previous night in the awful inn at Clayton – and wanted to lie down for a few hours. Rosie agreed to attend her. Murray hoped that Lady Akehurst never found out that he had employed her kitchenmaid to attend an established Cyprian. Meanwhile Harry and Ketchell maintained that they had come down to Brighton entirely to join the Akehursts and would stay with Murray until the Akehursts could be found.

'But I have friends in Brighton on whom I should like to call,' said Harry, considerably brighter than he had been that morning. 'So I'll leave you to your enquiries, Mr. Letho, and see you later at the inn.'

Ketchell also had some kind of business, its nature unspecified, about the town, and slid off before even he had eaten anything in their private parlour at the inn. Murray rubbed his face and ran his fingers hard through his hair, hoping that it would help him to make sense of the situation. He and Robbins ate some decent soup, and, revived, headed back on foot for the little road off the Steine.

The house on one side of the place the Akehursts had rented was also empty, and had been so for several weeks. On the other side, a lady of decent family but decayed means took in lodgers of a similar status. Robbins' application at the kitchen door brought them little information except that the Akehursts, around fifty of them in twenty separate carriages, to judge by the noise, had departed the neighbourhood at around six that morning without a word to anyone, servants and all.

'So it does sound as if all the guests went too, sir, at the same time,' said Robbins, 'even if we need to modify the numbers a bit.'

'Just a bit. I'll see if the lady of the house is at home. Perhaps she heard what happened, or where they went.'

As to where the Akehursts and their guests went, Miss Crockett was completely ignorant: there had been little communication between the households on this occasion.

'Though of course they have taken that house before, and are very charming,' Miss Crocket insisted breathlessly. She was a bony individual, and very excitable.

'No doubt you expected them to stay longer on this occasion.'

'Oh, yes, of course! They only arrived on … let me see … Wednesday, I believe. There were several guests with them, too: an old gentleman and a younger lady in their own carriage, and two gentlemen in another carriage, one very straight and smart and the other a younger man. And the Akehursts, of course.' She smiled sweetly, entirely unabashed at having such complete information.

'Of course.' It sounded as if Blair and Isobel had at least arrived in Brighton. As to the others, Murray had no idea: he trusted that neither of them had a green coat and a tendency to wear a mask.

'But of course, it was no real surprise when they left, I suppose,' Miss Crockett went on. 'Not when we heard what had happened last night! Oh, no, good gracious me, no.'

Her gaze was modestly directed towards her own knees, but at this she flicked a sideways look at Murray for his reaction. He was only too happy to provide it.

'What happened last night?'

'Well!' Miss Crockett sat forward eagerly. 'Of course I was not present on the occasion – not I! But the Akehursts attended a reception at the Pavilion last night, as did many others, and as I am informed by the most reliable, er, informants, Miss Akehurst was attacked! Attacked, Mr. Murray, and left for dead in a distant passage far from civilised society or any assistance! And when her dear grandpappa discovered her – well, quite a crowd of people discovered her, as I understand it – when he discovered her poor, beaten body, he took a fit and fell to the floor! Of course the King himself had to be told, and how terribly embarrassing that must have been for the poor Akehursts. And he is a Cabinet minister, of course, so that must make it – better? Worse? I have no idea.'

She finished with a nervous smile, clearly hoping for Murray's guidance in the matter.

'In what way was Miss Akehurst attacked?' Murray asked. 'Was anyone apprehended?'

'I have not heard that anyone was caught, but they are saying that when she was found, there was a man standing over her with a bloody knife! A bloody knife, Mr. Murray, in the Royal Pavilion! But he fled, before he could be caught.'

'I daresay, if Sir Joshua had collapsed. Is there any word on either him or Miss Akehurst? Are they likely to recover?'

'Oh, I believe the world expects the worst!' Miss Crockett's eyes were wide, but her expression was not authoritative. Murray left the matter.

'Do you know if he could be identified?'

'The assailant? I have no idea. He may have been someone from the kitchens, of course, which would explain the knife. They have an inordinate number of Frenchmen employed in the kitchens, you know. It could be any of them.' She sat back for a moment, nodding, happy with this assessment, before her eyes widened again in alarm. 'But, you know, they don't just stay in the kitchens. They come out of the Pavilion, and roam the streets – and who knows but that the man with the knife might be one of them!' She made it sound as though they had escaped from a zoo.

'I am quite sure,' said Murray, aiming for a comforting tone, 'that the good citizens of Brighton would apprehend on sight any Frenchman bearing a bloody knife in the street. I'm convinced you are quite safe, Miss Crockett.'

'Are you? Are you? Oh! Then that is a mercy!' She straightened again, quite relieved. 'Oh! I should have asked. Are you at all acquainted with the Akehursts? For I'm afraid I told you all about poor Miss Akehurst without considering that perhaps you are – that you might intend –'

'I have never met any of the Akehursts, to my knowledge, Miss Crockett,' Murray assured her. 'It is their guests I had hoped to find. A Mr. Blair and his daughter.'

'The lady and gentleman in the carriage, I daresay,' Miss Crockett nodded at once. 'And the two gentlemen in the other carriage?'

'I'm afraid I don't know them, either,' said Murray, unable

to gratify her curiosity. 'They made no mention at all of where they might be going? I suppose it could not have been far, if both Sir Joshua and Miss Akehurst were ill or injured.'

'Perhaps they thought it worth the removal, if Brighton was so dangerous!' Miss Crockett suggested, wide-eyed again. 'I wish they had said. If this grows to be a commonplace, Frenchmen wielding knives and attacking innocent ladies, I might seek a place of safety myself!'

Murray sighed: he had no particular wish to be the spreader of gossip, but Miss Crockett needed reassurance, and in any case it had been common knowledge in London.

'I believe this is quite a specific attack, aimed particularly at Miss Akehurst,' he said. 'She had already been attacked in London. This was almost certainly related. I'm convinced you are in no danger from this man.'

He hoped he was right. But one thing puzzled him, as he made his farewells and left to find Robbins: if the same man from the Park had attacked Miss Akehurst again last night, how could Ketchell have seen him following them eleven miles away at Clayton?

'In any case, we are not much further on,' Murray said to Robbins as they walked by the sea. He wondered if he should go for a bathe. 'It may be more evidence that it is the danger to this young lady Miss Akehurst that has distressed Mr. Blair, but there is nothing to tell us where they have gone. They could be anywhere: they could have returned to London.'

'Perhaps Mr. Holden will have some idea of where they might go,' Robbins suggested.

'Oh, Mr. Holden ... if he stays sober long enough to tell us. I had thought to look at them that Mr. Ketchell was the one more likely to spend his nights with a jug of gin to hand and a cheap mollisher on his lap, but it seems Mr. Holden can't be trusted near anywhere that sells spirits. I dread to think where he is today, and what his Brighton friends might be like: no better than his London ones, I daresay.'

'And then there is Miss Beatrix, sir,' Robbins put in, expressionless.

'Yes ... I should have been happier if I could have seen Miss

Beatrix on her way and returned young Rosie straight to Lady Akehurst's household. As it is – do you know, I believe nothing has been simple since we left Edinburgh?'

'I believe you may be right, sir.'

'I feel obliged to help Miss Beatrix as an old friend, even if I can't approve of how she now lives. I've borrowed Rosie without her mistress' consent, and now I can't give her back. And when I do, I pray Lady Akehurst never finds the nature of the woman Rosie was serving. I can't find the Blairs, and every time I think I've caught up with them they've vanished again. The man who seems to have attacked Miss Akehurst, for whatever reason, in London, appears to be here in Brighton to attack her again last night, despite the fact that he was also in Clayton – and if it turns out that there is a conspiracy, and more than one person is attacking Miss Akehurst, then that does not sound like something connected with an elopement but with something much more serious, and what has Miss Akehurst done to attract that kind of hostility? And how frightened must the Akehursts have been, that despite whatever injuries Miss Akehurst had and however ill Sir Joshua might be, they set off first thing this morning for somewhere else? And then there are Mr. Ketchell and Mr. Holden, who have wished themselves on us – and where did Young Donald go? And why? And is he back at Fitzroy Square or is he languishing in a gin house somewhere, no longer knowing where he is?'

'And where do we go from here, sir?' asked Robbins, manfully following all this.

'As good a question as any of the others, Robbins, and more pertinent. What do you think?'

'I think, sir, pleasant as the seashore is, we should probably go back to the inn and see if there is anything we can solve. Miss Beatrix's destination, perhaps, for one thing.'

'You're keen to rid us of her, aren't you?'

'Well, sir, yes.'

'You're right, of course. Though she knows how to behave respectably when she has to …'

'Still, sir.'

'Yes, I know.' Murray sighed, and directed their path towards the inn. 'At any other time, I might have been tempted to apply my mind to the reason her protector wants to kill her – no doubt at all it's connected with that semaphore tower she was so keen to see – but there is so much else going on that I'm barely interested. A matter of state business, she said, a government secret, that for some reason she should not know, serious and secret enough that a man who has taken her into his protection would rather destroy her than have her know. To protect the secret, or to protect himself, I wonder?'

'None of our business, sir, I'm sure.'

'But if she is still under threat …'

'Why should she be, sir? She is far from London – and forgive me, sir, but the whole thing sounds highly unlikely to me.'

'Well, as we know, the distance from London to Brighton was not enough to prevent Miss Akehurst from being attacked again. It's only fifty miles or so.'

'Aye, well, that's true, sir.' Robbins sounded reluctant.

'That was a truly awful inn last night, wasn't it?' Murray thought a change of subject might be good. 'I pray for better food and bed tonight.'

'Definitely, sir. And perhaps a sober Mr. Holden, returning at a more civilised hour. Though it is not my place to say so, sir.'

'Not your place? It's almost a moral obligation! Come on: let's see what they're serving for dinner. This sea air makes me hungry.'

But when they arrived at the inn, they found a new puzzle. Little Rosie was waiting outside, anxiously gazing up and down the road, tapping one foot impatiently.

'Sir!' she cried when she saw Robbins.

'What is it, Rosie? What are you looking for?' he asked.

'It's Miss Beatrix, sir: she went out hours ago.'

'She went out? Are you sure she didn't just go to meet her friends?'

'No, sir, she said she was going for a walk to clear her head. And that she'd be back in half an hour. And I know it's a lot more than half an hour, sir, for that clock over there chimes the quarters and it was before two that she left, and look, now, it's just chimed four and three quarters!'

Robbins looked at Murray.

'Has she taken her things?' Murray asked. 'I know she did

not have much, but she had Lady Akehurst's cloak, and her reticule, and … she bought a shawl in Kingston, didn't she?'

'She was wearing the cloak, sir, but she left the shawl,' said Rosie, directing her answer to Robbins even though Murray had asked. 'And she said she would see me later. She didn't have to. All she had to say was that she was off, and goodbye.'

Chapter Thirteen

It had been a horrible night.

The chaos that had followed the discovery of Amanda, and the collapse of her grandfather, had been deeply frustrating. Isobel, still kneeling on the scarlet carpet in skirts that would never be the same again, kept her hand over Amanda's bleeding throat, clinging to the hope of that faint pulse, but longing to be able to get up and fetch things and order people about. She knew that her father and Mr. Lawrence had gone in pursuit of the knifeman, Mr. Lawrence sedate but quick, Blair bumbling along the passageway, things catching his eye as he went. Useful things, no doubt, Isobel thought, watching him, but at that speed he was never going to catch anyone. And the crowds, servants and guests, dashing here, milling there, urgent and gawking – who could find one man amongst all that lot?

'That's it, Amanda, you're safe now,' she murmured, not even sure that Amanda could hear her. She huddled over to try to protect the girl from the feet of those pressing into the narrow passage to see what was going on. To her left, Lady Akehurst, torn between husband and grand-daughter, had simply sat down on the floor between them and stared from one to the other, moaning with equal fervour about her husband's weak heart and her grand-daughter's reputation, about as much use as a wax firescreen. It was Fussy, good reliable Fussy, who had called for help and was now kneeling with his knees under Sir Joshua's shoulders, regardless of his tight breeches, propping Sir Joshua's head up, rubbing his hands and generally encouraging him to wake up. Isobel did not like the colour of Sir Joshua's cheeks, but it was hardly surprising. He was at least starting to come round. 'Come on, now, Amanda, hold my hand. That's a good girl. Hold on. Help is coming.' She really prayed that it was.

In the end help had come from several directions at once. Blair returned bringing a physician, and only a moment later Mr. Lawrence appeared from the other direction with another physician. Both men had been guests at the reception, and as it turned out, they were professional rivals. Immediately a debate began between them as to what to do, which turned, as Lawrence and Blair watched them in disbelief, into a carping argument.

'That lady was perfectly well on the way to recovery when she left me!' cried one. 'And within two weeks you had her in her grave!' Isobel winced at the racket.

'After all the treatments you had given her, it's a wonder she lasted that long!' growled the other.

'Gentlemen!' She could not stand to address them, but she made her voice as ominous as she could. 'Since you are determined to be unhelpful, will you be so good as to be unhelpful elsewhere?'

The two physicians stopped and stared at her, and the corridor fell half-silent. It would have been gratifying, had Isobel not been crouching over a seriously-injured woman.

At that point some kind of senior servant appeared, fully liveried and wigged, but carrying a basin of hot water and a bundle of clean towels. He knelt on Amanda's other side, paying no attention to the doctors.

'There is more coming, madam,' he murmured to Isobel. 'How can I be of assistance?'

'I'm anxious about moving her,' said Isobel, 'but she cannot stay here. The man there is Sir Joshua Akehurst, her grandfather, who collapsed when he saw her. He, I think, could be moved to somewhere quieter.'

Already Sir Joshua was showing some sign of recovery, eyes open, forming words. His hands rubbed absently at his chest. A heart attack, Isobel thought, but apparently not a severe one.

'We can open a private room nearby, madam,' said the servant. 'There will be room for both of them. But should we make a pad for that wound?'

'Yes, we should – can you manage perhaps that smallish towel?'

The servant deftly folded the towel, and Isobel took a breath and shifted her hand.

'Here, madam.' The servant handed her a different towel,

already dipped into the hot water. Isobel cleaned some of the blood from Amanda's neck.

'It is not so bad as I feared,' she said. 'Look, he must have nicked her ear here. And ears do bleed.' She wiped off more of the blood, trying to assess the situation more clearly. Her father leaned over to see better.

'Her earring is missing,' he remarked. 'Wasn't she wearing two?'

Isobel gave him a half-smile for asking a daft question, but indeed only one ear sported a three-diamond droplet.

'That's what's injured her ear, in fact,' she said. 'It looks as if it was torn out.'

'A robbery, sir? In the Royal Pavilion?' The servant looked as if that would be a much more shocking event than a man drawing a knife on a young lady.

'Perhaps an accident,' Blair suggested kindly.

'Anyway, I think we can indeed move her, if we're careful,' said Isobel, padding both neck and ear with the dry folded towel. 'If you could move people back ...'

In the end they did not spend much time in the little room the servant had prepared for them. The physicians, waspish and irritating, tried to follow but Sir Joshua dismissed them, determined to summon a doctor of his own choice to the house. At least Sir Joshua was able to get to his feet, albeit with assistance from Fussy and Blair, and he sat in a soft chair with a glass of brandy, slowly turning a better colour. Lady Akehurst slumped beside him on another chair, while Amanda, a great heap of green and blackening silk, lay on a sopha with Isobel beside her to hold the towel against the wounds. Fussy laid over her a rug the servant brought, but it was not long before the servant returned to say that their carriage was ready if they wished to leave.

Amanda regained consciousness on the short journey back to the house, but seemed confused.

'Why are we leaving?' she asked, and then squawked as the movement hurt her neck. 'Ow! My ear! Where's my earring?'

'Hush, now,' said Isobel, 'you've hurt your neck and your ear, and you've bled quite a bit, so you'll need to stay quiet.'

'Oh ... I hope I didn't get any blood on my green gown,' Amanda murmured sleepily. Once at the house, Isobel, remaining mute on the subject of the awful green gown, saw her safely to bed with a maid to sit with her, and returned downstairs, where Sir Joshua and Lady Akehurst were seated, exhausted, in the parlour, attended by Mr Lawrence, Fussy, and Blair.

'Well, now,' Sir Joshua said, seeing her come in. 'I take it that the perpetrator was not apprehended while I was unconscious?'

'No, sir,' said Mr. Lawrence before Blair could say anything. 'The place was too crowded.'

'Would he not have been covered in blood?' asked Fussy. 'Sorry,' he added, looking at Lady Akehurst's face, 'but there was a very great deal of it, wasn't there?'

'Ears,' said Isobel, with a sigh.

'I believe,' said Blair, 'that from the angle of the cut, her attacker may well have stood behind her – and therefore most of the – issue – would have been blocked from him by – by Miss Akehurst herself.'

'And of course if he had been wearing, say, a black coat, it might not have been noticed,' said Sir Joshua, sensibly.

'Probably not in those conditions, no,' Blair agreed, eyes wide.

'Was he even seen? Identified? Would anyone know him again?' Sir Joshua looked exhausted, but his mind seemed alert. 'And are we, in point of fact, looking at someone who tried to abduct my grand-daughter in London, and has now tried to murder her in Brighton? Were we followed from Fitzroy Square?'

'Surely there can be no other explanation?' said Mr. Lawrence at once. 'How could it be that two separate parties might wish harm to Miss Akehurst?'

Ah, thought Isobel, but was it really Miss Akehurst to whom they wished harm? After all, Sir Joshua had been one of the Cabinet against whom the Cato Street plot had been formed. But then, she thought, it would be odd, if you had intended to slaughter the whole Cabinet as a political act, to try to harm members of it one by one by attacking specific members of their families. No, Mr. Lawrence was probably right. It was all to do with those peculiar love letters that her father had seen.

There seemed to be general agreement around the room now, except for Lady Akehurst.

'I cannot believe that any man might wish harm to my

darling girl!' she sobbed into what had to be one of Sir Joshua's handkerchiefs: it was the size of a dinner napkin. 'Why, you only have to look at her to see how dear she is!'

'Could it have been a robbery?' Fussy put in modestly. 'After all, Isobel said that her earring was missing.'

'A robbery!' Lady Akehurst seized on the idea with delight. 'Of course! Perhaps someone jealous of my darling Amanda's loveliness – snatching one of her jewels, perhaps as a token …'

'Ripping her ear as they did it?' Isobel queried. 'That seems a little excessive – and messy. Anyway, I found the earring on the carpet when she was lifted.' She handed the droplet, from which she had tried to wipe the blood, to Lady Akehurst.

Sir Joshua looked at her as if he had no idea who she might be. His gaze shifted to Fussy.

'Your idea would be a good one,' he said, 'if we had not already agreed that her abductor and her attacker tonight were the same person. Why would someone intending simple theft attempt to snatch her from my carriage? If they were that close, and that daring, they could have taken her necklace and ridden off, and it seems that no one in the Park would have lifted a hand to stop him,' he finished bitterly. Isobel had to agree with him: their fellow promenaders in the Park had been singularly useless.

'Then his purpose must have been abduction,' Lady Akehurst said firmly, and blew her nose. 'The scoundrel wanted to take her off and force marriage on her, no doubt! If Mr. Blair had not seized her we should not have seen her until he brought her back from Gretna!'

'That would have been a risky business,' said Sir Joshua. 'I might have disinherited her.'

'You could not disinherit your favourite grand-daughter!' cried Lady Akehurst in alarm at the very thought. 'But it is of course more than likely that he was prepared to take her in any case. He has probably fallen hopelessly in love with her. I tell you, she has charmed every young man in society.'

No one in the room was so ungallant as to disagree.

'He is a dangerous suitor, then, my lady,' said Blair meekly. 'For he was not gentle when he tried to snatch her, and tonight … well, I believe she was most fortunate tonight.'

Lady Akehurst began to sob again.

'Every young man in society …' Sir Joshua repeated his wife's words. 'Do we believe that he is someone in our circles? There seems a certain – assurance, shall I say, about this man.'

'He may be foreign,' suggested Mr. Lawrence. 'Someone mentioned that many of the kitchen staff at the Pavilion are French.'

'No idea how to behave,' Lady Akehurst muttered into her handkerchief. Sir Joshua sighed.

'Well, there seems little to be achieved tonight. My own physician will be here shortly, and I expect him to tell me that both Amanda and I will be fit to travel in the morning.'

Isobel was shocked. It had been traumatic enough to move both of them to the house from the Pavilion, and you could almost see the Pavilion from the front door. Why would they travel anywhere?

'Back to London?' asked Blair in surprise. Sir Joshua shook his head.

'I see no point in that: she is in as much danger there as she is here, and if he followed us from London he can, no doubt, follow us back. No: I intend to retire to our home, a house I have not long purchased and where, since we are but little known, I believe we might be safe.'

'And where is that?' Blair asked politely.

'Not far away: in Lewes. We leave at first light, and not a word to anyone, on your honour, what our destination is.'

'We don't have to go, I suppose,' said Isobel. She was watching Smith, her father's manservant, attempt to organise his belongings once more into his boxes. They had only been in Brighton a very few days, but Blair had a knack of spreading himself over all available surfaces and into every corner. Blair, quite contrary to Smith's wishes, was helping. It was not going well.

'We don't, I suppose. Lady Akehurst has still not told me what she wants of me.'

'Is that a reason to leave, or a reason to stay?'

Blair stopped folding a shirt into the tiniest possible lump of crumpled cloth, and considered.

'Both, I think.'

'I'd rather be in Lewes than in Brighton, generally speaking,' said Isobel. A grunt from Smith seemed to be a form of agreement, and Blair nodded, too.

'Though there are always curiosities to be seen in Brighton.'

'Father, you are capable of rooting out curiosities anywhere!' Isobel laughed.

'But Lewes is a more restful place,' her father said, blinking at her. 'And we are very familiar with it.'

'Mr. Lawrence will no doubt accompany us.'

'An argument against going there,' Blair sighed. 'Though Fussy is a pleasant fellow.' He squinted at Isobel, as if, like a good father, he wanted to assess her feelings about Fussy. Isobel had no intention of playing that game just now. Blair saw that, and gave up. 'But the main argument in favour of going – and of keeping in company with the Akehursts as far as is possible –'

'Or bearable,' Isobel put in.

'Is that I'm quite sure that taking Miss Akehurst to Lewes will not be anywhere near enough to protect her from whatever hazard threatens her – and I'm not even sure yet what that is.'

Isobel nodded. The same thought had occurred to her.

'Will you leave a note for Charles?'

Blair's flexible lips pursed alarmingly.

'I cannot!' he said, 'or nothing that would be of any use to him! I am on my honour, as are you, to say nothing to anyone of where we are going.'

'I'm not,' said Smith suddenly.

Blair and Isobel looked at him.

'No, you're not, are you?' said Blair. 'But then, I should not have told you where we are going. And since I have, I'm not sure that you should leave notes lying around for Mr. Murray where anyone could find them, any more than I should.'

'We could leave one in a code!' Isobel suggested. Blair frowned, considering the idea.

'No, I think that still goes against our promise. But Smith, if you were to stay in Brighton and meet Mr. Murray …'

'Of course, sir,' said Smith, 'if you're sure you can manage.'

'I fear I shall just have to. Isobel, my dear, are you all packed?'

'I am, and I've helped Amanda's maid to sort out Amanda's things – we may need an extra cart just for her boxes. But they are packed.'

'Then off to bed with you, my dear, and let us try to face tomorrow with as bright a mind as we can. Sleep well!'

And so next morning, as Murray was later to hear, the Akehurst family and household left Brighton as quietly and discreetly as ever a household of that size, with that many boxes of new gowns, pelisses, bonnets, wraps, muffs, boots, slippers and gloves, could. Sir Joshua, frail after his late night and illness, still managed the steps up to his carriage without assistance. His grand-daughter, however, throat swathed in scarves, was carried from the house and laid across the seat by two brawny footmen, sweating under their wigs. Lady Akehurst fussed over both invalids, but at last settled down beside her husband, having tired herself out. Blair and Isobel went to their own carriage, and if anyone noticed that they were not attended by Blair's faithful manservant Smith, they passed no comment.

The brawny footmen attended the entourage closely as it made its way back up the London road, and veered to the right outside the town. Isobel noticed with some alarm that they each had one of a pair of pistols, and however strong the two men looked, she was not confident that they had any idea how to use guns. The Blair carriage was not so well protected: Blair himself rarely carried a weapon, even when travelling, relying on Smith to be sensible – and Smith and his pistols were, of course, remaining in Brighton. Isobel had a knife in her muff as she always did when some distance from home. She had not yet had cause to use it.

It was a slow and miserable journey. Everyone could feel the tension: Sir Joshua insisted on stopping the convoy every couple of miles to see if anyone could be suspected of following them. It was raining heavily, and mud had slopped on to the road by Ditchling – chalky, clinging mud that made the horses strain in the shafts, the wheels twice their normal weight. The footmen had to dismount and shove the carriages in turn, then the baggage carts, and one lost his long boot in a puddle and had to hop back for it, ripping the other foot from the mud with each step and swearing under his breath. Ten miles had rarely been passed so slowly or in such tight-lipped, short-tempered anxiety.

Isobel had rarely been happier to see the sturdy little poorhouse by the road, and then the familiar flint-clad angles of ancient St. Anne's church loom in turn out of the rain on its mound to their right, one of the first clear signs they were arriving in Lewes. It was a gentle slope from there down into the town: ten miles had taken close to three hours, and already the worshippers were appearing at the church door, surveying the rain and giving the briefest of farewells to the vicar as they scattered to their warm homes. But if Isobel expected their entourage to continue into the town, she was to be disappointed: instead, Sir Joshua's carriage swung to the left, and their own driver followed obediently along a narrow lane. In a moment, they broke out into farmland again. Ahead was an extensive paddock, a few broad trees giving some shelter, and gardens lay to either side. Among them, Isobel saw, was a newly built house of more than modest size, stuccoed presumably over flint, bright white even in the rain. The carriages made their ponderous way up the curving drive, and Sir Joshua flung open his carriage door opposite the porch, impatient for his footman to help him down.

Fortunately the servants had made better time than their masters: there was smoke coming damply from the chimneys and inside the house was warm, the tea fresh and hot, and the promise of something to eat scented the air. Lady Akehurst sniffed.

'We must do something about those cooking smells! Take Miss Akehurst straight up to her chamber, John: the bed will have been aired.'

'But Grandmamma, I'm feeling much better! May I not lie in the parlour?' Amanda, in the footman's arms, pouted. The footman, poised to go wherever he was directed, staggered a little under her weight.

'Oh!' Lady Akehurst was indecisive. 'Well … But you'll need to rest after that awful journey.'

'I can rest on the sopha, Grandmamma, can't I?' The pout turned into something intended to be charming. It worked on Lady Akehurst.

'Well, I suppose so, my dear. But you must keep your head still: we must do our best to avoid a scar!'

'I know, I'll try!'

Sir Joshua had already gone to sit down in the parlour. Isobel thought he looked a good deal older than he had just the day before, and his cup shook on its saucer briefly as he set it down. Mr. Lawrence gave him a cautious look.

'Sir Joshua, Fussy and I can go to my own house on the High Street now, if you wish. We would not be far away if you needed us.'

Sir Joshua shook his head, decisive despite his frailness.

'If it does not inconvenience you, Mr. Lawrence, I should be pleased if both of you would stay here. Though I feel this must be a safer place than Brighton or London, I am still not convinced that we are entirely secure, and your presence will add another layer of safety.'

'Of course.' Mr. Lawrence bowed his head.

'Mr. Blair, likewise,' added Sir Joshua. A look of disgust passed across Mr. Lawrence's face.

'Oh! Oh, yes, yes, of course we'll stay,' said Blair, fumbling in his capacious pockets for nothing in particular. Amanda, on the sopha, sighed, and took another piece of cake. Lady Akehurst smiled fondly, and patted Amanda's hand.

By contrast with Amanda, Isobel was delighted to find herself alone in her room, on a floor that was not moving on heavy wheels on a muddy road, and to be able to take a good look through the window without being soaked by rain. Her room was at the side of the house and to her delight she could see the Castle on its steep mound, and the backs of the High Street houses, with just the tip of the spire of St. Michael's church among them. Lewes was a town well-endowed with places of worship, many of them quite ancient, each with their own particular charms.

She would have to see if she could winkle any information out of Amanda about her attacker – as far as she knew the girl had said nothing so far, but Isobel was sure that she must remember something, and Isobel or Blair would find out what it was. But here, she felt they could relax. This was Lewes, after all: this was her own mother's home town, a bustling, safe, busy market town. And for now that bed looked extremely soft and comfortable, and surely an hour's rest before dinner would do no harm? She would think much better after a little sleep.

Chapter Fourteen

'Do you know which way she went?' Murray could not believe that Beatrix could have gone out, gone out alone, placed herself in danger. What was she thinking of?

'I'm not sure, but I think it was that way.' Rosie pointed west, where the pale sun was already toying with the horizon. Murray sighed. Small houses, little shops, fishermen's cottages … and then fields, or shoreline. What had she sought there? And she had been gone for hours. She could be anywhere.

'Who would want to harm her here, sir?' Robbins asked quietly. 'She would not have been – um – raising funds, sir, would she?'

Murray almost laughed at Robbins' delicacy.

'I don't think she walks the streets, Robbins,' he said. 'She is a kept woman, or was.'

'Does she even have any acquaintances here?'

'None that she mentioned,' said Murray. But in his mind he could hear Barnabas Ketchell, back when they were stuck on the road before Clayton.

'Is there any reason why someone would be following us?'

Had the man in the green coat, on his good dark horse, come all the way to Brighton to attack Beatrix? But he had assumed that if indeed Ketchell had seen a man following them, it was the man who had tried to abduct Miss Akehurst in Hyde Park and then had presumably attacked her again last night. Could the same man possibly be the one who had tried to kill Beatrix? Was that a terrible coincidence, or did it in some way make sense? Well, if it did, it was beyond him at the moment. He shook his head at the tangle.

He glanced at Robbins. If he gave the order, Robbins would no doubt join him in a search for Beatrix. But neither of them knew the town well, and he had no idea how well Beatrix knew it or where she might have gone even of her own volition, let alone where she might have been taken against her will. And a small, irritable part of Murray thought that if Beatrix had wandered off on her own, knowing the danger she could be in, it was not high on his list of priorities to go and save her from whatever peril she had discovered.

Just as he was engaged in this silent quarrel with his conscience, he noticed a small, neat figure appear along the road down which they were staring. She had a bundle in her arms, but as she caught sight of them, she shifted it to wave. It was Beatrix.

'Good evening!' she said cheerfully, oblivious to their mixed expressions of surprise and relief. 'Goodness, I have been out far longer than I had intended! Rosie, help me with this: I found a wonderful second-hand clothes man, so I shall be able to change at last!'

'He was doing business on a Sunday?' Robbins was apparently unable to stop himself querying her story. Beatrix gave him a sharp look.

'He was Jewish. Aren't they all?'

Robbins' lips thinned.

'I'll take them, then, miss,' said Rosie, and disappeared with the bundle. She at least seemed pleased to see her temporary mistress safely back. Beatrix looked after the bundle longingly.

'I'll go and change in a moment. It must be nearly dinner time! Did you find your friends?'

'They've left Brighton, and no word of where they have gone.'

'Oh!' Beatrix looked more concerned than Murray would have expected. 'Back to London?'

'We have no idea. But I'll take you to your friends before we go anywhere, anyway.'

'Thank you!' That must have been her worry. She reached out a hand to touch his arm. 'I hope you don't mind that I have resorted to second-hand clothing in your company, but it would have taken far too long to have something made, of course, and I inspected everything he had to make sure it was clean. I'm certain it came from a respectable home.'

'You must do what you need to, of course,' said Murray. He knew he would not like to spend too long in the same clothes. And she would soon be gone to her friends. He found he was absently returning her smile, and moved a little so that her hand was no longer on his arm. 'I shall see you at dinner.'

Accepting that she was dismissed, Beatrix went into the inn, leaving Robbins and Murray alone outside in the roadway. Murray shivered. It was growing dusky and chill.

'I feel I have seen enough of inns in these last weeks,' he grumbled. 'But I daresay they will not bring dinner out here.'

'No, sir.' Robbins' lips twitched very slightly. 'Shall I go and order a bath?'

'Yes … that would help.'

Robbins disappeared into the inn. Murray perched on the wall by the side of the road, hands in his pockets and shoulders hunched. There was no one here who knew him, so his casual posture would hardly matter. The sideways rays of the setting sun seemed icy, gulls above him crying in protest as the dying light caught at their glowing wings. He tried to focus his thoughts, away from Beatrix and Young Donald and men in green coats and Harry Holden and Ketchell. Where was Blair, that was the immediate question, and how was he going to find out?

But even touching on the names of Holden and Ketchell in his mind seemed to have summoned them like demons to his presence. He heard them and straightened before he saw them, hurrying breathlessly along the road towards him from the direction of the centre of town.

'Mr. Murray! You will never guess – Amanda Akehurst was attacked last night! In the Royal Pavilion, of all places!' Harry gasped out the news.

'So I heard,' said Murray, taking the wind out of the young man's sails. He was pleased to note that both men seemed to be sober. 'Have you heard if they have apprehended anyone for the attack?'

'No,' said Harry, staggering to sit on the wall. Ketchell almost fell before he reached it. They were both out of breath. Murray thought that Ketchell was about his own age, but neither man was in good condition. 'No, I haven't heard. But that must explain why they have gone from the house by the Steine. Have you found them?'

'I was hoping you might have some idea where they have

gone,' said Murray. 'They left no word at all.'

'They must have gone back to London,' Harry said at once. 'Where else would they go?'

'But Miss Akehurst was attacked in London, too,' said Murray. 'Do you really think they would go back?'

Harry shrugged.

'It's London,' he offered. Murray did not think that was a good enough argument, and ignored it. Even in the fresh air breezing in from the sea, Harry and Ketchell exuded the aroma of old spirits: having one of them each side of him made him feel slightly ill. He wondered if Sir Joshua Akehurst would thank him, if Murray ever found him, for bringing Harry and Ketchell back to his household.

'Well,' he said, 'I think I shall go to my room before dinner. Will you both be joining us?'

'Is the delectable Miss Paterson still here?' asked Ketchell. Murray blinked, then remembered that that was the name he had used for Beatrix.

'Miss Paterson has not left us yet, no.'

'Then we'll see you at dinner,' said Ketchell, with a wink. Murray was on the point of protesting when he heard his name called.

'Mr. Murray, sir!'

He looked about, then spotted a familiar figure on the other side of the road. It was Blair's man, Smith. Murray could not keep a grin from his face: at last!

'Smith! Is Mr. Blair still in Brighton, then?'

Smith hobbled across the road towards them. Murray blinked: his feet were clearly giving him trouble.

'Ah, no, sir, he is gone. But he left me here to find you.'

'And you have.'

'Aye, well, it's not the first inn I've tried,' said Smith, which explained his hobbling. 'I'm that glad to see you, sir. Is Mr. Robbins about? I can go and communicate what I know to him.'

'Of course – I believe he's probably in the room I've taken here. I was just going in, myself.'

Murray abandoned the odious Ketchell and Harry without much ceremony, and led Smith into the inn. Upstairs, they found Robbins laying out clean towels, the bathwater just prepared.

'Go on, then, Smith,' said Murray, ready to wait for his bath if there was news.

'Mr. Blair and Miss Blair left this morning with the Akehursts. They are gone to Lewes.'

'To Lewes!' Murray repeated. 'Was that Blair's idea?'

'No, sir, as I understand it Sir Joshua Akehurst has a house there. Miss Akehurst was attacked last night, and the household left in great secrecy this morning. Mr. Blair did not wish to leave a note which might miscarry.'

'So he left you instead,' said Murray with a grin. Smith nodded.

'You'll travel on with us tomorrow, then?'

'Yes, sir, if you'll take me.'

'It'll be a squash, but you're very welcome.'

'We've a deal of people with us,' said Robbins, a little sourly.

'We do indeed,' said Murray. 'The two gentlemen you saw outside –'

'Mr. Holden and Mr. Ketchell,' said Smith, expressionless.

'Indeed. They seem to have wished themselves on me and are intent on finding the Akehursts, too.' He paused. 'But if the Akehursts left in secrecy, will they want Mr. Holden and Mr. Ketchell to know?'

'I wouldn't tell them where you were going, if I were you, sir,' said Smith. 'I mean, take them with you, but don't tell them before you leave. I wouldn't trust either of them to keep a secret – not when they had gin in them.'

'A fair point, Smith. We also have one of Lady Akehurst's servants with us, Rosie, a kitchenmaid.'

That caused Smith's eyebrows to rise.

'Rosie?' he asked. 'But …'

'We have a – an old acquaintance of mine, too, and Rosie is acting as her maid for the length of the journey. I hope the acquaintance will be delivered to her friends tomorrow, on our way to Lewes, perhaps.'

Smith looked at Robbins. Robbins' face was blank. Murray imagined that they would wait until he was out of the way before Robbins told Smith all Murray's misdemeanours. It would go no further, Murray knew.

'Well, why don't you leave me to my bath – no, I can

manage, Robbins – and order dinner for about an hour's time? We'll take it in the private parlour.'

'Aye, sir,' said Robbins. They left, and Murray quickly took to his bath before the water chilled. The fire was warm, the towels fresh, and he knew where Blair and Isobel had gone. Suddenly the world seemed a much brighter place.

It occurred to him that he had seen neither of the Blairs for ages. They had spent much of their time in Sussex lately, dealing, apparently, with some legal matter involving Blair's late wife's family, who had, as Murray remembered, come from Lewes. Murray had no idea how Blair came to be staying with the Akehursts, but perhaps there was a Lewesian connexion. Blair had ventured north with Murray last Christmas, but they had spent that time in Aberdeen and only seen Isobel briefly at Hogmanay. Murray had wondered, at the time, why she was not yet married – surely she must have had offers since her brief, unfortunate engagement years ago? She was not perhaps the prettiest woman he had ever met, he thought critically, but she was witty, talented (in art, at least – in the matter of music it was better not to ask), and very good company. Murray's daughter Augusta, currently in Fife with her cousins, adored spending time with Isobel.

Ah, well, perhaps she had formed an attachment in Sussex and that was her reason for spending so much time down here.

Murray wriggled down in the hot water, and wondered what was for dinner.

Dinner in Akehurst House was unimaginative, but probably hurriedly constructed of what had been available when they arrived in Lewes. Sir Joshua had retired to his bed, and Amanda Akehurst had announced that she found chewing painful, so around the table were Lady Akehurst, the Blairs, Mr. Lawrence and Fussy. When Lady Akehurst retired to the drawing room with Isobel, begging them not to be long, Blair found that the brandy had been placed in front of him, dropped with an awful clatter by the butler. Mr. Lawrence regarded Blair coldly, as if it were all his fault. Blair looked at the ceiling.

'So here we are, back in Lewes,' said Fussy, with a nervous glance at each of the older men. 'Isn't that nice?'

For a moment, neither responded. Then Blair cleared his

throat.

'Harvest all in?' he asked, indistinctly, not quite looking at Mr. Lawrence.

'As I told you in my letter,' said Mr. Lawrence. It sounded as if he were gritting his teeth. It made Blair nervous.

'Yes, yes of course.' Something about corn. He knew he had read the letter very carefully at the time: it was by way of being a business report. 'And the farm manager and his family, all keeping well?'

'The last I heard,' said Mr. Lawrence with precision, 'his youngest child had a slight cough. Other than that, as far as I am aware they are in excellent health.'

'That's good,' said Blair. 'That's very good. I'm very glad to hear it.'

Mr. Lawrence snorted.

'You'll be going to see Nathan Worthing, I suppose?' asked Fussy, with the air of a man drawn to the edges of precipices. 'Now that you're here. In Lewes.'

The name seemed to echo around the bleak Akehurst dining room. Mr. Lawrence was poker-straight, his face just a little pink.

'I daresay,' he said.

'Perhaps we should go together?' Blair heard himself saying.

'An excellent idea,' said Mr. Lawrence, after a moment. 'Yes, let us see him together. Then there will be no opportunity for – any nonsense.'

Blair sat back as Fussy shot to his feet.

'Shall we join the ladies?' he said, a forced smile on his face. 'Lady Akehurst did ask us not to be too long.'

'He's upset you again, hasn't he?' asked Isobel, seeing her father's face when he came into the drawing room. They were a little apart from the others. Amanda, having dined on soup, in private, had insisted on joining them or dying of boredom. She was flirting with Fussy, for want of anyone else.

'He didn't start it,' said Blair miserably, insistent on fairness even to Lawrence.

'And you did? Father!'

'No, no, it was Fussy. Poor Fussy, he was only trying to make conversation. And then he went and asked about Nathan

Worthing.'

'Oh, good heavens,' said Isobel. 'What is Mr. Lawrence doing here, anyway?'

'Well, dear, he lives in Lewes.'

'I know that – only too well! I meant what was he doing staying with the Akehursts? I have never known him like London, and he barely seemed to know the Akehursts. Yet … it feels as if he is doing his duty, doesn't it? A man with a purpose.'

'Perhaps Lady Akehurst summoned him, too,' said Blair with a sigh. 'I wonder if she has told him why yet?'

'I wish,' said Isobel with fervour, 'I wish that Grandfather had never made the two of you his trustees. Politics were always bound to come between you.'

'If it had not been politics, it would have been something else,' said Blair. 'He and I were never going to get on, whatever the subject. As for your grandfather, well, I think his intentions were good. He thought he could bring his two sons-in-law together after his death, if he never managed it in life. But alas! I think it makes it worse.'

Isobel patted his hand.

'I think I should go and rescue Fussy, Father. We cannot solve the problem of you and Mr. Lawrence this evening.'

'I simply wish I knew why he disliked me so much,' said Blair unhappily. It was true that Blair was so generally liked, it was a shock to come across someone who was not at worst bemused by him. But Isobel, who had had the chance to study the pair of them over the years – sometimes more than she would have liked – thought she could see the problem, even if she could not solve it. Mr. Lawrence was a pillar of convention: everything had to behave exactly as he and society expected. Blair was always unexpected, in his habits, his acquaintances, his sudden inconsequential observations – heavens, the contents of his pockets. Mr. Lawrence was, at heart, a good man, but Blair was simply more than he could cope with.

Blair retired to bed relatively early, missing Smith, undressing himself and leaving his pockets unemptied, for once. He was fairly sure he had not added anything living to them today, so their excavation was not urgent. But he felt disorganised and put out of his routine. There was a fire in the grate and the room was at least superficially warm: he climbed into bed, blew out his candle, and pulled the bedclothes over his head, pushing away dark thoughts. He prayed that Amanda's attacker would not find them, and that Charles Murray, led by Smith, would.

It was pitch dark when Blair awoke, shivering, and he pressed the repeater on his watch to find out the time. Its musical tone told him it was a quarter past three. The fire might as well have been put out with a bucket of water, for all it gave any warmth.

He should have asked one of the maids to fetch him a hot brick, he thought, and not been so forgetful. That was what happened when you grew older: you knew your mind was working away, on all kinds of things from last week and last year and last decade, but what you didn't realise was that it was filtering out all the really recent things that were still quite important, like remembering to eat breakfast or noting some announcement in the paper, or here, making sure that the bed was warm. He would catch a chill, and then Isobel would be cross with him. He really needed Smith to keep an eye on him, keep him right.

But there was no Smith here now, no one to ask for a warming drink or a hot brick.

But he could not sleep like this.

He reluctantly shed the bedclothes, lit a candle, and grabbed his expansive banyan, wrapping it quickly about him. This winter one was quilted inside but it took a little while to warm up: in the meantime he felt around with his toes and found his slippers. They, too, were icy. Rubbing his arms vigorously, he contemplated his plan, then picked up the candle and headed out of his bedroom.

Down two floors, he thought, or perhaps a third to the kitchens. He had not noticed whether or not the house had a basement level. Anyway, here he was in the entrance hall without mishap: he cast about, candlelight dancing, for the entrance to the servants' quarters.

There, that looked a likely door. He tried it, and at once found himself in a corridor painted acid green, with a cold stone floor he could almost feel through his slippers. After that it was easy to locate the kitchen, and to his delight there was still some heat left in the fire. A little guiltily, feeling that he was intruding where he should not, he filled a small kettle and placed it over the hottest point in the fire, chivvying the embers into life.

While he waited, never able to keep still for long, he meandered about the kitchen and, finding the windows too high to look through, he unlocked and gently opened the back door.

He had only intended to see which way the room faced, and what might be seen at the back of the house in the starlight. He had not expected to see a figure scrambling up a tree near the side of the house and apparently making for an upstairs window.

Hearing the movement at the kitchen door, the figure froze. Blair stared up at him, then yelled,

'You! What are you doing?'

If he hoped that someone inside the house would stir and come to see what was going on, he was disappointed. The figure, however, scrabbled for purchase, lost his grip and dropped to the ground, landing well. It was a young man. For a second he stared at Blair, then he ran.

'Oh!' said Blair, and without quite deciding to do so, he ran, too. He would know the fellow again, he thought, though he had no idea who he was.

The young man was quick, much quicker than Blair in his banyan and slippers. He headed for the lane down which they had driven earlier to reach the house, clung to the wall at the corner and rounded it, vanishing. Blair caught up in a moment. He could hear, even at this early hour, traffic ahead of them, up and down the Brighton road into Lewes. The intruder was making for that main road.

If Blair could only catch up a little, he might at least see in which direction the young man went. Kicking off his slippers he ran a bit more easily on the cold, hard stones of the lane, but he was an old man, he knew, and the young fellow was far too fast. Blair sought, and found deep within himself, a tiny well of power, and surged forward to the head of the lane, bursting out into the roadway with a wild look about from left to right.

The cart hit him hard, sending him spinning. He felt the road rise up and strike him, his back, his hands, his head. And where were his legs? The cart was still coming, the driver crying out, dragging back on the reins.

Blair seemed to fall again and again, each time more softly, pain surging and swiftly diminishing as he felt blood beating in his ears, behind his eyes, then slowly, slowly, ceasing.

Chapter Fifteen

Certainly Beatrix had been fortunate in her discovery of the second-hand clothes man: the gown she wore to dinner, and the second one she wore next morning for their departure for Lewes, both fitted as if they had been made for her. She looked perfectly appropriate, as Murray had assured Robbins she would do.

Brighton was dull and grey that Monday morning. From the inn's front door you could hear the suck and draw of the pebbles on the beach, and feel the sharp-bladed wind nip at your face. Not even the elaborate grandeur of the Pavilion could cheer the outlook as they drove past on their way along the Steine to the Lewes road. Harry Holden and Barnabas Ketchell had displayed very little curiosity about their destination: Harry had gone out again the previous evening and returned timely but drunk, and Ketchell was more interested in a bold examination of Beatrix's appearance. Beatrix seemed unaware of it, tucked into her corner of the carriage and quite comfortable, watching the Sussex world go by outside the little window. Smith had taken the empty place beside Old Donald, and Robbins and Rosie were once more on the back seat. Little Rosie had seemed in an odd humour this morning, quieter than usual and given to frowning. Murray wondered if Robbins could talk her into her usual cheerfulness on their journey, but was not sure that it was one of Robbins' skills.

For himself, he was eager to get moving: he had a nagging feeling that once more they would arrive at their destination to find it abandoned, and the Blairs gone on somewhere else. He was tense enough to be impatient at their slow progress through the busy Monday morning crowds on the London road, and only as they began to leave the town behind them did the traffic diminish a little.

There was a mist over the Downs, and specks of rain began to tap at the carriage. Murray knew that both Robbins and Smith would have good sensible coats, but wondered if Rosie had anything to protect her against the weather. Beatrix seemed unlikely to know.

And he had forgotten, in his thoughts of Lewes, to ask Beatrix where she wanted to be taken. He did not want to ask her in front of Harry Holden and Ketchell. Ketchell took far too much interest in Beatrix as it was. But Beatrix had not made any demur to climbing into the carriage this morning, as if she would simply go where she was taken. Well, he was not going to have that: she would have to tell him where her friends lived and where she needed to be.

Ten miles to Lewes. He had been there before, and knew it to be a smart, commercial little town, a little overshadowed now that the King had such an interest in Brighton – though he had stayed in Lewes, too. Despite that, or perhaps because of it, Lewes owned some political tendencies to the radical – Thomas Paine had gone to the Americas from the place. There was a prominent Norman castle and the low-lying remains of an abbey to the south, very picturesque, which Isobel had drawn and painted several times. Lewes rested its business credentials on a navigable river which took goods to the coast at Newhaven, and was possessed of respectable inns and a great number of ancient churches for its size. And Blair's wife, Isobel's mother, had hailed from the place. He had never found out quite how Blair had come upon a Lewesian lady for his bride, but then Blair knew people everywhere.

The Brighton road entered the town at what Murray thought of as the top, and would become the High Street after a dogleg in the road somewhere down the hill. Murray had no idea, for Smith had been unable to tell him, where the Akehursts' house was here, but if Harry Holden had no idea then he planned to put up at the White Hart and ask around. Though he very much hoped he would not have to spend the night at yet another inn.

'Mr. Holden,' he said, rousing the young man from his usual morning stupor, 'have you any idea where Sir Joshua Akehurst might have his house here?'

'Here? Where are we?' said Harry, with impressive confusion. Murray signalled a halt to Old Donald, and Harry jumped down from the doorway. Murray followed. They were just by the poorhouse on the outskirts of the town.

'Have I been here before?' Harry asked.

'I don't know. I hoped you might have been,' said Murray, with restraint. Harry looked about him blankly, turning on his heel. Robbins had already seen to the steps, and Murray wondered if he might take the chance to ask Beatrix where she wanted to go, but Ketchell leaned past her to see what Harry was doing. Beatrix clearly felt he was a little too close, and pushed around him to climb out of the carriage herself. Murray edged around to move her to one side for a private word, but Ketchell was too quick.

'This is Lewes, isn't it?' he asked, sniffing the air as though he could identify the town that way. 'Now why would you not have told us we were coming here? Or are we just greeting Sir Joshua and passing through?'

Murray opened his mouth to reply, but at that moment his attention was caught by a miserable looking figure approaching from another arm of the junction at which they stood. Coated in mud all down one side, with cuts half-bleeding, half-dried on his face and one glove flapping around his hand, the man – his age was difficult to determine, but probably older than Murray – was leading a horse, and both man and horse were limping. The horse looked a decent mount, and the man's clothes, what could be seen of them, appeared to have been respectable once. Murray wondered what could have become of him.

'Are you all right, sir?' he asked. 'Do you need help?'

The man blinked at him, the skin around his eyes unusually pale in his filthy face. He groaned.

'I'm nearly there,' he said, 'if the mud in my eyes hasn't blinded me.'

'What happened?'

'This fool of a horse put his foot down a hole, and I went over his head,' said the man. He was well-spoken – Murray would have put him down as perhaps a well-to-do merchant, or a middling army officer. 'I was sent to deliver an urgent message, but the horse has made a mockery of that.' Nevertheless he patted the horse's shoulder, a silent apology for insulting the animal.

'If you have far to go in the town you are welcome into my carriage,' said Murray, giving his own silent apology to Old Donald for the effect this would have on the leatherwork.

'You're a kind man,' said the horseman. 'Lieutenant Harold

171

Munnings, at your service. Royal Navy, retired.'

'Charles Murray, of Letho in Fife,' said Charles. They bowed, Munnings stiffly. Murray wondered what kind of urgent message required a retired naval officer to ride fast and alone to Lewes. 'Where are you taking your message?'

'To Sir Joshua Akehurst's house,' said the officer. He was too coated in mud and his own problems to notice Murray's surprise. 'I have no hopes of his being in the town, but someone there will get word to him at the Admiralty, I have no doubt. Probably has his own damned semaphore tower,' he added, clearly to himself. There was more than a hint of bitterness in his voice.

'That is fortuitous,' said Murray, 'for we are looking for Sir Joshua Akehurst's house and were not sure where to find it. This gentleman is Lady Akehurst's great nephew,' he added for qualification, 'but he has not visited here before, and I have friends who are staying with the family.'

'Then he may indeed be there?' said Munnings. 'That is more good fortune than I expected. It is not far – perhaps I could lead the way, rather than you have me bring all this,' he gestured at his filthy clothes, 'into your smart carriage.'

'Can you manage? Can your horse?'

'I can manage, I believe,' said Munnings, though he had been standing with all his weight on one leg all this time. 'But I'd be grateful if your groom could perhaps come behind us more slowly with poor Racer here.'

'Robbins?' Murray raised his eyebrows. But Robbins surveyed the horse and appeared to decide that Racer was not in a position to be too much trouble.

'Aye, sir. As long as I see which way you go.'

Munnings gave directions. Even with the horse taken care of, Murray could not persuade the Lieutenant to take a seat in the carriage, and instead they made a slow procession down the hill, with Harry, Ketchell, and Beatrix in the carriage, and Murray keeping Munnings company on foot. He had taken a liking to the man, and if he knew where Sir Joshua's house was, Murray was determined not to lose him.

There were gardens along the road to the north side, their left, and the walk was pleasant enough though the earth in the gardens was mostly bare. A wall of medium height broke off to allow for a laneway between plots. At the corner, a lad of about twelve was plying a stiff brush and a pail of water to the cobbles, while several of his like watched with interest.

'Lad, we need to turn the corner here,' said Munnings.

'That's as may be,' said the lad, not impressed by Munnings' appearance, 'but I've been told this blood's not to stay on the road a minute longer.'

Looking down, Murray saw that indeed, the water running down the street was pinkish.

'What happened here? An accident?'

The boy leaned on his brush in a practised manner. His friends edged closer. They seemed to know the tale, and want to hear it again.

'A madman, fleeing into the street in the middle of the night!' said the boy, eyes appropriately wide. 'Nothing but his nightshirt and a big thing like a coat, so I heard.'

'From an asylum?' asked Murray.

'The cart hit him solid, just here,' said the boy, not to be distracted. 'The wheels went on going, and drove him hard into the wall.'

If it did, there was no sign of it: the wall was clean and dry. Murray chose not to comment.

'There was a terrible cry, and the man dropped dead, right where you're standing,' the boy finished with lugubrious delight.

'He wasn't from any asylum,' added one of his friends, nodding and smiling at Murray. 'Oh, no!'

'Sim, whose story is this?' The boy with the brush lifted it a few menacing inches from the sodden cobbles. Sim backed off a bit. 'No, he came from no asylum, sirs. He were a gentleman.'

A cold hand clutched at Murray's spine.

'A gentleman? What was his name?'

'Don't know his name, sirs. He was a guest of Sir Joshua Akehurst, lives down the twitten yonder.'

'Down the ...' Murray's voice faded. A guest of Sir Joshua Akehurst. A madman. Many had thought Blair quite mad. Dead ... He had to know, and fast.

'Is the house down here?' he asked Munnings.

'You believe it's your friend? Yes: down to the end, turn right. Stucco, portico, only one.'

Already Murray was running. There were footsteps behind him: he did not look round, but he was sure it was Smith. Smith was too old to be running like that. Blair was too old to be running round at night on the street in his nightshirt and banyan. Blair!

The lane grew muddier. At the end, with fields before him, he seized the wall and spun to his right. Not far, and there was the house, just as Munnings had described it. He looked behind him. Smith and Munnings, were with him. Munnings looked abject, as though it had all been his fault. They ran in a pack up the curving drive, and Murray hammered at the front door.

In the pause that followed, Murray had a moment to wonder what would happen if it had not been Blair, if he was beating at the door of complete strangers to demand entry. But then a manservant, alarm on his pale face, opened the door and stood in the gap, clearly expecting an attack.

'Sir Joshua Akehurst's house?' Murray snapped.

'Yes, sir, but –'

'Who's that?' came a voice from the hallway within. The servant hesitated. Munnings nudged Murray.

'It's Harold Munnings, Sir Joshua, from Newhaven, with an urgent message.'

It worked more quickly than Murray's explanations might have. In a moment they were in the hallway, with a tall, thin gentleman peering at them crossly from a doorway.

'Munnings? What is it?'

'Sir Joshua, the Newhaven semaphore tower is burned to the ground. But also, this gentleman is here to see his friend who we believe is staying here.'

Sir Joshua stared at Munnings, then at Murray.

'My name is Murray, Sir Joshua. I have come to see Alester Blair.'

'Blair … The servant will show you the way.'

'Sir.'

Murray found he was shaking, following the pale manservant up the stairs. Smith followed, wordless. They climbed two flights, and went to a door across a well lit landing. It was ajar.

Isobel was seated by the bed. Blair lay flat on his back, attended by a young doctor with curly hair. A doctor. Murray stepped forward and Smith took his turn to stand and gape.

Isobel turned and saw them, and stood. Murray found he was embracing her, folding her in his arms for her comfort and for his.

'What happened?' he asked thickly. She bent her head for a moment, then straightened.

'He was hit by a cart – some time early in the morning. The carter brought him here, but there was a delay … no one knew who he was.'

'He was in his nightshirt, I heard?'

She nodded.

'He was. I don't know what he was doing!' Irritation surged in her voice even as she began to weep. 'He was so cold when they brought him back.'

Murray stared down at Blair, determined to see him breathe – and he did. The old man's lips fluttered, though nothing else moved.

'Will he live?' he murmured, afraid to hear the answer.

The doctor, packing up his bag, turned and shrugged.

'I won't lie to you, sir,' he said, 'I have no idea. The cold, the head injury, the loss of blood, the shock – any of these could kill a gentleman in his later years such as he.'

Murray nodded.

'Charles,' said Isobel unsteadily, 'he has lost his leg.' She leaned her head against his shoulder and sobbed. Murray could not remember seeing her cry since she was a little girl. His arm slid around her waist, and he held her close.

'He'll sleep for a while,' the doctor said, surveying his patient. 'Perhaps quite a while. The body needs time to recover, if it can. He'll need constant watching for signs of fever or difficulties in breathing.'

'Of course,' said Murray and Isobel together. She wiped hard at her eyes, breaking away from Murray's arm. There was a grunt from Smith. The young doctor gave them all an approving look, took up his bag, and went to leave.

'Mantell's the name. I am only on the High Street, not far away. Send for me if you need me.'

'Shouldn't have left him,' Smith muttered, already beginning to tidy the mess Blair had made of his room. He had rearranged Blair's discarded wig on its wigblock, and emptied the pockets of his coat into their usual bowl. The nightshirt Blair wore was clean: the bloodied rag he must have been wearing last night lay on the floor and Smith took it up delicately to dispose of.

'It's not your fault, Smith,' said Isobel at once. 'We divided our forces as best we could. And you know, even if you had been here it would not have stopped him – doing whatever it was he was doing. But you have done the best thing in finding Mr. Murray and bringing him here. Oh, Charles, I am so glad to see you!'

She took her seat again by her father's bed, and gestured to him to take one on the other side.

'What on earth has been happening?' Murray asked. 'I have had fragments of stories and distractions and confusions all the way from Edinburgh, it seems. Why did he call for me?'

'Well … if we only knew,' said Isobel, taking her father's hand and squeezing it thoughtfully.

'Then what are you doing with the Akehursts? Has he known them for long?'

'He barely knows them now.' Isobel sighed. 'Lady Akehurst sent to ask him to join the household in London, because she had a favour she wished to ask him. I was permitted to accompany him, partly because she has a grand-daughter for whom she is hoping to find a husband, and I was a useful companion.'

'I'm assuming from your expression,' Murray said with a smile, 'that the grand-daughter would not be your first choice of companion.'

'Hm. No, not really,' she admitted. 'Am I that careless with my expressions? Dear me.'

'It's only because I've known you for so long,' said Murray. He was surprised at how comfortable he felt, even here with Blair so injured between them. The journey with Beatrix, Harry Holden and Ketchell had left him tense and worried, but here in Isobel's company he could at last relax, and talk freely. 'So what was the favour?'

'We don't know,' said Isobel. 'He kept trying to find out, and she always avoided being in a position to tell him – you know, never alone with him, always busy. We couldn't imagine what the problem was. But then there really was a problem, though Lady Akehurst seemed to be unaware of it.'

'And that was to do with Miss Akehurst?'

'The lovely Amanda, yes. Heiress to her grandfather, Sir Joshua.'

'Ah, money. Is that why Blair thought she was in danger?'

'There's more to it than that.' Isobel told him about the peculiarly threatening love letters, and how they appeared under Amanda's chamber door at night. 'Or that's how she said they arrived, anyway. She was completely enamoured of the whole business: she believes every young man dotes on her, but this one in particular seemed to appeal. She's a sad romantic – addles her brain with novel-reading, I daresay.' Isobel met his eye. They were both partial to the occasional novel.

'But these things appeared under her door? So someone in the household must have put them there.'

'Yes – though of course the writer might not have been in the household. He might have bribed or persuaded someone to do it.'

'What are the staff like, Smith?' Murray asked, turning to see what the manservant was up to.

'It's not a very happy household,' said Smith at once. 'I'll be glad enough to be free of it. Doesn't help that they blame us for ruining a kettle – I'd guess the master went down to boil himself some water in the night, then saw someone outside. Did they expect him to toddle back and take the kettle off the fire before he chased after an intruder?'

'Would you say the staff are loyal to the family?'

Smith sniffed.

'Not specially. They take advantage a bit, you know, sir?'

'I see. What about Rosie and Jackie?'

'The brats? Too far down the pecking order to venture above stairs at all: I doubt either of them knows what the family even looks like.'

'All right. And the rest of the household?' He turned back to Isobel.

'Sir Joshua and Lady Akehurst. Both devoted to Amanda. He's at the Admiralty and considers his work more important than anything except Amanda, I believe. Lady Akehurst is not a sensible woman: she frets over Amanda's reputation and appearance, then forgets she is chaperoning her and gossips with her friends while Amanda flirts with every available young man.'

Murray grinned.

'I can see you've been enjoying yourself. How many sketchbooks have you filled?'

'Oh,' said Isobel, returning the smile, 'a dozen at least. And I could not show one of them to the Akehursts.'

'Who else was in the house?'

'Mr. Lawrence.'

'Your uncle Lawrence? What was he doing there?'

Isobel sighed.

'It seems to be complicated. You remember Adolphus Payne? Fussy Payne?'

'Oh! Yes, though I'm not sure I've met him more than once or twice. A pleasant man. He is some connexion of Mr. Lawrence, isn't he?'

'He's Mr. Lawrence's godson, and thinks highly of him – and I believe is very fond of him.'

'Not a sentiment shared by your father, I think.'

'Not at all. Anyway, Fussy is Lady Akehurst's great nephew, and if anything happened to Amanda I think a good proportion of the money might come to Fussy. But I cannot believe anything ill of Fussy: he's a very amiable man.'

'Hm, all right. Who else?'

'Oh, there is Harry Holden, another relative of Lady Akehurst, and a wastrel.'

'I have met Mr. Holden. In fact, he travelled down from London with me.'

Isobel raised her eyebrows.

'You mean he inveigled himself into your carriage? Why?'

'He said he wanted to join his aunt in Brighton. He, and his friend Mr. Ketchell.'

Isobel's face fell.

'Oh, no: don't tell me that loathsome man has come here, too!'

'I'm afraid so.'

'Lady Akehurst is very fond of Mr. Holden. I believe she detests Mr. Ketchell as much as anybody does, but she allows him to stay in the house because he is a friend of Mr. Holden.'

'Not much of a friend, I think: he uses Harry Holden's money to lead Harry into gin cellars and – and other places of disrepute.' Oh, no, thought Murray. I still haven't managed to find Beatrix's friends, and any minute now she would be arriving with the others at the house – might already be here. How would he explain Beatrix to Isobel?

'So which of these people do you think might want to send dubious billets doux to Miss Akehurst?' he asked, putting that problem to the back of his mind for the moment.

'I can't imagine Mr. Lawrence doing anything so undignified,' said Isobel, 'or why he would do it. Mr. Holden would lack the co-ordination, and Fussy is far too nice. My favourite candidate would be Mr. Ketchell. I don't trust him an inch.'

Chapter Sixteen

'But then things became serious, from all I've heard,' said Murray. 'Something that happened in Hyde Park?'

'Oh, dear: it won't please Lady Akehurst if it's the subject of rumour,' said Isobel.

'An abduction?' Murray prompted.

'Yes – it would probably have been frightening if it had not all been over so quickly.' She described the event, stroking her father's hand as she told how he had weighed Amanda's legs down to stop the horseman lifting her.

'He probably saved her, though I should think the horseman might think twice about trying to lift Amanda again. And when he realised he could not lift her, he just dropped her. She fell across the side of the carriage. I think she was probably quite badly bruised.'

'So that cured her romantic ideas,' said Murray, frowning. Isobel would not be so foolish, he was sure.

'Ah, unfortunately not, really. If you took out the bruises and the indignity, he was really quite dashing, in a highwayman sort of way. I don't think she saw him all that clearly, but she filled in the details very quickly for herself. How brave he was to swoop in through the crowds and seize her, how much he must desire her to take that risk just to be with her, you know.'

Murray made a face.

'Did you see him clearly?'

'I probably saw him better than anyone in the carriage. Lady Akehurst had no idea what was happening, Amanda was half-suffocating clutched to the abductor's manly breast, and my father was on the floor. The main thing I saw was the horse, which was very fine: almost black, well set up, a lovely creature. The man

181

himself wore a green coat and a black silk handkerchief across his face, and a black hat – I think his hair was dark, too, but there was not much of it for me to see. Gloves, lighter breeches, long boots – nothing he could not have taken off behind a bush and changed for something else.'

'But you would have known if it had been Ketchell.'

'Oh, certainly. He was younger, and I think probably taller. A better figure altogether.'

'All right … then worse happened – someone was murdered.'

'Yes,' said Isobel, 'poor Mr. Paulinson. That hardly seems real. We hurried away so swiftly afterwards – the very next morning – with no funeral, no time to miss him.'

'No time for investigation?'

She met his eye.

'That, perhaps, too.'

'Ketchell and Harry Holden told me a bit about it, but I had the impression they cared little for Mr. Paulinson. What was he really like?'

'I couldn't really say! But yes, he was not the kind of person who would much approve of Mr. Ketchell and Mr. Holden. They went out drinking and amusing themselves every evening, while Mr. Paulinson attended Sir Joshua at the House, or sat up late writing his letters for him. It would be hard to describe what he was like if you took away Sir Joshua: like a frame if you take away the painting in it.'

'Had he many friends?'

'I never saw any. Fussy, I think, spoke to him now and then, but Mr. Paulinson was rarely in company with us except for meals. He seemed always to be working, always in a hurry. But Fussy is a kind man, and does not like to see people left out.'

Fussy was indeed a kind man: Murray could not argue with that. He tried to imagine Paul Paulinson.

'Was there any thought as to who might have killed Paulinson?'

'Well … not exactly. But Father,' she squeezed Blair's hand, another flicker of fond anxiety crossing her face, 'Father did want to know why he was outside without any outdoor clothes, for one thing, and where he had been the previous evening.'

'Where he had been?'

Isobel looked back at him, surprised.

'Oh! You haven't heard? He was not seen from dinner the previous day: Sir Joshua sent up to his room for him but he was not there. Mr. Ketchell suggested he might have been hiding somewhere, and Father wondered if he had left the house already, but with no gloves or hat or cloak, at this time of year, it seemed very strange. And none of the servants had seen him leave, or let him back in. And then there was the note.'

'The note?'

'Mr. Holden and Mr. Ketchell clearly did not tell you much!'

'Clearly. I know he was left on the front step – there is still a mark – and that he was a tedious, boring young man who worked too hard and curried Sir Joshua's favour, possibly to inveigle himself into an inheritance.'

'That's not true!' Isobel cried. 'Or if it is, it was so subtly done that Mr. Ketchell could not possibly have noticed it! He did work very hard, no doubt, but my impression was that he was simply a hard worker who did not like to waste time on frivolity and believed that Sir Joshua's service was a worthy cause. If he simply wanted Sir Joshua's fortune he might have made a play for Amanda, but I don't believe he was even aware of her existence.'

'Would his suit have been acceptable?' Murray asked dubiously.

'Well, no. He was not of high enough quality for Sir Joshua, and not romantic enough for Amanda.'

Murray nodded.

'But this note?'

'I can't remember the exact words, but it mentioned Cato Street – the Cato Street heroes, I think it said – and said that this, Mr. Paulinson's death, was a warning.'

'That's interesting.' Murray sat back. 'A warning to Sir Joshua, presumably?'

'I imagine so.'

He folded his arms and stared up at the ceiling, thinking. Isobel did not interrupt. Between them, Blair snored lightly.

'And then what happened at the Pavilion?'

Isobel shivered.

'That was much nastier, in a way. I mean, Amanda didn't

die, but I suppose I know her better, and I saw her at the reception looking so happy, and then there she was bleeding on the floor.'

'You found her?' Murray sat up, concerned. Isobel nodded.

'And it's not nice to think – well, if it was the same man, then presumably he knew that we would be at the Pavilion – that Amanda would be, anyway. How did he know that? And how did they spend their time outside the reception hall? They must have been there ten minutes before we followed, and he was running away. What could she have been thinking?'

'What happened?'

He watched Isobel's face as she explained how she had followed and found Amanda. Her voice kept to the facts: her face added all the colour he could need. He saw her alarm at the blood, her frustration at the way the assailant had escaped, her annoyance at the staff and bystanders, her relief when the sensible servant came and helped. And her constant glances down to her father's face, grey and almost motionless on the white pillow. He felt a sudden urge to take her into his arms again and comfort her, but Blair was between them. He focussed on what she had been saying.

'That man at least could not have been Ketchell: he was at a country inn with me that evening,' he said at last. 'But he thought he had seen someone following us, and perhaps overtaking us – a man with a green coat.'

'Did he?' Isobel looked up at him in surprise. 'Then he did not dump the green coat behind a bush. But following you – why?'

'I've wondered that,' said Murray, 'and I think perhaps the abductor – or intending killer – the horseman, anyway, did not see you and the Akehursts leave London. He began watching the house in Fitzroy Square after you left, and assumed, correctly, that we were following you, so he followed us.'

'But could he have reached Brighton in time to attack Amanda?'

'He overtook us before Clayton – we were stuck behind a broken-down cart, and he was on horseback, if Ketchell saw him correctly.'

'And if Ketchell is telling the truth.'

Murray acknowledged the thought with a nod. Ketchell was not the kind of man one immediately associated with the truth.

'A man riding fast could have reached Brighton that night,

for he set off early enough while we were still stuck. We spent the night at Clayton.'

Isobel reached forward to straighten an errant eyebrow hair on her father's face.

'Sir Joshua tried his best to make sure we were not followed to Lewes. He would not even allow the servants to know where we were going. We left at first light, and he stopped fifty times along the way.'

'Probably sensible.' Murray watched her for a moment. 'The question is, are we looking at one person, or more than one?'

'It has to be more than one, surely.'

Murray raised a hand in acknowledgement.

'I meant, I think, is this one crime or two? Are the attacks on Miss Akehurst done for the same reason as the attack on Mr. Paulinson?'

Isobel considered.

'You could divide it another way,' she said. 'Mr. Paulinson's murder and the attack at the Pavilion – it sounds to me as if they had similarities. He tried to cut Amanda's throat, and that's what happened to Mr. Paulinson. The horseman in Hyde Park might indeed have been an unrelated romantic idiot, after her fortune.'

'And he, then, was the one who sent the letters?'

'Yes, that makes sense. Though it's a bit unfortunate for Amanda.'

'Indeed. Did you have any sense that Sir Joshua had been under threat before? He reacted very quickly when Paulinson was killed. Was it a culmination, do you think?'

'I have no idea. But he referred to the Cato Street incident a good deal, and he seemed to be under a deal of pressure in his work. Whatever he's involved in, he seems to consider it of vital national importance.'

A memory of Beatrix flashed into Murray's mind. Her protector, too, was working on something of vital national importance. An awful thought occurred to him: could Sir Joshua possibly have been her protector, the man who tried to kill her in Hyde Park? And if so, had he brought her unwittingly into his power again? And where was she, anyway? He had lost track, in the shock of Blair's terrible injuries.

Isobel was thinking of her father's accident, too.

'But then where was my father going last night? What was he doing out of the house, and on the High Street?'

'Let us pray that he wakens and is able to tell us,' said Murray, with feeling.

Smith had gone downstairs, perhaps to see what he could find out from the servants, perhaps to see that Robbins had arrived safely with the horse. Murray rose and wandered over to the window, staring out at the view of the paddock opposite beyond the drive and the road.

'Has anyone spoken to the carter?'

Isobel sat up.

'I don't believe so. I've been here since he was brought in.'

'Who recognised him?'

'One of the servants, sent out early for milk. It was his banyan she recognised: she had seen Smith cleaning it.'

'Fortuitous.'

'Yes: one of the sharper of the servants here.'

'I suppose Mr. Lawrence and Fussy have already left.'

'I believe Sir Joshua asked them to stay. In case there was another attack.'

Murray looked back at Blair lying in the bed.

'I must speak to the carter. How is Miss Akehurst?'

Isobel's mouth twisted.

'For the moment she is enjoying being spoiled – even more than usual. Soon, though, she will miss the attention of handsome young men. She has already started on poor Fussy. Even you will not be safe, I should think!'

'Well, I'm delighted to hear I'm not beyond the scope of eager young ladies,' said Murray. Nor Fussy either, he thought.

'You won't be, when you meet her. Where are you intending to stay?'

'The White Hart, I suppose, if there is room. I have barely spoken to Sir Joshua and I have not met Lady Akehurst: I should go and present myself.' Then a thought struck him. 'Did you say that Sir Joshua is in the Admiralty?'

'I did, yes.'

'Has he anything to do with semaphore towers? You know, the things with great arms that carry –'

'Yes, yes,' Isobel interrupted. 'I know exactly what they are.

Yes, you could say he has something to do with them. I'm not sure he was ever at sea, but he knows every semaphore tower ever built. Or planned to be built. Don't let him start you on the line they intended to take from Chatley Heath down to Plymouth.'

'Your father will have enjoyed that,' said Murray with a grin.

'Hanging on his every word, and taking notes. Weren't you, Father?' She gave the hand she held a little shake, as if to distract him from something. But he did not move.

'I'll sit with him if you need to go somewhere,' said Murray, watching her face.

'I know. Or Smith will. He'll not be left alone,' she said. 'But for now I'm content here. Besides, I have to give him a good telling off for going out in the middle of the night without telling anyone. Did you know he kicked off his slippers halfway up the lane? The carter found them and brought them back with him.'

'Silly man,' said Murray, with mock sternness. 'You're sure you'll be all right for a while?'

'I can ring if I need anything.'

'Sketchbook with you?'

'Always,' she said, but her smile this time was strained.

'I'll be back,' said Murray, and headed for the stairs.

The irritating fact of Blair kicking off his slippers teased at him as he reached the first floor. Had Blair's mind gone? Murray had had a much loved housekeeper who had been found wandering the streets of Edinburgh in her shift. Blair's mind was always so unconventional it might be hard to tell.

But there was another reason why he might have kicked his slippers off, and why he might have found himself in front of a moving cart. He had been running. But had he been running to something, after the intruder that Smith assumed, or from something? He had been running away from here, anyway, away from Sir Joshua's house. But why?

An enquiry of a servant on the ground floor helped him to discover that Lady Akehurst was in the parlour with Mr. Payne, and Murray asked to be announced.

'Charles Murray of Letho,' said the servant at the door. Lady Akehurst looked up in confusion. She was, he saw, not a lady anyone would try to lift out of an open-topped carriage. Not without special equipment.

'Please forgive my intrusion, Lady Akehurst. We have not met before: I am an old friend of Alester Blair.'

'Ah! I see, Mr. Murray. You are the young man my husband tells me ran upstairs to see the poor old gentleman.' Murray thought perhaps she was actually older than Blair, but of course made no comment. 'How is Mr. Blair?'

'Gravely injured, my lady. He has not yet recovered consciousness.'

'But what on earth was he doing on the street in the middle of the night? Most extraordinary behaviour!'

'A mystery I hope to solve, my lady,' said Murray with respect. 'Would your servants be likely to know the name of the carter who brought him back here?'

'They might.' She waved her hand rather vaguely. 'You can ask.'

'And I was not quite clear,' said Murray, 'what had brought him here? He wrote me from London asking for my help in some matter he did not wish to trust to a letter, and of course now he cannot tell me what it was, for the moment, at least. I did wonder if it might have anything to do with why he was in the street at night.'

'Really?' Lady Akehurst seemed astonished at the idea.

'He seems to have been running, my lady, though whether to or from something is of course obscure. If he sought my help in some matter – and he did mention the word "danger", my lady – might he not have been attempting to deal with it last night? I have been so delayed on my journey in one way and another, I fear he might have become desperate.'

'Oh, goodness!' cried Lady Akehurst. 'Such an idea had never occurred to me! What if the poor man was indeed … and I had never had the chance to sit down with him and tell him exactly what it was I wanted from him.'

'Then perhaps you could tell me now, my lady, and I could help?'

'Well … I don't know,' she said, puzzled more than reluctant. 'Mr. Blair did come especially recommended.'

'Recommended? For what? And by whom?'

'Ah, actually, that would be by me,' came a voice from near the window, and Fussy Payne rose from his seat.

'Forgive me, Mr. Murray,' said Lady Akehurst, 'I have not introduced Mr. Adolphus Payne.'

'We've met before,' said Fussy, with a friendly smile. 'Mr. Murray, do you remember?'

'Of course, Mr. Payne.' Murray's bow was just as friendly. Fussy was the kind of person who encouraged people to smile simply by being there. It was an enviable gift: he could see why Isobel liked him.

'I have a horrible feeling,' said Fussy, 'that if anyone is to blame here, it must be me. My Lady Akehurst,' he gave her a little bow, 'said that she had a – well, a mystery to solve, and though she did not confide its nature to me, of course, I said that I had met a man who was very able at solving mysteries, and mentioned Mr. Blair's name to her.'

'I see,' said Murray. 'And may I ask the nature of the mystery now, my lady?'

'It cannot have anything to do with what has happened here,' said Lady Akehurst, though her hands wrung each other awkwardly. 'It was – oh, I wish I had seized an opportunity to speak to him before this awful accident! I wanted to find out more about a rather unpleasant man who had attached himself to my nephew. I wanted to know about his background, and his motives, and whether he was out to bring disgrace upon us all. But the man was staying in our house in Fitzroy Square, and I could rarely find time to speak to Mr. Blair alone.'

'He was staying in your house,' said Murray.

'Yes, but of course he is not here now. We left him in London. He could have had no hand in what happened last night.'

'Was the man named Barnabas Ketchell?' Murray asked.

'He was!' From the expression on Lady Akehurst's face, you would have thought that Murray had produced Ketchell from his own pocket on the spot.

'Then he is here,' said Murray. 'In Lewes. But he was not last night: he was in Brighton.'

'In Brighton?' she repeated faintly. 'But how?'

'He and Mr. Harry Holden asked if I would bring them with me. But what made you suspect any ill intentions on the part of Mr. Ketchell, my lady?' Just looking at him would be enough, he thought, but persisted. 'I had the impression that he was a friend of

Mr. Holden, your kinsman.'

Lady Akehurst smiled indulgently.

'Oh, I am very fond of dear Harry! And he certainly brought
Mr. Ketchell into our house, but much against my better judgement!
I am sure he encourages Harry to spend far too much money on
drinking in places a gentleman should not be seen. I fear he will
draw Harry into trouble with the magistrates if he is not careful, for
Harry is a most obliging, gentle young man and easily led out of
kindness to his friends.'

Easily led by a jug of gin, Murray thought.

'And you know nothing of Mr. Ketchell's family or
background?'

'That is one of the things I hoped Mr. Blair would help with.
I know nothing about the man, only that I do not trust him.'

'Would it not have been more – convenient – to ask Sir
Joshua to do that?'

Lady Akehurst wriggled plump, frustrated fingers.

'Sir Joshua does not seem to see any harm in Mr. Ketchell.
Any time I have asked him for his support in this matter, he has
batted me off with excuses and unconvincing reasons. But I know
Mr. Ketchell is a man up to no good! And dear Fussy told me that
Mr. Blair was discreet and very helpful, and so I invited him and his
daughter to stay with us in London. He was very obliging, and came.
And the daughter – well, I'm sure he was happy to take a chance on
her finding a husband in London when her chances in North Britain
might well have been exhausted. And she is no competition for my
grand-daughter, of course, so I could not be worried on that
account.'

'I have yet to meet your charming grand-daughter,' said
Murray, restraining himself, 'but already I have heard that she is the
toast of London society.' Lady Akehurst was not, he thought, a
particularly bright woman. He noted with alarm the way her
expression changed from concern to calculation.

'Now, Mr. Murray, you must tell me all about yourself! You
are also from North Britain, I think: are you from Edinburgh, like
Mr. Blair?'

'I have some connexion with Edinburgh, yes,' he agreed,
'though I hail from Fife.'

'And you have arrived here, I gather, with your wife?' It was not a subtle question.

'I am a widower, my lady.' He drew a deep breath. 'My wife died some years ago.'

'How very sad.' She raised a speculative eyebrow. 'But perhaps she gave you an heir to your … estate?'

'I have a daughter, my lady. I daresay she will make a very fine heiress, when the time comes.'

'But a son would be so much better, would it not?'

Murray's lips parted to reply, thought better of his initial response, and paused. And at that moment, the parlour door burst open.

'Charles!' exclaimed Beatrix, in a whirl of skirts and a pretty bonnet. She saw Lady Akehurst and dropped into a neat curtsey. 'Oh – I beg your pardon!'

'And who,' said Lady Akehurst, eyes wide, 'is this person?'

Chapter Seventeen

Murray cleared his throat and tried not to meet anyone's eye.

'This is Miss Paterson, a young lady who is under my protection, on her way to stay with friends near Lewes. She was constrained to part company with her maid in London, and I must confess that we asked your kitchenmaid, Rosie, to accompany her here. I apologise for any inconvenience or distress that this might have caused, but I could not in all decency allow the young lady to travel alone with us.'

'Of course not – what an extraordinary thing!' Lady Akehurst looked bewildered. Murray wondered if she knew that she had a kitchenmaid called Rosie. He had been reluctant even to mention Beatrix to Lady Akehurst, but, since it had happened anyway, it seemed better to bring things out into the open before misunderstandings happened. Watching Lady Akehurst trying to absorb the information, he imagined that she was quite good at misunderstandings.

'Well, you must join us for dinner, Mr. Murray, with your young ward,' she said. 'Miss Paterson, I am sure you and my dear Amanda will get along prodigiously well! And, Mr. Murray, you will have the chance to make her acquaintance, as you requested.'

Goodness, thought Murray: he would have to watch his step, or he would find himself with a wife, one way or another.

He made their excuses to Lady Akehurst, bowed to Fussy, and took Beatrix back out into the hallway.

'Was there something urgent?' he asked her.

'Urgent? No – well, only that I heard about that terrible accident last night, the one the boys on the street told you about. It was a friend of yours, was it not?'

'Yes, it was. My oldest friend.'

'Is he – did he die?'

'No,' he said firmly, as if denial could help. 'No, but he is badly injured. I need to find out more about the accident. Where is everyone? Where is Rosie? Where is Robbins? What happened with the carriage?'

'Your man Robbins directed the coachman to take the carriage to, what was it now? The White Hart, that was it. But he brought that horse, the limping one, here, because it belongs to the gentleman you met on the road, so I came with him, and set out to look for you because I thought it would be easier for me than for him, and he could go on to the inn and see to things there. I hope that was helpful?'

He supposed he should be grateful she had not made her way upstairs and burst into Blair's bedroom. That would have taken some explanation to Isobel.

'Now we are in Lewes,' he said, guiding her to the front door, 'I can ensure that you reach your friends safely. Where do they live?'

'Oh, but I've accepted Lady Akehurst's kind invitation to dinner! I cannot go before that!'

'You won't have anything suitable to wear,' he objected.

'I bought more than one item from that excellent clothes dealer, remember? They must have come from the same household, for they are all the right size for me. Wasn't that fortuitous?'

'Very,' said Murray. 'But your friends – where do they live?'

'I shall write to them directly and make sure that they are ready to receive me,' said Beatrix. 'If I write now, from the inn, no doubt there will be a carrier to take it.'

Murray had had no idea of Beatrix staying at the White Hart. He wondered whether Rosie had gone back to the Akehurst household or not – but surely they would not need her for much longer? He rubbed his forehead, and replaced his hat.

'The inn is this way,' he said in resignation, and offered her his arm. She took it and smiled up at him from under the brim of her bonnet.

'Thank you, Charles!'

He managed not to smile back.

At the top of the lane he found, without surprise, that the lads who had been scrubbing the cobbles, and watching others scrub the cobbles, were still there, propped on brushes and gossiping about passersby. He stopped near them.

'Good work, lads,' he said, though blood was still to be seen around the cobblestones. 'Tell me, the carter that was involved in the accident: do you know who he was, or where he lives?'

The nearest boy eyed him with interest.

'Are you going to have him arrested?'

'Not at all,' said Murray. 'He helped as best he could. I doubt it was his fault that the gentleman ran out in front of him.'

The boys exchanged looks, a collective decision on whether or not to trust this stranger. Then one of them nodded, and they all turned back to face Murray.

''Snames Fields,' said the nearest boy, the spokesman. 'He lives down Cliffe. Near the river.'

'Thank you.' A solemn distribution of coins followed, and Murray carried on down into the town with Beatrix by his side. To look at her you would think they were out for a stroll, instead of, in her case, fleeing a murderous lover, and in his, trying to discover a vicious attacker.

'Down a cliff?' she asked. 'What a curious address.'

'It's not far,' he answered, not wanting to encourage her interest.

The high street was busy, lined with shops and fine houses and the gateway, just after St. Michael's stern flint church, to the Castle. Where the street narrowed again to accommodate the town hall, the White Hart stood, commodious and welcoming, to their right. Even as they approached, Robbins appeared in the doorway to see if they were coming. His face set when he saw Beatrix: Murray met his eye and Robbins gave the least nod – assurance and acknowledgement that the situation was in hand. At least, Murray hoped so.

'A room and a private parlour, sir,' he announced.

'Then please show Miss Paterson to the private parlour and have paper and ink brought, and I'll go to my room, thank you.'

But as soon as Beatrix was settled in the parlour with the door closed, Murray called Robbins and set out with him for Cliffe.

'We're going to try to find the carter that hit Mr. Blair,' he told Robbins as they descended the steep run of School Hill.

'May I enquire how Mr. Blair is, sir?' asked Robbins.

'Not good, Robbins. Not at all good. The physician who came would not commit himself one way or the other.'

'Maybe that's a good sign, sir. You don't want a physician that's over-confident.'

'True … He's lost a leg, Robbins. And a deal of blood, as we all saw. He lay a while before they worked out who he was, and that was thanks to an observant maid from the Akehurst household. Apparently she recognised not him, but his banyan.'

Robbins snorted slightly.

The town grew busier near the river and the bridge across to Cliffe, the industrial heart of mercantile Lewes. Beyond it rose the coombe that gave it its name, where chalk had been quarried time out of mind. Here in the broad hollow between that and the town on its hill, the air filled with the smell of mud, sawn wood, and brewing, not the worst of mixtures. Cranes shifted, bent and lifted. Men shouted directions or warnings as boxes and crates were shuffled and swung about the riverbank, and boys ran here and there with messages and deliveries. Boats filled with all kinds of cargo docked, emptied and reloaded, and continued upriver into the Weald or down to the sea and Newhaven – Newhaven, where Lieutenant Munnings had appeared from.

Again Murray thought of semaphore towers. Why had Beatrix been so keen to see the one at Coombe Warren, when it was in the middle of reconstruction anyway? What had her protector, her murderous lover, allowed her to overhear? Nothing about the towers seemed particularly secret: certainly not their existence, if Sir Joshua had lectured Blair on the subject. And Lieutenant Munnings had been quite open about his message to Sir Joshua, too. But why else would she have wanted to look at Coombe Warren? It was hardly a tourist site.

There were plenty of carters around the bridge and the riverside, with hand carts and horse carts, and even an ox cart taking up more than its fair share of the roadway. Presumably Blair had been hit by a horse cart, although certainly Murray had met some wildly driven hand carts in the past. He looked about for a likely one to start with, saw a bright looking young fellow in charge of a skewbald pony with a cartload of fat sacks. He was already stationary, so Murray had no qualms about causing him to stop and start again with a heavy load.

'Fields?' he said at once. 'Oh, yes, he's the one down there, with the smart grey.'

The grey was smart, for a carthorse, with an alert eye. Fields, who was overseeing the unloading of beets, had detailed a strong lad to hold the horse's head. Fields himself was solid and respectable looking, and inspired a good deal more confidence than some of the Edinburgh carters who would knock you over and trot off, their only concern to hide their cart number from you so you could not report them. Murray, followed by Robbins, stepped over to interrupt.

'Mr. Fields?'

'Aye, sir, that I am.' He turned without hesitation and looked Murray in the eye, then bowed. He wore a decent round woollen smock, in the local style, and a leather waistcoat over it that had been worn to softness.

'I understand you were involved in an accident early this morning?'

The man's face clouded at once.

'The old gentleman, sir? That were terrible. Nothing I could do, see. That's a fast horse, and no mistake, and though she's light on her feet there was no way she could miss him. She tried, mind, swerved out into the road when the first one come out, but the old gentleman and the cart was just doomed to meet, sir.'

'The first one?' This is what Murray had been hoping for.

'Yes, sir, there was two came running out from that twitten. And the wall there is too high for them to see me or me to see them until it was too late.'

'The older gentleman, the one who was injured – he's a friend of mine,' Murray explained, then saw the carter's face widen in alarm. 'No! No, if anything I'd like to say how grateful we are that you stayed with him, found Dr. Mantell and brought him back to the house. You probably saved his life.'

'Well, maybe, sir,' said the man, touched now by a pleasing modesty.

'But the other man, the one who ran out first – what did you see of him?'

Fields blew out sharply.

'Not much, sir, and that's a fact. He was younger than the

gentleman, and, begging your pardon, sir, he was fully clothed.'

'Which way did he go?'

'Why, down this way, sir, as far as I could tell. Straight down the High Street for as far as I could see him. Not that I was looking that much, sir, for the gentleman was in a bad way, as you'll know. He wasn't tall, though, I can say that much, and there was no weight to him. He moved fast.'

'Did he shout out at all?'

'No, sir, not at all.'

'Did you happen to see his face? Would you know him again?'

Fields considered.

'I didn't rightly see his face, no, sir. But I wonder if I might know him again, if I saw him run. I just might,' he concluded.

'Was he wearing a hat? Or a coat, or cloak?'

'No cloak nor coat, sir, no. As to a hat … I don't believe he was, sir, but I could not swear to it.'

'Boots, or shoes? You might have heard his footsteps as he ran, even if you did not see.'

'Then boots, sir, surely. Strange what you remember when you put your mind to it, eh? I couldn't have told you five minutes ago.' He managed a kind of smile. 'Will he be all right, sir, the gentleman?'

'We don't know yet,' said Murray. 'We pray so.'

'I'll pray too, sir, if I may.'

'Thank you. It would be very much appreciated.' Some coins changed hands, discreetly. Murray nodded farewell, and turned away. 'What's wrong, Robbins?'

Robbins was staring along Cliffe High Street. It was narrow and full of busy people.

'I just thought I saw … never mind, sir. It couldn't have been. Now what, sir?'

'Now I suppose I had better change for dinner at the Akehursts. At least it will give me a chance to find out how Mr. Blair is doing.'

'May I attend and speak with Smith, sir?'

'Of course.'

There was a pause. They crossed the neat arched bridge again over the river, and Murray glanced back to see Fields still unloading his cart.

'Will Miss Paterson be attending the dinner, sir?' Robbins asked.

'She has been invited.'

Robbins was silent.

'I hope there will be a swift response from her friends in whatever village they inhabit,' Murray went on. He did not want Robbins to think he was encouraging Beatrix to stay with them. At the same time, a lingering memory of the friendship he had once shared with Beatrix made him protective, still. 'But if Lady Akehurst has no idea of her – her situation in life, then it is unlikely to harm anyone. And I'm sure that Miss Paterson will not push the acquaintance.'

Actually he was not at all sure. Beatrix had demonstrated, long ago, that she would act according to her own interests, and even now was she not taking advantage of Murray's kindness to linger around Brighton and Lewes when she should be with her real friends? He wished his feelings about Beatrix were clearer: well, really he wished he had not met her again. Why had it had to be that moment that he and Robbins had crossed Hyde Park? But then, did he really wish that her attacker had not been interrupted? Of course not.

Whatever his feelings on the matter, Beatrix was ready and waiting when he came downstairs to depart for the Akehursts. Where she had changed her clothes was none of his business, but she was certainly suitably dressed for the occasion.

There was an air of grey normality about the Akehursts' house, as if Murray's oldest friend were not at death's door upstairs and the whole household on tenterhooks in case of attack. Murray could not imagine the panic that Isobel said had sent them spinning off so abruptly for Brighton. The closest thing to fear he could see was in the eyes of the butler, a nervy man who showed him and Beatrix into the parlour and looked as if he might lock the door behind them, just to be on the safe side. After a few minutes they were joined by Sir Joshua, followed by Lieutenant Munnings in borrowed dinner clothes: he had evidently been persuaded to stay. It was fortuitous, as he was able to perform an introduction between Sir Joshua and Murray. Sir Joshua, who was around Murray's height, nodded to him with the look that passes between unusually tall men: the look that spoke of a shared experience of bad jokes and bruised foreheads.

'You're Blair's friend, aren't you? The fellow that came in earlier.'

'That's right. Lady Akehurst kindly invited me back for dinner.'

'How's he doing, d'you know?' Murray had the impression that it was not much in Sir Joshua's nature to be sympathetic, but he was trying his best. He had begun to reply when Harry Holden and Mr. Ketchell appeared – Murray had not seen them since they had come across the blood on the lane. Sir Joshua looked twice at them: presumably they had not announced their arrival to him.

'Came down from town, then, eh?' was all he could manage in his surprise.

'Yes, Sir Joshua,' said Ketchell, with a smooth bow. 'Couldn't keep away. Sorry to hear of another attack on Miss Akehurst.'

'Yes. Yes, indeed.' Sir Joshua looked Harry Holden up and down as if checking for signs of drunkenness, but he regarded Ketchell with more respect. 'Good of you to say. Where did you hear about it?'

'When we were in Brighton, sir. It was the talk of the place, I'm afraid.' Ketchell, too, seemed to have tidied himself up for his arrival. Sir Joshua groaned.

'Of course it would be. I had no opportunity to pay the staff at the Pavilion for their silence.'

'Might not have worked anyway, sir,' said Ketchell. He caught sight of Beatrix, half-hidden behind Murray, and winked at her.

The parlour door opened again to admit Mr. Lawrence and Fussy.

'More men!' Murray heard Beatrix mutter, though whether she was pleased or dismayed it was hard to tell.

'Ah! Here we all are!' came Lady Akehurst's unmistakeable voice. Several of the men winced. 'Mr. Murray, may I present my grand-daughter?'

Amanda Akehurst advanced into the room, smiling at all around her. She curtseyed to Murray, who bowed. Murray had the impression she felt she could do better than him, which suited him very well.

'May I present my ward, Miss Paterson?' He gestured to Beatrix. There was a snort from behind him – Ketchell had overheard. Fortunately no one else seemed to have noticed.

Lieutenant Munnings was also introduced to those he had not met – he, too, was too old and too ordinary to be of much interest to Amanda, and so she lapsed into a sulk. Murray noted that she wore a scarf around her throat like a choker, and touched it now and again as if it were rubbing uncomfortably.

'Now, then,' said Lady Akehurst, almost in control of the situation, 'I sent Mr. Blair's man upstairs so that Miss Blair could join us for dinner. Ah! Here she is. Now we are all ready – though somewhat heavily weighted on the male side, I fear!'

Isobel had no chance to enter the parlour before she was swept aside by Lady Akehurst progressing to the dining room. Lady Akehurst had made no attempt to pair her guests, but Sir Joshua offered an arm to Beatrix, and Lieutenant Munnings followed suit with Isobel, catching her in the hall. Murray was left with Fussy, Ketchell and Harry Holden, none of them particularly interested in escorting Amanda. Murray was spared in a moment by Lady Akehurst reappearing in the doorway to claim him for herself, and Fussy kindly took Amanda on. Harry and Ketchell, sniggering like schoolboys, took up the rear.

The dinner was dull. Isobel, who could usually be relied upon to provide some kind of interesting conversation, spoke hardly at all. Sir Joshua and Lieutenant Munnings talked only of signals and flags and fires, even when the ladies left and the brandy circulated. In the drawing room, when the gentlemen appeared, Amanda gave only an impression of amusement at anything that was said, played the piano at her grandmother's request to a very low standard, and seemed altogether edgy and disappointed. Murray thought that his old housekeeper would have said she needed a good dose of salts. Isobel's toe was tapping on the floor beneath the hem of her skirt – no doubt she was impatient to be back with her father. Lady Akehurst did her best to charm each of the gentlemen on her grand-daughter's behalf, but Amanda was not co-operative. Conversation could not be said to flow: only Beatrix, chatting away with Fussy, seemed to be enjoying herself. To be fair, Fussy did not look as if he would be keen to break away.

Murray rose to his feet.

'My lady, I wonder if I might be excused to go and see how my old friend Mr. Blair does? I confess I am very anxious about him.'

'I shall go with you,' said Isobel at once, already halfway to the door. Their speed as they ascended the stairs had less to do with anxiety about Blair, however, and more to do with their eagerness to be out of the drawing room. No one else seemed to have moved as they left.

'Aren't they awful?' Isobel asked as soon as they had shut the door behind them. Smith, who had been sitting by his master's bed, rose stiffly to greet them.

'No change, miss,' he said. 'But no worse just as much as no better.'

'Then let us be thankful for that,' said Isobel. She went to take the seat Smith had vacated, and touched her father's face with light, painterly fingers. There was no reaction. Murray went to sit again opposite her.

'So,' said Isobel, without ceremony, 'when did you acquire a ward? And one of whom I have previously heard nothing? Paterson … a common enough name.'

'She's – don't say anything, but she's a relative of Lord Scoggie's.'

'That strange old man from the castle near St. Monance?'

'That's the one. When I lived there Miss Paterson was there as companion to Deborah.'

Isobel knew Deborah and admired her: Murray hoped it would stop her asking any more questions.

'But how does she come to be your ward?'

'Oh, it's a long story … and it is a temporary situation. She is going to stay with friends somewhere near here after a domestic problem in London.'

'A domestic problem,' Isobel repeated.

'Yes. That exactly.'

'And she is to stay with friends here?'

'Near here.'

'Where?'

'Somewhere near here. She has written to them to say she is

coming.'

'Oh, has she? Good.' Isobel kept her eye on Murray's face. Murray wished she would not.

'She'll be gone tomorrow, no doubt.'

'No doubt.'

'Look, I'd better see her safely back to the inn now.' He stood, so eagerly that he almost toppled the chair and had to grab the back of it. 'I'll be back tomorrow.'

'You'll be back and Miss Paterson will be gone. What an eventful day to look forward to!'

Murray hurried from the room, entirely disconcerted. Beatrix was much more trouble than she was worth.

It was nevertheless a dull recollection of the evening's activities that filled Murray's mind as he sat down to breakfast the next morning. He had not been able to find Beatrix the previous evening and had left without her, knowing that a servant could bring her back to the inn later. He was pleased to note at breakfast that Beatrix had not yet appeared – perhaps, if he were lucky, she had already left – and he could eat his meal in silent contemplation of Lady Akehurst's gaffes, Amanda's twitchy boredom, Ketchell and Harry's sniggering, Sir Joshua's irritation – and of course Blair's continued unconsciousness. He tried not to think about Isobel and Beatrix.

But he had hardly begun his meal when there was a clatter at the door, and one of the inn's serving maids came in, already half-curtseying in her rush.

'Sir, a Miss Blair to see you, sir.'

'Isobel!' Murray shot to his feet. 'Is it your father?'

'No!' she cried, though her face was flushed and her hair unkempt beneath her bonnet. 'No, I should not have alarmed you like this. But it is Amanda – she is gone!'

Chapter Eighteen

'Do you mean she's been abducted? Successfully, this time?'

'She left a note, but I'm not convinced. Can you come?'

'Of course.' He drained his teacup. 'Let me fetch my hat and gloves, and tell Robbins where I'm going.'

Isobel led the way quickly back up the High Street. It was indeed a beautiful morning: down the steep side streets to their left they could see the amber sunlight chasing the mists from the lower ground by the priory ruins, while behind them the hill beyond Cliffe loomed dark against the bright sky.

In only a few minutes they were back at the Akehursts' house by the paddock. At the gate, he was surprised to meet Beatrix, coming to the house from the other direction.

'Oh, Charles! Where are you off to in such a hurry?'

'Miss Akehurst has disappeared,' he said. 'Where were you?'

'Out for a walk: it's a lovely autumn morning. Lady Akehurst asked me to stay here last night. Oh, good morning, Miss Blair.'

'Good morning, Miss Paterson,' Isobel returned politely. 'I hope I may wish you a safe onward journey today?'

'That is very kind of you, Miss Blair, but I could not think of leaving if the Akehurst household is in such distress. Charles said that Miss Akehurst has disappeared!'

'Yes,' said Isobel. 'Well: it looks that way. It may be a false alarm.'

'One must hope so, of course,' said Beatrix sweetly. 'But at the very least I must go and present my sympathies to Lady Akehurst and offer any comfort I can.' She headed back towards the house, quite at home.

'Very well, then,' said Isobel. 'Charles, are you coming?'

Murray nodded, not daring to speak. He had known it would be a bad idea to bring Isobel and Beatrix together.

It was immediately clear that the household was more disturbed than it had been yesterday. Dr. Mantell was just ahead of them at the front door, servants scoured the autumn-weary grounds about the house, and Lady Akehurst stood in the hall, face tear-stained, berating Ketchell.

'You!' she emphasised with a stubby finger. 'You have brought some low person here to do this! There is no one else here who might have stooped – who might have *known* anyone who would do such a thing!'

'My lady,' said Ketchell, 'I have nothing to do with this.' He did not help his case by trying a smile. 'If you want the honest truth, I care not a jot for Miss Akehurst, nor, I imagine, would anyone of my acquaintance.'

If he had intended to help the situation deteriorate, he had gone the right way about it. Lady Akehurst, lost for words, seized him by the lapels of his coat and shook him like a dog, but she could not shake the knowing smile from Ketchell's face.

'My lady!' cried Isobel, hurrying to pull at Lady Akehurst's arm. 'My lady, this will do no good!'

At the same time, Murray drew Ketchell back out of reach.

'Perhaps you should go and sit in the parlour for a little,' he suggested. 'Out of the way.'

'Out of whose way?' asked Ketchell, with a knowing look. 'Yours, I suppose?'

'Oh! Dr. Mantell!' Lady Akehurst gasped, seeing him for the first time. 'My husband is in the drawing room.'

'I'll go at once,' said the doctor.

'Were you not here to see my father?' Isobel could not help asking. Dr. Mantell looked round, even as he hurried off.

'Later, if I may, Miss Blair. Sir Joshua is more urgent.'

'But –'

'He's collapsed,' said Ketchell. 'Fell off his feet.' Though his tone was disrespectful, Murray thought he saw some real concern in Ketchell's eyes. Lady Akehurst hurried after the doctor, plump hands flapping in distress.

'A heart attack?' asked Isobel in concern. 'His heart is not strong.'

'I have no idea. Well, no, I suppose I do,' said Ketchell casually. Murray was sure it was faked. 'He grabbed his chest and sat down, and went a very strange colour.'

'I should go ...' said Isobel.

'No, not while the doctor is there,' said Murray. 'Lady Akehurst is the best person to look after him.'

'And to look after Lady Akehurst?' asked Isobel, but her heart was not in it.

'Where is everyone?' Murray asked.

'Lawrence and Fussy Boy are out hunting for the girl,' said Ketchell, taking the chance to look Beatrix up and down. 'Harry's still in his bed, as far as I know – only he could sleep through all this rumpus.'

'What happened? When was the disappearance discovered?' Murray persisted.

'This morning, of course,' said Isobel. 'She went off to her chamber last night as usual – you saw her yourself at dinner – and this morning when her maid went to waken her she was gone.'

'She hasn't taken her maid?'

'No.' Isobel met Murray's eye. If Amanda had left with a man, and without her maid, she was abandoning all pretence at respectability. But then from what Isobel had said, Amanda was not very sensible.

'Was her bed made, or had she slept in it?'

'Why would you want to know?' asked Ketchell, with a sly look.

'It might give an indication of whether she left late last night or early this morning,' Murray explained.

'Oh, indeed,' Ketchell agreed. 'But why would you want to know that? What concern might it be of yours?'

'Oh, Charles is very good at finding out what has happened to people in odd circumstances,' said Beatrix suddenly. She turned a smile up at Murray. 'Aren't you, Charles?'

'Are you, indeed?' asked Ketchell. 'I wonder what odd circumstances you've come across?'

'Well, there was a very sad circumstance long ago, when

Charles and I were first acquainted –' Beatrix began.

'If you will excuse me,' said Isobel, 'I must go to be with my father.'

'How is he this morning?' asked Murray hurriedly.

'No different,' said Isobel over her shoulder, heading for the stairs.

'Such a shame,' said Beatrix lightly, watching her go. Murray had no wish to ask her what she meant. Should he follow Isobel or try to find out what he could here?

'My friend Mr. Blair,' he began to explain, 'was very concerned about Miss Akehurst's safety and, even before there was an attempt to abduct her in Hyde Park, thought that she might be in some danger. He had even some suspicion of who was responsible. He had written to me in Edinburgh to ask me to help.' He rubbed his forehead. He should be explaining himself to Sir Joshua and Lady Akehurst, not to Beatrix and Ketchell. 'I came as soon as I could, but at every stage I have been too late. Now I must do what I can.'

Ketchell looked at him for a moment.

'Did he give you any idea of who he suspected?' he asked sensibly.

'No, he didn't. But since he wrote to me from London, I suppose it must have been someone he had come across there, whether in the household or outside it.' He wanted to talk it through, but not with either Ketchell or Beatrix. He wanted to talk it through with Blair, but that was not going to happen. Robbins or Isobel, that was who he needed, and Isobel first. She would have more information for him, he was sure. 'I must go and see how Blair is doing. No,' he put up a hand as Beatrix looked as if she would follow, 'I'm sure Lady Akehurst would benefit from your comfort when she has spoken with the doctor.'

Beatrix smiled and nodded, as though that was what she had intended all along. Murray abandoned her in the hall, and tried not to run up the stairs to Blair's chamber.

Smith was sitting with Blair when Murray opened the door. He stood when he saw Murray.

'How is he?' Murray murmured.

'No change, sir,' said Smith, grumpy as ever, but Murray could see that his eyes were damp. 'And he'd be up and looking for the young lady if he could.'

'Of course he would. Is Miss Blair about?'

'I'm expecting her any moment, sir. She's more than pleased you're here, if I may say so.'

'I'm only sorry I was not here earlier. Oh, here she is.'

Isobel glanced from one of them to the other, and strode across to take her place at her father's side

'I went to fetch my sketchbook,' she said. 'There are pictures of Amanda in it: I thought it might be of some use. Smith, you must go and rest: you've been up most of the night.'

'Yes, miss.'

He left, and Murray took the other chair, as before. Blair was still pale, motionless, only a snuffling little snore telling them he was breathing and alive.

'Cursed, I tell you,' said Isobel. 'This whole household.'

'Do you think she's gone of her own accord?'

'I wouldn't be surprised,' said Isobel, 'but still, a decent man would not have taken her. If those letters are anything to do with it, she has been seduced. She's a silly girl.'

'Even after the incident in the Pavilion?'

'I'm not sure,' said Isobel, 'whether she convinced herself that that was a mistake, in panic, or whether it was some other man. She was a dreamer.'

'Was?'

Isobel looked directly at him for the first time since Beatrix had appeared at the inn. Her blue-green eyes were very bright and clear, and for a moment he was not sure what she was saying. He shook himself.

'I have a very bad feeling about this, Charles. I don't like it at all. Father was anxious, and that's why he called for you: he would not have expected you to travel all this way if he had not been worried. He looked for you every day.'

'I'm so sorry. I came as quickly as I could.'

She drew a hard breath, stopping tears.

'I know. I'm sorry, I didn't want to make you feel that any of this was your fault.'

'Nevertheless I have been too late at every point,' he said again. 'But now I'm here. He would want us to try and find her, wouldn't he?'

'And to find out what happened to Mr. Paulinson. He was

very distressed that we had simply been hurried away from London even before the funeral, let alone before we could find out anything about the circumstances. It felt very wrong.'

'Did he have any direct suspicions? He hinted in his letter that he did.'

Isobel sighed again, and squeezed her father's hand, watching for a reaction. There was none.

'He did, but he would never have written them down. He thought that Mr. Lawrence had something to do with it.'

'Mr. Lawrence?' Murray repeated in surprise. Mr. Lawrence was the face that came to his mind when he heard the word 'respectable'.

Isobel shrugged.

'That's the problem. He thought in his heart that Mr. Lawrence was to blame, not in his head. He knew how much he disliked Mr. Lawrence – I've never known my father dislike someone so much – and he did not trust himself in the matter. That's why he wanted you here. He knew you could be clear-headed about Mr. Lawrence. I think he thought that I, though I could be of some use, might be too loyal to him to see clearly, too. I'm not very fond of Mr. Lawrence,' she admitted, 'but I didn't really think he was trying to harm Amanda. Why on earth would he?'

'I found out why Lady Akehurst wanted your father's help.'

'Did you?' She looked at him in surprise. 'What was it?'

'She doesn't trust Ketchell. Thinks he's corrupting Harry Holden – which he might well be. Sir Joshua is not supportive and, according to her, seems sympathetic to Ketchell. Well, you saw her downstairs just now, blaming Ketchell for bringing reprobates into the household. Clearly that's her suspect.'

'I can't see even Amanda being seduced by Mr. Ketchell,' said Isobel.

'Well, no, but don't you think there's probably more than one person involved here? And Ketchell would be clever enough, I think, to write seductive letters.'

'Something I can't see Mr. Lawrence doing,' added Isobel, smiling very slightly. He was pleased to see it. He sat back, thinking.

'Was it someone within the household? That's one question.'

'There has to have been a connexion in the household,' said

Isobel at once. 'The notes were pushed under Amanda's door. If it wasn't one of the family or the guests, then it was a servant, and someone might have bribed them.'

'Right,' said Murray. 'So there is at least a link. And all those people are now here, aren't they? Except for Jackie.'

'Who's Jackie?'

'A small boy who works in the kitchens.'

'Oh. But not everyone was at the Pavilion. The servants weren't invited, of course – '

'Would they have been noticed if they had gone to the kitchen door?'

It took Isobel only a moment to consider.

'Probably not. There are armies of servants there. Most of them are in livery, of course, but I don't suppose everyone is, not the ones behind the scenes.'

'And did Fussy and Mr. Lawrence accompany you?'

'Yes, they did. All the Akehursts were there, though Sir Joshua seems to hate that kind of thing. And Father and me, of course.'

'But not Harry Holden or Ketchell.'

'Can we be quite sure?'

'Yes, if the dates are right: they were with me in an inn in Clayton. It's not far from Brighton, but I'm sure they would not have had time to go and come back. What time was the reception?'

'Nine.'

'And what time do you think the incident happened?'

'We had not been there very long. Perhaps no later than ten.'

'No,' said Murray, assessing his memory, 'they were both still at Clayton at half past nine, at least.'

'But you said we should be considering more than one person.'

'I know. But at least we can say that neither of them directly attacked Miss Akehurst at the Pavilion.'

Silence fell between them for a moment while they both applied their minds to the problem, or problems.

'Remember yesterday,' said Isobel, 'you thought it was two – parties, shall we say, one of whom tried to abduct Amanda then attacked her, and the other of whom killed Mr. Paulinson?'

'Yes, and you thought the two attacks went together, and the abduction was separate.'

'I said it might be. Anyway, how does this fit in? Amanda's disappearance?'

Murray reflected.

'I think it depends on what has actually happened. Has she been taken, or has she eloped?'

'You could be right: if she has eloped, it is one with the abduction. If she has been taken, it may well be part of the attacks. So we need to know. Well,' she said with a sigh, 'all the servants are out searching for her, and half the neighbours.'

'Maybe we need to look closer to home to find, not her, but the answers. You said she'd left a note, but you weren't happy with it?'

'Yes … you'd better ask Lady Akehurst. She's the one who saw it, she and Amanda's maid.'

'But Sir Joshua has collapsed: she'll be with him, no doubt. Perhaps I should ask Smith to ask the maid.'

Isobel smiled.

'I suppose she might tell him. Possibly.'

'Possibly?'

'I'm not convinced that Smith is that charming!'

'Perhaps not!' He rose, and put a hand out to her. 'Are you all right?'

She took the hand briefly. He felt – what? Something more than just her touch.

'I'm sure I shall be,' she said. 'But I never clung more to the saying that while there is life, there is hope.'

'I know.' He leaned over and touched her shoulder. 'I'll be back, if I may.'

'Please.'

Downstairs was still confused, full of bustling servants and wandering gentry, not quite sure, any of them, where they could be of the most use. Murray met Lady Akehurst by a French window, staring into the wilted autumnal garden. The butler Trent stood in silent attendance, as if he had slipped everyone's mind.

'I hope that Sir Joshua is improving in health, my lady,' he said.

'What?' She spun to look at him. 'Oh, Mr. Murray: I had

forgotten you were here. They are taking him upstairs. The doctor seems a good man, and I cannot help to carry him. Later I shall nurse him, of course.'

'Of course.' He let the silence lie for a moment. 'It must have been a terrible shock for him – for you both – to find Miss Akehurst gone.'

'Stolen!' Lady Akehurst laid a dramatic hand on the window frame. Murray heard the butler jump behind him. 'Stolen from us! And all our plans for her!'

'I understood she had, ah, left a note?'

'And what is that to the consequence?' she demanded. 'No doubt he forced her to write it – as he forced her to leave with him!'

'No doubt,' said Murray quickly. 'But such notes can tell us quite a lot, you know. Can you tell me what it said?'

'Tell you?' she cried. 'I can show you!'

And to his delight, she produced from her reticule a folded sheet of expensive paper, and handed it freely to Murray. He took it.

'Dear Grandmamma, He has such a passion for me I cannot resist! He means me no harm, I am quite sure. It is so romantic! When I know where we are to be, I shall send word for my things. My love to Grandpappa. Your loving Amanda.'

'It looks as if it had been written in haste,' said Murray. 'Are you quite sure it is her hand?'

'Oh, positive, positive!' Lady Akehurst flapped her hands, then seized the note back. 'This is the very way she writes her name. Oh, if her poor father were alive! He would fall dead to the ground! The very shame of it! And it's all very well for her to say he means her no harm, but how can she possibly know that? This was bound to happen! Oh, I knew she was too beautiful for her own safety!'

Or perhaps too rich, Murray thought ungallantly. He had the impression that the butler Trent was edging towards the door, keen to escape until he was remembered and summoned again.

'Who is this "he"? Have you any idea?'

'How could I possibly know? And yet she told me everything, Mr. Murray: she confided in me so sweetly. Oh, the dear girl – where could she be? Everyone is out there searching, you know. They are all devoted to her.'

'Do you think it could be the same man who tried to seize her from the carriage in Hyde Park?'

The butler paused. Lady Akehurst was appalled at the idea.

'Oh, no. No, she would never have gone off with him. No, whoever it is, he will be a most respectable young gentleman, I am quite sure. Amanda knows what care we have taken to find her the best of husbands. She knows quality when she sees it, you know. Oh, look: now one of the servants wants to ask me something. How can I possibly answer him at a time like this?' She flung herself into a chair and glared at the man who had dared to approach the French window. Murray unlatched it.

'Yes?'

'Please sir, we found this in the shrubbery. We didn't know if it was of any use.' He handed Murray a slip of paper with thick black writing across it. There was a sound at the door of the room, and Murray saw the butler, pale as milk, scrabbling for the door handle. What was his name again?'

'You!' he called, and this seemed to work. The butler paused. Murray thanked the other servant and sent him on his way, then turned his attention back to the butler. 'You don't look at all well. Come: you must take a turn in the garden. Fresh air will help.'

He marched the butler out through the French windows, leaving Lady Akehurst with her own thoughts, oblivious to the servants as ever. When they were a little distance from the house, he stopped.

'Dizzy?'

'Sir.' Trent nodded miserably.

'Have you been eating properly?'

The man shook his head.

'Sleeping properly?

'Hardly at all, sir.'

'And this would be since these notes have started arriving for Miss Akehurst, wouldn't it?'

The man squirmed.

'No ...'

'But you recognised the note that was just found, didn't you?'

'I don't –'

'This note,' said Murray, holding up what the servant had found in the garden. 'Like the ones that you delivered to Miss Akehurst's room in London.'

'Yes, sir …' It was almost a wail. Murray studied him: the man was a wreck. 'It was me. I didn't think it would do any harm. But if I didn't do it, he said he was going to tell Sir Joshua everything. And then, sir, I would have lost my place.'

Chapter Nineteen

Murray glanced back at the house, checking to see that Lady Akehurst was not watching their progress. He led the butler out into an area of open lawn so they could not be overheard unawares.

'You'd better tell me everything,' he said. 'I'd imagine it will give you some relief.'

The butler, staring at the well-kept grass, shuddered.

'I suppose it might, sir. I've had no one to talk to, no one at all …' He tailed off, but Murray knew better than to interrupt at that moment. Trent pulled himself together as far as he was still capable, and looked Murray in the face.

'I'm bad with the drink, sir. It's not a good thing for a butler, though it does happen to many of us, I believe: I saw it with my father years ago. And when you're the one with the keys to the cellar and all, and temptation is constantly in your way, it's very hard.'

'And someone found out about it?'

'It's worse than that, sir.' He cleared his throat. 'I began to think that Sir Joshua would soon see how quickly the household was getting through the brandy, and so I began to go out at night and drink gin. Only a night or two, at first, but then it grew to be every night, and now I can't stop, whatever I tell myself in the morning about not going that night, about taking a night off, at least, when the household has retired there I am, heading off to a handy gin cellar. I'm supposed to look after the household! Not abandon it in the hours of darkness!'

The hours, Murray thought, during which the secretary Paul Paulinson was murdered and deposited on the front doorstep. Had Trent's absence made that easier? And had the murderer known that the butler would be from home?

'Yes, you probably would lose your place,' he agreed, sticking to the principal story for now. 'So what happened with the notes?'

Trent swallowed hard, paling even at the memory.

'I was on my way home one night – not too far gone on that occasion, as it happens – when a voice came from behind me, very low and – and scary.'

'Scary?'

'It's the only word I can think of, sir. Sort of deep and whispery at the same time. And he told me not to turn round, said he had a knife, and that Sir Joshua would be delighted to hear about what his butler did at night. I – I tried to say that it was entirely innocent, that I'd just popped out for something, but he must have been watching me for he knew every night I'd been out that week, and which gin houses I'd been in, and when I'd gone home. Even I couldn't have told him some of the times and places. And then he said he wanted me to carry out a little service for him. He told me that there was a gap in the stones under the fence in the gardens in Fitzroy Square, and that he would leave notes there which were to be taken in and placed under Miss Akehurst's door without her seeing, preferably at night. I was to go and look for the notes every day, though they wouldn't be there every day. And I was to deliver them that night, without fail.'

'Or he would tell Sir Joshua about your nocturnal expeditions?'

'Exactly, sir.' He glanced around, as if the man would appear from the shrubbery and march straight off to his master. 'I couldn't let that happen, sir. Sir Joshua is most particular that his servants should not be compromised. Because of his work, you see, sir.'

'How many notes did you deliver?'

Trent had to think about that.

'Maybe a dozen, altogether?'

'Only in London? Or were there any in Brighton?'

'None in Brighton, sir. We were scarcely there long enough, but I thought perhaps we had shaken him in London.'

Murray could see the faded memory of hope in his face.

'What about here?'

'No, sir, none here.' He cleared his throat again. 'I thought to myself that maybe it was all a harmless prank, that it was an admirer of Miss Akehurst's and just a romantic way of delivering his love notes.'

'By threatening you?'

'Well, sir, not everyone thinks about how servants feel. And certainly not in this household.'

Nevertheless it had been a handy way of salving his conscience, no doubt. Murray sighed.

'Thank you, Trent.'

'I should go and pack my bags, sir.'

'You're leaving?'

'Well, sir, when you've told Sir Joshua ...'

'It's none of my business to tell him - and I think he has other things on his mind at the moment. Why don't you stay here and apply yourself to helping find Miss Akehurst? And if you have a dependable footman, why not give him the keys to the wine cellar – call it delegation, perhaps? Only you can break yourself of this habit, Trent, but you must try.'

Trent looked beyond miserable.

'But sir ... do you think the man who wrote the notes is the one she's run off with?'

'It looks like that, yes.'

'And I was responsible.'

'All the more reason to try to avoid putting yourself in that position again. Give it your best effort, Trent.'

He left the butler standing in the middle of the lawn, and strode back to the French windows, hoping that Lady Akehurst had not left the room. She had not: she was sagged in a chair very much where he had left her, and he had the impression that if one removed her stays, indelicate thought though it was, she would fold up completely. She was still clutching the note that had been found in the garden.

'May I see?' Murray asked, when he had rung the bell for brandy for her. She did not resist when he slid the paper from her fingers. The writing was bold and simple.

'Tonight,' it said, 'for I can resist no further. You will be ready.'

The very assignation, presumably. But if he had not used the butler to deliver it, how had Amanda's abductor delivered the note? And when?

He made sure that the footman who answered the bell brought brandy to Lady Akehurst and also summoned her maid to attend her. She should not, he thought, be left alone, and he needed to go and talk to Isobel. He wanted to talk to Fussy and Mr. Lawrence, too, but that would have to wait until they came back – with or without Amanda Akehurst.

'Well, now we know who delivered the notes, and why,' said Isobel. 'And that it was a man, but then we had not, I think, considered that it might be a woman.'

She was as before at her father's bedside, sketching his face. He seemed not to have moved since Murray was there last.

'No. And since Trent never saw him, and many people can assume a "scary" voice, we're not much further forward.'

'Does it prove that it was someone from outwith the household? No,' she answered her own question immediately. 'No, it doesn't – it might have been deliberately deceptive.'

'Indeed. In fact, someone within the household might have been more likely to notice Trent's problems.'

'He was certainly shaky. But who from the household would take the trouble to follow him around the gin cellars of London to gather all that information?' She waved her pencil as if she could summon the information from the air.

'I think,' said Murray, 'that if there's one thing we can definitely say about whoever is doing this, or part of this, it's that they are dedicating a good deal of time to their task. There's a deal of planning and attention to detail here, and a willingness to travel about the countryside that is impressive. Is that really because they wanted to kill Paulinson? Or because they are devoted to Amanda?'

'Devoted to Amanda's inheritance, perhaps,' said Isobel. 'Did you say you had the last note? The one that drew her away last night?'

'Yes – here.' He walked over from the window, pulled it from his pocket and handed it to her. 'Does it look like the earlier ones? Trent seemed to think so. It was the least sight of it that made him try to bolt.'

'I didn't see the earlier ones: Amanda showed them to Father, but not to me. Officially I knew nothing of them. But it certainly matches his description of them.'

'So the Akehursts know nothing of the earlier ones?'

'Nothing, as far as I know. Father couldn't decide whether or not he should tell them: he just did his best to protect her while he tried to make up his mind. Where was this found?'

'In the garden, blown into a bush, I believe.'

'Did you see it there?'

'No, one of the servants brought it in. Why?'

'Well,' she said, 'there's no sign that it was there all night, unless it was really sheltered. Look, the ink hasn't run at all, and the paper is quite dry.'

Murray took the note back, and sat down.

'You're right, of course. Now, there's a thing.'

'Isn't it?'

'Even if she had dropped it quite early this morning, rather than last night, it would have been caught in the dew.'

'Yes, it would. So who put it there? And why?'

'Not Miss Akehurst,' said Murray, 'since she was long gone, presumably. If it was her abductor, what were they trying to say? That it was an elopement, when it wasn't?'

'But she wrote that farewell note to Lady Akehurst. And anyway, could the abductor really have popped back here after the search had started, and stuck the note in a bush in the garden? The servants have been all over the grounds since she was found to have disappeared.'

'Oh,' said Murray, rubbing his forehead, 'my head is going round.'

'Mine too,' said Isobel, sitting back and sighing. 'Will you do something for me?'

'Hm? Of course – what is it?'

'I must pay a call on a man down in Cliffe. I cannot go on my own, of course, and Smith needs to stay here if I am not here. Oh, and I have just told him to go and sleep – it will have to be later.'

'Whenever you're ready. May I ask who it is?'

'Of course. You know that Father and Mr. Lawrence are joint trustees for Grandpappa?'

'For your mother's father? Yes, I think I had heard that.'

'The beneficiary of the trust, Mr. Worthing, lives in Cliffe. Father always goes to visit him when he comes to Lewes, and I think

I should go on his behalf to see that he is all right.'

'What manner of man is he?'

'Oh, quite respectable, a merchant, though he has been unfortunate.' She glanced down at her father, as if to ask how much more she should say. Discretion won, but Murray was still curious.

'Cannot Mr. Lawrence visit him, as the other trustee?'

Isobel made a face.

'Mr. Lawrence does not approve of Mr. Worthing, so any visit he made would not be a kindly one. Father always tries to make him feel – well, cared for.'

'In that case I am at your service,' said Murray.

Sitting at Blair's bedside, however, was not going to help him to find Amanda Akehurst or what had happened to her. Downstairs the house appeared to be deserted: even Ketchell had vanished. Murray walked about, trying to determine how Amanda and her lover might have left. Had the note been planted in the garden to direct their attention to the French windows? He went back out on to the terrace and stood looking up at the house. Had she left by the front door? Having met Miss Akehurst, he was fairly sure that any attempt on her part to climb down the side of the house from her bedroom window would have been unsuccessful, and besides, there was nothing to climb, no trellis nor ivy nor handy lower roof. No, a girl of her build would have been more likely to leave by a door, however romantically inclined.

He glanced round to find that Mr. Lawrence and Fussy were approaching from the direction of the summerhouse, round which several servants were still hunting.

'I'm not sure what they think they'll find there,' said Mr. Lawrence thinly, 'but it didn't stop us searching, too.'

'No sign of her, then?'

'Not since that fellow found a piece of paper in a bush,' said Fussy sadly, pointing to the servant who had brought in the note. 'But no doubt she's miles away by now.'

'Sir Joshua should be sending out messengers in every direction,' said Mr. Lawrence. 'But as Fussy says, it's probably too late. No doubt she will send word from Gretna, for I doubt if we will hear from her before then.'

'Oh, we might still catch her!' said Fussy, determined to be cheerful.

'It would be useful if we even knew what time she had left,' said Murray. 'Did either of you hear anything last night? Mr. Lawrence? Where in the house is your chamber, sir?' It was as well to prevail on Mr. Lawrence's friendliness while it lasted.

'I face the front, and I leave my windows wide open at night,' said Mr. Lawrence, subtly implying that anyone who did not was of a low moral character. 'I heard nothing at all, and I believe I should have had a horse or vehicle come near the house.'

'Even if it remained on the lane?'

'Even so, I believe,' said Mr. Lawrence with a frown. 'I have considered it at some length, and sat listening in my room an hour or so ago, and I think I should have heard a horse or a vehicle in the lane. I remember hearing an owl, for example, which must have been in the trees over on the paddock.'

'Interesting,' said Murray. 'What about you, Mr. Payne?'

Fussy grinned, ever friendly.

'I'm over at the side there, away from everything – and I had the windows tight closed! But I'm right over Amanda's room and I'm sure if she had screamed or there had been a struggle I should have heard something.'

Murray was not so sure: the house looked substantially built, and he had noticed that Sir Joshua's carpets were thick.

'When did you last see her?' he asked, and Fussy and Mr. Lawrence looked at each other.

'After dinner, wasn't it?' asked Fussy. 'When she played the pianoforte.'

'Oh, yes,' said Mr. Lawrence. 'Though she stayed in the drawing room for a little after that.'

Murray, who was musical, remembered it well.

'Did she leave the room before you both?'

'Yes,' said Mr. Lawrence, 'for Lady Akehurst suggested she should retire and continue her recuperation. You know she was injured in an incident in Brighton.'

'I had heard, yes.'

'I thought …' Fussy frowned.

'What's wrong, Mr. Payne?'

'Oh,' said Fussy, 'no doubt I'm confused. Did you also know that someone tried to snatch her from an open carriage in Hyde

Park?'

'Yes, I had heard that, too.'

'Oh, of course, Isobel will have told you. Well, I thought – but maybe I've taken it all up wrong – that the same person who tried to snatch her then was the man who attacked her in Brighton. Now, if that's the case,' he said, warming to his theme, 'would it not be more than likely that it was he who has taken her now?'

'I understood that she had gone of her own accord,' said Mr. Lawrence, disapproving.

'Well, yes, but … oh, I don't know,' said Fussy. 'Could she have been pretending to be upset after Hyde Park?'

'Was she upset?' asked Mr. Lawrence. 'I'm not sure I noticed.' Then, apparently feeling this was less charitable than the circumstances warranted, he added, 'But then Mr. Paulinson died, and everything was confusion, anyway. It was hard to know who thought what, and in a trice we were down here in Sussex.'

'I gather you were not able to attend Mr. Paulinson's funeral?'

'Good gracious, no,' said Mr. Lawrence. 'I can only conclude that Sir Joshua was most extraordinarily upset at the whole business, and wished to protect his family. Nothing else would account for it. Mr. Paulinson was, as I observed, a most devoted servant upon whom it was clear that Sir Joshua placed a great deal of reliance.'

'Do you know if he had been with Sir Joshua for long?' Again, Murray felt he ought to seize his opportunities where he found them.

'Years, yes,' said Fussy at once. 'I can't remember when he first appeared, but he must have been there ten years, anyway. Sir Joshua trusted him absolutely – he's anxious about servants, you know – and was as fond of him as he was of anyone but Amanda, I should say.'

'So was it out of character for him to vanish? I gather he went upstairs to fetch something and then could not be found.'

Mr. Lawrence shot him a sharp look.

'I hope you are not inclined to the same persistent curiosity as your friend Blair,' he said. 'I have never found such a characteristic either useful or appropriate. I have been out in this damp air for long enough: I must bid you good morning.' He stepped away as though finding the stones of the terrace not quite up to his standard. Murray looked at Fussy.

'I think it's terribly useful and appropriate,' said Fussy at once. 'That's why I told Lady Akehurst Mr. Blair would solve her problem – though I had no idea what it was. I'm sorry about my godfather. He and Mr. Blair have never seen eye to eye.'

'I know. But I can't help feeling that Blair would like me to press on with what he was being persistently curious about, particularly since he summoned me to London to look into at least part of it with him.' He sighed, at once weary of the enormity of the task and wary of talking too much, just because Fussy was sympathetic. 'I believe you and Mr. Paulinson talked, from time to time?'

'We did, yes – are you feeling the damp, too? Do you want to go indoors?'

'Not at all, if you are quite comfortable.'

'Oh yes! Perfectly. Yes, I did talk with Paulinson – I talk with everyone, you know? And I felt sorry for the fellow, always running about, barely time to sit through a whole meal without having to take some note or other for Sir Joshua, late nights at the House and early mornings writing letters and reading papers so that he could summarise them, and whatever else he did. I don't know what Sir Joshua paid him but I've no doubt it was nowhere near enough. But he was certainly valued.'

'And the evening he disappeared – did you speak with him then?'

'Only a word. I can't imagine how he vanished. It was the most extraordinary thing. And I'm sure if Sir Joshua had not been so eager to get to the House he would have stopped and made sure of what had happened, but we all thought that if Paulinson were not in his room, he must already have set out with the intention of meeting Sir Joshua at the House. When it turned out that he had not, we were all astonished.'

'Do you think he might have been hiding elsewhere in the house? In Fitzroy Square, I mean.'

'But why would he do that?'

'Did he ever mention any enemies?'

'He didn't have time to make enemies, I'm quite sure. Besides, he was a quiet, kindly sort of man. To look at him you wouldn't think he would have the energy to do all he did.'

'Subject to blackmail, perhaps?' Murray asked, thinking of Trent the butler.

'Good heavens, no! I cannot imagine anything he might have done to raise that spectre. But on the other hand, he didn't talk that much about himself – it was hard to draw him out, though I did try – so it's possible he had a dark past. But he didn't seem the type, at all. If anything, I'd have called him an innocent. I remember taking turn with him in the little park one day in Fitzroy Square – probably the longest conversation I ever had with him – and a couple of pretty young ladies passed us by. Paulinson hadn't a notion where to look, though he clearly wanted to. An innocent, as I say.'

'Oh, well … I'd better let you go and take a rest, anyway,' said Murray. 'If you think of anything, about Paulinson or about Miss Akehurst's departure, you will let me know, won't you?'

'Of course!' Fussy grinned. 'Be happy to. Anything to help Mr. Blair, too.'

When Fussy had disappeared back into the house, Murray wandered on, trying to imagine Amanda's movements last night. She was not someone who looked used to walking far, that was certain, but she had presumably walked out of the – perhaps not the front door. These French windows, then? And what happened after that? Had her lover brought a horse for her? Or a carriage? Surely that would have been very noisy if it had been close to the house – Mr. Lawrence was quite right, he would be bound to have heard it. Even a horse could have given the lovers away. But perhaps transport could have been left waiting somewhere a little further away? Not on the High Street, where it would no doubt have aroused some kind of curiosity. Where then?

He left the grounds by the main gate and glanced up and down the lane outside. To his left was the cobbled lane that would take them to the top of the High Street, where Blair had been hit by the cart. He swallowed, and added another to his manifold prayers for Blair.

The lanes were both almost empty. Only a figure that looked like Ketchell kicked around in the distance. No doubt any servants that had searched them were already further on in their exploration. Ketchell would be looking for any trace of Amanda Akehurst's passing by, presumably, like everyone else: carriage tracks, hoofprints, a dropped handkerchief – the stuff of novels. Had she gone willingly? The farewell note seemed to say so. Then why had someone felt it necessary to drop the other note in the garden?

He crossed the lane, and surveyed the extensive paddock over the wall – Shelley's, it was called, where the sheep fair took place in the summer. Lewes was a great sheep centre. But now it was quiet, with only a few horses grazing peaceably at the far end. To his right, where the lane curved gently around the edge of the paddock, there was a row of small cottages – plenty of ears there to hear a passing carriage in the night. He looked about again, and noticed to his left a gate in the paddock hedge. As far as he remembered, it led to a lane across the paddock towards the edge of the town. He strolled along – or at least, he went at the pace of a stroll, but really he felt a deep reluctance to walk any further, to look over the hedge or around the gateway, to bring an end to this unhappy search. But something drew him on, slowly, along the lane, drew his hand to unlatch the wooden gate, drew his feet on to the path, drew his gaze to the right and then to the left, and down into the ditch under the hedge, down to a black, lumpy shape bundled into the yellowing grass at the paddock's edge. He stepped delicately towards it, and crouched down, extending a long, gloved finger to pull back a fold of the black cloth.

It was Amanda Akehurst, of course, and she was dead.

Chapter Twenty

He stood for a long moment, a grim sense of the inevitable settling heavily about him. Though he knew he should hurry back to the house and tell Lady Akehurst the bad news, he was sure it would not harm her to have the tidings delayed for the moment or two it would take him to carry out a small investigation. Once servants had hurried about with stretchers and people had lifted and tidied her, little details could easily be lost, he knew. He pulled off his glove and laid the back of his bare fingers against her white cheek: she was quite cold, yet the night had not been particularly chilly. He was sure she had been dead for some hours. He closed her pale eyes gently, and surveyed the rest of her. Her hands seemed to be bundled beneath her as she lay on her stomach, as if perhaps she had fallen forwards and crumpled over them, but he pulled a little on her shoulder and found that she was quite stiff. Her feet, he discovered in a minute, were bare and grubby, as if she had walked a little distance but not through mud. Back to her head, he pulled the hood back gently to find her hair in a tousled plait, and beneath the cloak, as far as he could see, was her night dress. The back of her collar was white and fine with embroidery: the front was black with blood. It looked very much as if, like Mr. Paulinson, Amanda had had her throat cut, and thoroughly, this time.

He laid the hood back as best he could, tucking it under her, and stood, head bowed. Poor girl: whatever she had contributed to her departure from the house, she had not deserved this.

Back at the paddock gate, he looked about until he saw one of the Akehurst servants, recognisable by his livery, coming back down the lane from the High Street, still casting glances from side to side as though Miss Akehurst might be hiding behind a prominent cobble. He called him over.

'Stay here, will you, while I fetch … heavens, whom? Miss Akehurst is dead.'

The servant slapped the back of his sleeve across his mouth at the sight of the black bundle in the ditch, but drew himself up quickly and nodded, establishing himself by the gate. Murray ran back to the house, arriving just in time: Dr. Mantell was leaving by the front door. Stern-faced, he came to the paddock gate with Murray, and sent the servant for something on which Miss Akehurst could be carried back to the house.

'I fear breaking the news to either of the Akehursts,' he said to Murray, thinking aloud. 'He is in a very delicate condition as regards his heart, and she is already deeply upset by all this. Do you know the family well? Is there another person I could speak with?'

'I have only just met them yesterday,' said Murray, surprising himself. 'I believe Mr. Payne, a young man staying with them, is related in some way to the family.'

'Then perhaps he would be best, or would know best. They are quite new to the town and I've scarcely met them before,' he added as an excuse.

'As I say, I've only just met them myself,' said Murray. 'But I know Mr. Payne a little better. I'll go and find him.' He turned and was about to leave, when it occurred to him that Dr. Mantell, who was about his own age, seemed a sympathetic man and of some intelligence. 'Look, I've had some experience with this kind of business before – murder, that is.'

'In North Britain?' Dr. Mantell's eyes were bright, mind already at work.

'Yes – and elsewhere. If you are to examine her, will you please keep your eyes open for anything unusual? I am sure you would anyway …'

'Ha! There are many country doctors who would not!' said Dr. Mantell. 'Anything for an easy life. But you are right, Mr. Murray, I am afflicted with a nosiness not always shared by my colleagues. I shall indeed keep my eyes open.'

'Thank you,' said Murray, and went to look for Fussy Payne.

'Oh! Oh, good gracious!' exclaimed Fussy, agitating his waistcoat buttons in his distress. 'Are you quite sure – sure that it is Amanda?'

'Fairly sure,' said Murray. 'I only met her yesterday. It would be strange, though, for one person to be missing and another found.' He had been glad to find Fussy alone, and not in the company of his godfather Mr. Lawrence. One challenge at a time, he thought.

'And that would mean a tragedy for someone else, too,' said Fussy. 'No, if it is so I should not wish it on others. But oh, dear, poor Lady Akehurst! Poor Sir Joshua!'

'Will you be so good as to come, then, and look at her? Dr. Mantell is with her, but he knew her no better than I did, I believe,' said Murray. 'And at present I don't think I can ask either of the Akehursts.'

'No, no, not at all. Of course I'll come. Of course I'll come,' he repeated, as if to steel himself to the task. He pulled out a shining white handkerchief and swiped his forehead generously. 'Oh, this is terrible. Terrible.'

Murray led him outside and along the lane to the gate. Dr. Mantell was still with the body, crouched down. He had folded back the cloak rather further than Murray had, and it was very clear that Amanda was in her night clothes, now soiled and muddy. Fussy blinked, perhaps as much at the impropriety as at the presence of death. Then he pulled back his shoulders, and walked forward.

'Yes,' he said, 'that is Amanda. Oh, my poor girl! Oh, dear, dear me.' The handkerchief reappeared and this time he held to his mouth and nose, his eyes squeezed with tears. He turned away.

'Well, she was indeed murdered,' said Dr. Mantell to Murray, 'and most likely here where you found her. There's plenty of blood on the grass.'

'A cut throat?' Murray asked.

'That's right. There's bruising on her wrists here,' he added, for he had turned her on to her side. Amanda's jaw hung as it must have set when she fell. 'I think someone grabbed her by the wrists. I doubt she came out voluntarily in her night gown with no slippers.'

'No, though she is wearing a cloak. Perhaps that was convenient, though: it would be harder to see her in the dark.'

'When did she disappear?'

'Sometime last night. She was last seen by her maid when she went to bed, and only missed this morning when her maid went to waken her.'

'No doubt she went soon after the household retired for the night,' said Mantell. 'She's been dead for hours. Rigor is beginning to pass off.'

'I wish,' said Fussy, somewhat recovered, 'I wish she had said something about her plans. She must have known something was to happen. She left a note!'

That note, thought Murray. He was not entirely satisfied with that. Was it really in Amanda's handwriting? He had no way of telling, but he could see if anyone else agreed with Lady Akehurst's identification. But if it were definitely her hand, then why was she here in nightclothes and bare feet? Surely she would have been dressed, packed and ready to go?

They followed the sombre stretcher back to the house, with an old sheet covering their sad find. It was not, Murray was sure, up to Miss Akehurst's usual standards. She would not have liked this at all.

The servants took the stretcher into an under-used billiard room on the ground floor, and stood guard lest someone wander in without knowing. Murray and Dr. Mantell took Fussy into the parlour, and rang for brandy. Harry Holden was already in there, apparently talking with Beatrix and with Lieutenant Munnings. He turned, grey-faced, when they appeared.

'They tell me Amanda's disappeared. What's going on, Fussy?'

'My dear Harry, it's worse than that,' said Fussy at once, going to Harry and laying a hand on his arm. 'We've just brought her body back. She's been dead since last night.'

'Dead!' cried Beatrix. 'Oh, no!' She turned to Lieutenant Munnings, who took her arm at once to support her.

'My dear, do not alarm yourself!' he said, with a concerned look. Murray noted it: was Beatrix lining up a new protector?

'Amanda's dead?' Harry gaped, looking sick. 'Dead? Not eloped? I thought she had eloped. That's what they told me.' He glanced at Beatrix and Munnings, questioning and a little accusing. 'What happened – did the horse bolt?'

'I'm afraid she was murdered, Mr. Holden,' said Murray. 'This is the doctor who confirmed it.'

Harry sank into a chair, staring at nothing.

'Amanda dead ... This will kill Lady Akehurst,' he murmured, surprisingly. 'What will she do?'

'We'll have to break it very gently to both the Akehursts,' said Fussy, sitting opposite him. 'Sir Joshua's heart is so delicate.'

'We should tell Lady Akehurst first,' said Dr. Mantell firmly. 'She is stronger, and can help when Sir Joshua is told. I can do it, if you wish.'

'I certainly think you should be on hand,' said Fussy. 'Oh, this is very bad, very bad indeed. We should have a woman, too, when we tell Lady Akehurst.'

'Her maid?' suggested Dr. Mantell.

'A lady, too, perhaps, for strength,' said Fussy. 'Perhaps Miss Blair would come down? I know she is attending her father at present, but –'

'I could come,' said Beatrix, with a proper air of modesty. 'I have been with Lady Akehurst for a little time this morning and I believe she would trust me as much as she might trust any stranger. I should be happy to be of service.'

Murray saw Munnings squeeze Beatrix's arm encouragingly. Yes, she had certainly made a swift conquest there.

'Well, then,' said Fussy, 'there we are: Dr. Mantell, we take our lead from you, sir. Miss Paterson, lead the way. The sooner we do this, the better, before rumours spread.'

Sensible Fussy followed the physician and Beatrix out of the parlour, though Murray could see that he was clenching his fists in anxiety. They left the door ajar, perhaps hoping for a swift return. Murray did not envy them their task.

Harry Holden still sat desolate on his chair. Munnings stood by the window.

'If she is found, I should be getting back to Newhaven,' he said. 'If Sir Joshua no longer needs me. And if my horse is fit.'

'What happened to your semaphore tower?' Murray asked, as much for conversation as anything. He needed a moment to take in everything that had been happening.

'It wasn't even a semaphore tower, to be fair,' said Munnings. 'It was only half built.'

'Oh, like the one at Coombe Warren?'

'I believe so, yes. They are all at much the same stage – or were, until yesterday morning. I live in a small cottage next to the building, and in the early hours I woke to strange lights and a smell of smoke. And there, the whole thing was in flames. The timber is all gone, and the new brickwork damaged, too. We shall need to wait until we can get more wood.'

'An accident?'

Munnings met his eye.

'I don't believe so,' he said. 'For one thing, it was raining. For another, I smelled gunpowder straightaway, and there is none kept on the site.'

'That on its own would be enough to upset Sir Joshua, I should think,' said Murray, 'without everything else. He seems devoted to his semaphore towers.'

'That's why I came straight to him, or to a hope of communicating with him,' Munnings agreed. 'It has been under his personal oversight from the start. But you'll not find a naval man who doesn't approve: it's the quickest way by far to let the Admiralty know what is happening on the coast. And, of course, for the Admiralty to send its orders back.' He made this sound like a secondary consideration. 'It's an excellent system.'

'Why do you think anyone would have burned down the tower, then?'

Munnings made a face.

'It must be the French, I suppose. I mean, that's why Sir Joshua is building them: he thinks there is still a problem with French revolutionaries coming into England. Look at all that's been happening this year, after all: Cato Street, and the problems up in Glasgow and in the north-west.'

'Problems all over the place,' said Harry Holden unexpectedly. 'Europe and Brazil and everywhere. And the Royal Family dropping like flies. Paulinson dead. Amanda attacked and now she's dead, too. It's bad times, maybe the worst of times. That's why I drink,' he added. 'No point in anything else.'

Murray and Munnings stared at him for a moment. It had not occurred to Murray to ask Harry why he lived the way he did: if anything he thought Harry was under Ketchell's bad influence. He felt a little guilty.

'Anyway,' said Holden, stretching his legs and standing up slowly, 'do you think they've told her yet? Told my aunt?'

'I imagine they will have,' said Murray.

'Then I'd better go to her. There's nothing can be done, of course. Nothing at all.'

He left the room, pulling the door gently shut behind him.

'A melancholic?' asked Munnings.

'It seems so.'

'Well, as I said, I must go back to Newhaven if my horse is recovered. There's a deal of work to be done. Um, Miss Paterson expressed an interest in seeing the site: if she cared to visit with friends, I should be very happy to show her around and let her see – well, what's left, anyway.'

With a wistful glance across the hall to the stairs, in case Beatrix might appear, Munnings disappeared to the front door. Murray was left alone in the parlour, the miasma of the news of Amanda and Harry Holden's dark mood still lingering in the air. He decided to go up and see Isobel.

'It's what Father feared,' she said. 'He knew she was in danger.'

'I feel I've failed him.'

'Oh, and I, too!' She drew a deep breath. 'We have failed, but I'm not sure we could ever have succeeded. She was an obstinate, romantic, spoilt girl, God rest her soul: she would have broken away to be with whoever it is, whatever we had done.'

'Not if we had found him and shown her what he was, before she had the chance.'

'But how?' Isobel was nearly as miserable as Harry Holden. 'How can we find out who this is? He appears in the middle of the Grand Strut, in broad daylight, and tries to snatch her. He vanishes as if he has never been. He threatens the butler – the butler! Not a mere kitchenmaid, but the butler! – because he knows enough about the household to be able to. He follows us to Brighton and manages to get into the Royal Pavilion, during a reception, and attacks her again, and again escapes! Then he entices her down from her chamber in the middle of the night, in her grandparents' house, and takes her off in her nightclothes, with no shoes, and leaves her dead in a ditch. And no one even has the least idea who he might be! What is he, some kind of warlock?'

'You saw him,' said Murray, concerned to see her so upset. 'He must have seemed human to you.'

'He could have been a kelpie,' she said, crossly.

'I don't think kelpies wander as far as Hyde Park,' said Murray. 'They tend to stick to Scottish rivers.'

'Don't laugh at me,' she snapped. 'I'm not in the mood.'

'Of course not. But it wasn't the Park I meant. Didn't you see Miss Akehurst leaving the reception with a man?'

She sat up.

'No, I didn't, you know. But Fussy did. In all the drama about who was in the passage when she was found, I had forgotten that.'

'How clearly did he see the man?'

She frowned, trying to remember.

'I'm not sure. Not that clearly. But I imagine Fussy would have mentioned it if he had been wearing a mask, anyway.'

'Could he have been the same man?'

'I don't know. All he said, I think, was that the man was dark. And the man in the park was dark-haired, too. His brows were dark.'

Murray sighed.

'Shall we go and take that walk to Cliffe that you wanted to do? I think a little while away from this house would do you good.'

She blinked at him, forgetting for a moment.

'Oh, yes! I'll ring for my maid, and she can call Smith if he's needed.' She looked down at Blair on the bed. 'If he's needed, one way or the other,' Murray heard her mutter. 'Wake up, Father, please.'

But the shrunken figure on the bed did not move.

Out on the gravel circle that led to the front gate, Murray could feel Isobel's fingers gradually relaxing on his arm. They would have to return quickly, of course, even though Blair was in good hands, but an hour or so outside in the fresh air and away from the Akehursts and their problems would do Isobel some good, he hoped – and perhaps him, too. He was pleased to see that they had finally – or the rain had finally – washed the last traces of Blair's blood from the top of the lane. Isobel must have known that that was where her father's accident had happened, but she paused only briefly to look about her before she took a firm grip on Murray's arm again, and turned resolutely to walk down the hill into the town. He had walked with her many times before and felt easy with her there beside him, yet there was something more to it on this occasion: perhaps he sensed an extra level of responsibility for her, with Blair incapacitated.

They passed the White Hart, and to their surprise saw Barnabas Ketchell appear in the doorway. He was looking up and down the street as if expecting someone, and noticed them almost at once.

'Good day to you again,' he said. 'They serve an excellent ale in here, much finer than anything Sir Joshua's cellars can offer.'

'You've missed the news, I believe,' said Murray. 'Miss Akehurst has been found.'

Ketchell raised his eyebrows. His eyes were raw egg white yellow.

'Have they caught the fellow, then?'

'No. Unfortunately he had done his work: she was found dead.'

Ketchell's eyes flickered.

'Unfortunate, indeed. Sir Joshua will be – more than devastated.' He said no more, but Murray had the sense that he was genuinely concerned.

'The physician is with him.'

'I should return. I'm not sure what I could do, but I should return.' Ketchell seemed more disturbed by the news than Murray would have expected. He bowed and left them abruptly, striding purposefully up the High Street.

'I don't like him, I'm afraid,' said Isobel.

'I don't think we're required to. Not even by Mr. Ketchell,' said Murray. She half-smiled, and they walked on.

'Tell me about Mr. Worthing,' he said, after a moment of pondering a change of subject.

'Oh, I have never met him,' said Isobel, 'but I know my father likes him. He was the son of a clergyman – one of the dissenting brotherhood – who was a friend of my grandfather's. He was well-to-do, but lost his fortune in some financial scandal, I believe. And his wife died. My grandfather felt sorry for him, for – well, his politics have not altogether helped him, and he had trouble recovering.'

'Are his politics radical, then?'

'I believe so. Of course, my father does not mind any man's

politics as long as he believes he is an honourable man, but Mr. Lawrence was never going to approve. My grandfather was a bit of a mischief maker!'

'He may have thought it would be a good balance. Is there much money in the trust?'

'A comfortable amount in land, as I understand it. More income, I should have thought, than he requires to live in Cliffe. But he has lived here since he was in the depths of his poverty and perhaps he has an attachment to the place. It is an odd setting, I think, tucked under the headland like that. I should not like to live beneath an outcrop of land.'

Cliffe was as busy around the river as it had been the previous day when Murray and Robbins had come to look for the carter. Beyond the river, towards the cliff that Isobel so distrusted, the crowds thinned a little, but it still had the air of a place where people had plenty to do and were keen to get on with it. A church, St. Thomas', sat solid on their left, and on their right, in a row of decent but small houses, was the door that Isobel approached. For a moment they hesitated: from within that, or one of the close-neighbouring houses, came the sound of raised voices. But it was hard to tell where they were coming from, and in a moment they subsided. Murray knocked at a knocker.

'Is Mr. Worthing at home?' he asked, when a maid appeared. She was elderly, but neatly attired.

'Please to come in, sir, madam,' said the maid. 'I will go and see.'

Inside, they found themselves immediately in a small, bare parlour. One hard chair sat by a deal table on which a couple of books lay open: there would have been little room for more than two. The mantelpiece held two candlesticks of base metal and a religious print, depicting, as far as Murray could see in the dim light, Abraham finding the sheep to sacrifice instead of his son. A shelf held a Bible and a number of pamphlets, the nature of which Murray could not quite make out, but if Worthing were as radical as Isobel said, Murray could guess. Over the back of the chair lay an overcoat, carefully spread out as if it had been drying. To his surprise, it looked as if it might be the most expensive article in the room. The wool was fine, the buttons well made, the lining as good as he would expect in his own wardrobe, if not better. It was dark, navy or black perhaps, and made, as far as one could see, for a tallish man of good width in his shoulders. He was about to look more closely when the maid returned.

'I'm sorry, sir, madam, I thought the master was at home, but he seems to have gone out. I couldn't say when he might be back, though: he never mentioned that he was expecting visitors. He's not long back in town.'

'That's quite all right,' said Isobel, clearly conscious of the size of the parlour and how much they might be in the way if they stayed, 'we can call again. Please tell him that Mr. Blair's daughter called to see if he was well, and left her compliments.'

'Mr. Blair's daughter, of course, madam,' said the maid, with a curtsey. 'I'll be sure to tell the master the minute he returns.'

Back in the street, Murray and Isobel stood for a moment, at a loss for what to do now but return to the Akehursts'.

'Shall we walk as far as the cliff?' Murray asked. 'Just for exercise – then we can turn back.'

'Yes, why not?' Isobel turned in that direction. 'It's odd, though, isn't it? A house that size – you would think she would know at once when Mr. Worthing had gone out.'

'And he left his overcoat,' said Murray.

'Well, never mind,' said Isobel. 'I don't want another mystery bothering my head at the moment. Perhaps he hadn't shaved this morning and did not want to be embarrassed.'

Murray laughed. At the end of Cliffe's High Street they reached the cliff itself, and a junction with the road that led to Uckfield in one direction and Glynde in the other. They paused again, indecisive.

At that moment two figures appeared from behind a wall a little distance down the road to their right. They had their backs to Murray and Isobel, and for a moment Murray looked blankly at them, not expecting to know either of them. But then something about the smaller man caught his attention.

'Wait,' he said, completely taken aback, 'wait. That's my groom. That's Young Donald.'

Chapter Twenty-One

'Well – why not?' asked Isobel, even as Murray let go of her arm.

'Because he disappeared in London. What's he doing here? Excuse me, Isobel,' he gabbled, and took off at his best long-legged speed down the road.

Before he reached them, the two figures had separated, and the taller, dark-haired man, without even looking around, had vanished oblivious back down the lane from which they had emerged. Young Donald, though, turned at the sound of running footsteps, recognised Murray, and began to run towards him. Murray slowed, relieved.

'Sir!' cried Donald, 'Sir, I've found you at last! Thank the Lord!'

'Donald, how did you get here? Where have you been? What happened?' Murray slapped the young man on the shoulder, and drew him back at once towards Isobel. He could not leave her unescorted in the middle of the street. 'Come back to the inn: your uncle has been desperate to see you!'

'Sir, it's all my own fault: I'm so sorry, sir,' said Donald, hurrying after him. 'I was a fool – dazzled by London – I got lost and couldn't find my way back.'

'I thought that was probably the case. How on earth did you find us? You shouldn't have gone out on your own.'

'I know, sir, I'm so sorry. I thought I'd never see anyone I knew ever again!'

'Sorry, Isobel,' Murray said as soon as they were back with her. 'This is my groom, who seems to have taken a wrong turn in London but he's found us again. Well done, anyway, Donald.'

'Thank you, sir.'

'I'd better take you back to your uncle. Isobel, are you ready to go back? We could walk a little longer if you wish.'

'I'd better go back,' said Isobel, eyeing the groom with some curiosity. At least, Murray thought, that was one mystery solved. He offered her his arm and they walked back along Cliffe's High Street and over the bridge to Lewes again.

'Have you been all right?' Murray asked, looking over his shoulder at Donald. 'I'm sure you're starving. Make sure Robbins sees to it that you're properly fed, and perhaps a bath would be in order. Have you been sleeping rough?' He was still so taken aback to have found his missing servant that his head was spinning. Isobel was saying nothing.

'I met very kind people along the way, sir,' said Donald. 'I've been very fortunate.'

'That's good, that's very good.' He was starting to talk like Fussy, he thought, and made himself slow down and stop gabbling. 'Here, this is the inn – the White Hart. Don't lose it! Though Lewes is a good deal smaller than London, and without quite so many of the temptations to lure you out on your own. Your uncle will be round in the stables, no doubt.'

'Aye, sir.'

'Good to have you back, Donald!'

'Thank you, sir.' Donald nodded and grinned, then bowed and went round to find the stable yard.

'How did he lose himself?' asked Isobel dubiously.

'He went out to explore, I think, and missed his way.'

'At Fitzroy Square?'

'Yes – he was very excited about visiting London. In a way I was not entirely surprised, but he's the nephew of my coachman, and Old Donald was very upset about it.'

'But how did he find you?'

'He must have found his way back to Fitzroy Square and asked. We left word for him, but I did suggest that he should stay there and wait for us, not follow us down here, in case we missed each other on the way.'

'He's been very lucky, then.'

'Yes, indeed.'

'That's not a Fife accent, nor yet an Edinburgh one, I think,' she went on. He wondered a little at her curiosity, but then Isobel had inherited her father's interest in people of all stations and kinds.

'He's from the west, from Renfrew. He was living in Glasgow when the disturbances started, and had some connexion with one of the protestors, innocently. He decided it was safer to leave, and came to his uncle, my coachman. He's been making himself useful as a groom, though it wasn't his trade before – he's very good with the horses, and nimble about the carriage.'

'How these disturbances affect everyone in the end! Poor Sir Joshua, nearly shot in the spring by the Cato Street men, and now he's consumed with building semaphore towers to defeat a new French invasion.'

'And your father and Mr. Lawrence quarrelling over the politics of your grandfather's protégé.'

She gave a half-laugh, and shrugged.

'Oh, Father and Mr. Lawrence would find something to quarrel about even if politics had never been thought of!'

They fell silent, making their way up the gentle rise of the High Street with its smart new houses and eccentric old ones, brick, and sliced flint roundels, and proud stucco. There were plenty of obstacles to take up their thoughts: carters and cattle, and street sellers and sheep, schoolboys freed from their lessons, housewives marketing, and pensioners sitting out to take a little air in between showers. Murray slid a look sideways at Isobel and wondered if she were thinking still about her father, or if she were applying her able mind to the question of Amanda and her fate. No doubt, if she came up with any bright ideas, she would tell him. They knew that between them they had to do something to help the Akehursts. When Blair awoke – if he awoke – the knowledge that he might have told the Akehursts about Amanda's love letters, perhaps in time to save her from her fate, would hurt him badly. And even if they cared nothing for the Akehursts, to find the killer and bring him to justice would alleviate things for Blair. But helping the Akehursts was going to be difficult, if they were both wrapped up in Sir Joshua's illness.

As it happened, that was made easier for Murray the moment he stepped into the Akehursts' house. The butler, Trent, approached uneasily.

'Sir, Sir Joshua asked if you would come and speak with him on your return. At your convenience, of course, sir,' he added, as if Sir Joshua himself had tacked that on as an afterthought. Murray looked at Isobel.

'Of course,' he said. Isobel nodded, and made for the stairs to return to her father. Trent stood waiting. 'Where is he?'

'Oh, in the library, sir.' He began to lead the way, then stopped. 'Please, sir, you won't tell him?'

'About the notes? It might have to come out, but I'll not tell him unless I have to,' said Murray. He wondered what it was about the Akehursts that made it so easy to want to keep secrets from them: Blair had not told them about the love letters, and now here Murray was, siding with a butler he barely knew.

The library, as a room, was a disappointment. Most of the shelves were empty, freshly painted. The books must not yet have been unpacked. Crates were scattered about, some of them open. Sir Joshua caught him looking.

'I find it calming to dream of where I shall put everything,' he said. 'I like things to be organised.'

He was on a daybed in the centre of the room, feet towards a cosy fire, head and shoulders propped on a couple of very fine pillows. His face was still a very bad colour.

'I am glad to find you so much more recovered than report suggested, sir,' said Murray.

'Report is usually a very poor physician,' said Sir Joshua grimly. 'Will you take a seat?'

'Thank you.' The chair which had clearly been placed for him was upright and hard. He leaned back comfortably in it and crossed his legs.

'Now, I have an idea that it might be valuable for us to have this interview,' said Sir Joshua, 'though I have perforce seen little of you. Murray, isn't it? Of – er, Lethe?'

'Letho, sir, in Fife. A small estate. You'll know the Scotch way of naming men after their lands.'

'I suppose … And you are a friend of Mr. Blair?'

'I am. For many years. He studied law alongside my own father.'

'He seems a respectable, if outlandish, individual,' said Sir Joshua dubiously. 'I pride myself on being a good judge of men, but

Mr. Blair, I confess, has puzzled me.'

'He puzzles many,' said Murray with a smile, 'but he is both respectable and honourable.'

'I don't know,' said Sir Joshua with a touch of petulance that Murray put down to his illness, 'my wife wishes all kinds of people on my household. Fussy, of course, is a kinsman of my own – my late sister's grandson – but then there is his godfather Lawrence, and that creature Harry Holden, and then Mr. Blair.'

'Mr. Blair himself was not clear why he had been invited to join you,' said Murray, not mentioning that he had found the reason for himself.

'He was worried about Amanda,' said Sir Joshua, and his voice tripped over the name.

'He was. I believe that was why he asked me to come down from Edinburgh and meet him.'

'Why was he worried? Why did he not mention this to me?'

'She had told him that she had received notes from a man.' He drew in a deep breath to continue: the matter was open now. 'She was intrigued by them, but he was worried. He thought they were threatening and controlling. She, so I am told, found them romantic. I should imagine he encouraged her to tell you or Lady Akehurst herself.'

Sir Joshua gave him a sharp look.

'Is that why he accompanied them to the Park that day? Was he trying to protect her?'

'I have not had the chance to speak to him myself, of course,' said Murray, 'but yes, I believe he was doing his best.'

There was a long moment, where Murray waited for Sir Joshua's anger.

'And he did save her that day, from what I am told,' said Sir Joshua at last. 'My wife was taken aback at his actions, but I see now what he was doing. And there was some talk of Miss Blair attacking the assailant with her umbrella.'

'Was there?' Murray almost laughed. 'Good for her!'

Sir Joshua frowned.

'But in the end, of course … He could not be there to protect her last night. Mr. Murray, I will not deceive you: Amanda was the dearest person in the world to me. The hope of seeing her happily settled in her own household, one day with her own family about her

– that was my dream. Someone has taken that from me, and I will be revenged.'

He gritted his teeth, and Murray, braced to ring for a servant, wondered if he were suffering further pain, but he appeared to be struggling to calm himself. When he had drawn a long, sighing breath and relaxed again on his pillows, Murray ventured,

'Have you a plan, Sir Joshua?'

Akehurst gave Murray an assessing look.

'I am at a disadvantage,' he said. 'My secretary – my right hand man – was taken from me in London. There is no one here I trust to help, and I cannot do this myself.' He waved a hand in frustration, taking in the length of his frail body. 'Harry is completely unreliable, and Fussy is far too generous and kind: he would excuse anyone anything. I barely know Mr. Lawrence, though I understand he is to be a neighbour if we remain in Lewes.' He did not even mention Ketchell, Murray noted, which was fair enough.

'What about someone like Lieutenant Munnings?' Murray asked.

'Munnings has work of his own to do. The semaphore towers are of vital importance. Besides, he works for the Admiralty, not for me. No, I am asking you if you will help me. I am a good judge of men, as I told you, and I trust you, up to a point. Mr. Blair had already called on you for your help. Fussy tells me that you are reliable and intelligent. You must help me.'

Murray thought of Blair, helpless in his bed upstairs, and Amanda, foolish but innocent. He knew where his duty lay, and nodded.

'I'll do what I can.'

'Very well,' said Sir Joshua. 'Then off you go and make a start.'

'If I may, sir –' Murray raised a hand before Akehurst could dismiss him, 'if you are not too tired by the conversation, I can make a start by asking you some questions.'

'Asking me?'

'Of course. As the head of the household, and as Miss Akehurst's dearest kin,' he added, as delicately as he could. It would not do to have the master thinking himself above giving information.

'Well …' Akehurst considered. 'Well, I suppose it will help

you to establish some background. As you say, Mr. Blair has had no chance to tell you himself.' He seemed not to think of Isobel as a possible conduit of information, and Murray did not enlighten him. 'Amanda is the daughter of my late son, who died at Trafalgar. Her mother died at her birth. We have brought her up ever since. Needless to say, she has wanted for nothing, either material or emotional: what love a mother or father could give her, she has received in abundance from my wife and me.'

'Of course.'

'My wife has been in the business of finding a suitable husband for Amanda. There are, I believe, a number of young fellows interested, many of them titled, of course, and all of good family. There has been a good deal of social activity in London, and they were starting again in Brighton. This fellow put a stop to all that in both places. It was almost as if he did not want Amanda to marry.'

'And why might that be?' Murray asked.

'Well, it's obvious,' said Akehurst. 'They didn't want some husband getting his hands on my fortune. On Amanda's fortune, when I was gone. Only now she's gone first ...' He took a moment to pull himself back from that thought. Murray waited until he was ready again.

'And now that that will not happen,' he said gently, 'where will the money go?'

'Well, to Fussy, of course,' said Akehurst. 'Sister's grandson, remember?'

'No one else?'

'No one else left,' said Akehurst bleakly. 'Family's dying out. I suppose young Harry Holden – wife's grand-nephew, yes? – might think he has some kind of claim, but I'd leave nothing to him. Might as well hand it over to some cheap Cyprian directly, and have her spend it on gin.'

Murray was inclined to agree. But Fussy as the heir, now – that was an interesting thought. Not that he could see Fussy riding across Hyde Park to snatch Miss Akehurst from her carriage.

'May I ask, Sir Joshua, what happened to your secretary?'

A fleeting twitch of pain passed over Sir Joshua's face.

'Paul Paulinson? What does that have to do with Amanda?'

'As I understand it, they were both killed the same way. And both, of course, were closely connected with you.'

Sir Joshua's eyebrows rose high.

'You think it was the same man?' His breathing quickened. 'The same man killed Paulinson? And my grand-daughter?'

'It is only a possibility,' said Murray, trying to calm him. Sir Joshua looked away and again forced his own agitation under control with slow, concentrated breaths. At last he turned back.

'Paulinson disappeared one evening. He went upstairs to fetch something and was never seen again until he was found on the doorstep next morning.'

'But you sent someone upstairs to look for him at the time, presumably.'

'I did – I sent the butler to fetch him. Paulinson was not in his room.'

'Did the butler look elsewhere for him? In other rooms?'

'What would he be doing in other rooms?' asked Akehurst waspishly. 'When Trent didn't find him, I thought he must have misunderstood me and gone on to the House, thinking I had gone ahead. But when I arrived at the House I found he had not been there. I thought I must have missed him and returned home again, but Paulinson was not there, either.'

'Did you start any kind of search for him?'

Akehurst shrugged.

'I had no idea where to look, after dark – and he was the kind of man you thought must have had a good reason for whatever he was doing. He was eminently sensible. I assumed there would be an explanation on his return.'

'Had he ever done anything like this before?'

'Never – he was completely reliable. I would not have employed him otherwise. I trusted him in all my work. He was invaluable to me.'

Paulinson was invaluable, Amanda was the dearest person in the world. Sir Joshua had indeed been unfortunate recently.

'But then he was found dead. Have you any idea who might have done this?'

'Political radicals,' said Akehurst with venom. 'The same type as the Cato Street mob. Determined to undermine the Government, open the door to French republicans, destroy the country.' His breathing sped up slightly again, but he managed to slow it without a fuss this time. Either he was improving, or the thought of radicals was less disturbing than the thought of a conspiracy that could take from him both his secretary and his grand-daughter in the course of a couple of weeks.

'And Miss Akehurst?' asked Murray. 'Have you any idea who could have done all this?'

'Some suitor, after her fortune,' said Sir Joshua. He sounded tired, as well he might.

'That might work for an abduction,' said Murray, 'but someone after her fortune would not have killed her, would they?'

'Then what on earth were they up to?' Akehurst was definitely drowsy now. 'You need to find out for me, Murray. Go and make a start.'

'But I felt in dire need of some food and a moment or two to think,' Murray explained to Robbins. Back at the White Hart, Robbins had been overseeing some necessary laundry that they had been unable to accomplish in London or Brighton. He was happy to fetch some meat and bread for Murray. The White Hart was a superior kind of inn: the food arrived on china plates, the accompanying claret in rather good glassware. The parlour was panelled, well-furnished with comfortable cushioning and a neat little fire, and quiet – and entirely without traces of the Akehurst household. Murray began to relax just a little.

'We haven't been without distractions, sir,' Robbins agreed. 'That Ketchell was here earlier, too.'

'I saw him leaving. He said he'd been here for the ale.'

'I wasn't aware that they served ale upstairs to passing drinkers,' said Robbins primly. 'I met him on the landing, and I thought he'd come down from the top floor.'

'I always have the impression that Ketchell is up to more than he admits,' said Murray. 'I wonder what it is this time?'

'He has always taken an interest in Miss Paterson, sir,' said Robbins.

'Has she a room upstairs?' Murray had been reluctant to know where Beatrix was staying.

'She has not yet left the town, sir.'

'But she wasn't here in the inn earlier,' said Murray. 'She was at the Akehursts, flirting with Lieutenant Munnings and helping

Lady Akehurst.'

'Indeed, sir?'

'So it couldn't have been her that Ketchell was visiting, anyway. Is Rosie still here?'

'I suppose so, sir. I should find out: perhaps she has gone to the Akehursts' house.'

'Well,' said Murray, swallowing the last piece of beef, 'at least there is one mystery solved. Did you see that Young Donald is back?'

Robbins smiled.

'I did, sir. That was a great relief!'

'The lad has some intelligence, anyway, to trace us to here. I haven't heard his whole story: I think he was embarrassed at losing himself in London.'

'He should never have gone out on his own in the first place,' said Robbins severely.

'He was clearly excited at the idea of London. I should have suggested someone take him around safely to a few places, to calm him down.'

'You had other things to think about, sir. How is Mr. Blair?'

The joy at the thought of Young Donald's return immediately dissipated.

'He's in a bad way, Robbins. If you want to go up and see Smith again, then please do. He's much distressed.'

'Has anyone worked out what Mr. Blair was doing outside at that time of the night, sir?'

'No, I don't believe they have. Presumably he was pursuing the man who ran out in front of him, as the carter told us. And since Blair was in his night clothes he must have seen the man from the house – was he breaking in? Or perhaps he was looking the place over, preparing to abduct Amanda – why didn't I think of that before? That's obvious! What did the carter say he looked like?'

'Not tall and thinnish, wearing clothes but no cloak or overcoat, and boots,' said Robbins smartly after a moment's thought. 'It's not very helpful, sir.'

'Not very. It must have been someone not within the household, though, I suppose. Why did he kill Miss Akehurst, Robbins? Why did he kill her, when it looked so much as if he wanted to abduct her?'

'He tried to kill her in Brighton, though, sir, didn't he?'

'If it was the same person ... Well, let's think: what if he intended from the start to kill her? Why wait till now?'

'Too hard to get to her, sir. She's always with her grandmother.'

'Maybe. Isobel says that Lady Akehurst was not the most attentive of chaperones.'

'And it seems he did take her from under Lady Akehurst's nose in Brighton, sir.'

'Yes, though it's possible he was building on his earlier notes by that stage. Otherwise would even Amanda have gone out of the reception with a strange young man?'

'So the flirtation was all aimed at getting her away where she could be murdered, then, sir?'

'Maybe so. Maybe that's what Blair feared all along.'

'Well, sir, it looks that way. But then there's the other big question, sir: why? Why did he want to kill her?'

Chapter Twenty-Two

'That, indeed, is an important question. Who on earth would want to kill Amanda Akehurst?'

'Who is the next heir, sir?'

'Adolphus Payne – do you remember him?'

'I'm not sure I do, sir.'

'He's an amiable, friendly, sensible, competent sort of man. He's Sir Joshua's great-nephew, and Mr. Lawrence's godson. Mr. Lawrence was the husband of Mr. Blair's wife's sister. Both ladies are, of course, dead.'

'It's all very tangled, sir, isn't it?'

'There's certainly very little that is straightforward.'

'So is Mr. Holden Mr. Payne's cousin?'

'Only by marriage – he's Lady Akehurst's great-nephew.'

'And Mr. Ketchell?'

'Not related at all, as far as I know. He's just a friend of Harry Holden – and Lady Akehurst would rather he was not. He was the reason she invited Mr. Blair to stay, to find out what he was up to.'

'I wonder if Mr. Ketchell knew that, sir?'

Murray looked at him.

'You mean Ketchell could have lured Blair out at night and – and perhaps the cart was not an accident?'

'That carter, Fields, he looked innocent enough to me, sir. But any mischief could have been planned, couldn't it? Perhaps Mr. Ketchell was planning something worse.'

'Goodness, Robbins, it had not even occurred to me. Though it's true that Blair had no idea what Lady Akehurst wanted of him, it's possible that Ketchell might have known she had brought Blair into the household to find out about Ketchell. I wouldn't put it past him to listen at doors, would you?'

Robbins, with a sudden anxious look, crossed to the parlour door and opened it sharply. The corridor outside was empty. He closed it again, looking a little sheepish.

'Best to check, sir.'

'Always.'

'I haven't met the young lady, sir, but should we be limiting ourselves to money as the only motive? And money itself could be less straightforward than it seems.'

'Very true.' Murray stood and went to the window, where a bench had been softened with a well-stuffed squab. He sat, and surveyed the valley below Lewes over the roofs outside. 'She could have had a gambling problem. It's very fashionable.'

'A jealous rival, though, sir? That kind of thing?'

'A jealous rival is likely to be a woman, so she would have needed an accomplice. I'm not clear that Miss Akehurst had yet fixed on any particular suitor, though, and apart from her money she seemed to have few charms.'

'Oh?'

'She seemed to me – and Miss Blair endorsed it – spoilt, self-centred, naïve, and lacking the personal attractions that might have enabled some men to see past her character. But I'd only just met her. Despite what Miss Blair says, perhaps she had men falling at her feet. Or, well, if you're looking for a jealous rival then just the one man falling at her feet would be enough – it just had to be the man the jealous rival wanted for her own.'

'Then it's going to be hard for us to find out who that might be, sir,' said Robbins. Murray sighed.

'To be honest, I find it hard to believe that anyone was jealous of Miss Akehurst's charms, and I think Miss Blair would have noticed any particular devotion amongst her suitors. She's observant. And intelligent. She would have told me, too, I'm sure.'

'I daresay she would, sir, yes.'

'I think it's the money. But that leads to Fussy, and I can't believe Fussy would harm anyone. I know, Robbins, I know we've met people before who don't look the type to harm so much as a rat, but Fussy really does seem the most considerate of people. It's possible, but it's difficult.'

'I still favour Mr. Ketchell, sir,' said Robbins. 'He was in the household, so he could easily have begun his campaign to charm Miss Akehurst. He knew the butler and no doubt knew the gin cellars he frequented in London, so he was in a perfect position to blackmail him. I know he couldn't have done everything, sir – the Pavilion business, for example – but he knew, and only he and Mr. Holden in London knew, I believe, that the household had gone to Brighton. He could have made arrangements there.'

'Yes … but how did he arrange the attack on Mr. Blair here? At the time Blair was investigating whatever he was investigating, we were still in Brighton and did not know where the Akehursts had gone.'

'Were we, though, sir?' Robbins' eyes lit.

'Surely we were. Blair was attacked on Sunday night. We didn't arrive here in Lewes until late Monday morning.'

'True, sir, but we found out on Sunday afternoon about Lewes. Mr. Ketchell could have sent a messenger – he would barely even have needed an express, I think. In fact, if he has a conspirator, as he must have to achieve the Pavilion attack, then the conspirator could have gone on to Lewes as soon as Mr. Ketchell discovered the information and passed it to him.'

Murray considered. It all seemed to fit, physically at least.

'All right, then, say you're right – and it is convincing.' He stood, and began to walk about the room, but it was not conveniently laid out for striding. 'Come on: let's go out and talk. The notion of Ketchell listening at doors is all too realistic.'

Lewes was a small town: within a few minutes they were out of it and up on the chalky Downs, observed only by black-faced sheep. The walking was easy, where it was dry, for the sheep kept the moorland close-cropped and the turf was springy. The claggy bottoms, filled with mud that clung to your boots and trebled your weight, were best avoided.

'Ketchell,' said Murray at last, when they were undoubtedly alone. 'I agree: he's not a man to be trusted. And yes, he was in the household ready to ensnare Miss Akehurst and he could have sent his conspirator on to Lewes on Sunday night. But was he really in the household purely to entrap her? And why, and who is his conspirator? Someone seems to have planned this well in advance, if it is all linked.'

'The man in Hyde Park, anyway, sir: you said Miss Blair did not know him, and she would have recognised Mr. Ketchell, even with a scarf about his face.'

'She would, yes. And the conspirator, then, presumably is the one who attacked her at the Pavilion, and who was around the Akehursts' house doing something on Sunday night, when Blair fell foul of the cart. So he's middle-height and slim, with dark hair, and youngish, if you combine the various descriptions.'

'And if they needed Mr. Ketchell to be in the household, then presumably, sir, this man is not in the household.'

'Well, possibly. But anyway, the description does not seem to fit anyone Isobel knew, so that seems likely.' He poked his stick thoughtfully into a rabbit hole. 'I've said it before, but it still strikes me as odd. It's a huge amount of preparation to lure a girl out and kill her.'

'There's the secretary, too, sir.'

Murray looked up from the rabbit hole.

'So there is. Could that have been part of the plan? Or did – what's his name again? Paulinson – did Paulinson find out something he should not have? Again, Ketchell was in the household: he could have ensured that Paulinson was not discovered until the next day, or whatever happened. He could have hidden him in his own room until Sir Joshua had departed for the House, anyway. But again, you've got the conspirators murdering someone to prevent the discovery of their elaborate scheme to seduce and murder Miss Akehurst. Why go to all that bother?'

'It must be the money, sir. Are you sure Mr. Payne is the only one who will benefit from Miss Akehurst's death?'

'I think Harry Holden has some hope, but as I heard it is a faint one. He's Lady Akehurst's great nephew, as I said, not Sir Joshua's as Fussy Payne is.'

'And does Mr. Payne have an heir yet?'

'I don't believe so. Well, only in that many people do. I don't know what family he has. I should ask Isobel.'

They walked on a little. They were not at the top of the ridge, but the view across the Weald was as picturesque as one could wish for on a misty October afternoon.

'I am growing romantic in my old age, Robbins. I had a

sudden fancy for a cottage just up there, where I could waken to this view.'

'You're not thinking of staying in Sussex, sir, are you?'

Murray smiled at surprising such an immediate reaction from Robbins, staid and quiet as he was.

'No, Robbins, no, not really. Just at the moment I would return to Edinburgh in a shot, were it not for Mr. Blair and Isobel.'

'It'll be a while before Mr. Blair is able to travel,' said Robbins sadly.

If at all: the thought hopped up in Murray's mind, and he cast about quickly for a distraction.

'Oh, look!' he said, pointing with his stick. 'Someone is building a cottage up there, even if it is not for me!'

They strolled further up the slope to the rounded ridge, where bricks and timber were already assembled into a construction that looked at once rather familiar.

'It's an odd cottage, sir,' said Robbins, 'or anyway, it's odd at this end. The other end looks ordinary enough.'

'It's a semaphore tower, or it will be,' said Murray. He called up to a workman adjusting a window frame on the second floor. 'A semaphore tower?'

'So it is, master,' the man called back. 'Up and working soon as we can get the wires all sorted. And once they get the Newhaven one back and fixed up. Miraculous, master, that's what they are!'

'A semaphore tower,' Robbins repeated, gazing up at it. 'Like the one you went to see at Coombe Warren.'

'Yes, and the one that Lieutenant Munnings reported had been burned down at Newhaven.'

Robbins paused, then cleared his throat.

'Didn't Mr. Ketchell go up with you to the semaphore tower at Coombe Warren?' he asked. Murray stopped his perusal of the building works, and looked him in the eye.

'He did, yes. Though I thought at the time that he was more interested in spending time with Miss Paterson than with any signal mechanism.'

'What if that were just a blind, sir? What if that's the key?'

'Sir Joshua is in charge of the semaphore towers – this new line was his idea,' said Murray slowly. 'Did he work his way into the Akehurst household to find out more about them?'

'And perhaps Mr. Paulinson was able to tell him something of the matter, and lost his life as a consequence!'

'And then … Robbins, Newhaven is but a stone's throw from Brighton if you have a good horse –'

'And the man in the Park had a good horse,' Robbins put in.

'Indeed. What if the conspirator rode over to Newhaven after he carried out the Pavilion attack and set fire to the Newhaven semaphore tower?'

'You think they intend to destroy the line, sir?'

'Maybe! Maybe … And there was some talk that the servants at the Pavilion are mostly French. Who but a Frenchman would want to destroy the line that alerts the Admiralty to French activity on the coast?'

'Anyone else benefitting from that French activity, sir,' said Robbins. 'Smugglers, I hear. But also the kind of folk who are rising up against the Government here, there and everywhere. You read in the newspapers that the French are helping them, too. What if Mr. Ketchell is one of those? For he doesn't seem to be French himself.'

'He does speak French, for all that matters. Oh … and in Sir Joshua's household. No wonder Lady Akehurst was anxious. But Sir Joshua was not, she said: he dismissed her anxieties, which is why she wanted to seek help from Blair. But there's still a problem, Robbins.'

'There's plenty of them, sir. There's finding out who the conspirator is, and where they are, and proving your case against Mr. Ketchell. We've nothing but guesswork so far, have we, sir?'

'I wish Blair were conscious. I need his cleverness. But those were not the problems I was thinking of, problems though they are. It all seems to fit together very nicely, and perhaps if it's all true we'll find our proof. But where, in the midst of semaphore towers and radical conspiracies, Robbins, does that leave us with Miss Akehurst?'

It was dinner time when Murray returned to the Akehurst household. It was just as well that he had not expected to be served dinner, for Lady Akehurst had understandably not been in a state to give instructions and Sir Joshua was not fit to sit at the table. Harry Holden and Barnabas Ketchell had agitated some provision from the kitchen staff, and encouraged Murray to share it with them: socially it was not an appealing offer, but if Murray wished to find out more about Ketchell it was the perfect opportunity. At the last minute, the parlour door opened and Beatrix came in, followed swiftly by Isobel. Beatrix had found a black shawl to wear, but Isobel was – Isobel was – Murray was on his feet, of course, as the ladies came in, but for a moment he had to clutch the back of his chair. She was enchanting.

Murray felt as if he had been hit hard with a block of wood. He had known her all her life, had even offered her marriage once, when she would have benefitted from his protection. His oldest friend's daughter, that was what she was, someone happy to look after his own daughter from time to time, a witty artist, a clever companion, an easy friend, a wise adviser on occasion. But that was not what she looked like in that moment.

He made himself concentrate for a count of ten on her gown – was it just the gown? It was plain, white, short sleeved, and covered with a black gauze of some kind, long-sleeved and gathered at the cuffs, embroidered in black with flowers. Pretty, and appropriate in a house of mourning. His gaze wandered. Her hair was very simply drawn up into a pearl clasp. There was nothing new, nothing remarkable, he told himself objectively. Except how he was feeling.

The butler, Trent, was announcing dinner. He made himself hold back, shaking his head to clear it. Isobel took Harry Holden's arm to go in, and Beatrix, after a sharp look at Murray, submitted to Ketchell's support. Murray followed. He needed to watch Ketchell, without Ketchell realising his interest. That would be enough to take up all his concentration.

'We've had the magistrate here, Charles,' said Beatrix when the first course had been served. 'Asking all kinds of questions! Where were you?'

'Oh, yes, he'll be looking for you, Mr. Murray,' said Ketchell with a predatory grin. 'Particularly since you found the body.'

'Found Amanda, you mean,' said Harry Holden, with an unusually hard look at Ketchell. 'Found poor Amanda, not just a body.'

'I beg your pardon, Harry,' said Ketchell.

'It's quite terrible,' said Beatrix. 'And the magistrate seemed to have no idea what could have happened. I had thought – in fact I asked him – if there were some radical element in the town that could have wanted to attack her. But he claimed he knew of nothing like that. Why, everyone knows that Lewes has radicals! Don't they?'

Isobel glanced at Murray, daring him to say anything about Blair's protégé in Cliffe. Murray said nothing, and looked swiftly away from her.

'I thought we knew that it was the man who tried to abduct her in the Park?' Harry Holden objected. 'Some mad admirer?'

'Certainly mad,' Ketchell remarked.

'Well, he wanted to elope with her, didn't he?' said Harry Holden, his long forehead crinkling. 'He must have admired her. Or,' he added honestly, despite his clear reluctance to speak ill of the dead, 'he must have wanted her money, anyway.'

'Then why did he kill her?' asked Ketchell reasonably. 'Unless he brings proof that he married her, he can't inherit. And he could hardly have married her legally without her grandparents' consent – he wouldn't have had time to take her to Scotland, let alone bring her back again.'

'I should think,' said Isobel tartly, 'that a man turning up to claim Miss Akehurst as his wife just now would have some explaining to do regarding her death.'

Murray smiled, but did not quite look at her.

'He certainly would.'

'Then something must have gone wrong, I suppose,' said Harry Holden miserably. 'I cannot believe it. Only this time yesterday she was here, playing the piano and singing for us so beautifully ...'

Ketchell and Beatrix both exchanged looks with Murray. Murray tried to look bland, though certainly his memory of Amanda's performance did not accord with Holden's.

The soup had been perfectly acceptable, but the rest of the meal was perfunctory. Murray wondered how upset the servants were at Amanda's death: he would know when Robbins returned from his visit to Smith. Undoubtedly the dinner preparation would have suffered from the magistrate's questioning. One dish of vegetables did not appear until the dishes were about to be cleared, and an argyll of gravy accompanied an apple pudding.

'How is Lady Akehurst?' Isobel asked generally.

'She's taken some medicine and is lying down,' said Beatrix. 'I don't know how long it will be before she manages anything. I've told the housekeeper to do her best. The doctor has been in twice this afternoon, and to Sir Joshua, too.'

'I'm sure your presence is invaluable,' said Ketchell. 'No doubt one could not pay anyone to be more comforting in the bedchamber.'

Murray did his best not to look at either of them. What game was Ketchell playing? Or was Murray himself being oversensitive, finding extra meaning in his words?

Harry Holden was talking across the table to Isobel, asking her about her father, and Murray allowed the conversation to wander along while he thought. It almost sounded as if Ketchell knew exactly what Beatrix was. But if Beatrix had been the kept woman of one gentleman, how could Ketchell possibly know? Unless he knew the man …

How would that work? If Ketchell were doing as he and Robbins had postulated, if Ketchell were working against the Government, and if Beatrix's protector were, as she had said, someone important in Government circles, had Ketchell been watching him as he appeared to have been watching Sir Joshua? Again, a niggling thought came to him, that there was some link between Sir Joshua and Beatrix and the semaphore towers, but despite how Beatrix had described her lover, the lover could not possibly be Sir Joshua. Beatrix had fled her protector when he had tried to kill her. She would hardly have come quietly into the same man's house, sat at his dinner table and assisted him and his wife in their hour of need – would she? No, she could not possibly. But the man who was trying to kill her was more than likely someone known to Sir Joshua. Had Sir Joshua seen her before, or known of her existence?

Beatrix and Isobel retreated to the drawing room. Murray half-wished he could listen in to their conversation. It did not seem that the two women had fallen easily into friendship – nor, in fact, did Murray want them to. If Isobel realised what Beatrix was and that Murray had brought Beatrix into Isobel's acquaintance – or, heavens, if Isobel thought that Murray himself was Beatrix's protector, then … well, it did not bear thinking about. Would Beatrix mention Scoggie Castle? Say anything of her history to Isobel? He prayed not. If Isobel returned to Fife and talked of Beatrix to Deborah Scoggie, the whole story would come out. What on earth would Isobel think of him? What did she think of him anyway? It had never really occurred to him to wonder before.

Ketchell. He was supposed to be thinking about Ketchell, watching him, listening to him, finding evidence for anything Ketchell might have done wrong.

'Tell me more about Paul Paulinson,' he said suddenly, cutting across the desultory conversation going on across the table.

'Paulinson?' asked Ketchell.

'You mentioned him earlier, Mr. Holden,' said Murray. 'You seemed to think it was all part of these terrible times. Was there anything to link him with – well, with Lewes radicals, for example? Or with Miss Akehurst and her troubles?'

'Oh!' said Ketchell, with a sly smile, 'you're trying to make out that the same fellow did both killings, are you?'

'It's a reasonable thought,' said Murray. 'Unless you think that several parties are trying to attack Sir Joshua's household simultaneously.'

'I suppose he might have crossed whoever was trying to attack Miss Amanda,' said Ketchell, making a show of applying his mind to the matter, thoughtful fingers on his long chin.

'Do you think so?' asked Harry Holden. 'I can't picture old Paullie crossing anyone.' Paulinson could not have been more than a year or two senior to Holden, but it certainly sounded as if he had acted like an older man.

'I only mean he might have chanced on something. Maybe when he went upstairs that evening,' said Ketchell, 'he met someone, I don't know, trying to conceal themselves in Miss Akehurst's bedchamber?'

'Interesting thought,' said Murray. Was it Ketchell himself that Paulinson had found, somewhere he should not have been? But then Ketchell was part of the household. Had Paulinson come across Ketchell's conspirator? 'How do you think that might have worked? Would he have killed Paulinson on the spot, do you think?'

'He clearly didn't,' said Ketchell, leaning forward. His yellowish eyes met Murray's, and caught them there, watching closely. 'He was found outside, and he had not been dead for as long as that.'

'I hear he was not wearing outdoor clothes,' said Murray.

'He was not. If someone caused him to go outside, they did not give him the chance to prepare properly. But if he were going to be killed anyway, then a little chill hardly seems significant, does it?'

'You think Paulinson might have gone out knowing he was going to his death?'

'Oh, as to that, who knows?' said Ketchell casually. 'The thing is, Paulinson had nothing to do with Miss Amanda's death, did he? He was long gone. So who killed Miss Amanda?'

'Unless it was the same person.' Ketchell had looked away, but Murray kept his gaze on the man. 'Have you seen anyone acting suspiciously around the family, either of you? Anyone perhaps observing the goings on in the household?'

'No, no one!' said Harry Holden in surprise.

'Well, if you don't know,' said Ketchell, with a nasty smile, 'I don't know that we should tell you.'

'What do you mean?' Murray asked, confused.

'You brought her along, and now there she is, in amongst the family like a little cuckoo snuggled in its nest. Your friend Miss Paterson, Mr. Murray – who exactly is she?'

Chapter Twenty-Three

'I don't think Miss Paterson is observing the family!' said Murray, irritated at Ketchell's deflection. He tipped brandy into his glass, though he had hardly touched what was already there. 'Why on earth should she?' If Beatrix were inveigling her way into the Akehurst household, it was for her own safety and a respectable refuge, surely. And perhaps to procrastinate over joining her friends. Where were her friends?

'What do you know of Miss Paterson?' Ketchell persisted.

'She is an old acquaintance.'

'I note you do not say "friend". And yet she calls you by your Christian name.' It was true. Beatrix had been very familiar with him, and quite openly. Ketchell went on. 'Could it be that you are now trying to distance yourself from Miss Paterson, despite your lengthy *acquaintance*? Presumably you know what she is, but you do not seem very comfortable taking her around the country. If you've paid for her, then make the most of it! Don't mind us.' He winked at Harry Holden, who seemed bewildered by the whole conversation. He had propped his head on one hand, jaw loose, and was watching Murray and Ketchell as if he had strayed into a theatrical performance in Italian. Murray ignored him.

'I have not paid for Miss Paterson. I am taking her from London, where she had suffered some distress, to her friends in the country.'

'You're going about it in a very roundabout way, Mr. Murray. Where are these friends?'

Murray wished he knew.

'I'm not sure that it's any of your business, Mr. Ketchell. No doubt she will join them soon.'

'How long ago were you *acquainted* with Miss Paterson?'

Ketchell asked, leaning back in his chair, very much the relaxed interrogator. 'A few weeks? Months? Years? Were you childhood friends?' He invested the last with a mock sentimentality that made Holden laugh, even though his attention was more focussed on his brandy.

Murray considered. It was true that he had attempted to distance himself from Beatrix, even though he had been trying to help her. What else was he supposed to do? He had warned her years ago, with all the pomposity of youth, of the consequences of the path she had chosen. He could not in all conscience turn her away when she needed help, but he had no wish to become any better acquainted with her, on any level.

'A good number of years ago,' he replied at last. 'I know something of the life she has been living since, but as far as I am concerned I am simply an escort to take her safely to her friends. With whom I am not acquainted.'

'You know something of the life she has been living since,' Ketchell echoed. 'How do you know?'

'I know what she was setting off to do, and with whom,' said Murray, remembering that dark day at Scoggie Castle when Beatrix, whom he had liked and respected, confided in him that she was abandoning respectable society to live with a man who could only ever destroy her reputation. 'And I know what she has told me of her life since, which is in keeping with her intentions at the time.'

'Her intentions? Now that does surprise me,' said Ketchell.

'Well, I was shocked,' Murray agreed.

'Not every young lady sets out to be a middle-ranking prostitute in London, touting for custom around the Opera.'

'Just because you saw her at the Opera the night we were there –'

'Oh, not just that night, Mr. Murray. Miss Paterson – only that is an unfamiliar name to me: Miss Pirrie, she calls herself,' Murray was unexpectedly shaken by the use of Beatrix's real name. 'Miss Pirrie is a regular attraction at the Opera.'

'What?'

'Oh, yes,' said Ketchell, with that unpleasant grin of his. 'Of course she can look very respectable when she puts her mind to it, and removes her powder and paint. But that is where she makes her money. Or she did, anyway: I suppose she's growing old, for I haven't seen her there so much in recent months.' He looked at Murray again, and there was an unaccustomed hint of pity in his face. 'What was the story she told you, Mr. Murray? Or just the story the pair of you concocted?'

Murray swallowed. Concocted? What Ketchell said rang true – why would a woman who was an established mistress be in that room at the Opera? The man who was keeping her would hardly approve. But Beatrix would be old, by comparison with the girls at the Opera.

'She said that she was living under a man's protection – a man of some importance.'

Ketchell smiled, but it had a touch of kindness to it.

'The respectable side of the business,' he said ironically. 'Did she give you a name?'

'No!' Ketchell was pushing too far, anyway. Had Beatrix only lied to make Murray more likely to help her? She had clearly fallen further than she was prepared to admit, anyway.

'But presumably her domestic situation had suffered some kind of calamity,' Ketchell continued, 'otherwise she would not have had to turn to you.' He waited, but Murray did not reply. If Beatrix were not living with a protector, who was the man who had tried to kill her in Hyde Park? Ketchell sighed. 'Well, as to what happened in London … She seemed to have very little luggage, I noted.'

'She had to leave in a hurry.'

'With no maid.'

'No.'

'And no change of clothing.'

'No, nor that.'

'She was fortunate to meet with that second-hand clothing dealer in Brighton, then, don't you think?' asked Ketchell, nonchalantly.

'Well …' It had seemed very fortuitous. The way those clothes had fitted her …

'I happened to see her encounter with the dealer,' said Ketchell.

'You happened to?' was all Murray could manage. Holden had given up on the conversation completely and was draining the brandy decanter.

'On a roundabout route to meet Harry here. Or I followed her deliberately. Take your pick. I've never seen a second-hand clothes dealer with quite so fine a black horse,' he said. 'And just to be able to take a bundle of clothes and hand them to your customer, quite as if you were expecting someone of that exact shape and size – I daresay he was so pleased with his foresight that he forgot to charge her for them.'

'You're saying,' said Murray, 'that someone brought – Miss Pirrie – a bundle of her own clothes from London?'

'As to where they came from, I have no evidence,' Ketchell shrugged. 'I could not state in a court of law that the clothes came from London. But if you have any doubt as to the clothes being Miss Pirrie's, then ask that bright little kitchenmaid you brought along for her. I'd say she knew very well that those clothes came from no dealer.'

'You seem to have been watching Miss Pirrie very closely, Mr. Ketchell.'

'You have to admit that, given I knew where she came from, I was bound to find it surprising that you were taking her off in your carriage, in a manner that did not seem to indicate that you had purchased her services, even though you seemed to have some idea of their availability. It was bound to stir my curiosity. A nice Scotch gentleman like you? Something did not add up. And then,' his light voice continued, but something harder had entered his curdled gaze, 'you stopped on the way to admire a half-built semaphore tower. Not your last semaphore tower, either, Mr. Murray.'

The semaphore towers. They were back, full circle. Murray met his eye, trying to find the deception in Ketchell's conversation. But everything seemed to be telling him that Ketchell was sincere. And after all, hadn't Murray himself been asking questions about Beatrix from the start? And Robbins, wise Robbins, had not trusted her at all. So what was she up to? And what business was it of Ketchell's?

'You kept very close to Miss Pirrie when we went to see the semaphore tower,' he observed. 'Watching very closely, as I said.'

Ketchell gave a little smile.

'She was very close to the mechanism,' he said neutrally. 'She might have injured herself.'

'Or the mechanism?' Murray's mind made a leap. 'You

thought she might be there to damage – anything she could?'

'It crossed my mind,' said Ketchell. 'A woman leaving London urgently, under escort, and she asks to stop at a half-built signal tower. Curious, wouldn't you say?'

'She told me,' said Murray slowly, making a decision, 'that her protector had been a senior person in the Government, and I took her interest in the semaphore tower to stem from that. She had accidentally discovered some secret information, she claimed, and her protector had threatened to kill her.'

'Did she produce any evidence?'

'She was fleeing across Hyde Park when we found her.'

'How fortunate for her. To flee your attacker and fall into the arms of an old and sympathetic acquaintance.'

'It was just luck.' But was it? It was certainly something of a coincidence. If he had not seen Beatrix since long ago at Scoggie Castle, then that would be credible, if surprising. But when he had seen her just a little before, and she knew he was in London – was it possible that she had taken advantage of him? It seemed not only possible, but increasingly likely. 'Do you think she's – well, hostile to the Government? A radical? Sympathetic to the French republicans? If she's as deceptive as you think she is, then why?'

'Ah,' said Ketchell, 'that I don't know.'

'But you're trying to find out, aren't you? You went to look in her room at the White Hart, didn't you?' That was why Robbins had seen Ketchell coming down the stairs. If Beatrix were paying for her own room it was likely to be one up at the cheaper top of the building. Ketchell smiled.

'Oh, is she staying there? I was not so sure ...'

Murray fell silent, reviewing, as he knew Ketchell knew he was doing, his recent acquaintance with Beatrix. Everything Ketchell had said fitted the facts, and where there were no facts it reinforced his own suspicions. Her interest in the semaphore tower – and perhaps her flirtation with Lieutenant Munnings, supervisor of the Newhaven tower? – her luck in finding those neatly-fitting clothes, her reluctance to go to her friends ... but, as he had already asked, why was she doing it? He needed to talk to her.

'Time to join the ladies?' Ketchell asked, watching him.

'I believe so.'

But when they went into the drawing room, they found

Beatrix on her own.

'Miss Blair wished to return to her father,' she explained brightly. 'Of course she is very concerned about him.'

'Of course,' said Murray, trying to ignore the sudden deep sense of disappointment at not seeing Isobel. He sat opposite Beatrix. 'Sorry to have kept you sitting alone.'

'I have been content with my own thoughts,' said Beatrix. She looked very much at home there, sitting, ankles crossed, by the tea tray at the fire. Had that been her intention? To find a place in a decent home? Perhaps she had simply wanted to escape her previous life – no, that did not explain the man who delivered her clothes, nor the interest in the semaphore towers. He had to keep his mind on those facts. It was all too easy to believe in Beatrix, now that he was here with her.

Ketchell took a cup of tea in his hand as he stood, and drained it rapidly. A few rout cakes disappeared smoothly into his pocket.

'For later,' he commented, nodding at Murray. 'Harry, I think you and I need to investigate some business in the town,' he said. Harry Holden had already slumped into an armchair. Ketchell kicked his foot unsubtly, then grabbed him by the arm and pulled him to his feet. Ketchell was stronger than he looked.

'What?' Harry grumbled. 'Where're we goin'?'

'To find some gin,' said Ketchell, and dragged Holden from the room.

'Gin!' Holden exclaimed with satisfaction, as the door closed firmly behind him.

'Goodness!' said Beatrix with a smile, 'and now here we are on our own!'

'I'll walk you back to the White Hart,' said Murray, not liking the situation.

'Oh, Lady Akehurst has asked me to stay here. Rosie fetched my things yesterday.'

'In that case –' Murray broke off. He had no wish to find himself in a compromising situation, here unchaperoned, but at the same time no doubt Ketchell had cleared Holden out and gone to allow Murray the chance to ask Beatrix a few questions. He should take his chance, but where should he start?

'Your friends,' he said, 'no doubt you have written to tell

them you are in Lewes? You set out to do so yesterday.'

'I did,' said Beatrix at once, 'but I have received no reply as yet. I fear that they might be from home. Just when I needed them! I'm very fortunate that Lady Akehurst seems to find me of some use at present.'

'Indeed you are. Beatrix, do your friends actually exist?'

'Are you suggesting that I have no friends?' She smiled, teasing him.

'No friends to whom you have written, asking for help.'

'Well ... I do know some people in Brighton.'

'Is that people who might have been able to bring you some of your own clothes, perhaps?'

Her smile faded.

'What do you mean?'

'I mean there was no second-hand clothes dealer either, was there? There was your friend, a man on horseback, bringing you a bundle of your own belongings.'

'I have no idea how you come to think such things ...' But her voice was wavering. She clasped her hands in her lap, gazing down at them, shoulders tense.

'But it's true, isn't it?'

There was a long moment of silence. He managed not to break it, waiting patiently.

'I can see you are cleverer even than I remembered,' she said at last, looking up.

'You'd be better to tell me the whole truth,' he said. 'I don't like being tricked, Beatrix.'

'Of course you don't. But I can explain everything – and why I had to hide things from you, for your own good.'

Another pause, while she appeared to collect her thoughts.

'I recognised you that night at the Opera, of course. And I also saw who you were with, Harry Holden. I'd met him before, though he probably doesn't remember me, and I knew he was living with his aunt, Lady Akehurst. My – my protector works with Sir Joshua. You'll have seen what kind of man Sir Joshua is, proud and stubborn. And up to now he has thought himself invulnerable – avoiding the Cato Street conspirators helped, of course. But my protector knew that someone, maybe a party of people, was or were doing their best to get close to Sir Joshua, to his family, to his household, probably to find out more about the semaphore towers and Sir Joshua's work to protect the coast from the remainder of the French rebels. Sir Joshua had left town very suddenly, with a magistrate already trying to find out why his secretary had been left dead on his doorstep. But my protector had no idea where he had gone, and he needed to pursue him to continue trying to find out who it was putting Sir Joshua in danger – he knew who had killed Sir Joshua's secretary. When I said I'd seen you with Harry Holden, he asked me to presume on our previous acquaintance and see if you could take me into the household, find out what was happening, or at least discover where Sir Joshua had gone. Of course, being with you, I discovered instead that Miss Akehurst seemed to be the focus of their threat. It appals me that we arrived here too late to save her.'

'Then you weren't in danger that night in Hyde Park?'

She wriggled her shoulders, eyes wide and soft.

'I'm sorry, Charles. No, I wasn't. We had been keeping an eye on you through the day, and took our chance. He was in such a hurry he almost shoved me out of the bushes at you! The bruises were real,' she added ruefully.

'Perhaps if you had told me, if you had been truthful with me –'

'I had no idea where you stood, where your sympathies might lie. There seem to be radicals everywhere these days! Goodness, my protector is always rooting them out, seeing them in every corner! You'll know that – look at what has been happening in Glasgow and the west. And here, so near the coast – and with Lewes' history of politics …'

Murray stood sharply, and went to stare out of the window. It was dark outside, but the shutters had not yet been closed. The gravel drive was empty, and the paddock beyond it, where poor Amanda's body had been found, was invisible. His own reflection loomed against a picture of the lit drawing room behind him, candles in the chandelier and in the sconces, firelight dancing. Beatrix, whose chair had its back to the window, was leaning around its winged back, watching him, pale face and pale gown wreathed in the black of her shawl. For a moment he allowed himself to think of Isobel in her black and white gown. She would be sitting at Blair's side, praying for her father's recovery. Would her prayers – his prayers too – be answered? He did not want to see her so sad.

Beatrix. He had to think about Beatrix.

'What is your interest in semaphore towers, then?' he asked, but he knew she would have an answer ready.

'It's Sir Joshua's chief concern. I wanted to see one, to see what all the fuss is about. Our main line of communication from the coast to the Admiralty – the coast, as my protector tells me, where so much smuggling goes on, and where men and weapons can easily appear in our land from France.'

Her protector – yet Ketchell did not believe in such a man. Her protector, she now claimed, was not a threat to her life, but the man for whom she was working. Working closely, by the sound of it. He trusted her to do all this, discussed with her his fight against radicals, the activities of the French rebels. That seemed not unlikely: Beatrix, as a member of the Scoggie household, had been trustworthy and sensible, and probably discreet, too. But what had she been doing mixing with common Cyprians at the Opera? And doing so often enough that Ketchell recognised her as a regular? And by her own admission she had met Holden before – Holden, who frequented low houses and gin cellars more than anywhere else. Was she as devoted to her protector as she claimed?

'Where is your protector now, then?' he asked, still staring into the darkness as though the man might appear at any moment. Ketchell had mentioned the man's good horse – and the attacker in Hyde Park, the one who had tried to abduct Amanda Akehurst, he had had a fine horse, according to Isobel. Isobel …

'He's nearby,' said Beatrix, unwittingly breaking across his thoughts again, 'or so I believe. He'll be trying to find out how Miss Akehurst's killer came so close to the house – no doubt it's the same man that killed the secretary. Poor Sir Joshua has suffered so much. He may, of course, have gone down to Newhaven, though, to find out what happened to that semaphore tower. Lieutenant Munnings was good enough to tell me quite a lot about it, which I could pass on.'

'If he works with Sir Joshua, why could he not come to the house openly?'

'Are you not done with questions yet, Charles? Take another cup of tea – or there is more brandy here, if you would prefer.'

'But why?' Murray persisted stubbornly. 'Why could he not offer his help directly? No doubt he would be able to discover more about the whole business if he had direct access to the household, the family and the servants.'

Beatrix sat back as he crossed the room to her. When he poured himself a cup of tea, her mouth twitched as if she were holding back a wry smile. He returned with the cup and saucer to the window. Distancing himself, he thought.

'I understand that he and Sir Joshua are not on the best of terms,' she said at last. 'And he is somewhat junior to Sir Joshua. Sir Joshua has dismissed his warnings and concerns, and is unlikely to listen to him unless he can present better information as to the people perpetrating all this.'

Remembering how Lady Akehurst had complained of her husband's dismissal of her concerns about Ketchell, Murray could imagine this. But then Ketchell, too, seemed not to be quite what they had thought he was, whatever he was up to. Acting for the best for Ketchell was what seemed most likely.

'In fact, the more I think about it,' said Beatrix, 'the more I seem to remember that my friend said he was going down to Newhaven this evening, and would be away all night.'

'What's his name, this friend of yours?'

'His name? Oh, Charles, why do you want to know that? What use could it possibly be to you?'

He had not noticed her come so close to him. She was just behind his shoulder, and he felt her hand on his arm. She took the cup and saucer, and set them down, turning him gently towards her.

'Let us not think of him,' she said in a low voice – practised, he told himself. 'I was always very attached to you, Charles, you remember that. You were always my favourite.'

She had never, to his recollection, shown any interest in him as more than a friend – nor he in her. But if this was now her job, she was very good at it. Her hands seemed to have found their way up to his chest, her fingers sliding into the fabric of his neckcloth. He forced his own hands to stay by his side, but she was slipping a hand behind his head, reaching up to tilt his face towards hers.

Which was the point at which the drawing room door opened, and Isobel walked in.

Chapter Twenty-Four

Frozen to the spot, Murray waited for Isobel's reaction.

'I beg your pardon,' said Isobel, and crossed the room to pick up her sketchbook from a table. She returned to the door, but left it open as she went out. Murray could hear her laughing as she went back upstairs. He stepped back from Beatrix, and noted on her face a look of annoyance.

'If you're sure you're content staying here,' he said, 'I should head back to the inn. I wish you good evening.'

He did not allow himself a moment's hesitation as he crossed the hall. His coat and gloves could wait till morning. He crunched down the gravel sweep, and out into the lane, breathing heavily in his relief. The air was damp and cool, the night overcast, the cobbles slick as he made his way back to the High Street, pausing for a moment at the top of the lane. He had not enquired about Blair, though he knew Isobel would have told him if there had been a change. What had Blair seen that night, to take him out of the house in his night shirt? Who had he seen that he felt such a need to pursue that he had kicked off his slippers? Was it someone he had recognised, or had he only realised they were up to no good?

The timings were terrible. Had he himself unwittingly led the attacker from London to Brighton, and then perhaps from Brighton to Lewes? If he had, then whoever Blair was chasing was not the same man. But then, they were fairly sure that whoever was doing this, it was not one man working alone, even if it were really one scheme – the murder of Paulinson, the attempted abduction of Miss Akehurst, the attack in the Pavilion, Blair's pursuit of someone, the murder of Miss Akehurst. The parts seemed disjointed, yet it would be odd for them all to happen together, with common elements, too, without a connexion. And Ketchell seemed to think they were connected. How did Ketchell fit in?

He walked on slowly down the High Street. It was still busy enough, well-lit and scented with the smoke of cooking fires. He liked Lewes, and had enjoyed visiting it with Blair on occasion: it had always felt a safe place to him. It seemed to be changing.

Ketchell had made it his business to watch Beatrix, and did not trust her. If what he said was correct – and it seemed reasonable to believe him – that Beatrix did not spend all her time as a kept woman but also touted for trade at the Opera and presumably elsewhere. It was not a pleasant thought. To look at her, she had not yet suffered too much, but no doubt it would come. Murray had long ago cursed the man who had lured her into this dark world, but he knew it had been Beatrix's choice: if she had ever asked for help, the Scoggies would have protected her.

Well, and Beatrix still claimed to have a protector, and one who worked near Sir Joshua, and who was determined to guard him against these attacks. Which seemed to show that the series of misfortunes, to call them that, were aimed at Sir Joshua, and not, for example, at securing Miss Akehurst's fortune. It would explain why her murderer did not abduct her and wait, or demand a ransom. It might also explain Paulinson's death – he had been Sir Joshua's valued secretary, and his loss would no doubt hinder Sir Joshua's work. And that had to be at the heart of it, for the semaphore towers seemed to run through this mystery like the signal line they were. Someone, some political group, wanted them destroyed – presumably related to the Cato Street characters who had tried to attack the Cabinet.

He reached the inn and went up to his chamber, finding it empty. Robbins must not have expected him back so soon. He lit the fire for himself, and sat by the window, remembering.

Cato Street had been, they said, a fake assassination. The group had been genuine enough, a bunch of radicals wanting reform, meeting in a house in humble Cato Street – named, presumably, to Murray's amusement, after Cato the Elder or Cato the Younger, both remembered by history as deeply conservative politicians. But a police infiltrator had been the one to encourage the gang on to violence, and to plan the assassination: he had told them that the Cabinet would be at dinner at a certain house, and the gang could run in easily and shoot them all. But there was to be no dinner, and the gang were arrested, tried and hanged – not the police infiltrator, of course. But questions remained: would they even have thought of such an attempt, if the infiltrator had not suggested it and egged them on?

The whole thing had seemed outlandish to Murray: he could not help thinking that a gang running in and shooting gentlemen at dinner was almost bound to fail anyway. Guns jam; servants intervene; the wrong people are shot. If it had been a serious attempt, he felt, gunpowder should have been involved, and a slow fuse, like Guy Fawkes. But then the police infiltrator probably wanted as many of the gang members on the spot as possible. He must have been a persuasive man. Murray wondered what had happened to him. Presumably he had gone free, as it was suspected many of the conspirators had, too. Could it be that one of them was now intent on killing the Cabinet one by one? Or had other members of the Cabinet also been threatened? It would be helpful to know, though he was not sure who would be able to tell him. Blair would have the right connexions, he was sure. But Blair was not in a position to contact them.

So, with that avenue closed, he tried to work out what to do next.

He would have to talk to the magistrate, of course, but that was not likely to tell him much. He did want to talk to Dr. Mantell who had presumably examined Amanda's body. It seemed more than likely that the cut throat had killed her, but he needed to find out if there was anything else. Amanda must have left the house without planning her departure, or she would have been dressed and ready. He also wanted if at all possible to talk with Lady Akehurst, to find out what friends Amanda might have had, what genuine prospects of marriage, what – and that was very important – what Amanda might have said about the man she left the reception with at the Pavilion. Nothing had been mentioned about him at all. How had he persuaded Amanda to leave the room with him? She had been a silly girl, according to Isobel, but was the man Fussy had seen with her also her attacker? He needed to find out what Miss Akehurst had told her grandmother.

He needed more information from Beatrix, too, but he was wary. Was Beatrix's protector with the fine horse, the man who had brought her clothes to Brighton, was he the same man on a fine horse who had tried to abduct Miss Akehurst in the Park? She was unlikely to admit it if it were so. Ketchell was unlikely to know – he seemed to think that Beatrix's protector was non-existent. Anyway, if Beatrix were being honest about her protector trying to guard Sir Joshua and his household against attack, what on earth would he have been doing trying to snatch Miss Akehurst in the Park?

He shook his head. Nothing was making sense, and he was still not sure who he could trust. Apart from Isobel. For a moment he remembered her sudden appearance in the parlour, her swift departure, laughing. She had come back to collect her sketchbook. Since when, he thought abruptly, did Isobel accidentally forget her sketchbook?

Right, he thought, that was enough. He rang for Robbins, and decided to go to bed.

Wednesday morning dawned damp and muddy. Before breakfast, Murray decided to head for the stables and see how Young Donald was settling back in.

The stables at the White Hart were long-established and well kept, with a generous space for turning carriages and mounting horses. Old Donald, Murray knew, thought it a superior place to stay, and he was well in with the stableyard servants. Murray found him tucking into a substantial breakfast outside in the moist air, more at home outdoors than in. He set his plate down carefully on the stone bench beside him when he saw Murray approach, and stood politely, wiping his mouth on the napkin that had been tucked into his collar.

'Good morning, sir.'

'Good morning, Donald. Horses all well?'

'Aye, sir, no bad at all. The rest will be doing them good for a day or two, then I'll be taking them out for an airing, unless you want one to ride, sir.'

'I have no plans: carry on. I doubt you'll be exhausting them, and in an emergency no doubt I can hire.' He watched a spasm of pain pass across Donald's face at the thought of a hired horse. 'How is your nephew today? Recovered from his journey?'

'Aye, sir, I think so, though he's altogether ashamed of himself. Which is no bad thing, sir, in my opinion. He had no right to be off wandering at night like that without permission.'

'I suspect the temptation of curiosity was just too great, wasn't it? He's young.'

'He's not that young,' said Old Donald, cross now that he had no need to worry. 'He's old enough to know better. But young enough for a good skelping,' he added ominously. 'Here he is.'

Young Donald emerged from a stall where, to judge by the brushes he was carrying, he had been grooming a horse. The cool air did not seem to bother him, either, in his shirtsleeves and waistcoat: only Murray's appearance took him aback and he paused, a heavy blush spreading over his cheeks.

'I'm still here, sir!' he cried at once. 'I've no gone anywhere!'

'I didn't expect you would have,' said Murray with a smile. 'I should think you're too clever to make the same mistake twice. How did you make your way to Lewes?'

'I was lucky, sir, as I told you: people gave me lifts on carts and even a gig, once – that was a clergyman, I think, though they look different down here.'

He had been lucky indeed. Groom's boots were not usually designed for walking great distances, but his looked smart and polished, and barely down at heel. And he had made good time, it seemed.

'When did you arrive?'

'Yesterday morning, sir.' His hand holding the brushes gave a little twist. 'Not long before you saw me.'

Murray noted the twist, and frowned. Young Donald seemed to find some point just above Murray's left eye interesting.

'Who was the man you were talking to down in Cliffe? He looked a bit like someone we were looking for, but I think he could not have been.'

'He was just a man who had given me breakfast, sir. I didn't ask him his name. He had been out on the road and I happened to meet him on my way in. I think he was out looking for a lost dog, or something.'

'A lost dog? Poor fellow. Did he find it?'

'No, he didn't,' said Donald quickly. 'He said it was a young one, a bit daft, and would make its own way home sooner or later, no doubt.'

Too much information, Murray thought to himself. Something about Donald's story was not true, and he was trying to cover it.

'Sir!' It was Robbins. 'You asked me to let you know when breakfast was ready, sir.'

'Ah, yes, thank you.' It was all right: he wanted to have a think about Donald before he pursued his story further. Likely he had found some young lass to stay with, and was too shy to say.

But as he ate his breakfast, fortunately uninterrupted today, he considered. There was something much more tense about Donald than just some secret of where he had spent the night on his way from London.

From London. Was that it? If Donald had met that man in Cliffe, on his way into Lewes, where was he coming from? For if he was coming straight from London, how had he known to travel to Lewes? To know that, surely he would have had to have followed their path more closely, via Brighton? Even if Old Donald had written to him at Fitzroy Square to tell him where they were, it would not have reached Fitzroy Square before Young Donald had left to find them. How had he known where they were? And if he were skirting the truth over that part of his story, what else was he hiding? Murray was sure it was not, in fact, some cosy liaison. What was Young Donald up to?

'I'd go and tackle him straight away, sir,' said Robbins, when Murray shared his thoughts on the matter. 'I'd say you're right: there's something not right going on.'

'I want to go and enquire about Mr. Blair,' said Murray. 'I didn't ask before I left last night.' He wanted to see Isobel, too, but he did not mention that. Last night had not been the restful night he needed: there had been many images and memories intruding on his dreams. 'I think it's more urgent to sort out what is happening with the Akehursts, anyway: the magistrate is apparently looking for me, and I want a word with Dr. Mantell. And Lady Akehurst, if I'm lucky,' he added, remembering his own list from earlier.

'Will Miss Paterson be accompanying you today, sir?' Robbins asked without emphasis.

'Miss Paterson is staying with the Akehursts. Apparently Lady Akehurst finds her a great comfort.'

'Her friends will be disappointed, sir, if she delays any

longer.'

Murray gave Robbins a look.

'If they exist, yes. I had a very interesting conversation with Mr. Ketchell yesterday.' He outlined Ketchell's interest in the matter, though it was still not clear how it had arisen, then gave him a sketchy account of Beatrix's response.'

'And which of them do you trust, sir?' asked Robbins, his eyebrows high on his pale forehead. Murray shrugged.

'I'm beginning to think I don't trust either of them. But when I'm away from both of them, I have to say I find Ketchell's story the more convincing. What do you think?'

'It's a tough one, sir, but I think I'd agree.'

'But then you've never taken to Miss Paterson, have you, Robbins?'

Robbins' lips narrowed.

'I've never taken to either of them, sir.'

'A balanced view.' He set his cutlery on his plate and laid his napkin beside it. 'Right, I'd better get up to the Akehursts'. I don't want any more delay to visiting Mr. Blair.'

But there was to be a further delay. By the time Murray had found a muffler to keep him warm in the absence of his coat and hat, Robbins had a message for him.

'It's a Mr. Worthing, sir, waiting for you in the parlour.'

'Mr. Worthing?' Murray raised his eyebrows. How had Blair's protégé known where to find him?

'Good day to you, sir,' he said to the young man awaiting him. The man was tall and dark-haired, handsome, and courteous.

'Forgive my interruption, please, Mr. Murray,' said Worthing with a neat bow. 'Lewes is a small town, and my maidservant knew where you were staying. I believe you called with Miss Blair yesterday, and the whole town knows that Mr. Blair has been in a terrible accident. I had no desire to intrude on them at this time, and wondered if instead you would be able to convey my good wishes and hopes that he will make a full recovery. And my thanks to Miss Blair for venturing down to Cliffe to ask after my own health, at this time.'

'Please sit, Mr. Worthing,' said Murray, impressed. 'Will you take some refreshment? You'll know that the White Hart serves very passable claret, or a jug of coffee if you would prefer.'

'Thank you, sir, I should like that.' Worthing sat tidily at the table with Murray, and Robbins, who had waited at the door, went to order the coffee.

'I believe you are a business acquaintance of Mr. Blair's?' Murray asked. 'He was my father's great friend, and has been my own friend for many years.'

'It was the late Mr. Olliver I knew better,' Worthing explained. 'His daughters married Mr. Blair and Mr. Lawrence, and in his will Mr. Olliver, who was the kindest of gentlemen, instructed Mr. Blair and Mr. Lawrence to oversee a trust to my benefit. I had – I had been unlucky in business, Mr. Murray, putting my faith in a man who turned out to be undeserving of it. I was ruined.'

'That is most unfortunate,' said Murray. Robbins brought in the coffee, and poured them a can each, then stepping out of the room again. 'If it was a criminal deceit, were you able to press charges?'

Worthing shook his head.

'No, not at all. There would have been no hope of a conviction. But that is in the past: as you can see, I am not without resources now. With the help of Mr. Olliver's generous trust, I was able to build up my business again, and am now once again successful. For which I am perpetually thankful.'

'You must be. Mr. Olliver does indeed sound enlightened.'

'And Mr. Blair has interested himself in my case from the start. He has been more than good to me, always ensuring that I am comfortable and giving me the very best of advice.'

'It is one of his best attributes,' Murray agreed.

'You cannot imagine how devastated I was when I heard of his injuries. I pray every moment for his recovery.'

'You are not alone. His injuries are severe, but he seems to be stable: that is the best that can be said for the moment.'

'Terrible,' Mr. Worthing breathed. 'I heard that he was in his night clothes, running out on to the street when the cart hit him. What on earth was he doing at that time of the night?'

'No one knows,' said Murray. 'He has not yet spoken.'

'Not spoken? Oh, no.' He lapsed into thought for a minute. 'Do you think I might be permitted to visit him? Would Miss Blair admit me?'

'You can ask, of course,' said Murray. 'Miss Blair might feel that another, different voice might provide a stimulus that would arouse him.'

'Oh, that would be very good of her! I shall go and ask – unless you think it might be better coming from you, sir? As one well acquainted with the family?'

'I could certainly approach Miss Blair for you,' said Murray. Any excuse, he thought. Any reason to go and talk to Isobel.

Robbins appeared at the door.

'Sir, a Mr. Tebbitt to see you. He is the magistrate.'

'He is indeed!' cried Mr. Worthing, jumping to his feet and draining his coffee can. 'I must leave you. Thank you, thank you for everything, Mr. Murray. I shall return as soon as ever you wish.'

Murray stood as the magistrate appeared in the doorway. Mr. Worthing went to dart past.

'One moment, Mr. Worthing,' said Murray suddenly. 'Do you own a dog?'

'A dog? No. There is a cat in the house.'

'No, it was a dog I was interested in. Thank you. Mr. Tebbitt, will you sit, sir? Robbins, could you fetch more coffee, please?'

Robbins, with a glance at Murray that conveyed his curiosity about the dog, saw Mr. Tebbitt to the seat that Worthing had left, and went out again. By the time he returned, Murray was halfway through telling the magistrate all about the discovery of Miss Akehurst's body, and his memories of meeting her the previous evening.

'So you barely knew the family, Mr. Murray?' asked Mr. Tebbitt, a man who looked as if he had to control his natural joviality for the sake of his job. He drank his coffee with appreciation.

'Barely at all. My acquaintances in the household are Mr. and Miss Blair.'

'Ah, the gentleman who was hit by the cart. No doubt if he recovers he will want the carter to pay substantially. A man named Fields, I believe.'

'As far as I can tell it was an accident,' said Murray. 'I suspect that Mr. Blair will not pursue the matter. If he recovers.'

'Oh, very good, very good,' said Tebbitt. 'Fields is a decent fellow – no harm in him.'

'No, it seemed not.'

'Well, going back to poor Miss Akehurst – did you see anything nearby when you found the body? Anyone close to the place?'

'No, I did not, but she had been there for some time.'

'Oh, yes, so the doctor said. Some hours.'

'I take it this is an unusual case for Lewes? There has been no other attack on a young woman in the area?'

'No, none at all, not in my time,' said Tebbitt, rubbing his hands up and down his plump thighs thoughtfully. His breeches looked a little polished, as if this were a habit.

'I wondered,' said Murray carefully, 'if you had heard word, from your fellow magistrates, perhaps, of any other attacks on the families of prominent politicians? After Cato Street –'

'Oh! Yes, that was Sir Joshua's principal concern, sir. He is convinced that some political agitator sought to strike out at him through Miss Akehurst. In fact, as you'll find when you visit, Mr. Murray,' the magistrate leaned forward confidentially, 'he has taken some precautions. Half the servants have been given notice, and no one is to be admitted to the house without his express permission. I fear for his health, Mr. Murray – you'll know that his heart is not strong – but I wonder, too, if I may say so, about the state of his mind. If you have only just met them, you might not be in a position to judge, but I wondered if perhaps this matter, and I understand he recently lost a valued clerk, too, might have had some effect on his stability?'

Murray frowned. Could it be true? Was Sir Joshua now going out of his mind?

'I'll have to see him again before I can judge, I think, Mr. Tebbitt. If you have quite finished here, I'm eager to go and find out.'

Chapter Twenty-Five

But once again, there was to be a distraction before he could reach the Akehursts' house.

Halfway up the High Street he had to shift to one side to avoid a flock of the local black-faced sheep, and, pressed against a flint wall, he was surprised to hear his name called. He looked around to find Fussy Payne perched on a doorstep, waving to him.

'Good day to you, Mr. Murray! Will you step in here? At least until the livestock passes!'

Murray edged his way further along the street by a few yards, and reached the doorstep. Fussy urged him inside.

'This is my godfather's house,' he explained. 'Oh! No coat? You're a brave man!'

'I left it at the Akehursts' last night,' Murray said briefly.

'Then come straight into the parlour. Will you take some refreshment? I am just about to ring for some tea.'

'Thank you, that would be very welcome.' Murray felt he was awash with coffee already. Fussy tugged on a bell rope, then sat opposite Murray at a cosy hearth.

'I can't believe all that is happening,' he said, leaning his elbows on his knees. 'Poor Amanda, and Paulinson, and everything: it seems never-ending!'

'You don't think, then, that this was the man's ultimate goal from the start? That now that Miss Akehurst is dead, it might all be over?'

Fussy gave him a close look.

'I don't believe that you think that,' he said. 'Mr. Blair told me a few stories of things that had happened to the pair of you, and I know that it often does not end with one death. Or even two. And

I suppose that Paulinson's death is related to Amanda's, isn't it? Do you think he knew something about what was to happen to her? Was that it?'

'Or it may be a political attack,' said Murray, moving aside for a moment from the possibility of Amanda being killed for her inheritance. After all, if that were the case then the prime suspect was sitting before him.

'Political? Oh, you mean someone wanting to attack Sir Joshua? Goodness, that's a nasty way to go about it, isn't it? Threatening. I suppose they hope that he will step down from the Admiralty in fright and they can find a more radically-minded man to take his place – I'm not sure how all that works, though. I try to avoid politics if I can.'

'Difficult, here in Lewes, isn't it?'

'Oh, yes!' Fussy stopped and looked about him, as though radicals might creep out of the panelling. 'Such a town! And yet, I do like it.'

'I do, too ... Tell me, Mr. Payne, if you will, and please do not take this badly: now that Miss Akehurst is dead, you are Sir Joshua's heir, are you not? Not to the knighthood, of course, but to his fortune?'

Fussy sat back, surprised.

'I suppose I am. I'm not sure, but I think so.'

Only Fussy, Murray thought, kindly Fussy, would not take that as an accusation of murder.

'Have you made a will, Mr. Payne?'

'Oh, please, call me Fussy! Everybody does. When someone says Mr. Payne I look about for my father! Yes, I made a will several years ago: I visited France, just after Napoleon was defeated, and my godfather advised me to put my affairs in order before I went, just in case. I suppose it stands. Do wills go out of date? I'm not sure.'

'No, not unless you marry. Are you married?'

'Goodness, no! I have never yet found a young lady prepared to put up with me. I've often thought of asking Isobel, you know, Mr. Murray, but I'm sure she would say no. She has far too much sense to ally herself with someone like me!'

Murray was not sure: he knew Isobel was fond of Fussy. But he was not going to encourage the man, not at all.

'So, if I might ask, who would benefit from your death? Who did you name in your will as your beneficiary, or beneficiaries?'

'My godfather, of course. I have no brothers or sisters, and my parents are dead. I knew that if anything happened to me, Mr. Lawrence would see to it that any friend that might care to would receive some remembrance of me, and the rest of the little I had would be put to good use. A – a soup kitchen, perhaps, or something like that. Nothing radical, of course – that would be entirely against his own inclinations. I didn't specify, of course. Mr. Lawrence is far more sensible than I.'

Murray considered. Mr. Lawrence was not far off Sir Joshua's age, he thought. And Sir Joshua, and then Fussy, would have to die for Mr. Lawrence to lay his hands on the money. Murray had never thought Mr. Lawrence particularly short of money, but that was no matter: men with thousands could still desire more. Well, if Mr. Lawrence were part of this, Fussy would be safe for now – at least until Sir Joshua was dead. But Sir Joshua had a weak heart …

'Ah, Mr. Murray.' The parlour door opened, and Mr. Lawrence himself appeared, grey and humourless as ever. Only someone as kindly as Fussy could genuinely be fond of such a man, Murray thought uncharitably. He could understand why Blair, usually so tolerant, might find Mr. Lawrence more than he could bear. He rose, though, and bowed respectfully.

'Mr. Payne was kind enough to invite me in as a flock of sheep passed,' he explained. Fussy was also on his feet, waving instructions to a maid who had brought the tea tray.

'Will you take some tea, Godfather?' he asked. 'We have been having a most interesting conversation. Mr. Murray wonders if Amanda was murdered for her inheritance.'

'Does he?' Mr. Lawrence turned gimlet eyes on Murray. 'I see you really have taken on your friend Blair's eccentric compulsions. He is full of impertinent questions, always.'

'But Godfather, Mr. Blair is excellent at solving puzzles! And usually to someone else's benefit – isn't that so, Mr. Murray?'

'It is certainly my belief that Mr. Blair does substantially more good than harm with his questions,' said Murray.

'Then you must excuse me, sir,' said Mr. Lawrence icily. 'I have no wish to be the object of your idle curiosity. What Adolphus does is entirely his business.' He turned, almost sending the maid flying, and stalked from the room.

'I – um – I must apologise, Mr. Murray,' said Fussy, abject at seeing distress in anyone else.

'Not at all, Fussy. I know that Mr. Lawrence and Blair have never seen eye to eye, have they? A shame, for I have never known Blair to dislike anyone, and Mr. Lawrence seems an honourable man.'

'He is! He is indeed – and I know that Mr. Blair is just as honourable, though his habits may be very different. What interest would there be in the world if we were all the same?' he added nervously. 'Is there any word on Mr. Blair's condition?'

'None yet, which is perhaps as good news as we can expect for now. I was on my way to enquire. I met a man today, by the way, who made the same enquiry and knew both Mr. Lawrence and Blair – are you acquainted with a Mr. Worthing?'

'Oh yes! He lives in Cliffe, does he not?'

'That's the one. He came to see me at the White Hart.'

'He's the protégé of old Mr. Olliver – the father-in-law of Mr. Lawrence as well as Mr. Blair. You knew that?'

'I did – it was Isobel who made me aware of him.'

'Mr. Lawrence does his duty, I know, but he cannot abide the man,' Fussy admitted, with half an eye on the door. 'Mr. Worthing has radical sympathies. But this is Lewes!'

'Of course.' It confirmed what Isobel had told him. 'He seemed a very respectable businessman.'

'Oh, he is. He made the most of Mr. Olliver's beneficence and built his business back up after a substantial loss. I believe his contacts now extend from London to the coast, and of course Lewes is the perfect place to tie the two together. Well, the river is such a good route. If they could only clear the roads of mud in the winter it would be perfect! Mr. Blair is interested in drainage that could help with that. But then Mr. Blair is interested in almost everything. I do pray he will make a good recovery.'

Not a full recovery, ever, Murray thought. Not with a missing leg.

'I must go and see how he does,' he said. 'If I am admitted. Apparently Sir Joshua is fortifying his house against further attack.'

'Really? May I come with you? That sounds very strange.'

'Of course.' After all, even if Fussy had murdered Amanda for her money, taking him back to the house was unlikely to cause any further harm that Fussy could not do on his own. Murray waited while Fussy went to tell the maid where he was going, and found his coat and hat and gloves and muffler and boots, and popped his head around Mr. Lawrence's study door to let him know what was happening, and reconsidered the gloves and found other ones, and was finally ready and at the door. Perhaps it was true: Isobel would not take him on. Nevertheless …

They were admitted to the Akehurst household, but not until the butler Trent had subjected them to considerable scrutiny, as if he had never seen either of them before. Clearly losing patience, Lady Akehurst appeared behind him in the hallway.

'Oh, it's you, Fussy. And Mr. Murray – good. Let them in, Trent, for heaven's sake.'

The butler backed off, and began loading his arms with all Fussy's outdoor accoutrements.

'Good day, my lady,' said Murray, squeezing past. 'May I go and pay my respects to Miss Blair and ask after Mr. Blair?'

'Oh! Oh, of course. You know where they are, don't you?'

'Yes, my lady. May I crave the favour of a word with you later? At your convenience, of course.'

'Oh? Oh, yes – you spoke with my husband yesterday, didn't you?' She frowned, then nodded. 'Of course: I shall be in the parlour with Miss Paterson.'

He bowed, and strode upstairs. He had caught a glimpse of Beatrix in the parlour, and had no wish to linger.

His soft knock at Blair's chamber door met with an equally quiet summons to enter. Isobel was seated as usual beside Blair's bed. Dr. Mantell was washing his hands in a basin.

'I beg your pardon,' said Murray, turning to go.

'No, Charles, come in,' said Isobel. 'Dr. Mantell had just finished, I believe.'

'I think so,' said the physician, 'if you are happy for me to tell you what my observations are just now.'

'Of course: Mr. Murray is our dearest friend.' She must have said such a thing before: why was it that now that phrase made his heart jump? She was not even looking at him. He shook his head, and paid attention to Dr. Mantell.

'The amputation wound is very clean,' said the doctor. 'There is no sign of infection there or in the injuries to the other leg. Your man Smith is to be commended on his attention to his task. Mr. Blair's pulse is healthier than I have felt it, and you'll have seen yourself that his colour is improving. But it is still vital to have every care. He is far from out of danger, of course.'

'Of course,' said Isobel quietly. 'We'll take every care. Do you hear that, Father? We're looking after you – all you have to do is to make your recovery.' She stroked his hand. Was it his imagination, or did Blair's eyelids shift ever so slightly?

He turned his attention back to Dr. Mantell, tidying his things on the top of a chest of drawers.

'Have you been able to examine Miss Akehurst's body, doctor?'

Dr. Mantell turned, folding a towel.

'Yes, I have, to an extent. I remember that you wanted to know more about it. Sir Joshua mentioned that you had some experience of these matters, too.' He cast a swift look at Isobel, then tilted his head towards the window. Murray followed him to stand gazing out at the garden. 'She was not interfered with,' Mantell said in a low voice. 'She did die of the cut throat, probably where she lay, for there was considerable blood in her clothing and on the ground. Apart from that, there were bruises on her upper arms and bruises and scratches on her feet and lower legs, probably from walking outside with no footwear.'

'The bruises on her upper arms – would they have been consistent with being pulled along against her will? Dragged from the house?'

'Yes, I should say so,' said the doctor. 'There was one sharp bruise on her lower right arm that puzzled me a little – it was curved, as though she had been struck by something of a particular shape.'

'Could you draw the shape?' Murray asked, knowing there was little chance that he would be allowed to inspect Amanda's body for himself.

'I believe I could, yes.'

'Isobel, may we have a piece of paper, and something to draw with?'

Isobel brought her sketchbook over, and watched, curious,

while Dr. Mantell drew a smooth ogee with what seemed like a ball forming one end.

'Was it a recent bruise?' Murray asked.

'I should say so, yes,' said Dr. Mantell, handing the sketchbook over to Murray. Isobel took it to tear out the page, folding the book closed again with the loose page in her hand. 'As, of course, were the ones on her upper arms. There were older ones around her waist and ribs, I should say, particularly at the front.'

'That will have been from Hyde Park,' said Isobel. Dr. Mantell looked at her, and Isobel described the way the horseman had seized her, then dropped her across the side of the carriage. 'I'm sure it hurt.'

'I should have thought so, yes,' said Dr. Mantell thoughtfully. 'So this was not the first incident?'

'No, nor the second,' said Isobel. 'No doubt it was hidden by her later injuries, but someone tried to cut her throat before. A few days ago, at the Royal Pavilion.'

'When Sir Joshua collapsed?'

'That's right, yes.'

Dr. Mantell puffed out, eyes wide.

'A most unfortunate family,' he said. 'I must take my leave now, but call for me, Miss Blair, if you need me. You, too, Mr. Murray, if you have any more questions. Good Lord – most unfortunate.'

He took his bag, and left the room, shaking his head. Isobel returned to Blair's bedside, as if he might have done something while she had her back to him.

'He is a better colour,' said Murray, going to the other side as usual.

'Do you think?' She examined her father's face minutely. 'I think I agree, but I'm afraid to give myself hope, just in case ...'

'And you've spent so much time with him that you'll not see a gradual change so easily,' he countered. 'I'm sure he looks better now than he did yesterday.'

She flashed a smile at him, but looked away at once.

'Smith has tended him very well.'

'As have you: I'm sure he knows you are here.' Isobel did not reply, and he felt superfluous. But there was one thing he could do most easily from here. 'Do you think Smith would bring the kitchenmaid Rosie up here? I think I need to find out if she knows anything useful about her recent mistress.'

Isobel shot him a look which he could not interpret.

'Of course. I'll ring for him.'

Smith was efficient. In only a few minutes Rosie, with a curious glance at the Blairs, was standing by the window in Blair's room.

'Are you back to the kitchen, Rosie?' Murray asked, and she nodded. 'Happy to be so?'

'I want to be a cook, sir, not a ladies' maid,' said Rosie calmly.

'Not so keen on looking after gowns and hair and so on?'

'No, sir.'

'Not so many gowns to look after for Miss Paterson, though.'

'No, sir.' She frowned. 'She never bought those gowns from a dealer, sir. They were her own gowns. Her initials was in the back, "B.P." I seen them.'

'Well spotted, Rosie.' He took a breath. 'Did you wonder why she might have pretended that she bought them from a dealer?'

Rosie shook her head sharply.

'Are you sure? You're a bright girl, Rosie, I've no doubt.'

Rosie let out an exasperated hiss through her teeth.

'See, this is why I don't want to be a ladies' maid. Food is food, and you cook it well and send it up looking nice. Gentlefolk – they're a deal more complicated.'

'Aren't they just?' Smith put in. 'Never saw the like before I went into service.'

Rosie flashed him a glance and gave a tiny nod.

'There's more than the gowns, then?' Smith went on. 'There's always more, ain't there?'

'Well …' Rosie considered. 'Well, I didn't say nothing before, because I'd seen Miss Paterson before.'

'You had?' Murray could not help snapping. Was Sir Joshua Akehurst really Beatrix's protector?

'Oh, yes, sir, just the once. See when I venture up the stairs? No good ever comes of it.'

'That's the truth,' said Smith gloomily. 'Stay in the kitchens – much safer.'

'When were you upstairs, then, to see Miss Paterson?'

'I wasn't up to see her. It was one evening. The dinner had gone in, and Mrs. Lively – she's the cook, she's just wonderful – she saw that one of the footmen had taken her good big ladle by accident. "Run up the back way quick, Rosie," she said, "and keep to the dark corners. If that there ladle goes into the dining room I'll never hear the end of it – and I'll likely not get my best ladle back, neither." So off I went, but I'm barely up the stairs ever, Mr. Smith,' she explained, finding him the safer person to talk to. 'So I missed my way, and there I was in the hall. I near died! And then I saw Mr. Trent, and Miss Paterson, and he was taking her up the stairs.'

'Mr. Trent was?' Smith nodded. 'Aye, there's a thing.'

'He never saw me, or I'd have lost my place straight off,' said Rosie. 'But up the stairs they went, and I never budged until I heard them all the way up on to the second landing, well past me.'

'Have you any idea, Rosie,' said Murray as gently as possible, 'when this was?'

'Not long before the family left Fitzroy Square,' said Rosie firmly. 'It was the night afore the day they found Mr. Paulinson dead on the doorstep.'

'Was it indeed?' Murray glanced over at Isobel, who met his eye with raised eyebrows. 'That's very interesting. Thank you very much, Rosie. I hope you manage to become a cook, and avoid the perils of being a ladies' maid.'

For it struck him that Rosie might well have been in peril, the minute she ventured up those stairs.

And now he would have to deal with Beatrix, he thought to himself, as he went to the parlour door. This was the room with the French windows to the garden, though there was little bright natural light to flood the place this morning. Lady Akehurst was seated near the windows, trying to benefit from what little there was as she embroidered something subdued. Beatrix, on a stool at her feet, was sorting threads in a marquetry box, like a favourite daughter. She smiled up at Murray – as well she might, Murray thought. He had been instrumental in introducing her to this household, and they had taken her in without question. He prayed that she would not – what? Let him down? Let herself down?

'Ah, Mr. Murray,' said Lady Akehurst. 'Please, take a seat.'

He sat opposite, and watched her for a moment. The grey

light was not flattering: she looked twenty years older than she had at dinner when he had first arrived. But that was before she had lost her beloved grand-daughter.

'You were kind enough to say I might ask a few questions,' he said. If Beatrix's protector – if she had one – was really here to guard Sir Joshua, then this would help her, too.

'You may,' said Lady Akehurst, 'since my husband says you might be able to help us find out who did this dreadful thing.'

'I shall do my best, my lady.' He considered for a moment. 'I know Miss Akehurst will have talked with you all the time, but did she also have friends in whom she might have confided?'

'Friends? Outside the household, you mean?'

'Yes – I've noted how young ladies who attend assemblies and so on tend to cluster together and chatter. I wondered who might have been in Miss Akehurst's circle.'

Lady Akehurst looked puzzled.

'I don't believe she did. Of course, some girls know each other from school, or because they are sisters and cousins and so on. Amanda was educated by a governess at home.' She considered for a moment, perhaps anxious that she was portraying Amanda as a friendless, unpopular girl. 'She and Miss Blair were very close, you know. No doubt she spoke with her. Miss Blair admired her tremendously, I know.'

'Miss Isobel Blair?' Murray tried not to sound taken aback.

'Yes, Miss Isobel Blair. A quiet girl, but always with Amanda's best interests at heart.'

'Well, she would have, yes,' Murray agreed. He thought he heard Beatrix giggle, but ignored her. 'The reception at the Royal Pavilion – that must have been a splendid evening, at first?'

'Oh, very splendid! Everyone of any standing was there – it was packed, you know, with glittering people!'

'Did you see Miss Akehurst leave the reception room?'

'See her? Ah – ah, no, not exactly.'

'She'll have said where she was going, though, I imagine.'

'Well, no, not precisely. No, she didn't. I should think Miss Blair knew, though.' Lady Akehurst was quick to pass her chaperoning duties over to Isobel. But Isobel had not known that Amanda was leaving, until she heard that she had gone.

'What did Miss Akehurst say about it afterwards? She must

have told you who she was with when she left the reception room.'

'Oh, yes. She was with a young gentleman we'd just met – a perfectly pleasant young gentleman – the son of ... now, who was it again? She has so many young gentlemen interested in her, you know.'

'Someone who lived in Brighton?' Murray suggested.

'In Brighton? Now, then, was he? Do you know, I couldn't say? He was staying nearby, I'm sure, though.'

It was more than likely, Murray thought, if he had been attending a reception.

'I imagine, though, he was not, for example, the son of a Duke? Or even an Earl?'

'Oh, no,' Lady Akehurst chuckled, though it was an empty sound. 'No, I should have remembered that, I can assure you!'

Yes, that was what he had thought. Lady Akehurst had her priorities.

'But did he leave the reception room with her?' he asked. 'Or did he allow her to continue alone into the corridor?'

'Ah, now there I do know,' said Lady Akehurst. 'Or rather, I know what she said, for she could not remember clearly. She was attacked very suddenly, you see, and then she fainted, and she could not remember if the young gentleman had been with her or not.'

'If he were there,' said Murray, 'he did not make himself known to her friends, anyway.'

Lady Akehurst blinked at him.

'No,' she said slowly. 'No, you're right, he did not. That is odd.'

Murray looked away, thinking. Outside the French windows the garden was sinking into autumnal decay. A gardener, hunched in a woollen coat drawn tight into his waist, was raking leaves from the lawn. His focus shifted and he looked at the French windows themselves, wondering what had caught his eye.

It was the handles. Ogee shaped, with a little pommel on the end. Just like the bruise on Miss Akehurst's dead arm.

'Those are pretty handles,' he remarked casually. 'They look familiar – do you have them anywhere else in the house?'

'I'm sure they're everywhere, Charles,' said Beatrix with a smile.

'No, no, they're not,' said Lady Akehurst, 'for we had that

window put in when we took the house a few months ago, and I chose those handles because they are easier to open than the round ones, you know?'

'Perhaps I saw them in another house,' said Murray, quite as if it did not matter. 'May I return, Lady Akehurst, if I have further questions?'

'I suppose so,' she said, 'if you really think you can help.'

'I'll do my best, my lady,' he repeated. 'Now, if you will excuse me ...' He rose, and she waved a hand to dismiss him. This time he bowed much more properly, and left the room.

In the hall, he found Trent.

'Tell me, Trent,' he said, and caused the man to start shaking. 'Presumably you locked up the house on the night Miss Akehurst vanished.'

'I did, sir, most rigorously.' Murray could hear his teeth rattle.

'All the doors?'

'And the downstairs windows, too, sir. Sir Joshua has been most particular. He has made me get rid of all the staff who could not prove their support for the Government, sir.' His tone was an odd mixture of distress and pride.

'And yesterday morning, before her disappearance was discovered – you'll have unlocked doors again, presumably?'

'Yes, sir.'

'Did you notice any door already unlocked?'

'No, sir. I am the first up, and the last to bed. I've –' He looked about suddenly, and leaned a little closer. 'I've managed to stay away from the drink, sir, and my mind's clear. The doors were all locked, and the doors were all unlocked, by me, sir.'

'Who else has keys?'

'Sir Joshua, sir, and her Ladyship has some. But some of the doors have the keys in the locks overnight. Just in case of fire, really.'

'Which doors?'

'The front door, the kitchen door and the parlour French windows, sir.'

'The front door is solid wood. Is the kitchen door glazed?'

'No, sir.'

But the French window, of course, was. But none of the glass had been broken: no one had reached in to use the key that was there. Yet the bruise on Amanda's arm made it look as if she had been taken out by the French window, which had then been locked behind her.

And Murray was fairly sure he knew by whom.

Chapter Twenty-Six

He was about to turn and run back to the parlour, when a bell jangled uncertainly.

'That's the parlour bell, sir. I'll have to go.' Trent looked relieved at the excuse to get away, but Murray followed close on his heels.

Lady Akehurst's right hand was on the bell rope still, clutching it as though it had taken a mighty effort to reach it. Her left hand was on her chest, where the dainty loops of her embroidery scissors' handles stuck out like a crooked brooch. The French window was open. There was no sign of Beatrix.

'I'm not dead. I'm not,' breathed Lady Akehurst. 'I won't let myself be. Little cat,' she added, and even with her eyes half-closed it was clear she had glanced at the open window.

'Damnation!' cried Murray. 'Fetch her maid, then go for Dr. Mantell. Quickly!'

Without stopping to see if Trent had obeyed him, he made for the window. Outside, the terrace was damp but the stone showed no footprints. Which way had she gone? Off into the fields, or further down to the town?

Beatrix seemed like a town girl to him. He chose to make for the lane and the High Street. Not allowing himself to run, he strode quickly, trying to keep his wits about him. Beatrix was too canny just to bolt when she thought he suspected her. She would have a plan. But what was it?

Instinct took him up the lane and into the High Street, past the place where Blair had met with the cart. Beatrix had not been acting alone, of course. But she had let the fellow into the house to abduct Miss Akehurst, and had locked the door after him. She had lied to Murray, and used him. Her protector, or whoever the man was, had no sympathies with Sir Joshua at all, nor any wish to guard him from harm.

Even as he walked, looking about him, looking ahead of him – and sometimes, warily, glancing behind him – he tried to work everything out. Beatrix had used him to get into the Akehurst household, just as she had admitted, but for bad, not for good. Her ally, then, probably did not work in the Admiralty or the Government, and indeed seemed to be working against them. Beatrix would easily have been able to lay a trail for the ally to follow, to come down from London to Brighton and thence to Lewes – she could even have left notes, perhaps at Coombe Warren or – oh! anywhere, to say that Brighton was their destination, so that a man in a green coat on a good horse could easily overtake them on the road and be in Brighton before them, in time to attack Amanda at the Pavilion, in time to meet Beatrix with the bundle of her clothes he had brought from London. And then he could have ridden to Newhaven and set fire to the semaphore tower in mid-construction. And then followed them to Lewes, when Beatrix knew where they were going.

But in that case, he would not have been in Lewes in time to draw Blair out of the Akehursts' house in the middle of the night. Could that have been coincidence? Just a chance sneak thief, testing the doors to see if they were locked, and happening to catch Blair's attention? Not everything around a murder has to be linked with the murder, does it?

Yet he felt it should be, in this case. If it had just been a passing thief, would Blair not have called out for help? Summoned a few servants, and frightened the fellow off? And whoever the fellow was, it could not have been Beatrix's friend, for he would not have known where to find them.

Thoughts tumbled around in his head as he passed Mr. Lawrence's house, stopped, and returned. Could she have taken refuge here? Given Mr. Lawrence some sad story, and hidden in his parlour? Or would she just have gone on? Where was she going, anyway? He was bewildered, and found himself knocking at Mr. Lawrence's prim white door.

The maid led him into the parlour, and in a moment he was joined by Mr. Lawrence himself.

'Twice in one day, Mr. Murray? I should feel honoured.'

'Please forgive the intrusion, Mr. Lawrence, but I wondered if you had perhaps seen anything of Miss Paterson today?'

'Miss Paterson? Is that who you are after now?'

'No, sir: she left the Akehursts' house precipitately after an incident with Lady Akehurst. I think the magistrate will want a word.'

Mr. Lawrence's eyebrows rose with slow emphasis. But he was the kind always to be on the side of the magistrate.

'As it happens I did notice her, through my study window, not five minutes ago. Bonnetless, and wearing only a shawl over her gown, but then that is what young people are like these days, isn't it?' He eyed Murray's own head – Murray had not stopped to collect his own hat, either. 'It did strike me that perhaps she was taking urgent news somewhere – in fact, I wondered if she were going to the White Hart with a message for you.'

'She was heading that way? And you're sure it was her?' Murray was already halfway to the door.

'I'm quite certain,' said Mr. Lawrence. 'Even though I do not make it my business to poke into the affairs of others, I can be sure of my own eyes when I see something.'

'Thank you, sir. Please excuse me.'

'Of course. Good day to you.' Mr. Lawrence's thin tones followed Murray along the hall and back to the front door. He darted out on to the street, and stared down the hill. Was that her? That green dress? The dull autumn light made it hard to see clearly. He set off quickly again.

The hallway of the White Hart was empty: even the usual servant who kept guard at the front door was not there. Murray was not sure which room had been Beatrix's, nor where Robbins might be at the moment. He had talked of going to see Smith in case there was anything he could find out from the Akehurst servants. Murray left the inn and went round the corner to the stableyard, to see if anyone there had seen Beatrix.

The stableyard was quiet, too. Murray wondered where Old Donald was: it was rare for him to leave his horses for any length of time, finding them better company than any humans. Murray glanced into a stall or two, found his own horses, then found Young Donald. He was buckling a saddle on to Coalman.

'Are you intending to ride him out?' Murray asked. Young Donald jumped so hard he knocked both elbows on the wooden walls of the stall. Coalman whickered, not pleased. He looked up at Murray with a blank expression. Murray noted that in the neighbouring stall, another of his horses was sporting a cheap-looking saddle, too.

'I'm just – they need some exercise, sir. I hope you don't mind.'

'Hm. Good, good.' Young Donald relaxed a little. 'Tell, me, Donald,' Murray went on casually, 'it's an expensive place, these days. Where did you find to stay in Brighton?'

'In Brighton, sir? I was never in Brighton.'

'Were you not?'

Young Donald shook his head, clearly puzzled.

'Then I wonder,' said Murray, 'how you came to follow us from London to Lewes, without going the way we went?'

'I didn't – I don't understand, sir.'

'You weren't following us at all, Donald, were you? You came straight down to Lewes, for reasons of your own. It was pure bad luck on your part that we came here too, wasn't it?' Facts were slipping into place in Murray's mind. 'Let me think: how involved were you really in those disturbances in Glasgow? Your friend was arrested, wasn't he? You fled to your uncle, to avoid the same fate.'

'I never, sir,' said Donald, but his voice was faint.

'And when you heard you were going to London, you decided to join the radicals down here, see what use you could be to them. Your friends in Glasgow could give you names, maybe addresses. You wrote to them, didn't you, before we left? Not to your mother at all.'

'I would have written to her, too!' Donald protested, but Murray continued.

'So as soon as we reached London, you went to meet with your new fellow radicals. Is that where you saw Beatrix?'

'Who?'

'Miss Pirrie. Miss Paterson, as she is here.'

'Oh! Oh, you mean her! I mean, the lady that's been coming here?' He attempted to assume a bold, innocent look, but could not resist a glance at the horses. When he looked back at Murray, Murray's raised eyebrows were emphatic. 'I didn't meet her straight away, sir, no. But she was around.'

'She can't have told you she was going to Lewes, though. We didn't know ourselves until we'd been in Brighton for a day. So why were you in Lewes?'

'I was sent down here, sir,' said Donald, with surly resignation. 'Sent down with the instruction to wait, and make myself useful. There's plenty of people like us down here, you ken,' he added, with a flash of defiance.

'And a semaphore line to destroy, no doubt.'

'That wasna me, sir,' he said at once, but there was an air of disappointed truth to it. Donald would have liked to have set fire to a half-built semaphore tower, it seemed.

'What else was, then? You've been here longer than you told me before, it seems.'

At that, Donald's face flushed with shame.

'I only went to look at the house. It was pure chance I found the man he was after had a house in the town, so I went for a look. And that old fellow saw me, and man, he had a turn of speed!'

'What?'

'He ran after me, the old fellow, in some big coat and his nightshirt. The fool! But then that cart hit him, and I got away. How was I to know?'

'How were you to know what?' Murray asked carefully. Here was another question answered, though.

'How was I to know ... that he wasn't Sir Joshua?' Donald's eyes slid sideways. Was he lying? Murray was not sure how to dig the truth out from this one. He sighed, and let it go for now.

'So now you have two horses saddled. One for Miss Pirrie, and one for you?'

'Aye, maybe.'

'My horses, though, Donald.'

'Aye, sir. Well, Miss Pirrie said you wouldn't mind. And if you did, then, well, you were part of the establishment we want to bring down, ken, so it wouldn't matter.'

'Miss Pirrie said that?' Murray almost smiled.

'Aye, sir, and she's just off to fetch her things from upstairs.'

'And does your uncle know you're taking away his two favourite horses?'

'Och, dinna tell him, sir! He'll skelp me! And he'll tell my ma.'

'I suggest you unsaddle them, Donald, and leave them here. Quickly, now.'

He stood over Donald while the lad, fumbling and tripping, removed saddles and bridles again. Murray kept an eye on the back door of the inn, knowing it was likely that Beatrix would appear at any second. But somehow, somehow he was lucky.

'Right,' said Murray, 'come with me.' He made sure Donald was beside him as they left the stableyard. At the inn door, the servant had reappeared.

'Have you seen Miss Paterson, who was staying upstairs?' Murray asked.

'Yes, sir,' said the servant at once. 'She went out naught but five minutes ago, and turned right, if that's of assistance to you, sir.'

'Thank you.' Murray also went out and turned right. Donald scurried after, clearly torn between rebellion and obedience. Murray was not sure how long the conflict would remain unresolved, but was determined to use it as long as he could. 'Donald, where did you stay in Lewes?'

'Down in Cliffe, sir,' said Donald at once. 'A man in London said I could stay in his house for a night or two.'

'A man in London. Did he have a name, this man?'

Donald squirmed.

'I canna say, sir. I'm that … I canna say.'

'Was it Ketchell?'

Donald frowned, genuinely surprised.

'No, sir. I dinna think I've ever come across a'body with a name like that.'

'Then what was it?'

'I canna say!'

Murray stopped and gave Donald a searching look. The boy was afraid.

'You know what he has done, don't you?'

Donald wriggled again, looking down, sideways, anywhere but at Murray's face. He muttered something.

'What was that?'

'Killed a girl …'

'Yes, Donald, he killed a girl. A girl with no interest in politics at all. Why would he do that?'

'Don't know,' Donald grunted. 'See, Miss Pirrie and me, we were going to get out of it on those horses. Leave him well behind, and get off back to London where nobody would ken who we were.'

Murray opened his mouth to reply, but decided not to disillusion Donald just yet. He was pretty sure in his own mind that those two horses were for Beatrix, and for her friend. Donald would have been cast aside.

He took the road down to Cliffe, Donald hurrying beside him.

'You can show me the house where you stayed,' he said. 'You don't need to say anything: just stand across the street and point.'

'What if he sees me?' Donald sounded wretched. 'He'll do more than skelp me!'

'Not if you help me,' said Murray firmly. 'That way he'll be in no position to harm you. Come on, hurry up.'

At St. Thomas' Church, they paused. Donald lifted a wavering hand, and pointed, as Murray knew he would, to Worthing's little terraced house. The maid was cleaning the outside of the one downstairs window. Murray, with a warning look at Donald, crossed the street.

'Is Mr. Worthing within?'

The maid turned and recognised him, dropping a plump curtsey.

'No, sir, I'm so sorry. You've just missed him again – but you might be able to catch him up. He's gone up to Sir Joshua's house, to see old Mr. Blair.'

'Has he?' Murray was taken aback – then horrified. 'Has he, indeed? Donald, did the old fellow see you? The one hit by the cart?'

'Aye, sir, I should think he did.'

'Did you mention it to Mr. Worthing?'

'Aye, sir – he was gey angry. I dinna ken why.'

'Damnation,' hissed Murray. 'Donald, come on!'

The High Street had never seemed so steep. School Hill nearly burned out Murray's weaker knee, and the long run after that did nothing to help it recover. Donald, panting, stayed close behind, eager not to lose favour now. They ran, and at last spun round the corner into the lane with the broad pasture of Shelley's meadow in front of them. One more corner, and they were at the Akehursts' house.

All seemed quiet. From the gate, Murray stepped up the gravel sweep, as quietly as he could, wincing at the pain in his knee. Donald followed, pulling his breath back under control. They had not overtaken Worthing, and they had run along the direct route. Had Worthing taken some other path, perhaps to fulfil some errand on the way? Or perhaps, thought Murray, reaching the front door, he was already inside.

He was not in the hall, though, contrary to Sir Joshua's instructions, the front door was unlocked. But the hall was not unguarded: Trent was there, though he looked on the point of collapse.

'Oh, Mr. Murray!' he exclaimed, ignoring Donald, 'oh, what I would give for a glass of brandy! What a household!'

'It will have to be tea for now, Trent,' said Murray, though his tone was sympathetic. 'How is Lady Akehurst?'

'She will recover, likely enough,' came a familiar voice. Dr. Mantell, who seemed almost to have taken up residence, appeared at the head of the stairs. He gestured upwards presumably towards Lady Akehurst's room, and came quickly down to their level, dropping his voice. 'If I were to be permitted a moment's indelicacy,' he said to Murray, 'her corsets saved her. They are unusually robust.'

'I think perhaps, too, the assailant was in too much of a hurry to make sure,' said Murray.

'Miss Paterson?' Dr. Mantell asked. 'Lady Akehurst is alert enough to give quite a clear account of the assault, though she is in some shock. It happened, apparently, without warning.'

'Miss Paterson realised that she was about to fall under suspicion. It was she, I believe, who admitted the man who abducted Miss Akehurst.'

'Miss Paterson did? Good heavens! Why?'

'I believe the whole thing is political,' said Murray, with half a shrug. He glanced at Donald, who stood to the side of the hall but listened, face pale. 'Listen, has there been any sign of a visitor, a Mr. Worthing?' He looked from the physician to Trent. Trent nodded.

'Mr Worthing arrived some moments ago. I showed him upstairs to Mr. Blair's room. Mr. Smith was in attendance, as well as Miss Blair.'

'Oh, good Lord!' cried Murray, and made for the stairs. But he had barely reached them when a door opened, and Sir Joshua appeared. He was pale as chalk, and trembled, but his eyes were flint.

'More disturbance?' he demanded. 'Oh, it's you, Mr. Murray. Dr. Mantell, tell me how my wife does? Will you step in here to the library? You too, Mr. Murray – you need to know what has happened to my wife. More attacks! It is intolerable!' His words made it sound like a domestic disturbance, but the shake of his hands as he waved them into the room told its own story. He went to stand by the fire, supporting himself with a thumb on the mantelpiece. To Murray's surprise, Ketchell stood by the window. He nodded at the doctor and Murray as they came in.

'Good day to you, sirs,' he murmured.

'Sir Joshua,' said Murray urgently, 'I fear that there is someone hostile in the house. I was about to go upstairs to Mr. Blair, where I believe the man might be. I fear for the safety of Mr. Blair and his daughter. And his servant.'

'Someone in the house? Again?'

But despite Murray's move back towards the door, Sir Joshua seemed determined to stay in the way, hovering near the doorway, surveying Murray and Dr. Mantell with a confused air. Murray, in his agitation, wondered if all the shocks had addled his mind. He did not look at all well.

Then just as Murray had decided he would have to squeeze past Sir Joshua, several things seemed to happen at once.

There was a noise in the hall, and a sudden movement at the library door.

Something hurtled at Sir Joshua. Before Murray could do anything about it, a figure shot past him. There was a tremendous thump. Sir Joshua staggered back against the empty shelving behind him, falling over a crate of books as he went. Dr. Mantell, anxious for his patient, started forward, but Murray grabbed his arm. The nasty sound of fist hitting flesh, and a cry of pain, then a ripping noise and a shriek. And then Murray found his moment, darted forward, and seized two flailing arms, holding elbows as firmly as he could behind the man's back.

'It's over, Worthing,' he said, tugging the man backwards.

But as Worthing struggled against his grip, Murray looked down. On the library floor, slumped again the crate Sir Joshua had fallen over, was Ketchell, with a knife in his throat.

Chapter Twenty-Seven

But even as Dr. Mantell fell to his knees beside Ketchell, there was a cry from upstairs – a voice that Murray knew was Isobel's. He flung Worthing into the arms of Trent the butler, and bounded out of the room.

He ran unhesitatingly to Blair's room, and flung wide the door. Inside, Isobel was clinging on to the arm of Young Donald, the groom. And Young Donald, like Worthing downstairs, had a knife. It hovered over Blair's silent form, only kept back by Isobel's desperate grip.

Young Donald spun, and grabbed Isobel, holding her in front of him with the knife to her throat as he backed across the room. Where he was going was not clear – away from Murray and Blair, anyway.

'Let her go, Donald,' said Murray. 'You haven't killed anyone yet, and now is not the time to start.'

'I might of,' said Donald, defiant but shaky. 'I might of killed a'body. You ken nothing about me.'

'I know you're not likely to kill a defenceless woman.' If Murray had been anxious about Isobel's nerve, her sudden cross look at this description reassured him.

'I might, though,' Donald countered. His hand fidgeted on the knife handle, trying different angles. Murray swallowed. Should he push forward? Or hold back and allow Donald to calm down? Donald was right: he knew very little about his groom. Was he the kind to panic? Would he lash out if he were cornered? Donald might seem confident, but Murray did not like the way his eyes flickered, left, right, up, down, looking for a rat run out.

He stepped forward.

Not so much looking for a way out. More deciding on

priorities.

Donald flung Isobel down in front of Murray, and lunged for the bed, knife flashing.

Murray tripped on Isobel, but Donald had not taken into account his master's height. Even falling, Murray managed to tumble into and unbalance Donald. He fell with a crash against the night table, seemed about to surge up, then collapsed, dropping the knife from his senseless hand.

For a moment all was still. Then Murray reached out a long arm and picked the knife carefully off the floor.

'What? What's going on?' came a faint voice.

'Father!' cried Isobel, scrambling out from under Murray's feet. 'Father! I'm here!' She rang the bell for Smith, never taking her eyes from Blair. Murray, too, pushed himself up to see over the side of the bed. Blair was blinking, bewildered.

'Isobel?' he murmured. 'And Charles! Very glad to see you, Charles. Lots to do.' He beamed at both of them in turn, then closed his eyes again. But his colour was healthy, or nearly so, and he clutched Isobel's hand in firm fingers.

'Dr. Mantell is probably still downstairs,' said Murray, finding he was now sitting on Donald's legs. It seemed as good a way as any of keeping him in one place. 'Oh, downstairs – you won't know. I hardly know, myself.' He sat back and rubbed his face.

'Well, go on, then, tell me!' said Isobel, though even being impatient with him she could not keep the smile from her face.

'Mr. Worthing tried to stab Sir Joshua,' he said, 'I think, but Ketchell threw himself in the way.'

'Mr. Ketchell?'

'I think there is more to Ketchell than we realised.' Murray sighed. 'I'd better take this fellow down and see what's happening. And send Dr. Mantell up.'

'Are you not going to tell me why your groom tried to kill my father?' she asked severely.

'Oh – yes, that. He was the one outside the house that night, the one your father chased. He did tell me, but I suspect he thought better of his confession. If he made sure your father was dead, it would only have been my word against his – and no connexion to Worthing or to – to Beatrix.'

'Ah, yes, Beatrix,' said Isobel neutrally.

Murray sighed again.

'I'll tell you about Beatrix later. I will, I promise!' he said, seeing the expression on her face – her much loved face. How was he ever going to tell her that? 'I'm going to borrow this curtain tie, though,' he said, trying to focus on practicalities. 'I don't want Donald to escape, though I've a dread that Worthing might have.'

But downstairs, he discovered that Trent had been surprisingly efficient at holding Worthing, or at least at handing him over to one of those large footmen with a fixed expression and hands like shovels. Dr. Mantell was tending to Sir Joshua, who lay on the daybed, pale but conscious, and attended by Fussy and Harry Holden. A sheet covered Ketchell's body.

'We heard all the noise and came to see what was going on,' said Fussy to Murray. 'Saw you flying up the stairs. Everything all right up there? For it's far from all right down here,' he added, as cheerless as Murray had ever seen him.

'It could be worse,' said Murray. 'We have one of Mr. Worthing's friends tied up, too.'

Worthing, pinned in place by the footman, frowned.

'Oh, don't worry, Worthing, it's not Beatrix,' said Murray. 'But Donald decided to tidy up a loose end.'

'I knew he was a mistake,' muttered Worthing. 'Idealist.'

'What's going on here?' came another voice from the doorway. 'Worthing? What have you done?' It was Mr Lawrence, lip curled as he looked about him, from Worthing to Sir Joshua, from Harry Holden to the ominous sheet-covered shape on the floor. 'Who – who has died?'

'Ketchell,' said Sir Joshua, finally waving Dr. Mantell away.

'Doctor,' said Murray quickly, 'if you have a moment, Mr. Blair has said a few words.'

'Really?' With a startled look, Dr. Mantell hurried out.

'Has he, indeed?' asked Mr. Lawrence, but to Murray's surprise he looked relieved beyond measure.

'But why is Ketchell dead?' Harry Holden demanded. His face was wet with tears and wracked with confusion. 'Why did that man attack him?'

'Ketchell saved my life,' said Sir Joshua.

'He was working for you, wasn't he?' asked Murray. Sir

Joshua gave him a sharp look, then shook his head.

'Not anymore, no. He worked for us during the wars.'

'As a government agent,' said Murray.

'That's right. Blamed the Admiralty for wrecking his constitution – too much gin luring people into telling him their secrets, too many late nights and early mornings. And they refused him a pension. So when he turned up with Harry, well, I thought, he might as well stay.'

'Ketchell saved your life?' asked Mr. Lawrence. 'Do you mean there has been another attack? Oh,' he suddenly seemed to add things up in his head, 'oh, you mean that Worthing attacked you?' He turned a horrified look at Worthing in the corner.

'But ...' said Fussy, frowning over the whole problem, 'does that mean that Worthing has been behind the whole business? Did he attack Amanda? Did you, Worthing?'

'I'm saying nothing,' said Worthing, his handsome face hard.

'He did, though,' said Murray. 'Miss Paterson unlocked the French window for him, and locked it again afterwards.' Worthing flashed him a look, but pressed his lips shut.

'You brought Miss Paterson into the house,' said Mr. Lawrence, ominously.

'I did, in all innocence,' said Murray. Was he really innocent? He had known some of what Beatrix was. 'For which I apologise. Worthing was the man who attacked Miss Akehurst in Hyde Park. Neither Blair nor Mr. Lawrence, who would have recognised him, saw him clearly. He attacked her again at the Pavilion. Then he followed us to Lewes, and this time carried out his final attack.'

'You make it sound as if he planned three attacks,' said Mr. Lawrence dubiously.

'I think he did, didn't you, Worthing?'

'But why?' demanded Sir Joshua. 'Surely it's simply that he failed the first two times. He was interrupted at the Pavilion by Miss Blair, and Mr. Blair stopped him snatching her in Hyde Park.' He took out a handkerchief and unobtrusively dabbed his eyes.

'For the same reason that he killed your secretary, and that Miss Paterson attacked Lady Akehurst. To make you suffer, sir.'

Watching Worthing, he just caught sight of a nasty little

smile on Worthing's face. It confirmed his suspicions.

'Radicals, everywhere!' Fussy breathed. 'None of us is safe!'

'Is that really why you did it, Worthing?' Mr. Lawrence suddenly asked. 'Because you had another reason, didn't you, to wish Sir Joshua harm?'

'Did he?' asked Fussy, taken aback.

'I know Worthing,' Mr. Lawrence explained to the room, 'because my late father-in-law took pity on him before his death, and established a small trust to help him and his business to recover from a most disastrous loss. A loss which, I regret to say, derived, wholly, from the trust he placed in Sir Joshua.'

'What?' Sir Joshua struggled to sit up. Murray was also blinking. Why had Mr. Lawrence not thought to mention this before?

'I do not approve of Worthing,' said Mr. Lawrence, as stiff as ever, 'but I cannot deny, Sir Joshua, that you were responsible for Worthing's business collapse, and indirectly therefore for the death of his wife. No doubt this has made any political attack on you all the more appealing to him.'

'There was nothing political about it,' Worthing shouted, making them all jump. 'He ruined me. I couldn't believe it when I heard he had bought this place, in my own town! That I should be forced to see him, to share a street with him, to breathe the same air – it was disgusting! Repulsive! The man is no better than a thief!'

'So whatever we did you would have known to come to Lewes anyway?' Murray asked. 'And you sent Donald down here to wait for you?'

'Oh,' said Worthing, 'to try to get him out of the way. He was determined to destroy every man in Government. That was not my aim. When I went in with the fellows in Cato Street, it was only to destroy him.' He nodded at Sir Joshua.

'You were in the Cato Street conspiracy?' asked Fussy, aghast.

'You didn't think they'd caught everyone, did you?' asked Worthing disparagingly. Fussy flushed, aware that he was never quite up to current affairs.

'What about my secretary?' Sir Joshua demanded. 'What about poor Paulinson?'

Worthing laughed, then grunted. It seemed the large footman could squeeze quite hard with those huge hands.

'Beatrix kept him occupied while you left the house, and then we got him outside. That poor man – you should have encouraged him to get out and enjoy himself more. It took very little in the way of gin and blandishments to render him completely useless. It was almost a shame to take advantage of him – but if it hurt you,' he could not seem to bring himself even to mention Akehurst's name, 'it was well worth it.'

'The magistrate is here, sir,' put in Trent, who had briefly left the room.

'Bring him in. I need to hear all this again before you hang, Worthing,' said Sir Joshua.

Murray did not. He had almost the full picture, but one thing was missing. He needed to find Beatrix, though she was probably long gone by now.

At the White Hart, he tried the stables first. Old Donald was back, and anxious.

'Sir! I found that Miss Paterson trying to take one of the horses – was I right to stop her? I canna find Young Donald anywhere, sir: he might have helped.'

'Yes, you were right. And I'm afraid we've lost Young Donald again. Where did Miss Paterson go?'

'I didn't see, sir,' said Old Donald, already puzzling over his nephew. 'But she mentioned that she'd left a note, with Mr. Robbins.'

Murray turned and made for the inn.

'She appeared to be leaving, sir,' said Robbins, handing him the note.

'No doubt you didn't stop her,' said Murray.

'I'm not sure I could have, sir,' said Robbins.

'She might have done you some damage. I'm glad you didn't try. Robbins, I don't know where to start to tell you everything that has happened. Yes, I do: Mr. Blair woke and spoke a few words, and knew Miss Blair and me.'

'That is the best of news, sir.' Robbins' eyes seemed to light from within.

'It is, isn't it? I'll try and keep it in mind … So much has happened.' He summed up Worthing's attack, Ketchell's death and

Mr. Lawrence's revelation about Akehurst's part in Worthing's misfortune. 'And now I shall see what Miss Paterson – Miss Pirrie – Beatrix – has to add to that.'

The paper had been folded but not sealed. He opened it, and in a moment was back in Scoggie Castle, reading one of Beatrix's little notes sent to the schoolroom. But that was long ago. He began to read.

> *'Dear Charles,*
> *'You will not be expecting me to wait around to be arrested, of course, so this is farewell. I shall go and meet my friend, and we shall be married at last: he has promised me that in return for my help.*
> *'You'll have guessed, no doubt, that I have no important gentleman protecting me: I think Mr. Ketchell realised that, and he will give you some account of the places he has seen me before. Life has not turned out quite the way I expected when I left Scoggie Castle, but it has not all been bad. Meeting my friend, and consoling him for the loss of his wife, led from a business transaction to a deep affection, and once he has completed all he wishes to do here we shall spend the rest of our lives together. Most happily, I anticipate.*
> *'When I left Scoggie Castle all those years ago, you promised me that if I ever applied to you for help, it would be forthcoming. I hold fast to the hope of that promise now, Charles: do not betray us.*
> *'We are unlikely to meet again, so I take this chance to wish you a bright future as I hope for myself.*
> *'Your friend,*
> *'Beatrix Pirrie'*

'Too late, Beatrix,' he said quietly. 'For your bright future, it's too late.'

'It's an odd situation,' said Isobel, 'but I suppose it's for the best.'

She was seated in Mr. Lawrence's parlour, drinking tea.

'Well, as far as I am concerned,' said Fussy comfortably,

'you are most welcome.'

That was clear, Murray thought, but for himself he did not find it reassuring.

Dr. Mantell had declared that Blair could be moved, with care, and Mr. Lawrence had unexpectedly offered his hospitality. It was, as Isobel said, an odd situation, but Blair had been prepared to accept it and almost anything was better than staying on in the Akehursts' house of mourning and shock. Murray had suggested the White Hart, but Dr. Mantell had advocated peace and quiet as far as was possible. Isobel was free just now to relax in the parlour as Mr. Lawrence was reading to Blair. Murray was less concerned about the strangeness of that reformed relationship and more bothered by Fussy's attention to Isobel. It was impossible for him to stay in Lewes until Blair was fit to travel back to Scotland, for that could be months away. He would have to return frequently.

He decided not to mention the matter to Blair when he went to bid him farewell. Blair was remarkably cheerful for a man who had been so severely injured – his surviving leg seemed incapable of bearing weight – and had already ordered a pair of crutches with intricate carvings on the shafts.

'It will be most interesting to see what it feels like, my dear boy – imagine losing quite so much weight and all in one place! My balance will take some adjustment, no doubt. Dr. Mantell is a most interesting man, you know: we have discussed many scientific subjects already, and I feel there is more to come!'

'And if you lack conversation,' said Murray irresistibly, 'you have Mr. Lawrence.'

'He is trying very hard to be understanding,' said Blair, dropping his voice conspiratorially. 'You see, he's sure that if he had told you earlier about Mr. Worthing – he thinks that none of this would have happened.'

'Of course it would,' said Murray. 'Much of it had happened before I even arrived on the scene. Worthing was bent on revenge, and that was that.'

'Well, yes. But still – he's been awfully nice.'

'I'm so sorry it took me so long to catch up with you,' said Murray, not for the first time.

'Never mind, my boy – you were here in time to sort everything out very neatly. Tell me, did someone say that Worthing had damaged a semaphore tower, too?'

'He did, and Beatrix tried to damage another. They knew from Paulinson, I suspect, just how important they were to Sir Joshua. It was just another way of hurting him.'

'And adding to the impression that the attacks were political, of course.'

'Of course. But principally they wanted to strike the things he valued most: his secretary, his grand-daughter, his project, and in the end even his wife, before attacking Sir Joshua himself.'

'I always liked Worthing, you know,' said Blair sadly. 'I had no idea he was so intent on revenge. Though he was certainly cast down completely at the time.'

'It was Sir Joshua's appearance in Lewes that was the last straw, I believe,' said Murray.

'I should have gone to see him sooner.'

'You couldn't have – he was in London. You'd have found Donald instead.'

'Instead of finding him outside the Akehurst house. Poor lad: it wasn't his fault, you know.'

'It might not have been, but he certainly chose to come and try to kill you.'

'Which woke me up at last!'

'For which we should thank him, I know!' They laughed, gently in Blair's case: he was still in considerable pain.

'Anyway, you have to go,' said Blair. 'We'll follow when we can. I have seen enough of Sussex and London for this year. I think it's time to spend the season in Edinburgh, at my own hearth.'

'We'll all look forward to seeing you there. You and Isobel.'

And now, he was packed and ready to make a start on the long journey home. The carriage seemed pleasantly empty after the crowd on the journey to Lewes – no Ketchell, no Harry Holden nursing his head, no Rosie, no Beatrix. Old Donald, stony-faced, oversaw a temporary groom he had found and presented to Murray, insistent on a second opinion. Young Donald's betrayal had hurt him badly.

Fussy and Isobel came to see Murray off.

'We'll take a day in London on the way back,' said Murray. 'Robbins wants to see the elephants at the Tower.'

'Of course,' said Isobel. 'Good luck with that: it will be a while before I willingly go back.'

'Yes indeed,' said Fussy. 'Lewes will be a good place to rest for a while. For as long as you and Mr. Blair need,' he added, smiling at Isobel.

'Right, Donald, ready?' Murray asked, turning away. 'Robbins, all packed in?'

'Aye, sir,' said Robbins, nodding at the groom who held the door.

'Aye, sir,' said Donald, pulling himself up on to his seat.

'Then let us be off,' said Murray. He climbed into the carriage, followed by Robbins, and the groom packed away the steps and closed the door. Isobel turned from Fussy and began to wave, and Fussy raised a hand in farewell.

The carriage left the stableyard of the White Hart, and they set off for home.

Specimens of St. Giles Greek used by Mr. Holden and Mr. Ketchell

Beau-ideal – the perfect young gentleman
Blood – fashionable young gentleman
Bosky – tipsy
Buzmen – pickpockets
Corinthian – a person of fashionable perfection
Cyprian - slightly better class of prostitute
Daffy – gin
Knowing – in fashion
Lusky - drunk
Mollisher – cheap prostitute
On the fret – itching to go
Out and outer – outstanding, splendid
Pink – fashionable young man
Rainbow – liveried servant
Rhino – cash
Scran - food
Sluicery – gin shop
Ton – fashionable society
Traps – police officers

About the Author

Lexie Conyngham is a historian living in the shadow of the Highlands. Her historical crime novels are born of a life amidst Scotland's old cities, ancient universities and hidden-away aristocratic estates, but she has written since the day she found out that people were allowed to do such a thing. Beyond teaching and research, her days are spent with wool, wild allotments and a wee bit of whisky.

We hope you've enjoyed this instalment. Reviews are important to authors, so it would be lovely if you could post a review where you bought it! Here are a few handy links …

Visit our website at www.lexieconyngham.co.uk. There are several free Murray of Letho short stories, Murray's World Tour of Edinburgh, and the chance to follow Lexie Conyngham's meandering thoughts on writing, gardening and knitting, at www.murrayofletho.blogspot.co.uk. You can also follow Lexie, should such a thing appeal, on Facebook, Pinterest or Instagram.

Finally! If you'd like to be kept up to date with Lexie and her writing, please join our mailing list at: contact@kellascatpress.co.uk. There's a quarterly newsletter, often with a short story attached, and fair warning of any new books coming out.

Murray of Letho

We first meet Charles Murray when he's a student at St. Andrews University in Fife in 1802, resisting his father's attempts to force him home to the family estate to learn how it's run. Pushed into involvement in the investigation of a professor's death, he solves his first murder before taking up a post as tutor to Lord Scoggie. This series takes us around Georgian Scotland as well as India, Italy and Norway (so far!), in the company of Murray, his manservant Robbins, his father's old friend Blair, the enigmatic Mary, and other members of his occasionally shambolic household.

LEXIE CONYNGHAM

Death in a Scarlet Gown
The Status of Murder (a novella)
Knowledge of Sins Past
Service of the Heir
An Abandoned Woman
Fellowship with Demons
The Tender Herb
Death of an Officer's Lady
Out of a Dark Reflection
A Dark Night at Midsummer (a novella)
Slow Death by Quicksilver
Thicker than Water
A Deficit of Bones
The Dead Chase

Hippolyta Napier

Hippolyta Napier is only nineteen when she arrives in Ballater, on Deeside, in 1829, the new wife of the local doctor. Blessed with a love of animals, a talent for painting, a helpless instinct for hospitality, and insatiable curiosity, Hippolyta finds her feet in her new home and role in society, making friends and enemies as she goes. Ballater may be small but it attracts great numbers of visitors, so the issues of the time, politics, slavery, medical advances, all affect the locals. Hippolyta, despite her loving husband and their friend Durris, the sheriff's officer, manages to involve herself in all kinds of dangerous adventures in her efforts to solve every mystery that presents itself.

A Knife in Darkness

Death of a False Physician

A Murderous Game

The Thankless Child

A Lochgorm Lament

Orkneyinga Murders

Orkney, c.1050 A.D.: Thorfinn Sigurdarson, Earl of Orkney, rules from the Brough of Birsay on the western edges of these islands. Ketal Gunnarson is his man, representing his interests in any part of his extended realm. When Sigri, a childhood friend of Ketil's, finds a dead man on her land, Ketil, despite his distrust of islands, is commissioned to investigate. Sigrid, though she has quite enough to do, decides he cannot manage on his own, and insists on helping – which Ketil might or might not appreciate.

Tomb for an Eagle

A Wolf at the Gate

Dragon in the Snow

Other books by Lexie Conyngham:

Windhorse Burning

'I'm not mad, for a start, and I'm about as far from violent as you can get.' When Toby's mother, Tibet activist Susan Hepplewhite, dies, he is determined to honour her memory. He finds her diaries and decides to have them translated into English. But his mother had a secret, and she was not the only one: Toby's decision will lead to obsession and murder.

The War, The Bones, and Dr. Cowie

Far from the London Blitz, Marian Cowie is reluctantly resting in rural Aberdeenshire when a German 'plane crashes nearby. An airman goes missing, and old bones are revealed. Marian is sure she could solve the mystery if only the villagers would stop telling her useless stories – but then the crisis comes, and Marian finds the stories may have a use after all.

Jail Fever

It's the year 2000, and millennium paranoia is everywhere.
Eliot is a bad-tempered merchant with a shady past, feeling under the weather.
Catriona is an archaeologist at a student dig, when she finds something unexpected.
Tom is a microbiologist, investigating a new and terrible disease with a stigma.
Together, their knowledge could save thousands of lives – but someone does not want them to …

The Slaughter of Leith Hall

'See, Charlie, it might be near twenty years since Culloden, but there's plenty hard feelings still amongst the Jacobites, and no so far under the skin, ken?'

Charlie Rob has never thought of politics, nor strayed far from his Aberdeenshire birthplace. But when John Leith of Leith Hall takes him under his wing, his life changes completely. Soon he is far from home, dealing with conspiracy and murder, and lost in a desperate hunt for justice.

Thrawn Thoughts and Blithe Bits and *Quite Useful in Minor Emergencies*

Two collections of short stories, some featuring characters from the series, some not; some seen before, some not; some long, some very short. Find a whole new dimension to car theft, the life history of an unfortunate Victorian rebel, a problem with dragons and a problem with draugens, and what happens when you advertise that you've found somebody's leg.

www.ingramcontent.com/pod-product-compliance
Lightning Source LLC
Chambersburg PA
CBHW020335180626
46812CB00001B/216